# DIFFRACTION

## ATROPHY SERIES

# DIFFRACTION

## ATROPHY SERIES

# JESS ANASTASI

Entangled Publishing, LLC
2614 South Timberline Road
Suite 109
Fort Collins, CO 80525
Visit our website at www.entangledpublishing.com.

Select Otherworld is an imprint of Entangled Publishing, LLC.

Edited by Robin Haseltine
Cover design by Erin Dameron-Hill
Cover art from Shutterstock

Manufactured in the United States of America

First Edition January 2017

*For my Mum.*
*People are always talking about the need for strong heroines in books and movies, but I was lucky enough to witness a strong woman every day of my life as a child.*
*I don't know if I'll ever be as strong (and stubborn!) as you, but some days, the hard days, when I wish I could be a little tougher, I still tell myself "when I grow up, I'm going to be more like my mum."*
*Love you always.*

# Chapter One

Kira Sasaki wasn't sure she wanted to know what he was up to now. Because when it came to Rian Sherron, the captain of the *Imojenna*, often a person was better off pretending like she hadn't seen anything.

She came to a halt at the bottom of the ship's ramp, making way for the aforementioned Rian and his apparently-not-a-pirate cousin, Qaelan Forster. The two of them were dragging an unconscious soldier they'd seemingly removed from the *Swift Brion*, the flagship where the *Imojenna* was currently docked.

Considering all she'd seen in her years onboard as the ship's doctor, this latest of her captain's escapades didn't particularly surprise her. She wheeled the case she'd been lugging just inside the atmospheric doors as the trio passed her, Rian not bothering to ask what she'd acquired from the *Swift Brion*'s extensive and state-of-the-art medical deck. It'd been a rare treat getting to view the facilities and grabbing a few supplies she hadn't seen in years. Though she made do with what they could source in the outer systems, she couldn't deny there'd been more than one day when she'd wished she could go supply-gathering somewhere that didn't consider second-rate disposable gauze a marvel of modern medicine.

Abandoning her goodies, she tagged along after Rian and Qae as they headed across the cargo bay and hauled the soldier deeper into the ship toward the engines, instead of heading up to her medbay as she'd assumed.

By the time she caught up with them, they were dumping the soldier in Rian's makeshift brig. The man wore the dark blue military uniform of the *Swift Brion*'s crew, the shirt stretched taut across his broad shoulders and defined biceps. His light brown hair was chopped short but thickly spiked on top, and as his head lolled to the side, she got a good look at the square, masculine angles of his face. Well, he was a handsome one, no doubt about that.

"What's wrong with him?" She moved to just inside the cell door, putting aside her superficial assessment and casting a critical doctor's eye over the groaning man.

Rian stepped back, while Qae made a big show of stretching his shoulders, muttering about how heavy the guy had been.

"He and the new Reidar stunner didn't get along," Rian answered.

"It bitch-slapped him like a two-credit shag." Qae had one hand resting on the stunner in his belt. "If mine wasn't out of ammo, I'd be mighty agreeable to hit him with it again."

Her attention cut to the soldier's face, but he looked completely human. There was no hint of shimmery scales in his flesh nor the typical flatness over the forehead and bridge of the nose that the Reidar possessed in their true form. If the stunner had worked, she'd have seen evidence of a shape-shifting alien beneath his attractive form.

"Is he—?"

"Reidar?" Rian crossed his arms, staring down at the man

with cold detachment. "I don't know. Maybe. We don't know enough about how the stunner works yet to say either way. He could be an alien that's somehow resisting the change where others haven't been able to. Until I work out otherwise, everyone should consider him dangerous and keep their distance."

She nodded, though the doctor side of her brain had already taken over, cataloguing his condition: pale, clammy, tension in his body as if maybe he was in pain. And semiconscious—not with it, but mumbling and groaning as if he was having a bad dream or hallucinations.

She'd pulled the small palm-sized medical scanner out of her pocket automatically before her mind had even registered the decision.

"Before we leave him—" She stepped over and knelt down, holding the scanner above his chest and watching the readings scroll across the screen. "His blood pressure is a little on the low side."

"Fascinating." Rian's tone told her exactly the opposite. "He's still breathing, so I'd call that good for him right now."

"I don't like the idea of someone being down here in the brig under questionable health." She gently grasped the soldier's chin, tilting his head toward her. Maybe it was a coincidence, but he seemed to settle somewhat at the contact. At least she wasn't losing her touch out here in the barrens of space.

She gently lifted his eyelids, and with a startled half breath, found his eyes were an astonishing light blue, almost silver. She'd never seen that exact shade of blue before. It was utterly gorgeous. But she pushed the thought aside, noting that his pupils were reactive but a little sluggish.

"Since there's a chance he's not a *someone*, but an alien, don't make it your concern, Kira. When he wakes up, he just needs to answer a few questions and this can all be settled up—if he's human, I'll let him go. If not…"

Rian didn't need to spell out what came after *if not*. She'd seen the way he'd dealt with the Reidar, and it always ended bloody. Not that the sociopathic parasites didn't deserve it.

"And you think waking up in your brig will put him in a chatty mood?" She glanced over her shoulder, a low spike of annoyance cutting through her. Usually she took Rian's cavalier attitude toward people as it was, but for some reason, it'd started getting on her nerves today.

"Not to sound like a walking cliché, but"—Qae cocked a hip, patting the Reidar stunner—"we have ways of making him talk." The last words were uttered in an extra deep, foreboding voice.

She pushed to her feet, slipped her med scanner back into her pocket, ignoring how her annoyance was swiftly turning into frustration. "Let me know how that works out for you."

As she headed for the doorway of the brig, she paused to look up at Rian. "You'll comm me if his condition worsens?"

The captain gave a single nod, and it seemed like that was all she'd be getting from him in the way of agreement, which didn't leave her with much reassurance. The notion that the soldier might be a Reidar left a creeping sensation under her skin, like skittering insects, but her ingrained sense of compassion as a doctor pushed back against the anxiety, especially since, more than anything else in the universe, she hated seeing patients mistreated.

Her gut feelings had always gotten her a long way as a doctor, so she never ignored them. Something was up with this guy—not that she necessarily thought he was Reidar. As Rian had said, they hardly knew anything about the experimental energy weapon that revealed the alien's true form. What if he wasn't Reidar, but human, and for an unknown reason the stunner had seriously affected him in some way it hadn't done to anyone else so far?

If she hadn't heard anything by the following morning, she'd sneak back down for another check. Rian might want everyone to leave the soldier alone, but he surely knew her well enough by now to realize she wouldn't sit idly by in her medbay while there was a clearly unwell person within the bulkheads of the *Imojenna*.

# Chapter Two

Hell was an eight-by-eight-foot storage compartment converted into a brig by benefit of the bars in the hatchway instead of a door.

Varean groaned as he rolled onto his back, blinking against the bulkhead lights above him, eyes too sensitive, like his retinas had been burned by staring at a solar eclipse. Time had become a blur since he'd been stunned with that energy weapon, punctuated by periods of lucidness where Sherron's crew had locked him down, while his dreams had been more like someone else's memories—too real to be a figment of imagination, but so out of context and confusing he couldn't make any sense of them. Sometimes he'd gotten completely lost in those dreams, unable to find his way back to reality, battered by a language he didn't understand and places he'd never been but were familiar in some bone-deep way.

The only anchor had been a voice. The sound of it like honey soothing bitter acid.

The voice tugged at his consciousness and led him out of the dark. Her tone hadn't been wary and belligerent like the others, but steadfast and practical. And for some weird reason, the cadence of it had rippled through him like warm water. Except the few times he'd been conscious, had been able to crack his eyes open or with-it enough to sit himself up, he hadn't found a face to match the voice, and he put it down to one of the dreams he'd confused with reality. Probably a good thing too, 'cause someone with a voice like that probably had the power to get whatever she wanted in life.

Yeah, it was kind of hard to keep track of reality when that bastard marauder, Qaelan Forster, had made shooting him with the energy weapon his new favorite pastime, keeping him immobile and out of it like a junkie on a bender. The damn thing was like getting jacked by a thousand volts of electricity. It locked up all his muscles, leaving him rigid with rippling pain that just kept on coming, growing in waves, beginning from deep inside him and expanding outward like a tide of shattered glass shredding his insides to a pulp. The agony had taken over, become his only reality, melting and reshaping his cells until there was nothing left of him except a mass of inexorable torment, fighting the crushing darkness.

Varean half rolled and forced himself to sit up, leaving his head throbbing. It'd been a few hours since they'd last hit him with the stunner and, while he still felt like he'd been used as a landing pad for a battle cruiser, his mind was clearing a little. Enough that a good dose of pissed-off was feeding life to his muscles and limbs.

But something within him wasn't right, like a piece of himself had been knocked out of place. Or maybe that wasn't the right way to put it. More like something inside him had mutated, giving life to a kind of dark anger and need to lash out he'd never experienced before.

He'd always prided himself on being calm and collected, on remaining levelheaded and acting with logic. Even through the weeks of hell that'd been commando training, he'd kept his shite together. The more they threw at him, the more locked down and in control he'd become. But this—this dark mutation that had bloomed within him, it tempted him toward reckless violence.

His superior officer on the *Swift Brion* had put in a perfunctory attempt to stand up for him after he'd been stunned, but Sherron and Forster had dragged his half-unconscious carcass in here anyway. So what? He was their prisoner now? Well, he might have a goddamn opinion about that.

Footsteps echoed, and he lifted his head. Light tread, shorter stride, most likely female. He used the bulkhead at his back to steady himself as he pushed upright, his legs giving a good impersonation of undercooked pudding. But he locked his muscles and took a couple of unsteady steps, bringing him into the middle of the cell as a slight figure moved toward him, her features obscured by the shadows and half lighting along the passageway.

"Good, you're awake."

*That voice.*

A low shudder tumbled through his weak limbs, a chaser of relief like rain on the dry, cracked ground of a desert. It was the voice he'd heard in his dreams, the one that had constantly tugged and teased him back when he thought he was completely lost. His pulse kicked up, giving new energy to his dull, aching limbs.

Varean forced his feet to take him the last remaining steps across the space and braced both hands against the bars. The woman stepped closer, moving into a direct beam of light.

She was short, lucky to top out at five foot five, and a wavy mop of dark hair was haphazardly pinned back from her face of cinnamon-toned skin. When she glanced up at him, his heart jammed into his ribs as the light caught her unusual sage green eyes—made even more exotic by the wide, angular set of her thick lashes.

"When I came to check on you last night, you were totally out of it, so you probably don't remember," she continued, as though there wasn't a row of bars separating them and he wasn't being held here against his will. The new mutation within him stirred, mocking him with the idea of throwing himself against the bars in a rage like a wounded animal. He shook his head, dispelling the unsettling notion.

But he couldn't quell the low burn of anger starting up in his chest and spreading outward. Yep, he'd just run out of patience where this situation was concerned. He wrapped his hands around the bars and shoved at the door, making it clatter. "Let me out of here."

A flash of annoyance crossed her features as she folded her arms but didn't step back from him. "I'm a doctor. I'm here only to check on you. I can't let you out, but I can make sure you're treated well."

*"Treated well?"* He gave a harsh laugh and rattled his cage again. "Where were you yesterday?"

Her posture tightened as her expression took on an affronted edge. "You want out? Then give them what they want."

Frustration poured through him, and his fists contracted around the bars. "What do they want?"

There didn't seem like much point asking the question when he could already guess the answer.

"Rian wants to work out why the energy weapon affects you. He wants to make sure you're not Reidar."

Though he'd been expecting it, her words still landed in his guts, effective as a punch. He could guess why the energy weapon had knocked him on his ass—and it wasn't because he was a damned shape-shifting alien. Every man had his secrets, it was just that his went deeper than most. He'd worked hard to put his past behind him and build a life free of his heritage.

It wasn't the kind of thing he liked people to find out. So no, he wouldn't be giving Captain Rian Sherron War Hero shite about anything.

Thwarted aggravation gave strength to his legs and sent him pacing across the small space. When he came to the far bulkhead, he slammed the heel of his palm against the wall he'd woken up to earlier. Words on his lips he couldn't understand kept welling from somewhere unknown.

"I'm not one of those damned things. And what if I don't cooperate? Are Sherron and that pirate Forster going to keep me here against my will? Forcibly remove me from my post?"

The doctor didn't answer him, and he turned to face her. She was studying him, of that he had no doubt. He could all but see her dissecting him.

He crossed his arms and sent her a cutting grin. "You keep looking at me like that, Doc, and I'm going to start getting all the wrong ideas."

She tilted her head a little, gaze blatantly shifting down his body, considering, as if she were entertained by his taunt instead of intimidated like he'd intended. But then, maybe he'd imagined it, because by the time her attention came back to his face, she seemed nothing but detached. "I was planning on taking your vitals. They were a bit on the low side last night. But I'm going to assume that opening the door at this point wouldn't be a good idea."

The anger returned, harder and hotter this time, propelling him back across the short space of the brig to the bars. "Sure, if you want me to snap that pretty neck of yours. Because you and the rest of your friends aren't getting anywhere near me. Go tell Forster he can come down here and shoot me with that stunner until my brain turns to goo because I have nothing to tell you, and I refuse to spend another rotation locked up like a damned animal."

From the expression that crossed her face, it seemed she

didn't like his ultimatum. She stepped closer to the bars, either unaware or uncaring that she'd put herself within reach.

"If you're not Reidar, then why does the stunner affect you?"

Aggravation pounded him, burning through his stressed muscles. Was this some different interrogation tactic? Send a pretty face in here to soften him up? Did they really think he was that much of a moron? He was an AF-one commando, for jezus sake. Resisting torture one-oh-one was a basic requirement soldiers had to pass, or they got booted from the training unit like trash on garbage day.

"This is the last time I am having this conversation with anyone. So go tell that to whoever sent you down here. I don't know a thing about frecking shape-shifting aliens, and I don't know why in the hell that stunner knocks me sideways. You're a doctor, you figure it out."

A kindling flare of interest sparked in her gaze as she stared at him, leaving some kind of weird ripple chasing beneath his skin.

"If you're telling the truth, if this has been some unfortunate twist of fate, then I would like to help you. But you have to be straight with us. Rian has a short temper. Right now he's curious with a side of suspicious. If you don't cooperate, he's going to start getting suspicious with a side of pissed off, and then you're really going to be in trouble."

"Cooperating with Sherron means cooperating with Qaelan Forster. And considering the number of times he's pulsed me with that damned stunner, I definitely owe him a punch or five in the face."

A hint of anger touched her features, but not directed at him, more like she'd been unhappy with Forster's antics herself. "And I'm sorry for that. But if you don't fight Rian on this and tell him what you know, I can make sure no one shoots you with that gun again."

A low swirl of relief cut through the heat of his anger, loosening some tension within him. Maybe if he could get the doctor on side, she'd help him escape. Or maybe if he lulled her into a false sense of security, she'd agree to take his vitals, and when she opened the cell door… Well, either way, he was using her to get out of here.

A muted roar vibrated to life on both sides of him, making everything jump into a low rattle. He glanced around before looking back at the doctor.

"What's going on?" He raised his voice a little to make sure she heard him over the mechanical growling.

"We're disembarking from the *Swift Brion*."

Oh *hell* no. He was not leaving the *Swift Brion*, and he sure as dick wasn't going anywhere on this damn ship.

"Listen, Doc. I understand your people are a little wary of me, but can't you just leave me to my own? Let me be locked up in detention level on my ship until someone figures it out, but I'm not leaving my post—"

She shook her head and crossed her arms, glancing over her shoulder. "Sorry, it's too late. The *Swift Brion*'s crew were clearing the deck, getting ready to close the atmospheric doors and open the outer hatch when I came down here." The engine vibrations revved higher, and she gave a short grimace. "Sorry about the noise, too. You're right in between the engines down here. It might also get a little warm."

*Frecking great.* "How warm?"

She shrugged one shoulder. "Honestly, I don't know. I've never spent any time down here."

The doc went to step back, but he shot a hand out and clamped his fingers around her upper arm. "Not so fast."

She stilled beneath his grip and raised her eyes to meet his. For a long second they stared at each other, almost like enemies weighing up the advantage, but there was something far more dynamic and incandescent beneath the surface.

"You might want to think about removing your hand from me."

So the petite doctor had a pair, which for some reason he found way too intriguing. On first impression, he'd never have picked that, but of course, she worked for Major Captain Sherron, and he probably wasn't the type of guy to surround himself with wilting violets, or however the saying went.

"And you might want to think about opening this door before the *Imojenna* breaks dock."

Her expression hardened. "I told you, it's too late. Let me go."

He yanked her up against the door and grabbed her other arm, leaning in closer so that only the bars separated their faces. "Look at that, now I've got two hands on you. Open the door, before I start breaking bones."

He squeezed her right bicep just to make sure she knew he meant business. Really, he couldn't have hurt the woman—not with the way her voice was doing a number on his central nervous system and the way her green eyes were making his blood rush, heating him up in all the wrong places—but desperate times and all that shite. He had to get off this ship. There were things about him that he needed to keep to himself. Because if they got out, his life as he knew it would never be the same, wouldn't be his own any longer.

She stared at him; a spark of something in her gaze, he told himself, was all in his recently scrambled mind. "Is this really how you want things to go down? Because I'm telling you, if you leave the *Imojenna* now, you'll be vacuumed."

"I'll take my chances."

She huffed a short sigh. "Fine. I'll need at least one arm to release the door controls."

This time it was his turn to stare hard at her for a long moment. That had kind of been too easy. Did she have some ulterior motive? A weapon hidden somewhere she'd go for as soon as he let her go?

"How about a compromise?"

Her brow lowered over an impatient look. "What kind of compromise?"

"I'm not prepared to let you go, in case you've got a weapon stashed somewhere in that petite package of yours. Instead, we're going to tango."

Her expression morphed into skeptical confusion. "Tango?"

He pulled both her arms through the bars into his side of the cage. "I'm going to let you go one arm at a time, and you're going to keep them stretched out like this, until I've shifted sideways and reached around the next bar. Then we're going to move your arms out and around, one at a time."

"Aren't you in a hurry or something? This seems kind of excessive."

"Sure, I'm in a hurry, but I also don't plan on giving you a chance to shoot me." He let her bicep go and shifted to the side a little, reaching out and around to guide her arms around the bars.

Her body tensed beneath his touch. "I'm a doctor. I don't carry a gun. I aim to help people, not hurt them."

He glanced up at her as he shuffled sideways again to repeat his action. "Not even one of those stunner weapons?"

Her jaw clenched. "Not even one of those."

They were almost at the edge of the door, near the control pad. "Well, I'd love to take your word for it, but I'm just not the trusting type. I'll check for myself when I'm out of this cage."

Her lips pressed into a thin line, but she didn't answer him as they ran out of bars to dance around.

"Now, I'm going to keep a hold of your upper arm while you access the control screen, and you're going to keep your other arm stretched out just like this. If I see any funny business—"

"Yeah, yeah, you'll break some bones. Got it," she muttered darkly. Her gaze cut away from his as she slowly reached down and placed her hand on the screen.

Varean took the unguarded moment to study her profile. Funny, but she didn't seem the least bit afraid of him. She seemed more inconvenienced than frightened. She didn't even seem that intimidated by his threat to break her arm. Yeah, the doc was definitely intriguing. If only he hadn't met her on the wrong side of some bars feeling like he was coming off a hangover from being drunk on old-fashioned rocket fuel.

The locking mechanism clicked free, and the door swung loose between them. Varean pushed the doc back a few steps, keeping a hold on her until they'd created a wide enough gap for him to slip through. As he stepped sideways through it, he changed his grip on her fast so she didn't try to make a run for it.

"I did what you ordered. If you want to get off the *Imojenna* before she leaves the *Swift Brion*—if we haven't already—you better hurry."

Varean hauled her closer, sending a quick glance along the corridor to make sure no one was coming.

"And give you the chance to shoot me in the back? No thanks." He patted one hand over all the places people usually stashed weapons. Like she'd promised, he came up empty-handed. "How would you like to get acquainted with zero atmosphere? It hurts like a bitch's mother, but we can last for about thirty seconds before we lose consciousness and melt from the inside out."

"If you want to be technical about it, dying in space is really like boiling and freezing at the same time."

He glanced at her as he started towing her along the short passageway, looking for any kind of expression from her to work out if she'd meant that seriously or was actually making a morbid joke. But she simply stared back at him blankly, giving nothing away.

"Right, so we're going to do that between leaving the *Imojenna* and getting through the atmospheric doors on the *Swift Brion*, depending on how far open the outer hatch is."

"Aren't you worried about getting sucked out of the ship if the air is already venting?" She didn't sound concerned, more curious.

"Then I'll die in space. At least I won't be locked in a cage."

"Uh-huh. Wow, I'd heard AF commandos were crazy dedicated to their duty, but I thought it was just an expression. I didn't realize the crazy part was literal."

They came out in the back of the cargo hold, and Varean glanced down as he tugged her beside him. Hell, was she actually mocking him?

"Kira?"

The voice coming from the other side of the cargo hold sent Varean into full alert. He yanked the doctor in front of him and spun them toward the source of the sound.

Another woman and a man sat around a low crate, both with expressions of curiosity and concern on their faces. The guy had started to half stand, hand sliding toward his lower back.

"Kira, what's going on?" the woman asked. "Did Rian give you permission to let him out of the brig?"

Varean leaned down until his mouth was a few inches from the doctor's ear, the next breath he took laced with the sweet scent of her hair. "You knew they were out here, huh?"

"Yep." And she didn't sound the least bit apologetic about it, either. But she shifted subtly in his hold, so maybe she wasn't as cool and calm as she seemed.

Varean straightened, keeping an eye on the guy slowly but surely going for a weapon. "*He* has a name. And *he* is an

AF-one commando who isn't going to be forcibly removed from his duty."

"Command Donnelly thinks he can still make it back onto the *Swift Brion*. He's all ready to take on zero atmosphere," the doc explained, using the general title of "Command" people gave to commandos when they were unsure of their rank. And he didn't fail to miss the hint of dry humor in her tone.

So she thought this was some big joke? His whole life had been sucked into a nebula vortex and the woman thought there was something funny in that? He tightened his hold on her.

"And I'm taking the doc here for insurance. Whatever weapon you're thinking about laying hands on, buddy, I'd think again."

The man stilled.

"It's okay, Tannin. I don't think Command Donnelly wants to hurt us. He's just a bit annoyed about being locked up and wants to get back on familiar ground." The doc's voice was soothing and gentle. All kinds of patronizing, really. He tugged her closer until her back was flush against his chest and let go of her arm to wrap a hand around her slender neck instead. Though his adrenaline was pumping, with the doc's slight frame against him, an underlying calmness spread through him, the feel of her pressed in to him a little too enjoyable considering his circumstances.

"Someone get to opening the hatchway."

Tannin shook his head. "Sorry, *buddy*, it's too late. We've disembarked from the *Swift Brion*. So how about you make your way back to the brig and save us all a lot of trouble?"

A low, creeping dread skittled under his skin, the temptation of reckless aggression uncharacteristically rising within him again. But he set his other hand on the doc's stomach, pressing her more firmly against him, and clamped down on the sensation before it could get a hold of him.

"I'm not going back into that cage. You'll have to put me down first."

"The captain will happily take care of that for you," the guy muttered.

"Tannin." The other woman's voice held a note of warning.

"What, Zahli? Don't sit there and pretend like Rian hasn't been on edge lately, and I'm talking the knife's edge. One slip and someone is going to end up bloody."

Oh, so things weren't all confetti parades and shiny medals for the ex–war hero? Well, Varean could honestly say he didn't give a shite what kind of privileged problems Major Captain Sherron had, so long as they didn't interfere with him getting off the man's ship. And if they truly weren't docked on the *Swift Brion* any longer, he had to find another means of escape.

"Does this ship have emergency pods or some kind of evacuation craft?"

The doc glanced over her shoulder at him as far as his grip on her neck would allow. She still didn't seem overly concerned, but he could see a definite gleam of antagonism in her sage green eyes, feel the tension in the line of her body against his.

"There are two skimmer shuttles located on the top of the ship."

"Seriously, Kira?" Tannin muttered.

She shrugged, her shoulders brushing his pecs, leaving him too aware of all the places she was pressed against him. "Well, he asked. And anyway, he can't get to them without going past Rian."

Okay, this whole thing was verging on stupid. And stupid had a tendency to make him cranky. First, the doc hadn't seemed the least bit afraid of him since he'd grabbed her at the cell. And now, despite being a little wary, none of these people seemed to be taking seriously his plan of escaping and taking himself a guarantee in the form of the doc. For jezus sake, he knew over thirty ways to kill a person with his bare hands alone. If he wanted to take the lethal way out of this situation, the doc could be dead, and he'd have fingers on whatever weapon Tannin had stashed before her body even hit the deck.

Instead, he was trying his damndest to be polite...well, as polite as a man could be when he had his hand wrapped around someone's neck. None of these people were directly responsible for his imprisonment, so they didn't deserve to get hurt. But if he ran across Rian or that bastard Qaelan Forster, who *were* the accountable parties, he might have words that needed speaking, which would likely be punctuated with a lot of violence.

"I'll take my chances on avoiding Captain War Hero. Where's the access hatch to the skimmers?"

"You really don't want to do that—" the doc started in a low voice.

"No, what I really don't want to do is stay on this ship. So, point the way to our escape shuttle, Doc."

"What is he doing out of the brig?"

A new voice joined the conversation, and Varean glanced over to the metal stairs, where Sherron stood on the second-to-last step. While he didn't look particularly annoyed, he also didn't look any kinds of welcoming. Just stone-cold and lethal. Despite the impassive stare, Sherron had both hands relaxed on the butts of his holstered guns. And he'd seen what a freakishly fast draw the guy was. No doubt about it, this was the only warning he was likely to get that Sherron was thinking about shooting him.

"Nothing. Command Donnelly was just stretching his legs—doctor's orders. But he's going back to the cell now," the doc answered, leaning back in to him with full-body contact as though she expected him to start retreating.

"Like hell I— *Ow!*" Varean glanced down at the sharp jab in his arm to see the doc holding a small, slim dosing gun and an apologetic expression tightening her features. A single drop of blood beaded on his forearm. "*Son of a bitch.*"

Varean tried to tense as his arm suddenly went slack and his grip dropped away from her throat. The loosening of muscles and numbness shot through his body, until somehow the deck was at his knees. His head swam, and he blinked. Hadn't he been standing a second ago? And he'd been going to do something—something important. Thoughts flashed elusively out of his mind's grasp and a strange chemical warmth bloomed through his too-relaxed limbs.

He had to—had to—lie down. Yeah, that was it. *No!* Escape. Escape from— Where was he again? He forced his eyes to focus, and everything was sideways. *What the—?* Oh right, lying down. His vision shifted out of focus and when he strained his eyes, everything looked different. Voices echoed in his mind, words he couldn't understand, but were familiar nonetheless. The mutation within him—the one that wanted to act out with uncontrolled, wild hostility—it ballooned and eclipsed a bit more of the calm he'd always held onto like a lifeline.

A comforting voice came to him, pulling him back from the gray-and-yellow tinted shadows, and then a face appeared in his line of vision, cinnamon-toned skin and stunning soft green eyes. But a feeling of treachery accompanied the angelic vision. She'd done something to him.

"Going to pay for that, Doc." His voice slurred like he'd gone ten too many rounds at a bar. And why had he called her doc? Did he know her? Yeah. That voice. Lilting but firm. He knew her voice.

A light hand landed on his shoulder, the touch burning his oversensitized skin. "Sorry, Commando, but trying to escape is not worth getting yourself killed over."

He had a reply to that. Something he really had to say. But the words were dancing out of comprehension, and the lights along the upper bulkhead were flashing, burning his retinas all over again. He closed his eyes and rolled over to his stomach, the metal grate floor cool against the warmth radiating out of his skin.

Whoa, who'd turned up the atmospherics? Okay, he'd just lie here for a minute until someone fixed the damn heat, and then he'd remember what he was doing. Must be nearly time for his shift. Or was it after shift, and he'd gone and gotten shite-faced with his AF buddies? That would explain the way his head was sloshing.

"Get him back to the brig and leave him to come around. I want those questions answered before I decide what to do with him," someone said above him.

*Oh hell.* Was he meant to be escorting a prisoner to detention level? "Yeah, let's get right on that." He forced his heavy limbs to roll his dead weight back over and pushed up into a sitting position. "Where's the captive? And why in the hell is it so hot in here?"

Varean got himself upright, staggering into a bulkhead and then using it to push straighter. Had to keep his shite together. If his CO caught him totally wasted on duty, there'd be hell to pay.

"Right this way, Commando," a voice instructed.

Varean nodded and blanked his features, trying to pretend like the action hadn't sent his brain hammering about in his skull. Jezus, whatever he'd drunk must have been pure high-gravity toxin.

A slight figure had moved to walk in front of him, so he focused on a spot in the middle of her shoulder blades and set his uncoordinated legs into a march.

"That's far enough, Command Donnelly."

He forced his head up and saw nothing but bulkheads on all sides. Christ, it was even hotter here…wherever here was.

"Take a beat, Donnelly. We'll come back for you later," a different voice said.

*Yeah, that sounded like an idea. Need somewhere to sit.* There was a utilitarian cot shoved into one corner of the… wait. This place looked familiar. A brig. One he'd been in before. But that didn't make sense. Why the hell would he be in a brig?

"Hang on—" He spun around, way too fast for his floundering brain, and his heavy, clumsy movement unbalanced him, sending him over. Except maybe being down wasn't such a bad thing. The flooring was cool against his— huh. Hadn't he already thought this before? Well, whatever the case, he'd just lie here for a minute until someone fixed the damn environs, and then he'd get back to whatever the hell he'd been doing.

*Fight until there is no fight left.* That was the commando motto. He repeated the mantra as everything shifted, leaving him in that place that seemed like reality, but had to be a dream, where faces were misshapen and the words all garbled. But then the mantra that had defined his life these past years distorted into an abomination.

*Fight until they are all dead.*

# Chapter Three

Kira examined the dosing gun before slipping it into her pocket. She'd definitely hit the commando with a full dose of the sedative, but maybe she'd miscalculated his size. That shot should have put him out for a solid six hours. Instead, it'd only made him confused and somewhat unsteady. Unbelievable, but he'd even managed to walk himself back to the brig. Which maybe was a better result, because if Rian and Tannin had ended up carrying him, she'd never have heard the end of it. Considering how tall and broad he was—and she now had the extreme up-close-and-personal experience to go on—she had to imagine he weighed a ton.

Rian pushed the cell door closed and palmed the controls to lock it, then turned to pin her with a glare. She made sure her returning stare was as doctorly as possible to cover the very non-doctor direction her thoughts had been skipping.

"Why was he out of the brig, Kira?"

She glanced at the prone commando lying facedown on the floor and muttering something about the environs. "Because he threatened to break my arm?"

Rian's brow lowered at her question. "Was that your answer or a query as to whether or not I'd accept that as an excuse?"

"Both?"

Rian crossed his arms, stance intimidating. "Should I bother asking why you were standing within grabbing distance of an AF-one commando?"

"His vitals were low last night—"

"I said I didn't want anyone interacting with him until I had a chance to talk with him myself. Now it's going to be another few hours before I can do that."

"I understand, Captain, but I have my doubts about him being Reidar—"

"Possibly being a Reidar isn't the only reason I gave the order to keep clear of him." Rian headed back toward the main cargo bay where they'd left Tannin and Zahli.

"Then why?"

"Because he's a commando, and if they don't want to do something, like stay on a ship, there's not much that'll keep them there." He walked to the far bulkhead where he lifted open the lid of a crate, then grabbed something and made for the stairs.

"You have a theory, though, don't you?"

Rian was a hard person to read, but in the three years she'd been on the *Imojenna*, she'd come to learn he never did anything without a good reason.

For a second she thought he wasn't going to answer, but he finally passed a glance over them all.

"We know the Reidar have experimented on people, a frecking lot of people. But we don't know what most of those experiments were for, or how they might affect people. I can't be the only one who's ever escaped them."

"You think the commando was the victim of these experiments?" The hypothesis made a horrific kind of sense.

"Except, he claims he didn't know anything about the Reidar before we outed the ones on the *Swift Brion*."

Rian shrugged one shoulder. "So he doesn't remember, or he doesn't want to admit the truth to a bunch of strangers. If he's not Reidar himself, it's the only other likely explanation for why the stunner affects him. Either way, I want to know. Once I've got my answers, we'll cut him loose. But for now, I need him to stay put. Don't go near him again. He'd kill you to escape."

Kira crossed her arms, aiming an aggravated glare at Rian's back as he disappeared into the upper levels. Surely Rian was exaggerating. If the commando was willing to kill her to escape, he'd already had the chance and hadn't taken it.

She turned around to find Zahli watching her with an exasperated expression.

"No." Zahli's voice was hard, her tone scarily similar to the one her brother had just employed.

"No what?" Kira schooled her features into bland innocence. Might as well play dumb while she could.

"You are not going to check on the prisoner five seconds after Rian told you not to."

"I won't get within reaching distance of the bars, okay?" She shoved her hand into her pocket and pulled out a small bottle. "Besides, if he gives me any trouble, I'll just dose him again."

Zahli rolled her eyes. "Because drugging the man against his will isn't as bad as Qaelan shooting him with the Reidar stunner over and over."

"A sedative was better than the alternative," she answered, then headed toward the back of the cargo hold.

A small surge of contrition shot through her. Okay, Zahli might have a point. It wasn't like she'd *wanted* to sedate Command Donnelly, which was why she'd waited for the last possible second to use the dosing gun hidden up her sleeve.

Until Rian had turned up, she'd been hoping she could reason with the commando, which was why she'd gone along with his escape attempt even though she could have knocked him out as soon as he'd grabbed her through the bars.

Honestly, the scientist in her wanted to know why the weapon affected Command Donnelly, especially now, considering Rian's theory that he'd been a victim of Reidar experiments. But it didn't seem fair to keep him locked up. He hadn't done anything wrong. He wasn't their enemy. Even though it went beyond the usual bounds of a doctor's role, she couldn't help but feel for the situation he'd landed in.

When he woke up, she'd try again to convince him to answer Rian's questions. The sooner the captain got his answers, the better it would be for all of them. The stunner had obviously been painful for the commando, and she couldn't stand by and see him hit with it again.

In the brig, the temperature had risen now that the engines had been running for a while. She'd been telling the truth earlier when she'd said she didn't know how hot it would get in here. No one had ever spent any great length of time in Rian's brig, especially while they were traveling. Likely the heat wouldn't rise to dangerous levels, but it would certainly be uncomfortable.

The commando was still lying on his stomach in the middle of the cell where she'd left him. Even down on the floor, his body mass was intimidating. He was easily one of the tallest men she'd ever seen, topping out both Rian and Callan, who weren't exactly short in stature or muscle.

When he'd pulled her back against his chest earlier, using her body as a shield with his hand on her neck and fingers splayed against her abdomen, she probably should have been terrified, not just a little nervous—no doubt he could have snapped her neck with one hand. But despite his threats, he hadn't been rough with her. His hold had been light, and the longer she'd stood there, the sensation of his muscles pressed against her had started interfering with her ability to breathe.

She stared at him for a long moment before reaching over to unlock the door. And then she stood there for another few seconds, making sure he wasn't about to rush her for another escape attempt. He didn't move a muscle, and she couldn't see his face from this angle.

With a short breath, she pulled open the door and stepped into the cell. Maybe the sedative had at last knocked him out like it was meant to. Perhaps his body had taken longer to react to the medication, which was why he hadn't immediately gone down like she'd expected.

As she approached him, she pulled the med scanner out of her pocket. Sweat glistened along the line of his short light brown hair, but the commando's blue eyes were closed and she let out a low exhale of relief that he was still unconscious.

Kira knelt down and held the instrument a few inches above the middle of his back. Scanning the chest was more ideal, but the device would work either way; it would just take a little longer to pick up readings from different positions. While she waited, she reached down and trailed two fingers along the masculine line of his stubbled jaw. The man was handsome, but it was his startling light blue eyes that really made his looks. They were the purest, clearest blue she'd even seen, almost the color of silver ice, so easily distraction-worthy. She pressed two fingers into the crook of his neck, because no matter what her scanner or any other medical device could tell her, she'd always believed touch could impart information about a patient's condition a soulless machine couldn't.

The commando's skin felt clammy and, right away, the pulse lagging under her fingertips told her his heart rate was low. A rush of unease expanded within her, pushing upward, but she focused on the scanner screen, waiting for the results before she let the burgeoning alarm send her into action.

The device beeped at last, readings scrolling onto the screen.

*Damn it.* The apprehension she'd been holding back burst into a surge of adrenaline as she shoved to her feet and ran into the cargo hold, to the bulkhead where the emergency hover stretcher was clamped near the hatchway.

"Kira, what's going on?" Zahli came up behind her as she got the stretcher down.

"The commando's having a reaction to the sedative." She didn't wait for her friend's reply, but pushed the slim cot at a run through the cargo hold and into the short hallway.

Back in the brig, Command Donnelly hadn't moved, probably lucky, considering she'd left the door wide open in her haste. As she positioned the hover stretcher next to him, Zahli and Tannin appeared in the doorway.

"Help me get him onto the stretcher. If I don't get him up to the medbay, he's either going to stroke out or go into full cardiac arrest."

Tannin shared a quick look with Zahli then came forward to crouch down and help her roll the commando onto the stretcher. "Rian's not going to like this. Sure you can't treat him down here?"

Kira tabbed the controls on the stretcher to bring it up off the floor. "Since all my medical equipment is two levels above us, and he'll be dead before I can get up there and back down here, I'd say that's a no."

She brushed by Tannin as she pushed the hover stretcher into action, running the patient back out into the cargo bay and over to the freight elevator. As she loaded him on and then had to wait the few moments it took to go up two levels, she took a second to press her hand against his neck again while watching the too-slow rise and fall of his chest. The only other time she'd seen someone react this badly to a sedative had been back in medical school, and then she'd only observed other doctors treating the woman.

The elevator stopped, and she maneuvered the hover stretcher out into the passageway and toward the medbay. Zahli arrived, breath a bit short since she'd no doubt run up the stairs to get here so fast.

"What can I do?"

Kira stepped sideways toward the screen inset into the bulkhead at the head of the cot, touching the crystal display to bring it online. "Kick down the legs on the stretcher."

"On it."

Opening a recess below the diag-screen, she pulled out a conduit-cuff. Once Zahli had the legs down and turned off the hover mechanism, she snapped the device around the commando's wrist.

The cuff took a moment to scan and then insert a cannula needle into the patient's vein while the ship's med system performed a more in-depth scan, presenting readouts on the crystal display.

She ordered a shot of adrenaline and then stepped back while the drug was administered through the cuff.

"What's going on?" The rumble of warning in Rian's voice stiffened her shoulders.

"The prisoner had a bad reaction to a sedative," Zahli explained, her words short with tension.

No telling what their captain's reaction to this would be. They all knew he hated people defying his orders, and considering he'd given her one only a few minutes ago… She cut off the line of thinking, concentrating on the fluctuating readings on the screen.

"And?"

At the clipped word, Kira glanced over her shoulder. Rian stood just inside the medbay door, posture relaxed but palms resting on his weapons. Callan, the ship's security specialist, stood to one side with a stunner in hand, while Tannin was out in the passageway.

"And…" Zahli repeated, her tone a little unsure. "Kira brought him up here to treat him."

"Obviously," Rian muttered. "Except I seem to remember giving orders less than ten minutes ago that no one was to interact with the prisoner, let alone take him out of the brig."

Kira turned her attention back to the shallow rise and fall of the commando's chest, annoyance streaking through her. "He would have died, Captain."

"So?" The careless shrug came through loud and clear in Rian's tone. "Didn't he just threaten to take you on a spacewalk without a suit?"

"He was rightly insulted about being locked up and forcibly removed from his post. You want to be responsible for killing an innocent man? Because I sure don't."

"Wouldn't be the first dead innocent I'm accountable for." Rian's low words cut through the otherwise quiet medbay. "And since he threatened a member of my crew, if he dies, it's not going to ruin my day."

A spike of aggravation slashed through her, and she turned to glare at their captain. "Damn it, I'm going to treat him—"

An alarm sounded from the screen a split second before the patient started seizing. The commando arched up from the narrow stretcher, and Kira threw herself into his side to stop him from pitching off the cot. His eyes were open but unfocused, his expression twisting into confused rage.

An arm lashed out, and Kira ducked, narrowly avoiding a fist in the face. Damn, the adrenaline had been too much. The man seemed to have a hypersensitivity to any kind of medicine.

"Frecking jezus christ." Rian appeared on the opposite side of the stretcher and shoved both hands against the commando's shoulders, struggling to push him back down to the bed.

Tannin elbowed his way in, and Kira stepped aside as the two men fought to keep the flailing patient under control.

"If you're so set on doctoring him, Kira, do something before I tell Callan to treat him with a nucleon blast to the face." Rian huffed over the words, muttering a curse as the commando tried to rear up against him.

"The last sedative almost killed him." But, maybe a different one, at half dose — ?

"Do something. *Now!*"

She lurched the single step to the crystal display in the bulkhead and brought up a list of stored meds in the *Imojenna*'s system. The mildest sedative she had was in low supply; usually for kids, it often did nothing for adults, and they'd never had a reason to use it before. She ordered up a dose and then held her breath as she pushed the "administer" icon.

For a long moment, the commando continued fighting Tannin's and Rian's holds. But then he dropped like a stone, sending Tannin stumbling and Rian half sprawling across the patient at the sudden absence of resistance.

Heart tripping, Kira pushed her way in and pressed a hand to the commando's neck. A strong, steady pulse registered, and she blew out a short breath of relief. A quick glance at the display showed the patient's vitals returning to normal ranges.

She straightened and looked up at Rian, standing across from her.

"I'll save you the trouble of ordering me to send him back to the brig, because he's not going anywhere until I'm sure he's stable."

Rian's brow lowered over an unimpressed glare, and her heart skipped a beat. The captain hated ultimatums; maybe she should have worded that a little more reasonably.

"Then you better find a way to wake him up and make

him cooperate, because I will have those answers one way or another, even if it's from dissecting his dead body."

Sharp indignation sliced through her, but she kept her expression blank. She'd gotten used to his callous regard for life and lethal threats in the years since she'd signed on with the *Imojenna*'s crew, but that didn't mean she had to like it. Rian was a good guy, but this war with the Reidar that the wider universe didn't even know about meant he often walked a questionably moral line in his pursuit of the shape-shifting aliens. However, she'd never personally witnessed him kill someone who hadn't tried to kill him first. Whatever he'd done before she'd known him, well, it was all said and done. She wasn't in a position to be judging people on their history.

She clenched her fingers tighter where she held the edge of the stretcher. "I'll do my best. But only if he stays here in the medbay."

Rian gave a single nod, then glanced toward the doors. "Tannin, get some cuffs."

The ship's tech analyst disappeared along the passageway. The words to ask if restraints were really necessary tightened the back of Kira's throat, but she swallowed them away. Getting Rian to allow the commando to remain up here instead of the makeshift cell was probably as big a concession as she was likely to get. In fact, she was a little surprised he'd even agreed to it.

He returned his cool gaze to her. "If he tries anything, Callan will shoot him with a Reidar stunner."

And there was the punch line. Damn it, she'd promised the commando no one would do that again.

She nodded and focused her attention on checking the crystal display, making sure the patient's heart rate and breathing were still within a stable range. Tannin returned after a few silent moments, and she stepped back as the commando's wrists were secured to either side of the cot. Rian glanced up at her as he removed the commando's boots and then started strapping down the patient's ankles. Some kind of contrition or concern must have shown in her expression, because his gaze hardened as he stared at her.

"If you want him up here, Kira, then we've got to make sure he's not going anywhere." He gave the cuff around the commando's ankle a final tug while Tannin secured the other foot.

"After the hit he just took from that sedative, I doubt he'll be able to even sit up by himself, let alone go on a murderous rampage," she muttered.

"Yeah, well he's still an AF-one commando, and I can tell you from personal experience that they're tough sons of bitches with no fear of getting themselves killed."

Kira frowned as she glanced at the unconscious man. What kind of person didn't care whether or not he died? Okay, he'd seemed pretty serious about taking on zero atmosphere to escape the *Imojenna*, but part of her hadn't really believed he'd do it.

"I want to know as soon as he's awake and ready to talk." Rian sent her an implacable look, and she had to swallow a defeated sigh. He stepped away from the cot, pausing by Callan, who had finally holstered his gun and stood with his arms crossed in a defensive position. "He even twitches the wrong way, you shoot first and tell me second, got it?"

Callan nodded with military precision. The captain cut her one last warning glance and then left the medbay.

"Is there anything I can help you with?" Zahli asked from the opposite bulkhead, where she'd been standing during the commotion.

This time, Kira did huff a long sigh. "No. I think Command Donnelly will probably need a few hours to sleep this off."

"Comm me if you need anything." Zahli sent her a short

smile then walked over to Tannin.

Tannin dropped an arm over Zahli's shoulders as they left. Her heart gave a pinch at Zahli's calm and contented air, the same one she'd had since Tannin had come aboard and Rian had grudgingly consented not to kill the man with enough balls to touch his sister.

Out of everyone on the ship, she was closest to Zahli, so she certainly didn't begrudge her friend the happiness she'd found in these dark times. But still, in those moments when she caught the loving glances the two exchanged, it made a void ache in her soul for what she was missing, what she'd given up expecting from life after she'd left Capitol One Hospital on Jacolby in disgrace three years ago.

Thinking about the past and the life she'd left behind never helped anything, although it did remind her to be grateful Rian had landed on Auberon within a day of her arriving on the ruthless, almost lawless planet where people went to hide or get lost. She wouldn't have lasted two days if she hadn't seen the ad he'd posted at the spaceport trade center where she'd been loitering for over twenty hours, too scared to leave the relative safety of the spaceport, but not knowing where else to go or what else to do.

The first time she'd met Rian, when she'd gone to apply for the position of ship doctor, he'd frightened the heck out of her. He'd been ice cold, his eyes devoid of any emotion, weapons slung around his hips with deadly ease. He was the exact kind of person she'd been trying to avoid—one who she'd thought would kill her for looking at him the wrong way. She would have turned and run as fast and far as she could, if it hadn't been for Zahli standing next to him, a warm and welcoming smile on her face. With limited options, she'd figured the captain couldn't be too bad if Zahli was standing there looking at ease and relaxed, and when she'd found out the woman was actually Rian's sister, it had abated her fears even further.

Though there'd been some tough times, joining the crew of the *Imojenna* was the best thing that could have happened to her. Being on the ship under Rian was kind of like having a weird, dysfunctional family. Like her, the others didn't discuss their pasts too often, but she got the feeling she wasn't the only person who had no one else in the galaxy outside of the *Imojenna*'s bulkheads. And while she'd heard all kinds of conflicting rumors about Rian—from the reports of his actions that had made him a war hero and celebrity in the military, to his ruthless reputation of killing without prejudice—she'd come to see that even though he might be somewhat psychologically damaged from whatever had happened to him in those years he'd been missing, presumed dead, he was still mostly an honorable man who tried to do what was right.

Putting the unhelpful retrospection aside, she sliced a glance at Callan and shifted around the cot before setting her hand in the middle of the commando's chest. His breathing was even and heart pounded steadily beneath her palm. He no longer felt clammy or hot, though his shirt was damp. She checked the readouts on the crystal display and then went over to a nearby bench where she'd left her commpad.

While the commando was sleeping, she wanted to check the files they'd stolen from the abandoned Reidar lab on Nadira. The idea that this soldier had been a victim of the alien experiments, like Rian, had taken root in her mind.

Who knew how long the Reidar had been living among them, hiding in plain sight? For hundreds of years after the early technologists of Earth had mastered intergalactic travel and colonized space, people had searched for other intelligent life, but found only a handful of extinct remnants. Humans had thought they were alone, that the galaxy was theirs for the taking. And take it they had. Had these shape-shifting aliens been hiding among them the whole time, or had they come from somewhere else?

She'd taken a quick look at the files not long after they'd left Nadira and ever since had been avoiding the research, complete with repulsive details of the experiments and torture the subjects had experienced. Some kind of breeding program. It was the antithesis to everything she stood for as a doctor, and no amount of medical training could harden her against the monstrosities recorded in those documents. It had sickened her, imagining what those poor people had gone through at the hands of the sociopathic aliens.

But if she was going to help this man, and maybe even help Rian, she had to disconnect from the horror and search the facts for any clues that might aid her later, beginning with sensitivities to drugs.

As she walked to the doorway, she speared Callan with her best doctor-means-business glare. "I'm going up to Rian's office to download some files. I'll be back in a few minutes. Don't get any ideas about killing him and making it look like an accident while I'm gone, because I'll know."

Callan sent her a flat look. "Security on this ship comes down to me, and you know how seriously I take protecting the *Imojenna* and the crew. Besides, if I wanted to kill him, I wouldn't bother making it look like an accident, Doc."

"Of course you wouldn't," she muttered as she strode out into the passageway. At least she could say the ship's security specialist—or whatever title Callan used—remained constant in his liberal use of violence to solve his problems. That being said, he was almost overprotective when it came to the crew that called the *Imojenna* home—especially Rian. Out of everyone, Callan's dedication to their captain was second only to Zahli, Rian's sister. Of course, it was comparable to Lianna's loyalty. Kira had been waiting for the day the two of them would get into a who-bromanced-Rian-better argument.

She took in a few calming breaths as she made her way up to Rian's quarters, the familiar rush of a medical emergency gradually draining from her limbs. While working as the ship's doctor onboard the *Imojenna* wasn't as demanding or high-stress as her last position at a city ER on one of the Inter-Planetary Coalition's central planets, her career now definitely had its exciting moments and medical challenges, complete with things she would have never seen if she'd remained a big-shot trauma surgeon.

No, her life certainly hadn't turned out like she'd dreamed back in med school, but at least she had a home of sorts and could still practice medicine. She was happy enough, as long as she didn't think too closely about the threat of shape-shifting aliens who'd blow the *Imojenna* out of the stratosphere given half a chance to recapture Rian and the Arynian priestess, Ella. Their knowledge of the Reidar made them a target, but thus far, Rian had kept them a step ahead of the threat. Some days, though, she wondered just how much longer their luck would hold out.

# Chapter Four

Rian managed to make it to the bridge without any other minor calamities, though it was only a matter of time before the next disaster on his damned ship. These days, he couldn't go five minutes without needing to put out a fire.

"Oh good, you're back. I was just about to comm you," Lianna, his navigator-slash-engineer, said as he dropped into the captain's chair.

"Of course you were," he muttered. No doubt the next crisis was imminent. "What's going on?"

"Qaelan contacted the ship, wanting to speak with you."

He shifted in his seat and tapped his screen to life. They'd only just left his cousin and his smaller ship *Ebony Winter* still docked on the *Swift Brion*. Accessing the communications tab, he sent the comm-link to the viewport, then sat back in his seat as the image of Qaelan, along with Zander, flickered into sharp clarity. Zander was looking pretty good for a guy who'd almost been killed by his psycho Reidar twin a few short days ago. Thank christ they'd managed to stop at least him from being switched out by the aliens. But who knew how many other government and military officials were already lost?

"Miss me already?" He clasped his hands behind his head, kicking one boot over his opposite knee.

"And all the chaos you leave in your wake? Not a bit." Zander shot him a grin, taking the edge off the bite.

"So why the comm? Couldn't go an hour without me?"

"It's about getting more of the stunner weapons made," Qae answered, going straight to the point without any of his usual quips. "Which we've started calling razars, by the way."

"Razars?" Well, it was probably easier than calling them Reidar stunners. "Okay, I can live with that. What about them?"

Qae frowned, crossing his arms. "That contact I said we could use for the components we need? UAFA took him down a few weeks back for illegal arms trading."

"Damn it," he muttered. The Universal Armed Forces Agency were a galaxy-wide, privately owned military that contracted out to whoever could pay them the most. They operated with complete impunity granted by the IPC government and military, who governed the central planets and systems. UAFA had made up the ranks of the IPC military when the government had decided it was time to bring the outer independent planets under one ruling body. The resulting Assimilation Wars had spanned more than two decades—beginning before he was born. It'd been bloody, and very few independent planets had been spared. Only the most far-flung worlds hadn't been touched by the battle, but at the end—after what he'd done to give the IPC their victory—even those outer worlds had agreed to come under IPC governance.

So whoever had paid to have Qae's contact taken out could have been the IPC, who often sourced out warrants, or it could just as easily have been a rival illegal arms trader wanting to get the guy out of the way. UAFA didn't ask questions, they just took a person's money and were relentless in carrying out their contracts.

"So what's Plan B?" he asked, causing Qae and Zander to share a quick look.

"Actually, we were hoping you could tell us," Zander replied. "Once the *Swift Brion* goes off the grid, since I'll officially be AWOL and a traitor, it's not like I can use any IPC military contacts to get what we need."

"In other words, you want to know if I have any contacts we could use."

Zander knew about the short time he'd spent working for a big-time, illicit trader out of a legendary illegal bazaar after escaping the Reidar, when things had still been hazy, his blood lust unchecked and control nonexistent. He'd left all of that behind when Mae Petros found him and kicked his ass back into the IPC military, but there were probably more than a few favors from those days he could call in. "Leave it with me. I'll see what I turn up."

The end of his words were cut off as an alarm sounded. He glanced over at Lianna, who was frowning down at her console screen, a definite note of concern in her features.

"What is it?" He straightened in his seat, hand landing on the butt of his right holstered pistol by habit alone.

"Got a ping off an IPC transit policing ship. They scanned us, and as far as I know, the forged ident files are holding, but they're coming in for visual."

For the millionth time, Rian cursed his recently bestowed status as an intergalactic terrorist—one more way the Reidar were trying to screw him. It meant they'd had to start using ident files forged by Callan to fly through the IPC central systems so they weren't discovered and arrested on the outstanding warrant.

"If they get visual, they're going to realize we're not a Cephas class mining transporter. Are we still far enough away to make a run for it?"

Lianna cut him a worried look. "If we run, they'll know

we've got a reason to avoid them."

"Everything okay?" Zander asked through the comm call.

Already reaching for his screen to cut the subspace linkup, he glanced up at his cousin and oldest friend on the viewport. "Just the usual. I'll be in touch about those components."

Qae and Zander bade him good-bye, and he ended the transmission without answering.

"What's the closest place to go dirtside?" Even as he asked the question, he brought nav data up on his own screen, calculating the distance between the *Imojenna* and the IPC transit police.

"There's a quarry moon and beyond that, a resource trade planet, Braylon."

"Set a course for the moon. There'll be too much IPC presence on Braylon."

Lianna got to work altering their course, putting them on a trajectory to the small moon. The IPC trans-cops immediately corrected to pursue them. Damn it, he'd been hoping if they realized their pretend mining transporter was heading for the quarry moon, they'd be less interested.

Why they hell had they gotten so curious about his ship? And the bigger question had to be asked—was it just a transport of no-account IPC officers with nothing better to do, or was it a group of Reidar?

It was going to be close, but they should hit the moon's atmosphere just before the trans-cops got within visual range.

"When we hit atmo, scramble the ident files and get us lost in the biggest spaceport you can find."

He stood, planning to tell the crew they were making an unexpected stop and then heading to his office to start working on which of his old Huata contacts he might be able to hit up for some components to make a whole bunch of Reidar-stunning guns.

# Chapter Five

Varean tried to swallow, but his tongue stuck to the roof of his mouth like Velcro sandpaper. He coughed, his lungs aching like he had a boulder sitting in the middle of his chest. His eyes felt sticky and his body chilled with the aftereffects of sweating it up something fierce.

That now-familiar no-nonsense voice was the only relief in his current purgatory, and he hung onto the slight lilt of it, forcing back the weird, reality-like dreams that kept getting stronger and more confusing. Even more unsettling, the foreign language he kept hearing in his head was beginning to make sense, words here and there breaking through the confusion with their meaning and intent. It had to be some kind of nightmare induced by all he'd experienced in the past few days, added to whatever that stunner had done to his brain cells.

He lifted a heavy arm to wipe a hand over his face, but something tugged against his wrist, keeping it from going very far.

"What the—?" His voice scratched out at not much more

than a whisper, and he forced his eyes open to focus on the trapped hand. He was cuffed to a bed railing, and a tug at his other arm and legs told him he'd been tied down spread-eagled, with absolutely no slack to maneuver.

A spike of apprehensive fury cleared some of the fog from his brain as the events came back in a dizzying rush, ending with damn Kira sticking him with a shot of something that had made him girl-drink drunk before smashing his lights out with all the finesse of a sledgehammer.

"Command Donnelly? Just relax, you're in the medbay. Please don't fight the restraints. You'll only hurt yourself."

The doc's words washed through him, soothing the wildness with a power she shouldn't have possessed over him. She sounded so concerned, but had all the bedside manner of a Shivani pit viper—pretty to look at and deceptively tranquil until they decided to attack, then the moron who got close enough never saw it coming.

He rolled his head to the left and found her sitting on a stool, commpad in her lap and dark hair falling out of the pins. Despite her request, he yanked his arm against the cuffs, rattling the bed rail. That mutation of aggression within him had gained in size and strength while he'd been out of it, lending more credence to the idea of killing his way free, even though these people technically weren't his enemy, despite the fact they'd kidnapped him.

"Let me out, and I won't have to fight the restraints." Hell, he sounded about as threatening as a ninety-year-old, with the way his voice scraped over his dry throat.

"Water?" The doc arched a brow and stood, setting her commpad on a nearby hover trolley.

Varean clenched his jaw but didn't answer, watching as she poured water from a bottle into a clear plastic cup and then added a pink straw. As if he weren't being humiliated enough.

She brought the cup over, her movements wary but still efficient. Her green gaze sliced over him with brisk detachment as she poked the straw at his lips, her expression expectant. Part of him wanted to refuse, just because he was so pissed about her pulling that little stunt in knocking him out. And for apparently pandering to him like he was a dirt-licking imbecile. With that dosing gun in her possession—obviously missed when he'd done that quick frisk—she could have knocked him out any time after he'd grabbed her. Instead, she'd gone along and let him think he actually had half a chance of escaping. No wonder she hadn't seemed afraid of him.

Of course, refusing a drink of water when his throat had all the dryness of a desert in a heat wave would make him a total idiot. So he parted his lips far enough to accept the ridiculous pink cylinder sticking out of the cup.

As soon as the cool liquid hit his tongue, a wave of relief and then longing rippled through his body. He hadn't realized how parched he was until the water slid down the back of his throat. He greedily sucked down as much as he could through the thin straw and would have drained the cup if the doc hadn't pulled it away from him.

"Not too fast. You don't want to make yourself sick." She straightened and shifted back from him.

He stretched out his fingers and managed to catch the edge of her shirt before she retreated very far. "I'm still thirsty."

She stopped trying to move away from him, her clothes pulled taut against her tantalizing curves he couldn't help noticing, even when he was half dead. He tugged, trying to draw her closer.

"Just give it a minute."

Frustration pulsed through him, temper made shorter by the uncharacteristic urge to lash out fed by the thirst nagging at him. Damn it, did he look like a toddler who needed to be coddled because he had a boo-boo? "Water. Now."

She sighed and turned to top off the half-empty contents. "Fine, have it your way."

A moment later, the straw met his lips again, and this time she didn't take the cup away until he'd drained every last drop.

He sighed as he relaxed back against the pillow behind him. The doctor put down the cup and moved to the head of the gurney, accessing controls to make the top half of the cot rise, until he was in an upright reclining position.

Despite the slow movement, everything spun for a long moment, and he closed his eyes as the water in his stomach decided to pitch a revolt. He sucked in a long, slow breath, attempting to force the churning down, if only to save himself from an "I told you so" from the doc.

"What happened to me?" Maybe if he got his mind onto something else, his stomach would settle.

"You had a bad reaction to the sedative I gave you. Then you had a bad reaction to the adrenaline I administered to counteract the sedative. You nearly died."

Well, that would explain why he felt like fresh-churned shite in a bucket. And this conversation wasn't helping his roiling guts one bit.

"How long was I out?"

"Over twenty-four hours."

"*What*?" He snapped his eyes open. Except hell, he shouldn't have done that.

The doc shoved a plastic container in front of his face as the water came up again, leaving his stomach aching and empty.

Great. Now his head was pounding as well. He went to rub a hand over his face, but yep, he was cuffed to the bed. The newfound hostility within him stirred again, and he clenched his fists. He didn't understand where the fury was coming from.

He'd never considered himself an angry person prone to outbursts or unreasonable violence. His fellow AF commando buddies used to make jokes about him being a droid because, no matter what kind of shite had gone down, he'd always kept his cool. Ever since he'd first been hit by that damned stunner, it was like his much-prized self-restraint had up and left, to be replaced by an unpredictable cannon on a short fuse. Had the stunner affected him in some way, maybe because of the legacy within him that he'd spent the past decade hiding? It was the only answer he could come up with.

"Better now?" A hand lightly touched his shoulder, the contact rippling through him in bright, yet calming, waves. Which was damned ridiculous.

This was not him. He didn't get worked up over women he'd met five minutes ago. He didn't ever let anger or frustration take the helm and steer his actions.

He would get himself locked down and in control no matter what else these people did to him. Make sure they didn't find out the truth about him. He had to get free and disappear.

He cleared his throat and this time, when he opened his eyes, it seemed his equilibrium had got its shite together, because everything stayed exactly where it should be.

"You serious about the twenty-four-hour thing?"

The doc reached up with a damp, cool cloth and pressed it against his clammy skin. It felt too damn good, and he got the sense it wasn't only the administrations soothing him, but more the person doing the administering. Damned if he wasn't starting to suffer from Stockholm syndrome.

"Thirty and a half hours, if you want to be exact," she finally answered, the cloth moving to wipe down his hairline, taking away some of the lingering sweat.

*Goddamn.* Which meant they were light-years away from

the *Swift Brion*. Even if he found a way back, there'd be no point to it. He got the feeling that if Sherron didn't get the answers he wanted, the guy wouldn't stop pursuing him until he did. Disappearing was the last card he had on the table at this point.

Maybe he should have been more pissed that one anomalous shot from a weapon meant to reveal shape-shifting aliens had destroyed the life he'd worked hard to build within the military, because he sure as hell had nothing else beyond it. Growing up in the IPC foster system from a little over a year old after his mom had died, no knowledge of who he was or who his relatives were had left him with no family. The last ten years since joining the military, he'd been more interested in keeping a low profile and striving hard and fast through his career than making any kind of lasting personal relationships. Yeah, he had no life beyond his posting, this frecked-up turn of events making that fact more than obvious.

"What's going to happen to me?"

The doc shrugged one shoulder, lowering the cloth to stare intently at him, close enough that his gaze was drawn to the pink Cupid's bow of her upper lip.

"Depends. If you cooperate, Rian will let you go, though don't expect an apology. If you don't…"

She glanced away from him, her features tightening the slightest bit. But it was all the clue he needed. Sherron would get his answers one way or another.

"Should have let me die," he muttered, slouching down against the pillow.

"Sorry, it's not in my job description." Warm, gentle fingers landed on his forehead then slipped down to press into the crook of his neck, her touch echoing through him, leaving him fighting a shiver. "At least your pulse has regulated. I know this situation is not ideal—"

Varean let loose a cutting laugh and opened his eyes

to glare at her. "Not ideal? That's like flying within burning distance of a star and saying it's kind of warm."

Some of that resignation within him caught fire, flaring into kindling vehemence. He yanked at both arms, and the frame of the cot whined. "Whatever Sherron thinks I know, it's got nothing to do with him or any damned aliens. I just want to get back to the *Swift Brion* and be left the hell alone."

A little bit of deflection here and there—if he could get back to the *Swift Brion*, he'd be staying aboard only long enough to pack his crap and take the first shuttle out.

The truth about him was closer to being outed than it had been in a long time. Frustrating as it was, he'd have to disappear and start again, because if the government found out about him, they'd make sure he disappeared the permanent way. These people could think he'd been messed with by the aliens, or whatever theory Sherron was stuck on, as long as they didn't suspect the real answer.

Her gaze dropped, avoiding him. "Actually, I doubt at this point whether you could make it back to the *Swift Brion*."

"Oh yeah? Did they fly into a black hole or something while I was out of it?"

She returned her gaze to him, a definite flash of annoyance in her eyes. "Because Captain Admiral Graydon and the crew of the *Swift Brion* took the flagship and went AWOL."

Varean laughed, because how else would he respond to the most ridiculous thing he'd heard in his entire life. A whole flagship going AWOL? With Captain Admiral Graydon behind the decision—?

Except the doc wasn't laughing, and the steady stare she returned was too grave. His humor vanished as quickly as it had flared.

"What the hell are you talking about?"

She pushed up from the stool, avoiding his gaze. "Maybe this is a conversation we should save for later, when you're feeling better."

"Tell me!" He reared upright, yanking against the restraints, jerking the entire bed.

When she looked at him this time, her eyes were wide, her expression wary, for the first time since he'd laid eyes on her. Regret jerked his pulse along for a few beats, because he hadn't meant to scare her.

"Captain Admiral Graydon became aware of the fact that the Reidar have infiltrated the IPC government and military. In order to protect himself and his crew, he's taken the flagship somewhere in the galaxy where the IPC can't reach. And that's all I'm saying on the subject right now."

"It's more than you should have said, Kira."

Varean glanced over to see one of Sherron's men standing in the doorway, who seemed overly fond of adorning himself with more than a few lethal weapons, like a hooker wearing her sugar daddy's bling.

"Callan, I thought you were catching a few hours' sleep." The doc turned away from the bed, seeming to make herself busy at a nearby diag-cart.

"Kind of hard to get any shut-eye with all the yelling going on down here."

Her shoulders were tense. "Command Donnelly is understandably concerned about his situation—"

"Would you stop calling me that?" Varean gave another halfhearted yank at his restraints, wishing for a free arm if only to rub a hand over the tightening muscles in his neck. He sank back against the pillow. "Clearly I can't be an AF commando anymore, not if it's true about the aliens secretly taking over the military from the inside."

Callan gave a short laugh. "Then what are you, the Easter Bunny?"

Varean shot a glare across the medbay as the doc turned back to him with a medical scanner in hand.

"Callan, you know the rules of my medbay. Shut up or put up."

"I ain't never helped patch up another person in my life, so I sure as hell ain't going to start now."

"How altruistic of you," she muttered, pulling the stool over to sit down closer to him.

As she shifted nearer, a subtle whiff of a creamy vanilla caressed his senses, gone between one breath and another. But it left an echo of tightening through his body, a heating sentiment completely at odds with the anger he was fighting to control.

"I was told to comm Rian as soon as you woke. He has questions he wants answered. But you can tell me, if it would be easier. Let me help you."

"*Help me*? If you want to help me, then let me the hell go."

"I liked him better when he was unconscious," Callan mumbled. "Don't you have some kind of truth serum? Get him to spill his guts faster than a rookie recruit on his first uncontrolled reentry."

The doc sighed and sent Callan an impatient glare. "Because I took an oath when I became a doctor, and that included not drugging people just to get them talking."

"In case you haven't noticed, this isn't some fancy central-systems hospital. Rian gave you a direct order. He's already pissed about having to land. If you're not going to comm him, I will."

"I'll comm him in a second. Just give me one minute to make sure he's stable, or I'll be finding some laxatives for extra flavoring in your next meal."

"All right." He held up one hand; the other stayed wrapped around the grip of a holstered gun. "I'll shut up."

The doc turned back to him, a beseeching expression on her lovely features. *Oh hell.* No doubt she knew when she gave people that exact look, they went along with whatever spilled off her honey-poisoned tongue.

"We landed?" he asked before she could say anything. If he could distract her long enough to work out how to get free of these cuffs and then off the ship, he could start with his disappearing plan.

"Yesterday. We were being followed. Apparently they're still searching for us, but Rian is planning on leaving within the hour either way." No mention of who *they* were or why the ship had been followed. "Do you mind if I call you Varean?"

He clenched his jaw, sending her a hard frown instead of answering.

"Okay, despite the fact you're glaring daggers at me, I'll take that as a yes. I'm Kira." She paused for a short breath, then slowly lowered her hand to cover his. And damn it, why did he have to get that buzz every time she touched him? It was making it harder and harder to remember why he had to resist her. "It might not seem like it, but I only want to help you. Rian has been distracted with keeping us off the IPC's radar, but I can't hold him off forever. Eventually, he's going to want to question you. And if you don't cooperate, he'll find some way to force your hand."

"*Rian* can try, but he won't find me all that accommodating."

Kira made a frustrated noise. "What is it with you military guys and your damned supersized egos?"

Seemed the doc's gentle bedside manner didn't go very far. He grinned at her obvious irritation. "Sorry, but since I got forcibly removed from my post three days ago, I'm not feeling all that cooperative. Take me back to the brig, if you want. Hell, Callan over there can go tell Rian to vent me for all I care, but I don't owe anyone a single fact about myself."

Callan pulled the Reidar stunner in a slow, steady movement. "The cap'tin wants answers, and Rian Sherron tends to get what Rian Sherron wants. Maybe another pulse or two from the stunner will help that fact sink in."

The doc crossed her arms. "Because threatening him with a weapon is really going to help this situation. Besides, I promised him that no one else would shoot him with one of those things."

"Playing nice-nurse obviously isn't getting you anywhere."

Kira added a glare to her hostile stance. "Aside from the fact that I'm a doctor, not a nurse, screw you sideways, Callan."

A thread of cynical humor cut through Varean, and any other time he would have laughed at that charming comeback. Except not on the days he was cuffed to a gurney.

Judging by his frown, Callan didn't seem overly impressed by her retort. "Comm him now, Kira. That was his order. You know he'll be more pissed if I have to do it because you wouldn't."

She obviously didn't move fast enough, because Callan took a step forward and brought up the stunner.

Varean sent Callan a stay-the-hell-back-asshole glare. If that guy took one more step, they'd find out how this cot would stand up against a pissed-off AF commando. The temptation to let loose the wild, mutated fury within him was getting harder to deny. But he'd never lost control of himself in even the smallest way, and part of him feared what would happen if he did, that he might hurt someone who didn't deserve to get hurt. Like the doc.

"I'll make things simple by stating once and for all that no matter who asks the questions, I'm not telling you a damned thing."

Kira held up her hands in a calming kind of gesture. "Okay, how about we cool down a little. Varean only just woke up. Let's give him a minute to process."

She could give him all the minutes in a year—he still wouldn't change his mind. But instead of telling her that, he settled for glaring harder at Callan.

"Fine." Callan tugged a comm out of his pocket. "Don't say I didn't warn you."

Kira got to her feet and hurried over to Callan. "I'll comm him. But Rian also told me to make sure he was ready to talk. I can convince him. Probably quicker if you'd leave me to it."

Callan shook his head. "Sorry, Doc. Now he's awake, and it's a question of safety. If there's even the slightest chance he's Reidar, I'm not letting him out of my sight."

Varean straightened as far as the cuffs would allow, fatigue and ineffectual exasperation cutting his patience to a short end. "Yeah? Going to watch me take a piss in a few minutes? I'm sure that'll be real entertaining for you."

"Get frecked, asshole." Callan took another menacing step forward.

"How about you strip off all those weapons and say that to my face when I'm not cuffed down?"

The man sent him an easy, gloating grin, bringing up the Reidar stunner weapon again to aim at his chest. "Nighty-night, Donnelly. When you wake up in the brig, just holler if you still want that match."

Callan's finger tensed on the trigger as Kira yelled out and started forward. But the explosive, uncontrolled aggression inside him had burst free, and Varean wrapped his hands around the railings of the bed and hooked his feet into the corner bars, then threw all his weight and strength sideways, tipping the whole gurney over.

He swore as his fingers got jammed between the railing and the floor, though, from the other side of the medbay, Callan had started up a cursing streak much louder and more colorful.

Varean took a split second to brace himself for the inevitable pain and put his whole body into yanking his left arm. The cuffs snapped but sliced deeply into his wrists. Still, part of him hadn't expected to pull free so easily. A couple more jerks and he'd escaped the bindings altogether. He made it to his knees just as Callan got around the end of the bed. Obviously the guy had been expecting him to be lying there helpless, because the slack-jawed shock on the dick-hole's face would have been hilarious, except for that damned stunner in his hand. Freck him to hell if he was going to take another hit from that weapon.

He launched from his knees, tackling Callan around the legs. The guy roared his own fury as they both went down, knocking one of the carts, sending it crashing into the bulkhead and spitting instruments all over. As Callan tried to bring up the stunner, Varean scrambled to get a hold of his wrist. Clamping a hand around the guy's forearm, he smashed it down with all his strength, leaving Callan swearing and the stunner skittling away into a corner.

A fist rammed into his jaw, stunning his already aching head for a too-long second, leaving him vulnerable. He reached out blindly, finding Callan's throat and closing one hand around it. The guy bucked beneath him, but the mutated rage in his depths had taken hold, driving his fury-filled actions. And then, a trickle of hot power welled at the base of his skull—one he knew all too well but hadn't allowed himself to feel since he was a teenager. He should have realized this was going to happen. All the stress of the past days compounding until his instincts took over and released the abilities he'd worked so hard to conceal. The energy flowed out through his limbs on a precise vibration until it reached his fingertips. Callan's eyes widened for a split second, then the guy started going gray.

Something rammed into his chest, bringing a fiery burn of pain and loosening his hold. Callan shoved him and he fell back into the lower medical cabinets, glancing down to see a knife sticking out of his chest. Before he could react, Callan reared up, catching the handle to twist it, then yanked it out on a spurt of blood.

Acid-burning pain lit through him, and he couldn't breathe, couldn't swallow, couldn't do anything but slump to the floor.

"Callan! What did you do?" Kira came down next to him, tugging at his clothes, though he couldn't feel her rushed ministrations.

"Damn it, he was trying to kill me." The words came out hoarse, ending with a cough.

*Over. It's all over.*

For a second he floated on a bubble of disbelief. But it quickly burst, and his survival instincts kicked in, buoyed by the parts of him that had been tainted and forever distorted by the insistent, hostile mutation taking over more and more of the controlled person he used to be. He finally sucked in a desperate breath.

*No.* He refused to die like this.

It hadn't even been a fair fight. He'd survive this, if only to destroy Callan and his bastard of a captain, Rian Sherron. Might as well add Qaelan Forster to his vendetta while he was at it.

If a man could endure on the idea of vengeance alone, then he had more than enough to carry him through this injury and sustain him for the next hundred years.

Callan had gotten to his feet and come closer. Despite the pain ripping through his chest, Varean shot out a hand to wrap around the man's ankle. "You're a dead man."

Though he'd wheezed the words, they must have held a definite bite, because Kira paused in shock, then shook her head and pressed something against his wound.

Callan seemed taken aback, but then laughed. "*I'm* a dead man? I'd tell you to take a look in the mirror, but by the time I actually got one and came back here, you'd already be a corpse." He kicked free of Varean's weakening grasp. "I'm going up-ship to tell Rian about the commando's unfortunate demise."

As the gorilla stomped out of the medbay, the doc muttered a few choice words.

"You're not going to die, all right? So don't listen to him. Just hang on until I can get you hooked up to the ship's diag systems. You know that would have been much easier if you hadn't tipped over the gurney."

A somber laugh escaped him but turned into a cough. "Sorry, but the plan was to avoid being shot. Obviously that didn't pan out so well."

"And he's got a sense of humor even when he's dying," she muttered, shoving some medical supplies out of the way that had gotten knocked about during the scuffle.

"Thought you said I wasn't going to die." Funny, but the pain seemed to be fading, although his body felt heavy all of a sudden, his mind slow and tired.

"I'm the doctor, that's what I'm supposed to say." She finished shoving equipment out of her way and turned back to him.

For a moment, he focused on her gorgeously disheveled mop of dark hair and those soft green eyes. She really did have the face of an angel hiding the core of pure metium-reinforced steel inside her. Right at that moment, she looked like an angel who'd been put through hell. A sheen filled her eyes, leaving her blinking rapidly. He grabbed her hand covered in his blood, leaving the grip slippery.

"You're not actually upset over me, are you?"

She speared him with a pissed-off, indignant glare. "Of course I'm upset! You don't deserve to die just because Rian wanted his damn curiosity sated."

His muscles rapidly weakening, he reached up with his other hand to cup her cheek. "I'm not worth it, Kira. I'm a commando; it's the only end I had coming."

She leaned down, tugging her hand free to press the cloth harder against his injury. Her other hand came up to grip his chin. "I am not letting you die."

Warm vibrations erupted from deep within him, his inherent abilities fully blooming. She was right, he wasn't going to die, but when he survived, Rian was going to have even more damned questions.

The truth would be much harder to conceal.

The low reverberations streaming through him reached the wound, taking away the pain and leaving him breathing easier. But it was getting harder to keep his eyes open. Just before he succumbed to the healing sleep, Kira's eyes widened, her hand releasing his chin to lift and cover where he still had his palm against her cheek.

"What in the stars—?"

He let his hand fall away from her cheek as she stared down at him with a mystified expression. At least she wasn't looking at him like he was a freak.

# Chapter Six

"I thought you said he was dead." Rian shot a glance over his shoulder as Callan brushed past him, stepping into the medbay. He and Lianna had only just gotten the *Imojenna* to burn hard and fast off the quarry moon to avoid the IPC trans-cops still hovering in orbit when Callan had come to report the latest trouble with their guest.

Callan crossed his arms and glared at the unconscious commando on the gurney hooked up to the ship's medical life-support system. "Hell, Kira, you saved him? The frecking bastard tried to strangle me."

"I know. I was here, remember?" Kira paused in setting various instruments onto a diag-cart and half turned to aim a frosty glare at Callan. "But did you really think I was going to stand by and just let someone die in my medbay if there was a chance I could do something about it?"

"Yeah? Well, you just wasted your time." Callan didn't seem overly concerned about Kira's obvious annoyance. "Because when he wakes up, I'm going to pay him back in kind."

Kira slammed a tray onto the cart, rattling the instruments.

"Captain, I understand you have security concerns about Command Donnelly being in the medbay, but I refuse to have *him* in here any longer when the result is this." She flung a hand out to indicate the half-cleaned-up mess from what had obviously been a dirty fight. "The commando is not and never was our enemy, but we're doing a really good job of treating him like one. And the next person who gets any ideas about using that damn Reidar stunner will have to go through me."

Rian glanced from Callan to Kira and then to the half-dead commando. *Huh.* Kira had always been passionate and hard-lined about her views on saving people. They all knew she was more than willing to put herself in harm's way if it meant helping someone else, especially anyone she considered innocent. That zeal and fortitude made her a great medic and part of the reason he'd taken her onboard. However, in this case, her fierce defense of a man she didn't even know seemed a little excessive.

Of course, it might have something to do with Callan destroying her medbay. She could be kind of OCD when it came to her corner of the ship. The crew all knew not to go in and mess around with anything, so she was probably about ready to dose up Callan's lunch with a laxative for his part in the fight.

"Ha!" Callan scoffed, hooking his thumbs into his belt. "I've never seen you hold a weapon even one time in all the years I've known you. And we're supposed to take that threat seriously?"

Kira's expression turned almost sweet, except it was underlaid with metium-reinforced determination. "I took down a tier-one AF commando. And unlike you, Callan, I *can* kill people and make it look like an accident."

His eyebrows shot up and his mouth opened, no doubt with some kind of poetic comeback along the lines of *freck you.* But Rian stepped forward before he could get one word out, holding up a hand to cut Callan off.

"When he's stable, send him back down to the brig. And this time, chain him up."

Callan grinned and saluted him, while Kira's expression went from annoyed to downright infuriated.

"He doesn't deserve to be chained!" She abandoned the tidying up and crossed her arms. Though she'd voiced opposition to his opinions once or twice in the past, she'd never outright defied him before. A small, dark thread of anger trickled down the back of his neck.

"He threatened to space you the day we left the *Swift Brion*, and just now he did his damndest to choke the life out of my security specialist. You told me you don't want Callan in your medbay. The commando is dangerous, Kira. I'm not going to explain that to you again."

"Here's a novel thought. Why don't we let him go? In fact, what business did we have in taking him off the *Swift Brion* in the first place?"

"You know why. He reacted to the stunner. If he's not Reidar then the aliens did something to him. I want to know what it was and why. The guy answers my questions, I'll let him go."

Kira clenched her jaw, shooting an aggravated frown at Callan then turning her back on them. "And I still think I can talk him around if I'm given half a chance. I was just about to try when Callan so rudely butted in."

He clenched his fists, about ready to tear a verbal chunk out of her. But this was the first time she'd caused him any problems in the three years since she'd come aboard. So instead he took a second to suck in a breath. Look at him, all controlled and respectable-like. Well, almost anyway.

"And what makes you so special that you think he'll take any heed?"

A slight flush of color stained her cheeks, but she kept her expression impassive. "Varean obviously isn't going anywhere while he's unconscious. I'll comm Callan when he stabilizes."

Callan took half a step forward. "No way—"

"Roarke." The low warning in his voice was enough to make the ship's security specialist take a step back. "We're aiming to dock on Kalaheo Two station in around forty-eight hours. I need you to review a few things for me."

"Yes, Cap'tin." Callan cut a thwarted sideways glance at Kira then headed out of the medbay.

Her shoulders dropped a touch, and she let out a low sigh as she bent and picked up a stool.

"I know it's in your nature to see the good in people, Kira, to give them the benefit of the doubt and save them even if they don't want saving." He set his palms on his weapons and focused on the still form on the gurney. Something about Donnelly sent hot, prickling vibrations rippling down his spine. Every instinct told him the guy was far from a simple commando. "But I'm telling you to be careful with this one."

Her already tense expression tightened the slightest bit, but she didn't reply, simply nodded and turned her attention back to sorting out her medbay.

Rian cast one more look over the patient to where the broken ankle restraints hung off the end of the bed, before leaving the medbay. Maybe someone desperate enough could have snapped those binds on an extreme adrenaline high and damn near broken their ankles in the process. However, according to Callan, the commando had simply flicked them off like they were string cheese.

Despite his orders sending Callan up to the bridge, he didn't plan on leaving Kira alone with the prisoner. The next sensible choice security-wise, besides himself or Lianna—who needed to be on the bridge—would have been Tannin, but she'd see right through that and send the tech analyst packing.

So it'd have to be someone less obvious.

On the upper level, he stopped by the galley-communal room where some kind of damn tea party was taking place. Ella, the Arynian priestess, had half his crew hooked on that frecking Jasmynah tea, leaving his entire ship smelling all flowery and perfumed to the point the last trader he'd had onboard had commented on it. Everyone else said the scent had a kind of calming effect. But he sure as hell didn't find the scent calming. Not one damned bit. It amped him up until sometimes it felt like his skin was itching from the inside out.

In fact, some days it was all he could do not to take a shuttle and fly himself into the nearest star, because dying in some spectacularly messy crash or bloody chaos was about the only way he could see this all ending. But not yet, not until the Reidar had paid for the weight of his sins in rivers of blood.

So that meant putting up with Ella and her damned Jasmynah tea, until he figured out once and for all what the Reidar had wanted with her when they'd abducted the priestess from the peaceful temple planet of Aryn. Before he could focus on *that*, however, he had to keep a promise to his sister's tech-analyst fiancé and take a suicidal trip to one of the IPC central systems to find out what had happened to one of Tannin's childhood friends who'd probably gotten too close to the truth about the Reidar and then gotten dead.

"Did Callan really kill the commando we brought onboard?" Zahli asked as he stepped into the galley. Ella and Nyah, both seated with their backs to him, turned to look over their shoulders, though Ella had likely sensed his presence well before he'd walked into the room.

He shoved the niggling awareness of her mysterious powers into the compartment where all the other crap he didn't want to think about went. "Not quite, though he did make a decent mess in Kira's medbay."

Zahli's lips lifted in a half smile, a definite edge of wickedness to the expression. "Then Callan might need to employ a food taster for the next few rotations, otherwise he might end up paralyzed or unconscious somewhere for a few hours."

"Or getting intimately acquainted with the head." Lianna hadn't been seated at the table, but behind the galley bench, making a coffee. "Are you sure it's worth stopping at Kalaheo Two? No one else wants to say anything, but it's bad enough we're flying right into one of the IPC central systems and heading to Barasa to chase up a guy we don't even know. Adding a pit stop to that is just giving the government or UAFA one more chance to realize there's a ship of wanted intergalactic terrorists flying right up their noses like a bunch of morons."

He stopped in front of the table and leaned over to grab a muffin from the tall stack sitting in the middle of several other baked treats. Still warm. And his mouth was not watering. No, because he was eating it only for the fact that his other choice was repli-rations, and he couldn't be frecked making himself anything else.

"We'll dock and then launch before the engines even have a chance to cool." He turned to face Lianna, who'd come out from the galley bench holding a second cup to hand over the coffee she'd made for him. At least some people still remembered who the captain was around here. "All I need to do is call in a favor with a guy who owes me. Figure I might as well cash in my chips, since we won't be returning to this region of the galaxy anytime soon, especially now that we've aligned ourselves with Rene Blackstone."

"I'm still trying to work out how cozying up to the psycho pirate who runs the Barbary Belt is our best option," Zahli muttered.

"Because it was our only option." He took a bite of the muffin and almost wanted to groan at the soft, fluffy, cakey goodness. Hell, it should have been a crime that something so simple tasted so good. He leaned over and snagged a second treat then glanced at his sister. "Zahli, I need you to go hang in the medbay with Kira and comm Callan or me when the commando wakes up."

She nodded and pushed her teacup away, but snagged a cookie before rounding the table and heading off to follow his orders.

He backed up a step, casting a glance over Ella and Nyah. "We're docking at Kalaheo in just under forty-eight hours. We'll be keeping a low profile, so that means I'll be going to make the meet while everyone else stays onboard and doesn't attract any attention to themselves."

Nyah uttered a low affirmative while Ella simply inclined her head. And he didn't fail to notice the gleam in her unusual moss-hazel eyes, one that told him she either had her own opinion on his dictate or was possibly considering doing her own thing no matter what he said. Technically, since she wasn't one of the crew, she didn't have to listen to a damn word he said. For her own sake, and the sake of the thin threads of his temper, he hoped she kept whatever was going on in that head of hers to herself.

He stuffed the last of the muffin into his mouth and washed it down with a gulp of coffee—laced with a generous amount of brandy, just the way he liked it—as he left the communal room and headed up the short steps to the bridge.

Lianna cut him a brief glance from her console as he sat in the captain's chair but, smart girl that she was, didn't say anything else, instead made herself busy reviewing the flight path to Kalaheo Two.

Yeah, they'd all heard about his run-in with Ella a few days back, one in which he'd somehow ended up on the losing end. Apart from one incident, he and the priestess had managed to avoid speaking directly to each other ever since, and he didn't doubt the rest of the crew had noticed.

He'd been battle-and-blood high, beyond reasoning, the demon inside him riding the dark tide from the short but vicious fight to retake the *Swift Brion* from the Reidar. It'd been years since he'd waded through a skirmish like that, and he'd forgotten exactly how loud the blood lust roared. He'd been all ready to go ten rounds with a bottle of Violaine until he passed out in drunken oblivion, but damn Ella had found him.

He still had no idea what she'd thought to do for him in that moment, but he'd turned on her, coming so close to unleashing his dark urges. Tannin and Zahli had hurried in, trying to intervene, but apparently Ella hadn't needed any help. She'd used her Arynian abilities and put one hell of a whammy on him. The memory of it could still make him shudder. Whatever power she wielded, he'd felt the full force of it in that moment—warm, seductive, and euphoric in a way nothing else had ever been in his existence. And it scared the living hell out of him. The fact that she could take him down so easily and in a way that would leave him begging for more—maybe the Reidar weren't the ones mankind should be fearing most in this galaxy.

While Ella had always been unpredictable around him, in the past few days, she'd been somewhat reserved in her treatment of him, when before, it had seemed she'd appointed herself his minder and personal savior.

Maybe he'd finally succeeded in scaring her despite her claim otherwise. Especially since his mind had finally supplied him with a clear memory of his time with the Reidar—one where he'd been sent to kidnap her years earlier, except her touch, her powers, ended up being the catalyst that broke the aliens' hold on him. One more gossamer thread to the growing ties between them.

An uneasy sensation roiled in his guts.

Guilt? No. He couldn't remember what guilt felt like, and

he had nothing to feel guilty over…if he were so inclined to waste his time on such a useless emotion. He'd warned Ella every moment since she'd come aboard to leave him alone, but she hadn't heeded his words. Perhaps she finally viewed him as the surly, unhinged bastard the rest of his crew already knew him to be.

His attention caught on Lianna as something in her posture changed, tension in the line of her shoulders.

"Something wrong?"

"Not sure." Lianna moved her hands over her console, bringing the information onto the main viewport of the bridge. It showed the asteroid field they were shadowing, which stretched through two entire systems, in case the trans-cops had tracked their exit off the quarry moon. Some might argue they were traveling suicidally close to the debris that could destroy an engine or punch a hole in their shields and hull at the right velocity, but Lianna was a genius at knowing the *Imojenna*'s parameters, what she could take and what she could do for them. The engineer and navigator was walking them right down the thin line between the asteroid field giving cover and leaving them to a fiery end.

At first, all he saw were rocks, chunks of ice, and space dust. The *Imojenna*'s sensors were picking out larger meteors and scanning them, then moving onto the next, one after the other at nanosecond speed.

"What are you looking for?" He leaned forward in his chair and braced an elbow against his console.

"Initial scans picked up an anomaly in the asteroid field. Something that wasn't an asteroid. I'm trying to find it to see what it is."

Someone lying in wait for them—had the trans-cops laid some kind of ambush? Or maybe a ship full of marauders waiting on an easy mark? But anyone who flew a ship deeper into the asteroid field had to know they'd more likely explode than fly out again.

"Think we've still got company?" He shoved his hair back then gulped the last of his coffee.

Lianna shook her head, attention focused between her console and the viewport. "That was my first assumption, but I scanned for heat and life signatures first and got nothing."

His suspicions eased a fraction. So maybe it was just a hollow chunk of rock or abandoned shipping crate. Probably nothing they needed to waste their time finding. Every minute they spent traveling through the IPC central systems, they were at risk.

"If there's no reason to suspect someone's waiting to intercept, let's keep going. I want this business on Kalaheo Two taken care of ASAP."

"Okay, but just give me one more—" She straightened, her fingers tapping the console to stop the sensors. "There."

The *Imojenna*'s viewport stopped flashing through the scans and zoomed in on a hulking form jutting off the side of a midsized meteor. The lines and edges were too clean-cut and smooth to be rock or ice, yet the shape was dark and indefinable in the shadow of the meteor. A scroll of text dropped down the side of the viewport showing a composite materials list.

"It's a ship." Saying that aloud was probably redundant, since Lianna would no doubt be able to work that out on her own from the information.

"A dead ship." Lianna accessed the composite list, highlighting and scrolling through the contents, her expression thoughtful.

Though few and far between, dead ships weren't that unusual. However, in most cases they were literally floating skeletons, salvagers and marauders having stripped them of anything even remotely useful. This was showing to be fully functional and airtight. There could be a lot of useful stuff onboard, but a heavy feeling had parked itself in his gut, one of deep foreboding. He always got antsy traveling through the IPC central systems, but with the added threat of them being wanted intergalactic terrorists and the brush with the trans-cops, the skulking sensation of being in immediate danger was riding him harder than usual.

Lianna swiveled in her chair to face him. "We should send someone over to check it out."

He arched a brow at her. "Usually I'm the one making a suicidal suggestion and you're the one giving me the look that says you think I'm being a moron with a death wish again."

Lianna's expression creased with a faint trace of indignance. "I would never give you that kind of look. You're probably mistaking it for my he's-going-to-get-us-all-killed expression."

He cut her a glare that probably landed somewhere toward exasperated. "We don't have time to play explorers."

"We all know what we're risking by flying to Barasa to search for Tannin's friend, but any supplies we find on this ship means one fewer stop we have to make down the track."

He wanted to argue against the too-frecking-sensible logic, but she was right. The fewer stops they had to make on any worlds or stations before they got back to the Barbary Belt, the smaller their chances of getting caught.

He blew out a short breath, the beads on his left wrist clinking against the crystal display of his console. "Fine. We'll go take a look. But if we get over there and it's a bust, we're coming straight back. I'm not going to spend the next two hours here while Callan rummages through the bowels of the ship looking for weapons or you crawling under the consoles pulling out microcrystal components."

Her lips quirked in a not-quite smile as she turned back to her console. "Yes sir, Captain. I'll prep the portside skimmer shuttle."

# Chapter Seven

She should have been reading those files she'd downloaded from Rian's office, or even tidying up the remaining mess in her medbay, but Kira hadn't done anything since Rian and Callan left, apart from stare at the commando and watch the readings on the screen above his bed.

There was something about him, some anomaly her gut told her existed, but her logical, medical mind had no answer for...not yet anyway. The readings from the ship's R and R unit were mostly normal, with the occasional irregularity that could be written off as interference or momentary miscalculation as the patient's vitals changed. But she took note of every one, pieces of a puzzle she didn't have the full picture of yet.

The penetration of Callan's knife into the dead center of Varean's chest should have killed him. It would have killed anyone else almost immediately. But he'd survived and, according to the ship's diagnostic computer, he was in recovery mode. Rapid recovery. Way out of the normal human body's response in terms of improvement.

And then there was that moment before he'd passed out, when he'd had his hand against her cheek. At first, nothing but the warmth of his palm, the slight callouses on his fingers had registered, and the sensation of it had struck her much deeper than it had any right to.

Medicine was all about logic and science, though she'd always relied on her instincts as much as cold hard facts. And she didn't doubt herself now.

She'd felt a power emanating from him. A warm, rippling vibration that'd brushed beneath her skin as surely as an ocean breeze on a hundred-degree day. Not only that, but his eyes—

She had no logical explanation for his eyes. The blue had nearly faded out to be replaced by a mercury-silver color, swirling and bright sure as the volatile element had bloomed in the irises. She'd never seen anything like it in all her years of being a doctor. And while she couldn't remember reading any accounts of such a thing, something tugged at the back of her mind, like she should know what his mercurial eyes meant.

Besides the fact that she hated to see any vulnerable person mistreated—not that Varean could exactly be described as vulnerable—the growing mystery of him had her hooked.

The doctor and scientist in her wanted to find the answers of him, while strangely, the woman in her, the part of herself she'd let lay dormant for too long, was undeniably and inappropriately interested in him for completely different reasons. Some indefinable quality about Varean struck a chord. Maybe seeing what Zahli had found with Tannin had awoken some spark within her, and it was basic human instinct to not want to be alone.

But obviously that side of her was completely irrational. She couldn't have found a more unsuitable interest. Apart from the fact that the man was practically their prisoner and understandably unimpressed with all of them, he wouldn't be sticking around once Rian got his answers. Maybe that was why she'd noticed him as more than just a patient—he was totally unobtainable, and she didn't need to worry about things getting complicated.

Satisfied at her conclusion, she pushed the introspection aside and picked up her commpad containing the Reidar files, determined to find some clues that would help her work out the answers to Varean. But just as she tapped the screen, her comm trilled, ID showing either Lianna or Rian were calling from the bridge. *Great*. Rian was probably already wanting to know if the commando was awake. Her finger hovered over the screen. Just how pissed would he be if she pretended she hadn't heard her comm?

The idea was tempting, but not worth it. With a short sigh, she tapped the connect button, only to be unceremoniously summoned to the bridge with no niceties or explanation. At least some things on the ship never changed, no matter what latest crazy was getting splattered all over the bulkheads.

• • •

Rian finished checking his weapons—more out of habit than expectation he'd need to use them—as his sister stepped onto the bridge, followed by Kira.

"What's going on?" Zahli asked, glancing from him to where Callan was similarly kitted up, ready to head out.

Lianna gestured to the main viewport. "We found a dead ship in the asteroid field. We're taking a skimmer and going to check it out for supplies."

Rian thrust his pulse pistol back into the holster on his weapons belt. "Zahli, I need you to take the bridge while we're over there. Kira, you're coming with us to sweep the ship's medbay. If you find any supplies, take as much as you need or want."

Zahli moved to sit at Lianna's console, while Callan and Lianna headed off the bridge, Kira following reluctantly. Probably didn't want to leave her patient. He didn't like the way she'd gotten so protective of him, so attached and defensive. Once he got his answers and got the damned commando off his ship, they'd need to have words about her actions.

With one last glance at Zahli, he brought up the rear to trail the others down the short flight of stairs to the upper corridor of the ship. One side held the galley and communal area, while the opposite side was entirely taken up by the captain's quarters—his cabin, sitting room, and office. At the far end of the passageway, just beyond where the stairs dropped off, were two other sets of upper stairs that were so steep, they might as well be ladders. Each led to one of two skimmer shuttles on top of the ship. They didn't use the skimmers very often, mostly reserved for emergency escapes or traveling between ships in zero atmosphere when there was no docking option, like they were doing now.

Rian waited while the rest of them climbed up into the portside skimmer, coming aboard last and pulling the hatch shut. The skimmer was a fairly good size for its type. At the front were two seats before a single viewport and two consoles to fly the ship. Directly behind were two rows of double seats to sit eight other people, and in the back were ten fold-down, narrow bunks on the bulkheads for what doubled as the cargo space. The only flaw was they couldn't fill the cargo bay and fold down the bunks at the same time.

He and Lianna took the seats behind the consoles, firing up the shuttle as Kira settled in the seat behind him, quickly pulling on her harness. Callan slouched down in a seat in the opposite row behind Lianna, a huge nucleon gun across his knees.

"What exactly do you think you'll need to shoot with a gun that big on a dead ship?" Kira asked. "You'll just as likely punch a hole in the hull with that cannon."

He shrugged one shoulder. "I like to be prepared. Especially for zombies."

"Zombies? Really?" Kira's voice was heavy on the exasperated disbelief. "Sure, if zombies were real, I'd want to walk around with a gun that big, too."

Rian glanced over his shoulder. "Callan has a dire fear of zombies."

Callan pointed at him with the metium knife he was holding in his other hand. "Hey, you're the one who introduced me to the world of frecking shape-shifting aliens. Far as I'm concerned, it's only a matter of time before some witless frecking twat discovers Planet Living Dead and starts the zombie apocalypse."

"And you figure the bigger your gun and the more weapons you've got, the safer you'll be?" Kira asked.

The guy did have a pretty impressive arsenal strapped and holstered.

Callan gave a single nod. "I plan to be the last man standing."

"And when the universe is repopulated from your sterling gene pool, mankind will be saved," Lianna interjected, not taking her attention from the console as she guided the skimmer away from its mooring locks.

He sent Lianna a suggestive smirk, though she wasn't looking. "Stick with me, McKenzie, and I'll repopulate with you any time you want."

"How can any woman resist such a romantic proposal?" Kira asked, grinning as Lianna made a face.

He could make as many suggestive remarks as he wanted, because there was no substance to them. For a start,

Callan and Lianna definitely weren't interested in each other, and secondly, Rian had strict rules about his crew and fraternization. They'd all seen the results of that when he'd kicked his own sister off the ship after finding out about her and Tannin. The only reason he'd eventually accepted their relationship was because of the danger to Zahli being offship, since the Reidar could grab her to get to him. And after Zahli and Tannin had gotten engaged and fully committed to each other, he had no choice.

He sure as hell wouldn't tolerate his crew having any type of casual relations. That caused too many problems and tension.

The shuttle rumbled as Lianna slowed to navigate the asteroid field. Going in with the skimmer was a much smaller risk than an entire ship. Still, the mood among his crew abruptly sobered as they got deeper into the asteroid field. Lianna carefully guided the skimmer along a projected path that could change in the blink of an eye as rocks and ice drifted—or in some cases streaked—through the other debris. He rode point, double-checking her trajectory and using the illegally mounted nucleon guns to blast anything that got too close.

There were a few edgy moments when the engines sucked in chunks of ice, or rocks big enough to take them out sliced past too close for comfort, but they made it to the dark ship, which sat on a flat section of a large meteor as though someone had parked it there.

That heavy feeling that'd landed in his guts when they'd first seen the ship on the viewport turned into an arctic churning. Something burgeoned in the depths of his mind, pushing against the fortifications where he kept all that bad shite from his past buried and locked down. He didn't know what it was about this ship, but there was definitely something hitting all his nerve endings.

Lianna backed up the skimmer to the ship's hatch, and it vacuum sealed and equalized the pressure. He grabbed in a quick breath then got up and pulled out several full-face masks. He handed them around, but as he went to put his on, his hands quaked. *Goddamn it.* He tightened his grip on the mask, locking his muscles to force them under control. But his body simply kept up the rebellion; the tremors stopped, except a cold sweat broke out on his lower back.

For half a wild second, he wished Ella had come along. Last time he'd faced his nightmares, walking into an abandoned Reidar lab and fighting not to lose his shite, she'd used her Arynian abilities and stolen away the panic.

Though she'd done it without his permission, and he'd been pissed about her butting into his private hell, even having her stand beside him now would have made this more bearable. *Jezus.* He'd been doing fine before Ella came along, and he'd be fine after she decided to sashay right back out of his existence.

He damn well didn't need her or anyone else.

Holding onto the driving resentment, he gave Kira and Lianna sensors to measure the air for any toxic substances or life signs. Not that he expected to find anything living onboard. Unless Callan's zombie theory came true.

He stepped over and pounded a fist against the hatch release, ignoring the final spike of icy warning slithering down his spine.

"Lianna, you're with Callan. Kira, I'll take you to find the medbay. You see anything out of the ordinary, comm me and come straight back to the skimmer."

The others nodded, not seeming overly worried as they fitted the masks on their faces. But something had happened to this ship's crew, probably something bad. People didn't just abandon perfectly good ships in the middle of nowhere.

The hatchway opened, letting in a puff of air that would

no doubt be stale. They stepped cautiously forward into the deep darkness.

Callan fitted a flashlight to the top of his huge-ass gun, shoulders set, tensed for action. Rian fell into step behind him, hands on the grip of his guns, but not drawn. Wouldn't make a difference if they came face-to-face with any kind of danger—he could draw faster than his enemy could blink.

Inside was pitch black, and Lianna flicked on a bigger, heavier flashlight. Unsurprisingly, the first thing the beam of light swept over were corpses lined up in the middle of the otherwise empty cargo hold. The sight of those bodies sent a deeper, harder surge of ice through him, and he signaled for them to stop. Lianna stepped sideways and accessed some kind of panel. A moment later, light flooded the ship.

"This ship didn't die; it was powered down." She pressed the panel closed again. "And this isn't just any run-of-the-mill galactic transport, this ship has full circadian lighting and an integrated solar simulator for UV daytime."

"So whoever these dead bastards are, they had money. If I'm not mistaken, this is a Kingswell class, b-line. Not top of the range, but anyone who can afford any line in this class is sitting damn pretty in life." Callan hadn't lowered his gun, only switched off the flashlight on top. "UAFA personal security division."

Rian strode closer to the bodies, all six lined up neatly as though ready for transport somewhere else. A pounding started in the base of his skull in time with the rapid beat of his heart. Dark sensations scrabbled at the barrier in his head. But he didn't need the remnants of memory to know what his mind was trying to tell him. He could feel it in the tips of his fingers and the ache of his limbs, like sensory recall in his very muscles.

"They're bodyguards?" Kira stepped by him, the doctor in her obviously overcoming her hesitation. She walked along their feet, and he could all but see her cataloguing the few wounds and the injuries that had caused death. They'd been executed fast and clean. And they'd been dead a long time, maybe six or seven years. Bodies didn't decompose the same way in space, especially when a ship was dead or powered down. They were kind of half decomposed, half mummified, and definitely gross looking.

"Yeah, they're glorified bodyguards," Callan confirmed. "The type employed by politicians and anyone else rich enough to pay UAFA's exorbitant fees. Evidently these guys weren't very good at their job. I'm betting we'll find the mark dead somewhere else onboard."

"Great. Just what I want to see. More dead bodies," Lianna muttered.

The others all moved forward to a wide set of stairs, but Rian had trouble getting his heavy feet to cooperate. In his mind's eye, he could see the layout of this shuttle like he'd meticulously memorized every bolt and plate. This ship wasn't even half as big as the *Imojenna*. With only two levels and limited accommodation cabins, it was the type of ship for shorter, infrequent trips, despite the obvious luxury.

His crew was already halfway up the stairs when he finally forced himself to follow after them. His mind was blank as he reached the top, which opened into a bridge and conference-type area. Like the cargo hold, there were bodies lined up in neat rows. Ten dead up here. Two were in uniform—the captain and navigator who'd been flying the ship. The rest were dressed in civ clothes.

He stopped two steps in, not able to take himself any farther, breath cutting too shallow in and out of his lungs. Random pictures flashed through his mind, nothing he could understand or put in context, just ruthless violence and the dark gratification of taking life with precise strikes of his weapon.

Kira continued over to the first row of bodies, pulled a compact modified medical scanner out of her pocket, and crouched down next to the first civilian. She slowly passed the scanner over the hand, presumably hoping to get a bio-ID. After a second, the unit beeped, and she held it up. The scanner would still be connected to the *Imojenna*'s onboard systems and linked into the IPC's database—a neat little permanent hack Tannin had organized for them.

The doctor frowned down at the screen when the unit chimed. "That can't be right."

"What does it say?" Lianna asked from where she'd remained near the stairs, a few steps from him.

"It says this man is the vice-chancellor of Freemont, Gustaf Pavin. I don't remember hearing he'd been killed. In fact, I'm pretty sure I saw him on a newsreel at a summit on Yarina not that long ago."

"Check the rest." His voice was flat and frigid, instantly sobering the already tense air in the room as the others cast him wary looks. But he didn't need the scanner to tell him who lay here and how they'd died. He already knew, the knowledge an innate sense more than an actual memory.

Without a word, she checked the rest of the bodies in civilian clothes one by one and then stood.

"According to the bio-IDs, we're looking at the entire top echelon of the Freemont government. Which is impossible unless—"

"This was a Reidar hit, and now a bunch of meat puppets are in control of the entire planet of Freemont." Callan knelt down near one of the bodies. "But there's something familiar about the pattern of wounds. I've seen this before. I know I have. The death strikes aren't sloppy, they're precise. The killer would have been calm and in control the entire—"

Callan shot to his feet, disbelieving gaze cutting to him.

"This looks like…" His voice came out slightly hoarse.

"My handiwork." Rian set his palms on his weapons with measured movements, the familiar grips anchoring him in reality as the slashing memories struggled against his fraying hold. "And you'd be right. I killed these people."

"What in the holy mother of all hell?" Callan stepped back from the bodies, his own grip tightening on his nucleon rifle.

Without saying another word, Rian turned on his heel and stalked down the steps, the heavy tread of his boots the only sound echoing throughout the entire ship.

# Chapter Eight

They weren't dreams. They were something else. Too vast and too real to be Varean's imaginings. Yet nothing was familiar. Places and objects he didn't recognize and had no reference for. It would have been easy to get lost in the infinity of it — snatches and figments that were as fascinating as they were daunting. Being in this place fed the mutation within him, making him want to escape the yellow-and-gray shadowed reality as much as he wanted to see more.

An entity always hovered like a celestial being, a brilliant blue light. He'd first thought it was a sun or a rare ultra-blue star. But the more lucid this dream state had become, he'd come to realize it was something else. What, he had no idea. Although he'd spent time tracking it, it forever remained frustratingly out of reach.

Only two things kept him from completely sinking into the oblivion. *Her* voice, though he couldn't hear Kira now, the memory of her constantly teased the edges of his awareness. And some small part of him warned that if he wanted to again experience the ripple of her voice like sunshine on cold skin, he couldn't become lost.

His abilities may have saved him physically, but she'd saved him in the ways that mattered most—when she'd told him *I am not letting you die* he'd wanted it to be true for her and no other reason, which was completely stupid. He barely knew her—they lived totally different lives—and had been thrown together by a twisted kink in the fabric of circumstance. They didn't mean anything to each other and never would. However, that logic didn't stop his craving to hear her voice.

The conflicts of her—woman and doctor, caring, yet with inner fortitude like the most stalwart military commander—sparked something inside him. Maybe it was simply that she'd been his anchor in a sea of confusion and pain since he'd first been hit with that damned stunner. Maybe it was her petite figure at odds with the size of her personality and tenacity. Whatever the reason, she was starting to seem more and more like his own personal guardian angel, wanting to protect and save him no matter what anyone else thought.

Time passed differently here, and he couldn't have said how long he'd been under, but a buzzing like a damned insect in the back of his mind finally got loud enough to pull him out to the real world.

Varean forced his eyes open but couldn't focus on whatever the hell was right in his face. He went to reach up, intending to push it away, but his arms were locked in place. Turning his head to the side, he saw a crack of light, his brain registering that he seemed to be in some kind of pod. A warm kind of humming sensation poured over his entire body like water, accompanied by a low whir. He inched his hand to the side, trying to get a grip on the seam, but couldn't find purchase or a gap large enough to stuff his fingers into.

A moment later, the whole thing lifted, flooding him with blindingly bright light. He threw his arm up to shade his eyes but froze when he felt the business end of a gun pressing into his neck under his chin.

"No sudden movements, soldier."

Tension rippled through his muscles as he slowly lowered his arm to focus on the man standing next to the bed with another one of those stunners. Tannin, if his memory served. The guy was like a tech analyst or something. While he couldn't imagine a tech-head would be any match for him, the guy currently had all the advantage with the way that gun was giving him a hickey. The frecking things were becoming the bane of his existence.

Tannin dropped a pair of cuffs on his chest. "Put 'em on."

He picked up the restraints—metium-reinforced—and clicked them onto his wrists. If they made the guy feel better, sure, he could have his illusion of control and safety. No need to tell the tech-head that escaping cuffs and killing without use of hands were basic commando training.

Once he'd finished, Tannin stepped back but didn't lower the gun. "You weren't supposed to wake up for at least another twenty-four hours."

The statement didn't make sense, until his brain helpfully bombarded him with his last few seconds of consciousness. That security moron had skewered him dead center of his chest. He glanced down to see his skin healed and pinked through the ragged edges of his torn, bloody shirt. Damn it, Sherron was going to be like a terrier on a rat over how the hell he managed to survive that.

Despite it being a decade since he'd buried his inherent abilities, apparently they were working no problem. He felt like he'd come off a restless night's sleep, not that he'd almost taken a one-way trip to the hereafter. A thwarted kind of frustration lit up within him as the helplessness of the past days returned like taking a sucker punch to the solar plexus. After this, hiding the truth of who he was would be nearly impossible. Damn Sherron butting into his life as if he had any frecking right to it.

Behind Tannin, the doors to the medbay opened to reveal the doc steering a hover-pallet stacked with crates.

"Oh, you're awake." If her tone hadn't given away her shock, the surprise on her face would have. She positioned the pallet out of the way and came over, her gaze sweeping him before she looked up at the screen above his bed. When her eyes returned to his face, maybe he was imagining it, but he could have sworn there was a hint of relief in her features. Why that should matter so much, he didn't have a clue. Or maybe he did, and didn't want to admit he was starting to care what she thought.

"How are you feeling?"

"Considering I should be dead, pretty damned alive." She went to pass a handheld scanner over him, but he reached up with his cuffed hands and caught her wrist. "You don't need to worry about that."

For a moment her sage green eyes studied him, then a stubborn gleam entered her gaze. "Sorry, but when you're in my medbay, you do things my way."

"Hands off, soldier boy." Tannin had moved closer with that damned stunner again.

Varean made a big show of letting her go and holding out his hands in surrender. The doc finished her scan, her expression satisfied and somewhat mystified by whatever readings she got.

"Has Ella been here?" The doc glanced over her shoulder at Tannin, who shook his head in response.

She turned back to him, picking up the ragged edges of his shirt and running light, cool fingers over his skin. A ripple of tingles spread across his chest from her touch, and he locked down his muscles against the shudder chasing up the sensation.

"Then how is this possible? It doesn't make sense." The words were a mumble, seeming more for herself than the benefit of the room.

No, it wouldn't make sense. Not to anyone else. For him, it was no big surprise and right now, more of an inconvenience than anything else.

She pulled away and took half a step back, making herself look busy as she picked up her commpad from a nearby trolley. But she had an underlying uneasiness to her stance that hadn't been there before.

"You're entirely healed from a wound that should have killed you."

He shrugged one shoulder, aiming for a nonchalance he wasn't feeling. "So? You put me in the life-support pod."

She shook her head, not meeting his gaze. No doubt the doc had a theory, but he couldn't ask her without arousing more suspicion.

"It should have stabilized you so your body could heal naturally in time, not perform a minor miracle. But we've seen this before. I just have to check with Ella."

That was the second time she'd mentioned that name, a note of near reverence in her tone when she said it. Someone else with some kind of healing abilities? "Who is Ella?"

"None of your damned business," Tannin snapped. The tech-head glanced at the doc, who appeared kind of annoyed. "So, he's awake. You know what Rian's standing orders are."

She gave a short sigh, cutting a sympathetic glance in his direction as she set down the commpad. "Okay, let's do it before Rian comes in here and decides to take care of the matter as violently as possible."

He sent her a hard look. "I told you I'm not answering any questions—"

"We'll talk about that later. Right now, I have to get you back down to the brig. Believe me, Rian is not in a mood to be messed with."

Shadows darkened her eyes, gaze haunted as though she'd experienced something horrible since the last time he'd seen her. An inexplicable flash of white-hot fury burst through him, and he straightened on the bed to catch her arm.

"Did he hurt you?"

The doc froze, her gaze clashing with his, confusion and a touch of awe crossing her lovely features. "No, Rian didn't touch me."

"I mean it, Doc. You tell me if he even laid one finger on you—"

Tannin's derisive laugh cut him off. "You got taken down by Callan, tough guy. He's a cuddly teddy compared to Rian. You wouldn't stand a chance against the captain. In fact, I'm pretty sure there's no one in the universe who could take on Rian and live to talk about it."

The admiration and respect behind Tannin's words were more than obvious.

"What is he, some kind of demigod?" he muttered.

"Might as well be. Short of it is, he's one guy you don't want to piss off. The best thing you can do for yourself is cooperate, unless you want to get vented."

"That's enough, Tannin." Kira's voice was quiet, but no less hard, as she shot the guy a glare.

Tannin's threats didn't bother him, but that cagey gleam in her gaze did. He'd cooperate, but only for her sake, only so it saved her from whatever Rian's bad temper might entail.

"Back to the brig it is then." He swung his legs off the edge of the gurney and shuffled his ass forward. The doc set a hand against his shoulder when he put his feet on the cool metal floor, as though she thought he might be unsteady. She needn't have worried; he felt fine, not even the slightest twinge of light-headedness.

"I'm sorry about this. I can't imagine the brig is the most

comfortable place to be when recuperating from injuries like yours." She kept her voice low, the words just for the two of them as she shifted beside him, her hand firm and secure on his shoulder as he stood. She reached over to a nearby trolley and grabbed a bundle, never shifting her grip from him. He probably should have told her she didn't need to be so solicitous, but damn if he didn't like having her hands on him a little too much.

"Makes no mind to me. I've had it worse."

She sent him a dubious glance as they started toward the doors of the medbay, Tannin bringing up the rear.

No one attempted any other conversation. Varean studied the layout and components of the ship, cataloguing every bit of information he could use later when he escaped. If he wasn't mistaken, this was an old Nirali classer with a damn lot of modified upgrades. The ship had been a staple of the Assimilation Wars, legendary for flying supplies in under fire. After the war had ended, they'd been decommissioned and either scrapped or entirely refitted to become unarmed Feint Class long-haul shuttles. He hadn't guessed any of them might still be puttering around the galaxy in their original incarnation.

The rest of the crew seemed to be scarce as they went down two flights of stairs and through the cargo hold. Obviously they'd made a stop while he'd been out of it—crates that hadn't been there before were stacked along the bulkheads and strapped down to the floor.

When they reached the brig, he didn't hesitate as he walked through the hatchway, leaving Tannin to clang the bars shut behind him. It was much warmer in the brig now than it had been when they'd first put him here.

Kira glanced at Tannin, a hint of impatience in her gaze. "You can go. Between the cuffs and the bars, I don't think Command Donnelly is going anywhere."

The tech analyst didn't say anything, simply nodded then strode away.

Once Tannin disappeared, she approached the bars. "Sorry about this, but after what happened with Callan—"

A swell of contrition rose within him. For the first time in his entire military career, he'd lost control, let the anger drive him into attacking Callan. Worse, his abilities had been freed, and he'd nearly killed the guy with nothing more than an enraged thought. Despite remorse at his reckless actions, a part of him, that hostile mutation that'd taken root in his psyche, was glad for what he'd done. Wished he'd finished the job and watched the life fade from the bastard's eyes. He took in a half breath, loathing the malicious gratification.

*What the hell was wrong with him?*

"Well, anyway," she continued when he didn't say anything. "I suppose it's not surprising Rian ordered you back in the brig."

"I probably would have done the same thing if I were in his position." His words came out rough, and he swallowed over the gravel in the back of his throat. Hell, he was starting to think he would have locked himself up in here to protect everyone else until he figured out how to destroy what was inside him. What if he lost control again?

What if next time Kira was the one who got hurt?

Bending down, she set her bundle on the floor inside his cell. "I brought you a change of clothes and some water. I'll go up in a minute and get you a meal, plus some extra water. You're going to need it down here with this heat."

Yeah, he could feel a fine sweat starting to bead over his skin. Kira's cheeks were slightly flushed, a light sheen glistening down her neck into the line of her shirt.

A pulse of heat cut through him that had nothing to do with the engines, and he couldn't help but step forward. He half expected her to back up after their last encounter on opposite sides of these bars. But she stood her ground, her gaze not tainted with suspicion or fear like others whenever his abilities had surfaced in the past.

She had to be putting the pieces together—the vibration when he'd touched her cheek, surviving an injury that should have killed him, his rapid healing. And his eyes—when his abilities swelled, they turned mercury. She'd been staring right at him, their faces inches apart. She had to notice, and now, no doubt, they were back to their usual color. But she hadn't mentioned a word of it to him.

"You're still trying to figure it out. Why I healed so fast, why I'm not dead."

Her expression closed off slightly. "Accounting for your extensive injuries, you should have needed the R and R unit for at least another twenty-four hours, if not longer."

Not really an answer, just a statement of fact. "Maybe my injuries weren't as bad as you thought."

"Maybe." The word was a concession, but her tone signaled doubt.

He closed the remaining distance to the bars and glanced down at the pile of clothes near his feet. "I appreciate the sentiment, but I'm going to have a little trouble doing anything with these on."

He held up his hands, causing her attention to shift to the cuffs.

"Lucky pickpocketing is considered a life skill onboard this ship." She produced an electronic key from her pocket and then reached through the bars.

But, before she passed the key over the lock sensor, she hesitated, regarding him intently, the color of her eyes a darker green in the low lighting. His attention got caught by those eyes, by the way her short dark hair brushed her neck and the very tops of her shoulders, by the plump shape of her mouth, and the slight dimple in her lower lip. A man would have to be blind not to see how gorgeous she was, and though he'd realized from the first that she was attractive, now he was noticing her on an elemental level that could lead nowhere but trouble.

"Will you promise not to try anything when I take these off?" she asked, interrupting his wayward thoughts.

"I think the better question is, would you take me at my word?"

She gave a single nod. "Despite everything, I get the sense that you're an honorable man, and you took your duty as an AF commando onboard the *Swift Brion* very seriously. I've heard that a commando will die to keep his word."

He inclined his head. "It's true. When a commando gives his word, he will do everything in his ability to keep it, including sacrificing his life. Which is why I don't give my word lightly or easily."

Her posture relaxed. Stretching her arm the remaining distance, she held the key up to the sensor. The cuffs clicked then dropped free to clang on the metal grate flooring. Before the doc could retreat, he caught her hand in a gentle grip.

He drew her closer to the bars, even as he moved to lean against the metal separating them. Despite the background noise of the engines, he heard her breath hitch.

He'd lived with hiding the truth about himself for so long, he didn't know any other way to exist. People wouldn't understand, would start looking at him differently. But maybe Kira wouldn't. Besides the fact she was a doctor and probably a little more open-minded, a pure light shone within her— one that helped her see the good in people, no matter who they were or what they'd done. Still, the fear of discovery was so deeply ingrained within him, he didn't know how to get to a place where he could bring himself to tell her, no matter how he told himself he could trust her.

"You're trying to find the answers, right? To why the

stunner affects me. To how I healed."

"I think I already know." Her words weren't much louder than a whisper, her gaze roaming over his face. She shifted closer until nothing but the scant few millimeters of the bars separated them.

"You do?" Apprehension about anyone knowing the truth, a flicker of surprise, flared. Could she have really worked it out?

She nodded, hands coming up to wrap around his on the bars. "The Reidar. They took you, did some kind of experiments."

Unexpectedly, disappointment streamed through him just as potent as the relief that his true heritage was safe for another day. It'd been a stretch to think she'd come to the right conclusion, because it was almost even farther from the realm of possibility than the shape-shifting aliens. If Kira couldn't work it out, he had no worry anyone else would.

"Is that what Rian thinks as well?" Maybe he could latch on and ride it for as long as it took to escape.

Her hands tightened on his. "If you don't want to tell us the details, don't want to relive that, I completely understand. And the details aren't what Rian wants from you. We just need to know it happened."

Christ, he wanted to let her think it was the reason behind everything, but stupidly, he couldn't bring himself to lie to her. "That didn't happen to me."

"Maybe you don't remember—"

"No, Kira. It's not the answer."

An almost pleading, empathetic gleam lit her eyes, and she set her face nearly against the bars, leaving her mouth too temptingly close. "Then what is the answer, Varean? Tell me so I can help you."

He lifted a hand to cup her cheek. "It's not you I don't trust."

"Then trust that I can handle whatever it is for you."

"I can barely handle it myself," he murmured. He needed to let her go and move back. He could feel his abilities stirring at the base of his skull, a warm, deep vibration, like listening to a blues guitar riff on a balmy evening. But for all the pain and confusion of the past days, for all the fighting of the newly awakened, aggressive, uncontrolled parts of himself, the sensations expanding within him were simple. And even better, they smothered that hostile mutation that'd been getting stronger and harder to ignore.

So instead of letting her go, instead of doing the smart thing and putting some distance between them, he tilted his head and touched his lips lightly to hers.

He'd expected to surprise her, to find her hesitant or to simply pull away from him. She reacted, but it was to press against the bars and deepen the kiss, her hand finding the back of his neck, shooting sensation down his spine, along with a bursting reverberation of his abilities. It lit up his body like a flash grenade, making him shudder from head to toe. Kira gasped against his mouth and pushed away, but only far enough to stare at him.

Before she could say anything, he shifted from the bars, shuffling back a number of steps as he tried to catch his breath and shove his powers back into the recesses of his mind where he'd kept them with no trouble for the past decade. It was just another demonstration of how far out of control he was getting. For someone who'd prided himself on always being bound and stalwart, the downward spiral he was on was almost laughable.

Kira stepped back from her side of the bars, fingers lingering over her mouth. There was no doubt in his mind she'd just gotten a hint of his abilities for a second time.

"Get changed while I go get you some food, because I'll have to make sure you put the cuffs on when I come back."

He glanced at the pile of clean clothes, then scanned the sweat and blood covering his skin where his ruined shirt gaped open. "I don't suppose a shower is on the cards?"

Her expression took on an uncertain edge.

Before she could refuse, he pressed, "There's no point in putting on clean clothes when I'm still sweaty and blood-spattered."

Her lips tilted up in a half grin. "Who would have thought a commando would be so picky about personal hygiene? I can't bring you up to any of the wash facilities. The best I can do is a bucket."

"I'll take whatever I can get."

"Okay. I'll return in a few minutes." She turned and hurried off down the passageway.

Though Kira and her life were clearly none of his business, he was starting to feel more than a little concerned about the doc and her situation. Kissing her certainly hadn't helped that sentiment.

She was obviously a highly trained and skilled surgeon. He'd seen enough military medic hacks in his time to know a first-rate practitioner when he came across one. And her accent had the definite upper-class, rounded elocution of someone who'd grown up in the central systems. So how and why had she ended up playing nurse to a bunch of sociably and legally questionable people like the crew of the *Imojenna*? Maybe he needed to take those facts into account against his blind desire to trust her, which was certainly led by a senseless appendage south of his belt.

He sighed and wiped at a trickle of sweat running down the side of his face before taking a long swallow from the bottle of water.

Another, heavier tread of steps came toward him, accompanied by a metallic clanging noise. Callan appeared carrying a length of chain, a hard, wary expression on his face.

"I heard you done some miraculous healing while we were offship." Callan stopped a few steps from the bars—smartly out of reaching range—swinging the heavy chains back and forth.

"No offense, but I'm sure you'll understand if I'm not in the mood for chitchat with the guy who carved a hole in my middle."

Callan nodded, almost thoughtfully. "Yeah, that was some real pretty knife work. 'Course, you deserved it, the way you were trying to crush my windpipe."

He crossed his arms, the sight of those chains starting to make his skin itch. He wasn't against being locked in the brig, but he damn well didn't need to be leashed.

"You know what it's like in the heat of battle, in that moment when the fury gets the better of you. I went too far, but you stabbed me. I'd say we're even."

"This ain't about getting even." Callan clinked the chains into the bars as he stepped up to the lock. "This is about what's smart for the people of this crew security-wise, and you've proven yourself to be a threat."

"And I can agree with that." He worked to keep his tone reasonable, but anger was beginning to stir, tensing his muscles. That uncontrolled belligerence within him getting free too fast and too easily. "So I'll stay in this brig and won't try to get out until Rian decides to cut me loose. The chains aren't necessary."

"See, I think they are. And what with the homicidal mood the cap'tin's in right now, I'm pretty sure he'd agree."

The rage inside him was like a low growl getting louder until it became a roar. "You step one foot inside this cell, friend, and this time I won't be the one in the ship's R and R unit."

Callan pooled the chains into his left hand and slowly drew the stunner with his right. Goddamn it. He'd frecking had enough of getting pulsed with those things.

"Sorry, *friend*, but I'll be stepping foot inside that cell, all right, and you'll take it like a stoned waystation whore."

He started to take half a step forward, but Callan let off a single round from the stunner.

The pulse hit his midsection and sent him staggering back under a wave of burning hot pinpricks exploding in every cell of his body. *Jezus*. He stumbled to his knees, trying to suck air into lungs that had stalled. Distantly, he heard the cell door open, and no matter that he wanted to drag his head up and lunge for the scum bastard, none of his muscles were connected to his brain. Goddamn, but the stunner hurt more every time they used it on him, like an electrical burn ripping through each atom.

The cuffs were unceremoniously slapped around his wrists, then came the hissing jingle of the chain. His arms were pulled above his head, and his whole body jerked upward.

He clenched his jaw, forcing his jellied muscles to harden so he could bear his own weight and take the pressure off his wrists. His knees buckled twice before he could brace himself. But even though he'd managed to get up, the pulling on his arms continued until they were stretched uncomfortably above him.

"Callan! What the hell are you doing?" The doc's pissed-off voice cut through the haze, pulling him out as effectively as a lifeline on a dead ship, and he lifted his head far enough to see her rushing into the brig. "This is not necessary."

"Yeah, well I say it is. People who try to kill me get chained up. End of story."

She shot Callan an angry glare as she passed him. The doc came over to grip his chin, flashing a light in front of his eyes, then pressing her fingers to his throat just above his collarbone.

"What did you do to him?"

"Used the stunner. You think I was dumb enough to step in here without neutering the bastard first?"

She turned on Callan with a furious expression. "You stunned him with an experimental weapon less than an hour after he came out of the R and R unit from suffering a critical wound? Just how dumb are you? Who knows what it's done — ?"

"What it's done is subdue the guy who tried to choke me. Not to mention he threatened to space you the first day he was aboard. Or are you forgetting how that went down?" Callan stepped closer, looming over her in a way that was meant to be nothing but intimidating.

While just the sight of the gorilla was enough to make him furious before, seeing him trying to frighten and terrorize the smaller doc made the last of the stunner's effects drain away like a retreating wave.

He straightened, clenching his hands around the chains at his wrists. But Kira didn't seem too worried about Callan's antics, staring at him with just as much ferocity in her expression.

"Take those chains down."

"If you want him out of those chains, you can take that up with the cap'tin. But a sane person would have to be hankering for one hell of a death wish to be pushing him on anything right now."

With one last glare, Callan pivoted and stalked out of the cell, disappearing into the shadows of the passageway that ran into the cargo bay.

Kira sighed then turned to look up at him. "I'm sorry. This is unacceptable. But Callan's too shifty to get pickpocketed, and considering the mood Rian is in, I shouldn't risk it anyway. I'll get you down as soon as I can, but for the time being, you're going to have to stay like that."

"Don't get yourself in a tizz about it, Doc." His voice

came out hoarse, the back of his throat dry. "This isn't the first time I've been chained up."

An unfortunate truth—there'd been an entire week's worth of training dedicated solely to getting tied up. The memory of getting chained upside down in a tank of icy water still had the power to make him shudder.

With a look of stern determination, she went over to where Callan had secured the chains. From this angle, he couldn't see how it had been done, but he heard enough of the doc rattling around and muttering under her breath to know she couldn't loosen it.

She returned to stand in front of him, shoulders slumped. "I hate to leave you like this, but if I'm going to fix this situation, I can't do it from here."

"It's been at least a week since I hit the gym. I'll do a few pull-ups and we'll call this extreme resistance training."

She glanced up, exasperated. "How can you still have a sense of humor after almost being killed twice and being chained in the bowels of a ship that's lucky if it's a step above a garbage compactor?"

"You make it easier to bear." He clamped his lips closed after the unintended words slipped out. *Goddamn.* Obviously his brain still wasn't firing on all cylinders after taking that hit from the Reidar stunner.

She stilled, staring up at him with green eyes that would probably haunt his dreams for years to come. As they took a moment to really look at each other, the realization that the words were entirely true sank into the depths of his being. This situation was a hell the likes of which he'd been trained for, but hoped to never face. Yet Kira, with her metium-reinforced backbone and contrasting tender compassion, made this whole thing an anomaly, like some weird dream that kept swinging back and forth between a nightmare and a fantasy.

"I won't let them keep you like this." The fierce determination was back in her expression, like a warrior preparing for battle.

But the uneasy ripple through his stomach for her well-being returned. "Don't put yourself in the firing line over me. I'm not worth it. Everyone I've seen in the last hour keeps mentioning how the captain is in a killing mood. I don't want you risking his temper."

"Rian would never hurt any of his crew." The words sounded confident, but the way her gaze dropped away told a different story.

He pulled forward against his chains, getting as close to her as he could, leaning down until his next breath was laced with a creamy vanilla scent, one he thought he must have imagined earlier.

"I mean it. I can survive a few hours chained up. Promise you won't push the issue with Sherron."

She looked back up at him, chin tilting at a defiant angle. "Fine. I promise not to push things with Rian. But like I said, I'm not just going to leave you like this."

And probably would still get herself into trouble. But from what he'd come to learn of Kira since coming aboard the *Imojenna*, she wouldn't be persuaded from doing what she thought was right, no matter what anyone else said on the issue. Damned if that wasn't half the reason he'd become so taken with her. No doubt about it, he wanted nothing more than to follow the woman into more trouble, the last place he needed to be right now.

# Chapter Nine

Kira stomped up the stairs, more furious than she'd ever been since setting foot on the *Imojenna*. While Rian and the crew of the *Imojenna* had done a lot of questionable things in pursuit of the Reidar, they'd never locked and chained anyone in the bowels of the ship before. Yeah, there'd been a handful of shady traders and other morally lacking persons stuck briefly in Rian's brig simply for the intimidation of it, but no doubt those goons had deserved it, and she'd actually always seen it as a bit of a joke, as had the rest of the crew.

On the second level, she ran out of steam. Just where did she think she was going, and what did she plan on doing? She didn't have a sound argument against Callan's reasoning. Her concern for Varean had gone beyond the usual doctor-patient care. Beyond even her deep-seated loathing of seeing a person mistreated or taken advantage of. She'd let it go to a place where she couldn't be sure her decisions were ruled by logic, or if she was blindly following her tangled emotions, driving her to help Varean for personal gain instead of professional obligation.

How could she have come to care so much about someone she knew so little about, especially one who had secrets, one who might prove to be a danger to her and the rest of the crew?

Besides, no one except Rian had the power to order Varean released, and she'd promised she wouldn't push him on the subject.

After the short, tense trip back from the dead ship, Rian was about the last person she wanted to speak with. He'd walked away without a word, hadn't looked at any of them, but there'd been a rawness to his manner she'd never experienced before. Honestly, it freaked her out, like looking at an entirely different man.

Knowing about Rian's shadowy past and seeing it firsthand were two very different things.

They all knew the Reidar had captured and held him prisoner for years, but that was the only confirmed detail anyone had. If the people on the ship had been dead six or seven years, it put the incident right in the middle of the time frame. While they'd assumed he'd been tortured, no one had ever speculated exactly what that might have entailed.

If Rian had been about in the galaxy carrying out executions on the Reidar's behalf, what the hell else was he keeping from them?

She'd never once second-guessed her decision to join his crew, even after she'd found out about the Reidar. She didn't want to doubt her choice or the man who'd returned her purpose in life. But his treatment of Varean, and the discovery onboard the dead ship, left her feeling shaky.

As she reached the stairs leading to the upper level of the ship, she spotted Zahli coming down. Relief crossed her friend's face as she reached the landing.

"Oh good. I was just coming to find you."

"Something wrong?" She braced her hand on the rail as

she faced the captain's sister.

Teeth worrying her lower lip, Zahli pushed back her thick hair. "I need you to tell me exactly what happened when you went over to that dead ship."

A shot of dismay streaked through her. "Haven't you talked to Lianna or Callan? Or better yet, go see Rian—"

Zahli shook her head. "I tried. You know how loyal Lianna is to him. She told me Rian would tell me himself if it were something I needed to know. And Callan flat-out shut me down. Rian locked himself in his cabin the moment he got back, and from past experience, no matter how much I bang on his door, he won't come out until he's good and ready. I could get Tannin to override the captain's codes, but I'm worried enough about Rian's frame of mind that I don't want to put anyone else in his sights." Zahli beseeched, "Please, Kira, you're my closest friend—"

Any resistance failed in the face of Zahli's blatant cajoling. "Okay, okay, don't pull the friend card. There's probably no one to overhear us, but I don't want to talk about it out here."

She headed halfway back along the corridor and swiped a hand over the small crystal screen sensor to open the hatchway to her cabin.

The space was identical to every other crew cabin on this level of the *Imojenna*—a double bed pushed up against the bulkhead below a high, long viewport in the outer side of the ship. Adjacent to that was a padded bench running along the side bulkhead, with a small table set toward the hatchway end. Across the room from that were two smaller hatchways, one the privy facilities and the other a closet. The personal possessions she'd added over the years had slowly given the place a homey feel—a couple of plants that survived in low lighting, a colorful, hand-woven blanket from a market on Shivani, a hanging display of glass and beads in varying shades of purple, and an enlarged picture of a sunset over an ocean on her homeworld of Jacolby on the only blank wall. She didn't know why she kept that final piece of her old life, only that it was a picture of a beach she used to visit as a child with her parents, sister, and two older cousins—memories of a happy, simple life.

She went over and plonked herself onto the bed, dragging a corner of the soft blanket over her lap as exhaustion hit her like an asteroid. She'd been running the past days with only a few naps to sustain her. She was beat, but hadn't realized it until she'd sat down. Now she didn't know how she was going to get back up again.

Zahli had sat down on the padded bench opposite and leaned forward, her hands resting on her knees and posture full of tension.

"So, what happened? I haven't seen Rian with that exact expression for years, not since he first came back after—" Zahli clenched her hands together. "Well, you know."

Actually, she didn't know, not really. Over the years, Zahli had offhandedly mentioned what Rian had been like when he'd first returned from presumably being dead. He'd been cold and emotionless, detached, and always within a hair trigger of violence to the point she'd refused to sleep in the same house. The shadows in her eyes suggested there was more to the story, but Kira wasn't about to ask, and truthfully, she didn't think she wanted to know, especially after what they'd found in that ship.

"Are you sure you want to hear this? It wasn't pretty."

Lines of tension bracketed Zahli's mouth and the corners of her eyes. "I have to know. I *need* to know. No matter what he's done, he's still my brother."

She fingered the soft edge of the blanket while she attempted to put the words together in a way that would be less traumatic to hear. But damn it, there was no easy way to tell a girl that the sixteen dead bodies on the carefully abandoned ship were the sole responsibility of her older brother.

"The ship hadn't been abandoned…by the crew anyway. They were all dead. About seven years by my guess."

Zahli gave a jerking nod, sitting forward a bit more. "So? Rian has seen dead bodies before. What about this made it so different? Were the Reidar responsible?"

She slid her gaze away from her friend. "You could say that. Indirectly, I suppose."

Zahli's hand dropped over hers where she'd nearly frayed the edge of her blanket. "Come on, Kira, just tell me already. The suspense of not knowing has got to be worse than whatever the truth is."

"No, actually, I don't think it is." The words came out clipped, almost choppy, as though her mouth didn't even want to form the syllables. "He killed them."

"Who killed them? You mean Rian?"

She nodded, pressing her lips together as the image of those coldly, perfectly, freakishly laid-out bodies slapped at her. He could have simply killed them and left them where they'd fallen. Instead he'd *arranged* them. Sure, it looked similar to how the military lined up their dead for transport after a battle, but it still sent a shiver along her spine, made her wonder why Rian had taken the time to do that, and what state of mind he'd been in all those years ago.

"I thought you said they were already dead." Zahli's features took on an edge of frustration.

"They *were* already dead. Rian killed them all seven years ago."

Zahli blew out a sharp breath. "Okay. So maybe they were Reidar. Maybe they—"

"No. They were all human. The leaders of Freemont. Pretty much all of their top governing council, actually."

"So the Reidar have replaced the Freemont government."

Zahli's hands clenched. "And if Rian killed them…"

The end conclusion to that was shockingly simple, though not one member of the *Imojenna*'s crew would want to believe it.

"He was a Reidar assassin," Zahli whispered, her face paling.

Heart squeezing at her friend's distress, Kira reached over and wrapped her hand around Zahli's clenched fist. "We don't know that for sure."

"Yeah, but it frecking explains a lot." Zahli closed her eyes, taking a slow breath, then opening them again. "It doesn't change anything. Rian isn't that person anymore. I knew whatever happened during those lost years was bad, but—"

"You assumed he was locked up somewhere being tortured, not flying around the galaxy…"

"Not flying around the galaxy assassinating people? Yeah, that never factored into the equation." Zahli sent her a bleak smile, unclenching her fist to give her fingers a quick squeeze. "Thank you for telling me. I know it's the last thing you wanted to do."

Zahli released her hand and slouched back on the padded bench as though she had the weight of a world on her shoulders.

"Since I did you a favor, maybe you can do me one." The words came out almost before she'd thought about them. Now was the worst time to put any more burden on her friend, but Varean's situation was winning over her reservations, and Zahli would understand. Out of all the crew, Zahli was the one she could count on to always take her side. "I need you to talk to Rian about Varean. If Rian ever wants him to cooperate, locking him up is not going to achieve that, and neither will being chained to the wall."

"Why are you so bothered about what happens to some

random soldier Rian took off the *Swift Brion*?"

She worked to keep her expression neutral while her mind raced to come up with an excuse, but apparently she wasn't all that successful. Comprehension dawned on Zahli's face.

"Kira—"

"It's nothing, I swear. But you have to admit he doesn't deserve to be treated like a criminal when he hasn't done anything wrong."

Zahli crossed her arms, giving her head a slight shake. "I'm sorry, Kira. I don't think it's a good idea to cross Rian about even the smallest thing today."

A small swell of disappointment washed through her. It'd been a long shot and probably not fair to press Zahli just because she was the captain's sister. Rian had proven that in matters of ship and crew, he wouldn't treat her any differently than the rest of them.

"I just can't stand knowing he's chained up down there."

Zahli stood, expression sympathetic. "I don't like it either. But the best thing you can do is give Rian some space and find some other way to help the commando."

"Thanks."

"I should be the one thanking you." Her friend took a couple of steps toward the hatchway, then glanced back with a rueful smile. "I might not agree with the way Rian handled this thing, but I think you need to be careful. I get the feeling this commando is going to bring nothing but trouble, and then some."

Not waiting for a response, she left the cabin.

Pushing to her feet, Kira winced at her stiff muscles. What she really needed was a hot shower and a few solid hours of sleep. But that wouldn't be happening until she sorted something out with Varean.

Zahli had said to find another way to help Varean, but

truthfully, her options were limited. She was a doctor, not a soldier or a psychologist. She didn't know the first thing about getting someone to talk—because talking was the only thing that would get him out of this. If he were injured, she could fix his wounds no problem. If he were sick, she could run tests and administer medication—

Her brain stumbled, and she paused at her cabin hatchway. *Tests.* Of course, why hadn't she thought of it before? Surely, if the Reidar had done some kind of experiments to Varean on a genetic level, it would show up in his blood work. He didn't need to tell them anything, he just needed to let her take a blood sample.

With renewed energy, she left her quarters. The ship was quiet, apart from the rumbling hum of the engines, no doubt because everyone was wary of Rian's mood. It would have been almost easier if he yelled or smashed a few plates in the galley. Instead, the eerie, still tension in the ship, like humidity rising before one mother of a storm, was much worse than any violent outburst.

She went to one of the storage cupboards and got a bucket. After that, she went to her medbay to fill it with warm water, grab some antiseptic liquid soap, and a few cloths. Though everyone seemed to be keeping themselves scarce she was still surprised she made it down to the brig without anyone intercepting her. Someone had been down here, however, because she'd left the barred doorway standing open, and now it was closed and locked. The sight reignited the spark of anger. Seriously, the guy was chained up. Was it really necessary to lock the bars as well? He looked like he could barely hold himself up, let alone orchestrate some superhero-esque escape.

She set the bucket down with an aggravated clunk, sloshing some of the water and gaining Varean's attention. He lifted his head and straightened from his slouch as she unlocked the door.

"What are you doing back here?" He adjusted his shoulders, wrapping his hands around the chains on his wrists, holding himself up. A sharp stab of contrition cut right through the middle of her chest, making her heart skip a painful beat. She'd strayed into uncharted territory in letting her emotions get mixed up with him and his situation. She was so determined to help, but barely knew how. Getting him cleaned up seemed superficial when taking into account his current circumstances.

"I seem to remember someone wanting to be clean." She hefted the bucket over and set it down by his feet.

The upward quirk of his lips couldn't be called a smile, but there was definitely a brief flash of cynical amusement. "Belay that order, Doc. No quarter for this prisoner, which definitely includes a sponge bath from the naughty nurse."

"Naughty nurse?" If anyone else had said that, especially Callan, she definitely would have added a little extra something to their next meal in revenge. But coming from Varean, and considering his predicament, she found it humorous. "Lucky you're already chained up or I might have taken exception to that."

Stepping closer, she pulled out a small pair of scissors and cut away his torn, bloody shirt, holding her breath as his chest and shoulders were bared. The way he'd healed was nothing short of staggering. Where there should have been a gaping, bloody wound from the large knife Callan wielded, there was nothing but a healthy-looking pink scar, as though the injury had been sustained months ago, not a day past.

She hadn't found the chance to talk with Ella yet and still held out minor hope the Arynian priestess was responsible for the healing. However, there was a marked difference between his wound and when Ella had done the same for Rian. After Ella had finished with the captain, there hadn't been any hint of a scar, whereas it looked as if Varean would be left with a permanent reminder.

Putting the thought out of her mind, she crouched down to wet one of the cloths and add a dab of liquid soap, then stood and focused on the streaks of blood across his chest. Beneath that, his muscles stood out in sharp relief under the bulkhead lights. She had to take a second to grope for her professionalism. She'd given plenty of sponge baths when she'd been an intern, but that had been a lot of years ago, and none of her patients had looked like Varean. None of them had put her in a tailspin of impetuous emotion and deep kindling heat.

Instead of this being a chore, part of her was a little too eager to get the slippery wet cloth all over his glistening skin. Oh god. That thought had been so wrong. She had to find her sensible side, wherever it had flitted off to.

"Kira."

The sound of her name in the low rumble of his voice jarred her entire body, including her lungs, leaving them to stall on a half breath. She glanced up to find him staring down at her. Sweat dripped down the side of his face, his bunched shoulders and biceps glistening from a damp sheen covering his skin.

"You'd be doing me a better kindness to simply leave me alone. I'm starting to get the feeling none of this is going to end pretty, and I don't want you in the middle of that."

Her fist contracted around the wet cloth, water dribbling over her hand as she squeezed.

"I can't do that." The words came out as not much more than a whisper.

He shifted forward, as far as the chains would allow, which was scarcely half a step. "You have to."

"Let me take a blood sample." She hadn't meant to blurt out the words so bluntly, had planned to ease him into the idea, talk him around to seeing reason. "Let me run some tests. I understand why you've been refusing to talk—you don't owe us anything. But if you want to help yourself, if you want to help *me*, then let me take some blood and run a sample. It's the only way you're going to get out of this."

He glanced away, a muscle pulsing in his cheek as his jaw clenched. She deflated a little, the stubborn angle of his head telling her he was going to refuse again. But he closed his eyes and blew out a short, sharp breath.

"What if the results make things worse?"

Her heart thumped a few painful bursts with apprehension and confusion. "How could they—"

He returned his gaze to her, light blue eyes burning with a cold light of foreboding. "What if I'm something else?"

"Something else?" She resisted the urge to step back as she processed this piece of conjecture.

He heaved a sigh, closing his eyes for a long moment.

"I'm not what I seem," he finally said, his tone harsh.

She swallowed, wanting to ask what he meant, but was unable to form any words. Was he actually Reidar? One who was different from the others and could resist the stunner's effects to change him? Or what if he truly meant *something else*. Some other undiscovered type of alien? If there was one other species besides humans out there in the universe, who was to say there weren't another hundred? The idea was almost too much to grasp, and she got her wild imaginings under control.

He opened his eyes again, resignation in the silver-blue depths, along with hints of pure mercury. "I wasn't surprised that I survived the stab wound or how fast I healed. The truth is—"

His words broke off with a low, ragged curse and she closed the remaining distance between them to reach up and set her hand on his jaw. Despite her rampant conjecture a moment ago, the explanation would be the most logical one—his healing abilities were similar to Ella's, so maybe he was somehow related to the Arynians.

"Whatever it is, if it has nothing to do with Rian and the Reidar, then I'll keep your secret. We can convince Rian together that you don't know anything, especially if I run these tests and nothing shows up."

"But that's the thing. I don't know what the sample will show. I've never been tested. When I joined the IPC, I switched out what should have been my blood with a sample a buddy of mine gave me, no questions asked. Since then, if I happened to get injured—"

"You healed yourself and never sought medical attention," she concluded. "But why?"

"Because I've been running from my birthright ever since I was a kid." He closed his mouth, clenching his jaw.

"You've never told anyone?" She could see it in the edge of vulnerability in his gaze.

He shook his head. "And if it gets out, it'll change everything."

"But it won't change the way I see you. I can promise that." She didn't know why she made that vow. Why should it matter to him what she thought? They were almost complete strangers thrown together through an unfortunate domino chain of events in a game far larger than the two of them.

But he released a low breath, as though her insistence had been exactly what he needed to hear.

"I have…" He paused, clearly trying to choose the right words. "I have abilities. Powers. Healing is just one. You felt it when I was touching you after I'd been stabbed. And just now when I kissed you."

"That vibration? It was warm, like a tropical breeze."

"That's it, yeah."

On the verge of finally getting the answers, her pulse

spiked, like riding the high of a medical emergency and knowing just what to do to save a life.

"Can you heal only yourself, or others as well?" Yep, the scientist within her had perked right up, wanting to know all the details. Ella was the only other person she'd met with these abilities, but since the priestess had come onboard, she'd tried to be circumspect about grilling the poor woman for information. "And what else can you do besides healing?"

"That's just it. I don't know. I didn't *want* to know. When I was fourteen, I accidentally started hearing thoughts from my foster parents and other kids. I'd always known I could heal myself and even kind of influence people into doing things. But when the mind reading started, I knew I was in trouble, so I buried the abilities as fast and deep as I could."

"Trouble?" she repeated, not understanding why a kid with next-gen evolutionary abilities would want to get rid of them.

"Because of what would have happened to me if anyone else had figured out the truth. I would have been sent to Aryn and forced into training to become a priest. I might not have known much at fourteen, but I sure as hell knew that wasn't the life I wanted to live."

"Would it have been so bad? You would have been taught about your full potential, and, as I understand it, you would have always had a safe place to belong, maybe even an important role—"

"And not a single damn choice about anything again in my life." He glanced past her, as if worried someone was going to appear or overhear their conversation. "The IPC don't like people with any kind of abilities floating around the universe unchecked. They've got an agreement with the Arynians. That's why the kids are taken and trained, because the Arynians can influence their beliefs and keep them in line. If an adult is discovered, they disappear. An adult with my kind of powers, who hasn't done Arynian one-oh-one, is viewed as a potential threat."

She'd never thought too closely about the Arynians. Even after Ella had come aboard, she hadn't considered the details. It seemed ridiculous to think the government would simply kill anyone with extra-evolutionary abilities simply because they hadn't been given the extensive training of the Arynians. But a few years ago, she would have said shape-shifting aliens were ridiculous.

"You don't believe me." His disappointed words brought her attention back to him.

"I do. It's just taking a second to sink in." She shook her head, putting the information away to think about later. "So you think that's why the stunner affects you, because of your abilities?"

"At first, yes. But now, it's like my insides have been scrambled. There's something in there, Kira, deep down. Something new. Something aggressive, hateful, and destructive. Something that wasn't there before. It's getting harder and harder to keep it down. When I almost strangled your security guy, it was because the hostility had taken over. I'd lost control. And I've been having dreams of places I've never been, but they're so real they're more like a memory. And the language spoken, something I can't understand but know—"

He dropped his chin, releasing a harsh breath. Tension rippled through every line of his body, as though he was trying to get hold of himself. Finally, he brought his head up, eyes drowning in shadows of both apprehension and self-loathing.

"I need help. If this keeps up, I don't know where it's going to end. Next time I lose control, you might be the one I attack."

It was no small thing, the trust he was placing in her and asking for help. She shouldn't read into it, shouldn't think it was anything other than the fact she was a doctor who'd done everything to help him since he'd come aboard. Except the part of her with no sense wanted it to mean more.

Considering everything he'd just told her, she should be backtracking out of this brig as fast as she could. But instead, she pressed forward, setting her hand lightly in the middle of his chest, right over his pounding heart. There was no point questioning her motives. She had no explanation for leaping headfirst into what would no doubt amount to more danger, apart from the undeniable fact that she'd abandoned all logic to follow her instincts.

"I can help you, Varean. No matter what happens, I will help you."

"If you do the tests, how long will it take for the results?" A hint of stubbornness entered his expression, telling her that he was still ready and willing to fight.

The medbay was her domain, the unspoken rule on the ship that no one messed with her things. She could run the tests on her commpad completely separate from the onboard systems so no one would know, though it might take longer on the limited power of the small tablet. Or, she could run an isolated program in her medbay systems and hope no one noticed.

"I have no idea how long it will take. The *Imojenna* isn't exactly a flying genetics lab. There are probably entire DNA components missing in the computer's medical program. It could take a few days."

One side of his lips lifted in a crooked, grim smile. "And how do we keep Sherron or his gorilla from questioning me in the meantime?"

"Gorilla?"

"The security guy. Callum."

She gave a short laugh, letting some tension go with it. "Oh, you mean Callan. Well, for a start, don't call him a gorilla to his face, no matter how appropriate it might be."

"I'm not making any promises. Being chained up tends to make me a little cranky." He grimaced as he adjusted his shoulders, though the movement was restricted, due to the way his arms were stretched above his head.

"Don't worry about Rian or Callan. I'll find a way to run interference until the results come through."

He gave up on trying to improve his position and speared her with an intense look. "Guess at this point I don't have much of a choice, do I?"

She returned his stare with a steady, implacable one of her own. "You have a choice. This is about what's smart."

He glanced upward, biceps flexing as he tightened his grip on the chain, like maybe he was thinking about simply yanking himself free the way he had on the gurney in her medbay. But while he might have found enough desperate, adrenalized strength to break the cuffs, the metium-reinforced chain connecting him to an upper bulkhead brace was an entirely different story.

After a long moment, he blew out a hard breath and returned his gaze to her. "Okay, Kira, do what you have to. Take the sample and run the tests."

She gave him a quick nod, forcing herself not to outwardly react, despite the relief blasting through her like a ship's slipstream. She hurried from the brig and headed up to her medbay for the equipment she'd need.

Once she'd returned, Varean watched her with all the intensity of a caged tiger when she approached, muscles coiled as though he'd spring into deadly action the second he got free. Ignoring the shiver chasing over her skin, she stopped a few steps away and studied him with clinical precision.

"Considering your current situation, I'm going to have to take the blood from your ankle, since I can't get your arms down. It's not ideal but—"

"It'll be fine. Let's just get it over with." The words were loaded with apprehensive impatience so, before he could change his mind, she knelt down and pushed the bottom of his cargo pants midway up his calf.

It took three tries to find a useable vein, but Varean didn't so much as make a noise or shift. She took four vials of blood, not really sure how much she'd need, deciding it would be better to have too much than have to come back later and ask him for another sample. When she was done and withdrew the cannula, the small pinprick didn't bead with even a single drop of blood. In fact, she couldn't even see where the needle had gone in. Well, that healing ability definitely came in handy.

"All done. Now let's see about getting you cleaned up a bit."

Varean didn't say anything, still didn't move, just continued to watch her with predatory intent. She took his silence as an agreement and bent down to retrieve the cloth, rubbing it between her hands to work up a lather with the soap.

She studied the streaks of blood, forcing herself not to notice the sculpted muscles standing out in stark relief. Who was she kidding? She'd gone way beyond the point of being able to shove him back into the neat confines of the usual doctor-patient relationship.

Thick whiskers now dusted his angular jawline and, despite the fierce expression on his face, the burn of frustration in his silver-blue eyes, and the fact he'd clearly been run down hard in the past few days, he was undeniably sexy. The thought rammed itself into the forefront of her mind and wouldn't budge.

Though she'd never been attracted to overtly muscular, powerfully built men before, Varean wasn't a typical brainless macho soldier. She'd also very definitely never been attracted to one of her patients. She'd never wanted to ride that cliché, and yet here she was, in way over her head with him with no warning. One second she'd been floating like usual, the next she'd found herself drowning in too many confusing emotions.

Swallowing down a ripple of awareness, she forced herself to disengage—made easier by years of practice. When it came to patients who were severely injured or distressed, like most doctors, the easiest way to cope was to turn to the side of herself that didn't see anything except a subject, a problem, or an issue that needed solving, one piece at a time.

Her mind back in familiar territory, she shifted forward and set the cloth against his skin, just below his collarbone. She focused on nothing except the dark red streaks of dried blood until the cloth and water in the bucket had turned red, and Varean was clean.

Last, she took a second cloth and patted down his damp skin—not that it made much difference. He was sweating all over from the heat of the engines. The fabric of her own clothes had started sticking to her skin, but at least she could leave here, take a cool shower, and put on something fresh. Once again, thinking too closely about Varean being chained down here made frustration rise through her in a hot pulse.

"I know I've already said it, but I'm sorry about this." She took half a step back as she glanced up at him. He had his eyes closed, a tense expression on his face. Fatigue or pain? Either would be likely, considering everything he'd been through, ending with him chained up like a rabid animal.

"Stop apologizing, Kira. You've got nothing to be sorry for." His voice sounded a little strained.

Offering him some pain relief crossed her mind. But for one, he'd probably pull the macho I'm-fine-don't-need-no-damn-pain-meds trick, and second, after his extreme reaction to both the sedative and adrenaline, she was hesitant to give him anything in case he had yet another reaction. His body had been through so much, next time she might not be able to save him.

"You should get on. Go do whatever you have to with that gallon of blood you took." He opened his eyes to focus on her, taut lines around his mouth. Still, his exaggeration made a smile tug at her lips.

"It wasn't a gallon."

He raised an eyebrow.

"Fine, it was more like two gallons."

The left side of his lips quirked upward. "Thought so."

Bending down, she tossed all the cloths and Varean's ruined shirt into the bucket, tidying up what little mess she'd made. After that, she retrieved a bottle of water, screwing off the lid and holding it up.

"Think you can keep it down? I could get a drip set up if you prefer—"

He cocked his head in a gesture to indicate she should come closer. "I'll be fine. I should probably count myself lucky to get this. I'm pretty sure I could guess Rian's opinion about you setting up a drip."

A week ago—heck, maybe even yesterday—she would have made some flip comment about how Rian could take his opinion and vent it out the nearest hatch. But after the revelations of that dead ship…

While she hadn't lost her faith or trust in the captain, she was taking all the rumors about him more seriously.

Pushing aside the uneasy sensation, she stepped up and held the bottle to Varean's mouth, tipping it slightly so he could drink. A rivulet of water escaped and trickled down his neck, right between his pecs, and it took a long nanosecond to realize she'd watched the progression of the droplet with too much mesmerized fascination. Snapping her gaze back to his face, relief flared since it seemed he hadn't noticed. Still, a light flush crawled upward through her chest. At least if her cheeks were going bright red, she could blame it on the damn heat.

When he'd had enough, she lowered the bottle and screwed on the lid.

"I'll come back in an hour or so to give you more water. It won't take much for you to end up dehydrated in this heat."

By the tightening of his jaw, he didn't appreciate the observation. Or maybe it was her statement about returning he didn't like, worrying she would get herself in trouble with Rian. Either way, if she hadn't already seen him more than half dead and saved his life two—or was it three?—times over, the uncompromising set to his face would have been intimidating.

"I already told you, if playing doctor with me is going to get you in trouble with Sherron—"

"Who said anything about *playing*?" She stooped down to grab the bucket. "I'm not some backwater hack who got her doctor's license online after watching half a dozen medi-vids. I'm a real doctor; I trained at a real medical school and interned at a real hospital."

Varean winced. "I didn't mean—"

"And I'm sure as hell not going to sit up-ship with a coffee and snack while someone gets dehydrated," she continued right over him. "So for what it's worth, I'm telling you not to waste any energy trying to escape. Get some rest, don't draw attention to yourself, and maybe I can keep Rian from questioning you until the tests are done."

That little slice of hope was hollow at best—like using paper to make a ship hull. It wouldn't hold out for any time and was foolish to consider in the first place.

Before Varean could argue, she left, not bothering to close the barred door. No doubt he'd totally ignore her and start trying to work out a means of escape before her feet even hit the stairs. So maybe she should have locked the brig.

Despite what he'd said about losing control, she trusted him and didn't think he'd hurt anyone on purpose if he did escape. If they tried to stop him, that might be a different scenario. And yeah, maybe there was a small part of her that hoped he would get free, sneak through the ship without encountering anyone, and steal one of the skimmers to find his freedom. It wasn't very likely, though. The chances of him not getting caught were minuscule.

Hopefully, he'd listen and stay exactly where he was, getting what little rest he could.

In her medbay, she put all personal thoughts aside as she discarded the cloths and water before taking the sample tubes and labeling them with a micro-crystal stamp. On each label, the thumb-sized screen flickered to life and catalogued the contents, then scanned and confirmed they were all workable samples. She put three in a coldstore, but kept out the fourth. In another half hour, she'd separated various components of the blood and started the *Imojenna*'s computers working on DNA and genetics sequencing.

But when the estimated time flashed in the bottom right-hand corner of her commpad, she groaned. Five days? How was she going to keep Rian from questioning him for that long? Worse, how could she expect Varean to languish down there for all that time?

# Chapter Ten

Despite Kira ordering him to get some rest, Varean wasted a good half hour trying to figure out if his chains or the bulkhead brace had any weaknesses he could exploit to get himself free.

Unfortunately, he'd take a safe bet on the gorilla chaining up more than a few people before him, because even with his extensive commando training, he couldn't find any flaws in the way Callan had attached him to the brace.

He muttered a few choice curses under his breath, wiping his face against his biceps, trying to stop some of the sweat dripping into his eyes. Whatever good Kira's sponge bath had done was well and truly wasted now. Although, at least he wasn't half covered in his own blood anymore.

Speaking of that sponge bath, he was not going there again. No way sir. Living through it had been hard enough without his mind supplying him a play-by-play rerun. But damn him to Erebus, he couldn't stop the thoughts from coming at him like an avalanche, no matter his determination to the contrary.

She'd soaped him up and oh-so-innocently cleaned him

down with all the precision and detachment of cleaning a battlecruiser. There shouldn't have been anything sexy about it. Yet for all the pain and injury he'd suffered recently, it seemed his body was primed to soak in any kind of ministrations like a damned soppy sponge.

Never mind getting shot with the Reidar stunner, chained up, locked up, or put down. If anyone ever wanted to torture him, apparently all they needed to do was send in Kira with those wet, soapy cloths a few times, and he'd be begging for mercy.

It had taken her maybe ten minutes to get him cleaned up to her satisfaction—every touch completely, frustratingly professional and impersonal—but they'd been the longest ten minutes of his life. If he'd been sweating by the time she was done, the heat from the engines hadn't been the cause. He'd been left with the small dignity that, while he'd been dealing with some serious swelling below the belt, at least he hadn't been fully standing at attention. And apparently she'd been so unaware of him as anything but an object, he didn't think she had a clue just how intensely she'd jacked up his entire system.

But all that aside, it'd probably come time to admit he did need to shut himself down, let his abilities do their thing, and regain some strength after taking another hit from the damned alien stunner. His body was still buzzing from it, like he'd been hit by lightning, leaving residual burns licking under his skin and his head throbbing with each beat of his heart. Though being upright with his arms stretched above his head wasn't ideal, he closed his eyes and made his mind go quiet, forcing himself into a semi-relaxed state as if he were taking a combat nap while stuck in live action.

But with his abilities now running rampant, his body and mind separated, leaving his physical self in a healing state while his consciousness remained mostly alert. *Whoa.* So he had no idea he could do that. Weird. Like floating in a dark pool of water where he knew he existed, but there was no sensation.

Gradually, he got the sense he wasn't closed in a dark, sensory-deprived bubble, but opening to—something bigger and more complex than his own mind, something that had become familiar. It was that place he'd been unwillingly drawn into when he thought he'd been dreaming. Now he could see there was actually a way to enter, a rippling horizon of yellow and gray shifting light. And above him, always unreachable but present, was that blue star. What this all meant, he had no idea. Did it come back to his heritage? Things he would have learned if his mother hadn't died and left him to the foster system?

It seemed he was gaining more control over this augmented reality, choosing to tap into the mysteries himself instead of simply being inundated by them.

Yet once he'd become immersed, the antagonistic mutation within him stretched, latching onto his newfound feelings toward Kira. Images came at him like asteroids.

He wanted her, saw, felt himself kissing her, but there were no bars between them. This time she didn't pull away, this time he didn't *let* her pull away. He took control, took what he wanted. The shadows drove him to take everything from her. Claiming her body wasn't enough; he wanted her pleasure and her pain. Her very life. Instead of touching her like a lover should, he was hurting her, he was going to kill her, because that's what the shadows demanded.

He recoiled, distantly feeling his body jerk as though he were fighting to get free. But there was no escape. He'd been dragged too deep and couldn't break the suffocating hold.

• • •

Rian leaned on his console, watching as Kalaheo station loomed. Lianna took them underneath one of the four protruding external docking bays before swinging back around and maneuvering the ship toward an empty berth.

Being a large station in a central system, Kalaheo was busy, and they'd had to cool their jets for three hours before anything had even opened up. Station law required a ship to stay docked for two hours, something to do with authorization checks and cooling engines. But he didn't plan on hanging around that long. For a start, no matter how good at forgery Callan might be, he couldn't be sure some tie-wearing form-filer wouldn't realize they were flying under a fake registration. And two, if his luck ran the usual crappy streak, they'd more than likely need to make a quick getaway.

Lianna sat back as the engines started winding down. "Docking complete. Pressure equalizing in the cargo bay hatch."

Though her voice held its usual note of perfect professionalism, and outwardly she hadn't treated him any differently in the last twelve hours, he was getting a definite chill from her that hadn't been there before. At least she wasn't outright avoiding him like some of the others. Even Callan seemed to have an extra wary glint in his eyes the few times they'd spoken.

He couldn't decide if the crew's new, guarded, tiptoeing-through-the-frecking-tulips attitude was hilarious or downright aggravating. He'd never lied to any of them about his true nature, never tried to hide the darkness inside him. They'd all been witness to him killing some frecking mother-loving son of a whore at one time or another over the years. They knew him for the destroyer he was.

So maybe he'd never told them about the whole Reidar-assassin bit, but that was mostly because he didn't remember all that much about it himself. There were flashes; most often they came at night, in his dreams. He never could tell what was real memory and what was simply his damaged mind creating gruesome, bloody images. And while he didn't remember the specifics of killing the entire Freemont government, the simple, undeniable fact that he had done it was lodged in the dark recesses of his mind like knowing his own name.

Maybe a normal or remotely sane person would have felt guilty when faced with the stark reality of their vicious, malevolent past. And sure, a cold kind of creeping sensation—one that was familiar and desolate—had burrowed into the back of his neck and refused to let go since he'd stepped onto that dead ship. But he didn't feel bad. He was sure as frecking hell angry, like he was giving birth to an arctic vortex that would raze everything in its path. Yet he let the frigid fury feed his resolve to pay back those shape-shifting freaks in kind—kill two of them for every life they'd directly or indirectly had a hand in destroying.

"McKenzie, you're coming on station with me." He pushed back from the console, but tapped the comm icon and ordered his sister's fiancé, Everette, up to the bridge.

"What about Callan?" Lianna asked once Tannin had arrived to take over the helm and they'd started down to the cargo bay.

"He's coming, too."

Lianna gave a single nod, clipping her gun belt around her hips and double-checking her weapons. Usually he would have taken only one or the other, not both. He'd like to say they wouldn't expect trouble on a nice, civilized station like Kalaheo, but lately trouble found him like a black hole found any matter dumb enough to get near its event horizon.

Callan was waiting for them on the cargo bay deck. Though it didn't outwardly appear the guy was toting as many weapons as usual, it was just an illusion. No doubt he had an impressive number of guns and knives stashed.

As he hit the hatchway release, he glanced up the stairs, fully expecting Ella to come waltzing down, all soft eyes, swaying hips, and metium-reinforced attitude to tell him she was coming along on this little jaunt. But by the time the hatchway had fully opened, there was no sign of her. He was almost disappointed, which was idiotically ridiculous. Actually, maybe disappointed wasn't the right sentiment. More frustrated that she kept him so far off-kilter he could never guess her intent. Hell, she hadn't even come to see him after he'd returned from that dead ship and locked himself in his cabin with a bottle of Violaine until the frecking tremors in his hands had stopped.

Obviously, their last encounter had convinced her to stay away from him, even though he definitely hadn't been the victor in that little skirmish.

Putting the priestess out of his mind, he stepped through the atmospheric doors and into the short metal tubeway leading into the docking arm. He, Callan, and Lianna came out in a wider passage with a gangway running down the middle, multiple tubeways leading to each berth in this section of the station. People strolled up and down the wide gangway, some coming, some going, some towing luggage or directing small, compact hover carts, some groups standing and chatting.

Rian kept his head ducked but his attention sharp. The last thing he needed was someone recognizing the ex–war hero. For a start, he was trying to keep a low profile and get out of here before either the authorities or Reidar knew he was dumb enough to set foot on a central system station. And second, he frecking hated it when people tried to congratulate him or stared at him in awe like he was something special.

Once they'd left the gangway and made it to the inner station, he stopped to access a directory. It'd been years since he'd come through this system. The public station logs he'd checked had listed Grigor as still residing and trading here, but often the information was outdated by months or occasionally years. However the directory aimed him toward a sector on the upper trading side of the station. Seemed Grigor had moved up in the universe since last time Rian had dealt with him, when his base of operations had been at a hole-in-the-wall, dingy stand in the bowels of the station.

Then, Grigor had acted as one of the many cogs in the larger syndicate of drugs, weapons, and prohibited tech run by an illegal trader named Uzair, who operated out of Huata, the legendary illicit bazaar on the Rim. When a rival organization had snatched Grigor's son and sold him into slavery, Grigor hadn't contacted Uzair for help—not that the ruthless trader would have helped anyway—but instead had contacted Rian. Liberating that frecking slave ship had earned him one more gold star in the legend of Rian Sherron, War Hero. He'd left the slave traders bloody and broken and had abandoned the ship at an aid station used by the IPC military for relief works before taking Grigor's son back to Kalaheo.

In return, Grigor had offered him an open-ended favor. Rian had never thought he'd need to call in the voucher, or if he did it would be something minor. What he planned on asking for today was no small thing.

The Reidar stunner weapon—or razar as Qae had started calling them—was the only weapon they had, the single toehold they'd found in the flawless wall of assault the aliens had erected. They needed to produce them fast, on a mass scale. Which meant parts, components, devices, and materials. A lot of which were tagged, catalogued, and tracked by the IPC. It'd be impossible to buy or trade for the amount they needed without attracting attention.

They already had UAFA charges of intergalactic terrorism hanging over their heads. And they were about to be associated with ex-Captain Admiral Zander Graydon and the huge-ass IPC flagship he was stealing—once the IPC military realized he'd gone off grid. So catching the IPC's attention by stockpiling materials used to make weapons wasn't something he wanted to add to the list. Besides, if the IPC knew, the Reidar would know. And until he could nuke the entire galaxy and show people the truth of what was hiding right under their noses, he didn't want them to realize he'd found a firearm that could out the bastards to their true form.

He took note of the directions and moved off, motioning Lianna and Callan to follow him.

Some places were more crowded than others, and as they passed through each sector, Rian took note of the security cameras and tried to keep his head angled down or away. One decent facial scan and the station alarms would be wailing themselves into a lockdown.

Ten minutes later, they were standing outside a large, reputable-looking storelet, complete with offices on either side and decals on the crystal display panes announcing GRIGOR AND ASSOCIATES COMMERCE EXCHANGE.

"Fancy digs," Callan muttered as they stepped toward the wide, three-panel doorway, which slid smoothly into a recess.

"Don't touch anything, Callan." Lianna shot the security specialist a quick, impertinent grin. "Knowing you, it'll get broken, and I'm guessing everything in here is worth more than a grunt like you makes in a year."

Callan hitched his weapon belt with its single, visible gun. "We can't all be fancy-pants engineers, now, can we?"

"All the kiddies get the same sized slice of cake," Rian put in before Lianna could reply. "Which means you all get the same cut of the take. Now, can we keep an eye out for station security or maybe any Reidar looking to freck us upside down and backward?"

Usually the crew's tit-for-tat didn't bother him. Sometimes it was even entertaining. But right now, the way his skin was crawling, he wasn't in the mood for it.

Inside, high-end clientele browsed over everything from robotics and biometric upgrades to jewelry and kitchen appliances. More than a few took a double look at them. No doubt because their functional, shipbound clothes made them stick out like a garbage compactor in a sub-light racer lineup.

A woman came out from behind a counter and walked over smiling, but her tense gaze gave up the truth of her pseudo-friendly expression.

"Can I help you with something?" She clasped her hands in front of her as she stopped, seeming all manner of solicitous and polite.

He hooked a thumb into a loop on his belt. "I'm here to see Grigor. Tell him it's Rian. That's all he'll need to hear."

The woman's smile became over-patient with a touch of brittleness. "Mr. Grigor isn't available today—"

And there went the small quarter of patience he'd saved up for this little outing. His hand landed on the butt of his pulse pistol. "I didn't ask you if he was available. I asked you to tell him Rian is here to see him."

She opened her mouth, but Callan half stepped in front of the woman, gaining her attention as he shot her what could only be described as a suave smile. His eyes, however, remained hard.

"I'm sure you don't want any kind of scene in front of all these fine customers. Doesn't take much for word to get around and damage a business's reputation. This looks like a nice place, so I'd hate to see it all scorched and broken, what with the pulse pistol fire and fleeing that's sure to happen if you don't go back there and find Mr. Grigor."

The woman's eyes widened, her lips pressing together as she swallowed, before darting a glance over Lianna and ending on him. He lifted his lips in a quick, crooked smile, one that had just a tad of lethal added to it, and pointedly moved his other hand so he had both palms on weapons. Truthfully, shooting up the place hadn't factored into his plan, but it didn't hurt to let the woman think he was more than willing to go all kinds of postal on the no-doubt expensive merchandise.

She cleared her throat and waved a hand toward the spot she'd left a moment ago. "If you'll come with me?"

Without waiting for a response, she led them past the long bench to a frosted-crystal pane door, where she paused for a palm scan. Inside was a kind of anteroom. A couple of plush chairs were arranged around a low table with three doors leading off in various directions.

"If you'll take a seat, I'll go find Mr. Grigor."

Rian nodded, but she didn't see, since she was too busy fleeing through the door on the far right. Lianna sat and helped herself to a glass of water from a chilled pitcher on the table, but he stayed where he was, scanning the room for any cameras or other security measures.

After Lianna was done with the jug, Callan took it and gulped straight from the pitcher, then made a face.

"Jezus. You reckon a place this fancy could at least have decent water. This tastes like it came out of the *Imojenna*'s decontamination tanks."

Lianna sent the guy a flat look. "It has lemon slices in it, that's what you can taste."

"It's got *fruit* in it?" He set the jug down with a grimace. "No wonder it tastes so frecking terrible."

The woman came back less than two minutes later, avoiding Callan and him to angle herself toward Lianna. "Mr. Grigor is on a call, but he'll be out in a few minutes, as soon as he's finished."

Lianna gave a single nod, then took a sip of the water. The woman shuffled a few steps sideways and rounded the far side of the chairs. "If you'll excuse me, I'm needed out front."

When she broke for the main doorway, Rian stepped into

her path, blocking her exit and forcing her to look up at him. He smiled down at her, even though he never got anywhere near looking friendly. The woman took half a step back, only to bump into Callan, leaving her looking even more nervous.

Maybe he was a paranoid sonuvabitch—actually, no *maybe* about it—but on the small chance she'd worked out who he was, he didn't want her leaving here and calling the station authorities while he negotiated with Grigor.

"I'm sure they can do without you for a few minutes while you keep us company."

The woman glanced past him at the door, as if maybe she was thinking of leaving anyway.

"Take a seat." He nodded toward the cluster of chairs. If she wouldn't cooperate, forcing her to stay would no doubt end with Lianna giving him some kind of disapproving glare over the way he treated people. Although, after the revelations of the dead ship, maybe his nav-engineer wouldn't even call him on that today.

Callan clamped a hand on the woman's shoulder, steering her over to perch on the edge of a chair and then all but standing at attention beside her. She clasped her hands in her lap, posture tense, and shook her head when Lianna offered to pour her a glass of water. Yeah, he wouldn't have drunk it, either, considering it now had Callan's slobber in it.

"Don't let them intimidate you." Lianna finally shot him a chiding look, putting them back on familiar ground. "My name is Lianna."

"I'm Nyomi." The woman raised her arm to shake Lianna's offered hand, a slight tremor in her fingers.

"How long have you worked here?" Lianna sounded genuinely interested, but Rian immediately tuned out as the pair launched into small talk.

He re-scanned the room, double-checking he hadn't missed anything the first time. After finding that dead ship and then coming onto a central system station, his senses were already jacked way up. Standing around here, it felt like the walls were closing in on him, like the bulkheads above him were going to come down and crush him in a trap. Bad things were skittering under the thin-ice surface of his calm.

He wanted to believe it was just a culmination of factors causing the creeping sensation in the back of his neck to rake like talons down his spine. But his instincts had kept him alive and one step ahead of the Reidar for a long time now. Something wasn't right about this situation—something way more wrong than just being on a central station where the Reidar, IPC, or UAFA could nab him without expending any resources. Just as he was about to start demanding Nyomi here take her ass back out that door and find Grigor, the hatchway slid open to reveal the man himself.

"Rian. I thought there must have been a mistake when Nyomi told me, but it really is you." Grigor stepped into the room and stopped by the chair his assistant sat in, not sparing a glance for Callan or Lianna. "I never thought I'd see you on Kalaheo again."

"Why? Because I'm a wanted intergalactic terrorist?"

Grigor shook his head. "You never did let anything get in the way of what you were doing. But I'm sure this isn't a social visit. What do you need?"

*Good.* Down to business, just the way he liked things to go. "I'm here about the favor you owe me."

Grigor raised both brows. "The favor?"

Asked as if the guy had no clue what he was talking about. Which only sparked his fraying temper. "You're not reneging, are you? Because we both know—"

"No, no." Grigor held up both hands. "I just—I suppose I thought maybe you wouldn't ever call that marker in."

"Is it going to be a problem?" His voice had gone the way of an arctic breeze, and Nyomi stood, making a show of clearing the glass Lianna had used, smartly putting herself out of the firing line. Callan had an eye like a terrier on the woman, leaving him free to concentrate on Grigor.

"No, no problem at all. I'm a man of my word. I promised you a favor, and so you'll have it."

Something in the man's tone was a little too blasé, and the talons in his spine dug in harder until a cold sweat prickled his skin. He slowly shifted his hand to the butt of his razar. "You remember what that favor was in return for, right, Grigor?"

Grigor's gaze dropped down to where he gripped the gun and then sliced back up, nervous tension in the lines around his eyes.

"Of course. It's not something I'm likely to forget." But sweat had started beading along the man's hairline, his skin washing out to a paler color.

*Frecking christ.* Rian yanked out the razar, and across the room, Nyomi squealed as Callan mirrored his action and Lianna surged to her feet. But that was all happening in his peripheral, not impacting his awareness locked onto Grigor as he fired off a round from the razar.

Grigor stumbled and went down to one knee, a hand braced against the floor while he shook his head, as if to clear it. When the man looked up, Rian wasn't surprised to find himself face-to-face with a Reidar.

They'd replaced Grigor? *Frecking Grigor?* Because of his connection to the man, or had it been another awful coincidence of his luck continuing to run the crappiest streak in the history of mankind?

"Well, Sherron, that was a mistake." The Reidar formerly known as Grigor reached behind himself, but Rian palmed his nucleon gun in his left hand, getting off a shot before the alien had brought his weapon halfway up.

The shifter took the shot in the middle of his chest with not much more than a flinch, but it threw off his aim. Rian sent his second round of ammo into the alien's arm, causing him to drop the weapon.

He took a slow step forward, keeping his aim true. "I'm more than happy to kill you if you're looking to die today, or we can have a nice chat, because there's a few questions I've been meaning to ask you scum bastards. Unfortunately, every time I run across any of you, you seem more interested in getting dead than having a civilized conversation."

The Reidar had clamped a hand over the wound in his arm, expression a mix of disdain and fury. "I'm not the one who's going to die today."

Going low, the alien went for the weapon where it had fallen on the floor. Cursing under his breath, Rian lit up with the nucleon gun, Callan letting loose with his own weapon, firing until the shape-shifter fell still and half pulped on the floor.

"God-frecking-damn-it," he muttered, holstering his guns. One of these days, he was going to catch himself an alien for a nice long chat. But right now, they needed to get offstation before someone sent the authorities up here for a report of weapons fire.

Glancing around, he found Lianna standing half in front of the Nyomi chick. But the frightened woman wasn't staring aghast at the dead alien carcass—which was swiftly liquefying as alien carcasses tended to do—but had her freaked-out gaze fixed on him like he was the boogeyman in this scenario. And when those dots connected, he almost couldn't believe it, but didn't have a doubt he was right.

He stalked over and reached around Lianna to yank the cowering woman out from behind his nav-slash-engineer.

"You knew." The words weren't much more than a snarl, because either she was a Reidar herself, or worse, she was human and helping the frecking invading aliens.

"Rian, what are you—" Lianna reached for the woman,

but Callan intercepted her.

Rian jerked Grigor's assistant away and shoved her so she stumbled then dropped into one of the chairs.

"You knew what he really was."

Nyomi's mouth opened and closed, but no intelligible sound came out. He tugged out his razar for the second time in a matter of minutes and pressed it to the middle of her chest.

"No! Wait, *please*, I—" Nyomi blubbered, but it didn't make him hesitate for even a second before he pulled the trigger. Except nothing happened. The pulse of energy passed through her with no discernable effects.

"You're *human*." The word conveyed all his confusion and disgust that she could know the truth and be working happily alongside him. "And you knew what he was."

She held up her hands, whole body shaking. "Yes, I knew. I know all about them."

His fury snapping through the remaining threads of his control, he reached down and grabbed a handful of her hair, yanking back her head and leaning over her.

"Why did they replace Grigor?"

Nyomi flinched from him. "I don't—"

"Don't tell me you don't know." He tightened his grip, forcing her deeper into the cushions of the couch.

"Rian!" Lianna shifted closer—as near as she could get with Callan still holding her arm—but didn't touch him and didn't make a move to Nyomi. No, his nav-engineer knew him better than that. "She's not the enemy."

"No, but she was sure as frecking hell sleeping with them. She knows something, and she's going to tell us."

"Okay!" Nyomi held up her hands and he eased the tension in his hold on her. "All I know is that when I told Grigor you were here, he called someone…someone named Niels. They told him to alert the authorities and station-jack your ship until the nearest IPC vessel could get here."

Callan muttered a string of curses—the same ones he was thinking—as he let Nyomi go and stepped back.

"We have to move." This sector of space was crawling with IPC military ships and UAFA vessels. If there wasn't already someone docking to take him and the rest of his crew down, there would be within minutes.

Callan had already headed for the door. Lianna's features were tense, but she didn't say anything as they left Nyomi where she sat frozen on the chair and stepped out into the main storelet—empty, of course. No doubt the shooting had sent everyone fleeing.

He set his hands on his guns, grip light, as they hurried out into the main thoroughfare where red emergency lights were flashing but no alarm sounding.

"Contact the ship. Get Tannin working on that station-jack right now." If he wasn't already. Hopefully his tech analyst was earning his keep and knew about security clamps locking them onto the berth.

Lianna had her comm out, the conversation with Tannin short as they came into another section and plunged into a milling crowd, only just slipping past the station security officers who went running toward Grigor's storelet.

"Tannin's on it," Lianna reported.

"Good, with any luck he'll have it freed by the time we get back."

None of them said anything else as they continued through the station, making it back in half the time it had taken when they'd set out.

Zahli was waiting for them and hit the hatchway controls the second they set boots on the ramp.

"Tannin said the IPC flagship *Marshal Beacon* docked three minutes ago. They're on the opposite side of the station, two berths up, but it won't take them long to get here."

"Has he kicked those detainment clamps yet?" He hit the stairs without waiting for an answer.

"Not when I came down here a minute ago," Zahli answered from behind him.

Up on the bridge, Tannin was standing at the captain's console, leaning over the screen and working with fast fingers on the crystal display. But his expression was grim and definitely not the look of a man who was about to get them free. Callan had followed him, but stopped at the back of the bridge in the process of adding more weight to his arsenal, getting weapons strapped and ready.

"Report?" He shot at Tannin, glancing over the tech analyst's shoulder and seeing nothing but gibberish.

"It's Reidar. It's all frecking Reidar. Some kind of coding I've never seen before. I can't get through it."

Zahli came up on Tannin's other side and put a hand on his shoulder. "Just take a breath. You'll figure it out."

He shook his head in a sharp movement but hadn't paused in navigating the program or even looked up from the screen. "No, I won't. Not before the officers from the *Marshal Beacon* get here. I'm tracking them through the station. We've got ten minutes until they're on the other side of our hatchway."

A calmness born of the deep-seated, permanent glacial fury toward the Reidar settled over him as he gripped Tannin's arm.

"Everette, can you get the *Imojenna* free before the IPC officers get here or not?"

Tannin finally paused and glanced over at him, his gaze heavy with a defeated, grim shadow, similar to how he'd looked the day they'd taken him off the prison planet, Erebus.

"If I had more time—" He clenched his jaw, glancing down at the screen. "No. Not before the officers get here. But I can lock down the ship. Maybe give us a chance to—"

"Shut it down and wipe the system." He stepped back

and turned, tapping open the console in the side of his chair and pulling out his spare weapons.

Tannin didn't need to be told twice, diving straight into a full system cleanse.

"Everyone else, grab anything you can't live without and head up to the skimmers."

"What are you saying?" Zahli moved away from Tannin, her gaze locked on him, burning with denial.

"Abandon ship." He slammed the empty console closed and threw one of the bigger nucleon rifles to Callan.

"We can't leave the ship." Her voice went up a notch in strident disbelief. "This is all we've got left."

"We've still got our freedom, which is worth a hell of a lot more. If the IPC have us, that means the Reidar have us. And whatever those frecking aliens have in store for us, it's certainly not worth standing our ground here. So grab anything you need and head up to the skimmers."

He didn't wait for Zahli to reply but took one last glance at the viewport, flashing with the words "total system erasure," before stepping off the bridge, trying not to let the thought that it would be for the last time swim through the furious, burning fog of his thoughts. The Reidar had taken nearly everything from him, including his ever-damned soul.

Right in this second he was giving ground, because he had to protect his family and crew. But he sure as hell didn't plan on letting this stand. Somehow, someway, he'd get this ship back. And if the Reidar unscrewed so much as a single bolt on the *Imojenna*, he wouldn't just kill the scum-sucking parasitic bastards. No, he'd get inventive. And then he'd get messy.

# Chapter Eleven

Kira rolled out of bed at the pounding on her door, body going into automatic action before her mind had even fully awakened. She stumbled over her shoes on the way, tugging her T-shirt straight and then pushing her hair out of her face as she swiped a hand over the controls to open the hatchway.

"What happened?" she asked before the door had even finished sliding open. Zahli was already retreating across the hallway when her bleary eyes focused in the brighter light.

"We're abandoning the ship. We have to leave *now*. Grab anything important; I don't know when we'll be coming back."

*What the hell?* She scrubbed a hand over her face, forcing the last tendrils of foggy sleep to clear. They were abandoning ship? What the freck had happened while she'd been sleeping?

She turned and scrambled for her shoes and then rushed to the locker and grabbed the emergency medical bag stashed in the bottom, flinging a spare pillow and other shoes out of the way to reach it. She tossed a single change of clothes on top, but when she left her cabin, instead of heading up to the skimmers, she sprinted down all the flights of stairs and through the cargo bay.

The door to the brig was open, like she'd left it, Varean still chained up. But now he was slumped, his chin on his chest. For a wild second, the panic that he'd gone and died on her ripped the air right out of her body. She rushed in and dropped the bag at his feet.

"Varean!"

His body twitched at her voice, bringing relief as she gasped in a quick breath.

She pressed her fingers into the crook of his neck, his pulse registering as fast but steady.

Cupping his jaw, she ducked her head to see his face more clearly. "Varean, wake up."

He mumbled something she couldn't understand, something definitely not in any language she could recognize. But he was definitely responding to the sound of her voice.

"Come on, that's it," she coaxed as his eyes opened, taking a second to focus as he lifted his head.

"Kira?" Confusion colored his tone as he straightened from the slump. "What's going on?"

She didn't give herself the time or luxury to dwell on the relief rushing through her. "I have no idea. But we're abandoning ship." She shifted around him to examine the chains, except they didn't look any better than they had last night when she'd failed to release them.

Callan had wanted to make damn sure Varean wasn't going anywhere and had double-wrapped them around and through the thick outer metal frame of a brace on the bulkhead above him, securing it all with two separate electronic locks she didn't have the keys for.

Cursing under her breath, she moved back to face Varean. "I can't unlock this without Callan. Just give me a minute."

Before Varean could reply, she ran back out of the brig, but only as far as the cargo bay, where Callan was flipping the lid off a crate and pulling something out, shoving it into the bag he held.

"Callan! Give me the keys to unlock Varean."

He glanced over his shoulder at her, slamming the crate shut and then bending over to pick up a huge nucleon rifle that had been leaning against another crate.

"Sorry, Doc, it's every man for himself, and since that cocksucker tried to kill me—" Callan headed for the stairs with an uncaring half shrug, but she darted over and reached the bottom landing before him, blocking his way.

"Give me the keys."

"Rian didn't say a word about releasing the commando. Unless you want to get left behind, get your ass up to the skimmers."

She crossed her arms. "I'm not leaving without Varean."

Callan elbowed her aside with a disgusted glare. "Fine, have it your way. I'm sure we can find another medic. One who actually follows orders."

He jogged up the stairs, disappearing into the upper levels. A rumbling started up above her, both skimmers being brought to life on top of the ship.

Rian would leave without her. He rarely gave the same order twice. If a person didn't follow the rules, they got left out in the cold. But she couldn't abandon Varean, chained up and defenseless in the bottom of the ship.

She swept a glance around the cargo bay but didn't find anything worth a damn. Urgency clamped onto her, and she ran into the engine room, colliding with the bench and scattering tools, searching for something to break the locks or chains. The ship's mechanic, Jensen, had things all over the place with no order whatsoever.

She grabbed a small power saw, knowing it would take ages to cut through, but finding no other options. Back in the brig, she couldn't meet Varean's gaze as she rushed by him and fired up the blade.

"Get out of here," Varean said, his voice hard, with more than a hint of order to his tone.

"Shut up. I'm not leaving you." But even as she touched the saw to the chain, the stupid piece of crap tool sparked and died in her hands.

"Damn it!" She threw the useless hunk of parts and pushed to her feet. "I'll find something else—"

"*Kira!*" Varean's expression was just short of furious as he stared down at her. "Get out of here before they leave without you."

Despite that being a very real possibility, her heart palpitated harder at the thought of abandoning him and what he might face alone with the IPC authorities or Reidar bearing down on this ship, more so than the notion of the crew flying off without her.

"Maybe they don't want to take responsibility for what we've done to you, but I will, no matter what."

He gripped the chains around his wrists, making his biceps and shoulder muscles tighten. "You're being stupid. You don't even know me, but I can sure as hell tell you I'm not worth getting caught or dying over. Do what the captain ordered and get the hell off this ship."

Though he obviously intended the opposite, his words only made her dig in, made the stubborn anger and drive to do the right thing burn hotter.

"I'm not leaving."

"Damn it!" Varean yanked furiously against the chains, and the metal above his head whined. They both glanced up, the brace where Callan had threaded the chain now bent.

She took half a step closer, a spark of hope making her heart skip a beat. "Do that again."

He locked his grip on the chain and tensed, then pulled against the links. The metal whined again, slowly turning into a low screech.

"Varean, you've almost got it!"

He lowered his head, entire body taut as he strained another tortured step forward until the brace half popped on one side, less than a finger's breadth away from snapping free. He took another step but, with a muted crack, his shoulder dislocated, yanking out of the joint.

"Oh my god." She started forward but, apart from clenching his jaw on a grunt, he didn't stop, putting all his weight into his good arm and giving one final, vicious tug. The brace broke, and Varean collapsed forward to his knees, chest heaving as his arms dropped with the chain.

She wanted to examine him, make sure the dislocated shoulder was the only thing he'd damaged in the desperate escape, but they didn't have time and, even as she reached for him, he was already pushing to his feet.

She grabbed her bag off the floor as he looped the chain in one hand while keeping his injured arm close to his chest. They sprinted out of the brig, running up into the ship. Halfway there, she detoured into her medbay. Varean didn't say anything, just waited as she pulled a second medical bag out of a recess and snatched the blood samples she'd taken from him out of the coldstore, shoving them into a thermal-lined case that would keep them at optimal temperature.

Not letting herself dwell on the fact that she was leaving half her life behind on this ship and what might happen to it after she was gone, she brushed by Varean and continued upward.

As they hit the top of the stairs, she found Zahli waiting at the bottom of the ladder-steps leading into the left skimmer. Her friend's expression relaxed with relief, before she turned to climb up. "Another few seconds, and Rian would have ordered us to leave you behind."

Frustration at everyone's lack of concern over Varean's

welfare almost had her snapping at her friend, but she clamped her teeth over the words while she waited for Varean to go ahead of her, up into the skimmer. Considering he was one-handed and still chained, he climbed surprisingly fast. She'd barely pulled the hatch closed behind her before the craft started disengaging from the *Imojenna*.

Lianna was at the helm, Tannin beside her, along with Zahli. Which meant Rian, Callan, Jensen, Ella, and Nyah had taken the other skimmer. Once, a few months ago, the entire crew could have all fit together on one skimmer, but now they had no choice but to take both.

Varean stood tense and wary not three steps from the hatchway, injured arm cradled against his chest, the other hand braced against the bulkhead as Lianna maneuvered the skimmer away from the *Imojenna* and amped up the throttle.

"Where are we going?" She set her two medical bags and the case containing Varean's blood samples into a nearby recess. Through the single viewport at the front of the shuttle, the other skimmer with the rest of the crew split off in another direction.

"We're going on to Barasa to follow up on Quaine Ayden like we'd planned," Lianna answered, tabbing off the comm as the heated voice of a station tower controller ordered them to return to port or risk injunctive weapons fire. "Rian and the others are heading to Dunham. Apparently he's got an acquaintance there he wants to try for the stunner components."

"Because the last contact worked out so well," Zahli muttered, crossing her arms. Though she had a dark glare on her face, Kira could see the worry in her friend's gaze as the other skimmer disappeared from view.

So, by reason of deduction, it seemed Rian's contact on Kalaheo had screwed him over, which is obviously what had led to them abandoning ship. Well, that made her twice as glad she hadn't ended up on the other skimmer with the captain. If he'd been coldly lethal since finding that abandoned ship, she couldn't begin to imagine what kind of deadly mood he was in now that they'd had to leave the *Imojenna*. She wasn't the only one who believed captaining the *Imojenna* was one of the only things keeping Rian from going off the psychotic deep end.

She turned to Varean, stepping closer as she studied the dislocated shoulder and the chains dragging from his wrists.

"We obviously need to do something about that." She turned her attention to the compartments, rummaging around until she came up with a pair of laser bolt cutters from a toolbox Jensen had left at some stage. If only she could have found something so easily a few moments ago before Varean had needed to dislocate his shoulder to escape. With a few quick snaps, the chains fell to the deck with a clank.

"Now for your shoulder," she said as she dropped the cutters back into the toolbox.

Varean clenched his jaw and nodded, stepping forward to brace himself against the back of an empty chair, exactly in the stance she'd been about to direct him.

"Something tells me this isn't the first time you've had a dislocated shoulder."

She moved up beside him, gently shifting his arm out and away from his body so she could work the joint back into place.

He gave a single nod. "First time I put it out was in basic training. Ever since then, the damn thing has never been the same. I've lost count of how many times I've had to put it back in. At least this time I've got someone else to do it for me."

She winced at the image of him popping his own dislocated shoulder back in. Not many people would have been able to do that successfully.

"Okay, then you know the drill." She set her hand against his skin, still slightly damp from the heat of the engines in the brig. "I don't suppose there's any point asking if you want some pain relief before we do this?"

He glanced back at her, a glint of amusement in his gaze as though she'd made a joke instead of a sensible suggestion.

"Let's just get it done."

"Fine. You want me to count it down?" She tightened her hold, manipulating the muscles in the top of his shoulder with firm fingers.

"No, just—"

With her other hand just above his biceps, she squeezed with a gentle but forceful pressure, and the joint put itself back into place.

"Is that it?" Varean's brow creased as he straightened, rotating the arm with a mystified expression. "That didn't hurt at all."

She sent him an exasperated look before turning to her medical bags. "If it's done properly, it's not supposed to hurt. You macho guys who are always going around shoving the joint back in are probably only doing yourselves more damage."

Unfastening the nearest bag, she rummaged around until she came up with a sling, but even as she turned to Varean, he was shaking his head.

"I don't need a sling, it's fine." He slipped past her and disappeared into the privy, clearly dodging any more doctoring on her behalf.

With an annoyed sigh, she tossed it back into the recess. She couldn't even be bothered arguing and, from what she'd learned of him, it wouldn't get her anywhere.

"How long until we get to Barasa?" She dropped into the seat Varean had been leaning against.

"Two days," Lianna replied in a short tone.

*Great.* Being stuck on the *Imojenna* with all the crew for days and weeks and months on end sometimes grated, but at least they each had their own space when they needed it. Onboard this shuttle, where there was virtually no privacy, the next two days were going to drag.

But at least she'd gotten Varean off the ship. She glanced over her shoulder to where the case with the blood samples peeked out from beneath the haphazardly tossed sling. When they got to Barasa, maybe she needed to call on some contacts of her own, see if she couldn't get into a lab and learn the answers she'd promised.

# Chapter Twelve

Varean shifted in his seat, an ache echoing through his recently dislocated shoulder as he tried to get comfortable. They'd been on this shuttle for nearly a day, and while maybe he shouldn't have been surprised, everyone had been pretty civilized toward him. No guessing needed, to know it would have been an entirely different story if that gorilla had been on this skimmer with him.

Kira had volunteered to take dead watch, since she'd gotten a few hours of sleep right before they'd abandoned ship. The others had all retreated into the back section of the shuttle a while ago and pulled narrow bunks down along the bulkheads. He probably should have done the same, but didn't want to make the displaced crew of the *Imojenna* feel like they had to sleep with one eye open because the guy they'd been keeping chained was now their bunk-buddy. Plus, his mind was working itself over, so even if he had gotten horizontal, he doubted he would have found himself hitting the sleep zone.

Because he had a decision to make. Now he was off the

*Imojenna* and away from the frecking deranged captain and his leashed muscle, escaping would be that much easier. When they reached Barasa, he could easily overpower Tannin, Lianna, Zahli, or all three of them, to make his getaway. He didn't think Kira would get in his way, so he didn't count her in his liberation scenarios.

The problem was, while he came up with some damned entertaining ways to set himself free, he'd failed to come up with a next step. He couldn't return to the commando military base on Yarina.

If he believed what Kira had told him, the *Swift Brion* and the entire crew had gone AWOL, because apparently half the universe was being run by shape-shifting aliens. Could he make the choice to defect and rejoin the ship? But Rian Sherron was all buddy-buddy with Captain Admiral Graydon, so if Sherron wanted to go round two with him about getting those damn questions answered, it would be too easy for the guy to find him if he went back to his berth on the flagship.

Outside of the military he had absolutely nothing, leaving him with nowhere to go and nothing to do. And if that wasn't one mother of a depressing realization, then call him a son of a bitch for a month of Sundays.

He dragged a hand down his face and closed his eyes; a stress headache began to pound his skull like it was roadkill. Exhaustion finally caught up with him, and he slipped into a doze. After the last hallucination while he'd been chained up in the bridge—they weren't dreams, not when he was so conscious of everything happening—he'd tried to keep himself awake as long as possible. Christ, even recalling them made his guts churn.

That new vicious part of himself had gotten a foothold and twisted every good thought he had about Kira. Not only had he hurt her, he'd enjoyed doing it. Now, more than ever, he feared if or when he snapped like he had when Callan attacked him, Kira would be the one to get hurt, and he wouldn't be able to stop himself.

And the thought had stuck in the back of his mind like a burr—what if Sherron had been right, and at some stage, the Reidar had done something to him without his knowledge or recollection? The notion was beyond horrifying.

As the doze inevitably dragged him into the not-quite reality, he cut off all thoughts of Kira, pretended like he didn't know her, like she didn't exist, if only to save a repeat of the last abhorrent visions.

It seemed to work, because this time he simply got dragged into some kind of disconnected narration, flashing pictures of people and places he'd never known, but were inherently familiar. As always, that distant blue star hovered, and though this time it seemed closer and brighter, he didn't bother trying to pursue it. Voices ebbed and flowed around him, and, while he didn't understand a word of what they were saying, he got the sense the translation was just waiting to burst free from the depths of his mind.

A familiar, quiet voice called his name, a hand touched his arm, and he instinctively reached down and clamped on, twisting the grip off and away. The low, startled gasp yanked him out of the trance, and he blinked open his eyes to find Kira crouched in front of him, frozen to the spot and regarding him with a wary gaze.

He straightened in his seat, abruptly releasing his grasp once he realized he had a too-tight hold on her wrist, a surge like lava ripping through his body. *Jezus*. Had he hurt her?

She rubbed at the red marks on her skin as she shifted back, but before she could get too far, he landed a hand on her shoulder to stop her escaping.

"Let me see."

For a second she cradled her arm against her lower ribs, but then slowly extended her hand again, turning her wrist upward so the light caught the already-bruising fingerprints he'd left on her flesh.

"Damn it to hell, I'm sorry. I was asleep—"

"So I noticed," she returned in a dry voice, not sounding the least bit upset. "It's not your fault. I should have known better than to grab a sleeping commando. But stage-whispering your name wasn't working, and I didn't want to wake the others by yelling."

"Next time try dumping a bucket of water on my head and stay out of reaching distance." He traced the marks with a light finger, wishing he could take the bruises back, guilt stabbing a wide hole right through the middle of his conscience.

"So, what were you dreaming about? The confusing ones you mentioned before?" She moved to sit on the seat next to him.

"Honestly? It was all a jumble, and I couldn't understand a word anyone was saying."

"Kind of like I couldn't understand a word you were saying?"

A jab of trepidation stuck him, like he'd taken a hit from one of Sherron's alien stunners. "What do you mean?"

"You were speaking a language I've never heard before, repeating the same few words over and over. It sounded something like *kei n'sum sicurua.*" Kira shrugged one shoulder, the motion careless, but her guarded gaze told an entirely different story.

"I don't understand," he blurted out automatically.

"Neither do I," Kira replied.

"No, I mean those words. What you said. It means *I don't understand.*"

But how did he know that? Until now, he hadn't been able to comprehend a single syllable of the weird language. But it was like his brain had finally rebooted, and words and phrases poured into his mind, translating until he understood everything.

A secondary rush of uneasiness caught him, trapping the breath in his lungs. "What the hell is happening to me?"

Kira leaned forward, reaching out to take his hand, fierce determination in her gaze.

"I don't know, but I want to help you find out." She shifted closer, glancing to where the others were sleeping then returning her attention to him. "Listen, I can guess what you've been thinking since we left the *Imojenna.*"

"Oh yeah?" He shot her a half smile, totally believing every word. Of course she knew what he was thinking—the woman was nothing if not scary-smart.

She sent him a small frown, as if not impressed with his smart-assery. "It's kind of obvious, cowboy. Anyone with half a brain would have to know you're planning on hightailing it outta here as soon as we hit dirt on Barasa. I know you've got no reason to trust us—"

"*Them.* I don't trust them."

She blew out a short breath, some of the tension leaving her shoulders. "Okay, then, maybe you'll take what I have to say into consideration."

"I'm listening." He might as well hear her out. If anything, the last twenty-four hours had made him realize he sure as shite didn't have any better prospects for now.

"When we get to Barasa, instead of running off at the first opportunity, I want you to come with me. I've still got a few contacts in the medical community, and I'd like to see if we can get ourselves into a proper lab or hospital to run those blood samples I took. See if we can get an answer to some of your mysteries."

Most of them weren't mysteries as far as he was concerned, just an aspect of himself that he'd spent his whole life running from. But this new, appalling facet of ruthless aggression was something he'd never guessed he might possess. Added to the strange waking-dreams and the language that'd basically just downloaded itself into his brain, then perhaps it was time to stop running and face his heritage—whatever that may be.

His fighting instincts, the ones that were still pissed as hell about being kidnapped, were telling him that before the engines even cooled on this skimmer he needed to cut out and go to ground until Rian Sherron either forgot his name or got himself killed.

However, Kira had stood up to Sherron about his treatment. He knew seasoned soldiers who'd play Russian roulette with their own gun before taking on the legend that was Major Captain Rian Sherron. Despite that, Kira had put herself on the line for him.

Would it be selfish of him to take advantage of her offer to help him get the answers when he was becoming increasingly worried that he might be a threat to her, might accidentally hurt her like he had as he'd woken up? That ran right into the concern that things were clearly becoming more dangerous for her anyway, considering they'd just been forced off the ship. He didn't have a clue what'd gone down, but guessing the Reidar had something to do with it didn't seem like such a stretch.

No matter the niggling misgiving that he might be the one to hurt her, the threat of whoever was after the crew of the *Imojenna* seemed like a bigger problem. So maybe he'd sleep only when he absolutely had to and work to keep his temper in check until Kira had run those tests, and he could see her somewhere safe before he disappeared.

Anyhow, now that Sherron and his gorilla buddy, Callan, were no longer with them, the chances of him losing his cool and either getting shot with the Reidar stunner or committing frequent acts of violence were that much lower.

Kira stared at him expectantly, as if his answer really mattered. He gave a slow nod, watching relief creep into her features.

"I need to know what's going on with me. Whatever the answer ends up being, I'd prefer if you were the one breaking the news." He had no doubt the results were going to make his life that much harder, but for all she'd done for him and the way he'd started getting all giddy over her, Kira could probably tell him he was terminal and it wouldn't seem that bad. He'd be too distracted by her eyes and the way she looked at him, or those lips as she formed the words, leaving him thinking about how they'd feel on his body.

Kira blew out a short breath. "Good. That's good."

He glanced over his shoulder, but no one in the back had moved, still sleeping soundly. "What about the others? I doubt they're going to be happy about leaving me alone with you."

"Yeah, that's going to cause an argument. But I'll deal with it when we reach Barasa." She settled back in her chair in a more relaxed slump. "For now, I'm just going to enjoy the quiet of dead watch and try not to think about everything I left behind on the *Imojenna*."

He half turned in his seat to face her, matching her slouch. "What was that all about anyway?"

She stared out the viewport at the front of the skimmer.

"Apparently Rian went to meet an old contact to negotiate for some components we need that can't be bought through the usual channels. My guess is that whoever it was screwed Rian over and called the authorities. Which is pretty much suicidal. If the guy isn't already dead, then his days are numbered, because Rian is nothing if not methodical about payback."

He sent her a short frown. "I thought Sherron was some big war hero. Why are the authorities after him?"

Kira threaded her fingers through her hair, pulling some pins free. "A few months ago, Rian got Tannin to hack into the data streams of Kasson Three, a supposedly abandoned station that should have been sucked into a nearby black hole years ago. Rian suspected it was some kind of Reidar base. Baden Niels, a multiversal corporation CEO, who's actually an alien himself, ordered a warrant issued for our arrest. He claimed his company had turned the station into a research outpost. We're now wanted intergalactic terrorists."

While the charge was obviously quite serious, and he was a little shocked to find he'd been nabbed by a band of wanted criminals, the idea of Kira being an intergalactic terrorist was pretty damn amusing. The more he thought about it, the harder it was to stop the grin yanking at his lips.

Kira glanced over at him, confusion crossing her features. "What's so funny?"

"You. Being some badass, hardened criminal on the run from the authorities."

She crossed her arms, trying for a stern expression but totally failing, her gorgeous eyes giving away her amusement. "Hey, Mr. Big, Bad, Tough Commando, I took you down, didn't I? I'm totally rocking the fugitive lifestyle."

"Then I guess I don't need to feel so bad about things if I got decked by one of the IPC's most wanted. When I account this story later on, I'm going to tell people you were a butch, six-foot-tall, backworlds hack-medic who dosed me with an untested cocktail of synthetic drugs."

She gave a short laugh and patted his arm. "Whatever saves your fragile ego, soldier boy."

"Thanks," he muttered, a little too charmed by the spark in her gaze and the way the unguarded smile made her that much more gorgeous. "How many hours until someone else takes over watch?"

She checked the time then slipped her comm away. "About two hours, maybe three if I'm feeling generous. Tannin said he'd take the next shift."

"If you're tired, let me take the next two hours. I promise

not to fly us to the nearest IPC outpost, as tempting as it might be."

A half grin kicked up one side of her lips. "If I was tired, I'd let you take over the helm, but I'm really not. Well, not sleepy, anyway. Truthfully, I am feeling kind of drained. I had this really difficult patient in the last week who seemed determined to get himself killed. You know I had to save his life two and a half times."

"Two and a *half*?"

She gave a decisive nod. "Yeah, I'm calling it two and a half. Don't tell anyone, but I nearly killed him myself with a sedative."

"Sounds like the bastard deserved it."

"Maybe." She gave a quick shrug. "That's still up for consideration."

The next smile that crossed her face had just a hint of mischief to it. He'd been wrong—her earlier, unguarded smile he'd thought was beautiful had nothing on this one, and it hit him right in the middle of his chest and rippled outward.

A low billow of desperation swirled through him that she'd see him as something other than some guy she had to save or a mystery to solve for Sherron. For so long he'd been nothing but a soldier, a part of a bigger whole that kept the IPC military operating, which had been fine when he'd been looking for somewhere to fit in life. Before that he'd been a kid with no family, terrified every day that someone would work out the truth about him and send him away.

Right in that second, he didn't want to be any of those things any longer. He wanted to forget. He wanted simple. He wanted a rush.

He wanted Kira.

*Freck it all.*

No doubt it was selfish as all hell, but he was going to steal one second of pure rapture from her and not be sorry about it in the least.

He twisted out of the seat, setting his knees on the floor in front of her chair and clamping a hand on either side of her on the armrests. Her eyes widened a touch, breath catching on a half inhale.

"Varean—"

He leaned in closer. "Unless you're about to tell me this is a really good idea, I think you should put that mouth to better use."

Indignant shock flashed across her features.

"That is the most insulting—" She reached up and grabbed a handful of his short hair, tugging in a way that told him she meant business but left nothing except a ripple of pleasure shooting down his spine. "You talk to me like that, it's going to end badly for you."

"Yeah?" He closed the distance, leaving not much more than a breath of space between them. "No second chances with me. I won't be letting you get near me with the dosing gun again."

"Who said anything about the dosing gun?" Her words were low, a little rough over her uneven breath. "I've got other ways of getting my own back."

"You don't have to tell me that. I've already experienced your particular brand of torture firsthand."

An edge of confusion crept into her green eyes that were otherwise charred with desire. "What do you mean?"

"If you don't know, then I'm not going to tell. I've got to retain some balance of power in this skirmish."

"I didn't realize we were in combat."

He grinned, knowing there was probably too much self-satisfaction in the expression. "Then you've already lost."

She shifted closer, until he could feel her next exhale brush over his lips like the kiss he was becoming more and more determined to take. But she skimmed by his mouth, using her hold on his hair to tilt his head the slightest bit. Her lips trailed like stardust over his cheek and upper jaw until she reached his ear.

"I'm not the one on my knees."

*Jezus.* He'd never thought a few simple words could send burning lust—the likes of which he'd never felt—erupting through him like blazing hydrogen. There was no doubt about it. She had him on his knees both figuratively and literally. He wanted her to keep him there, if only she'd work him up and take him down until it didn't matter that he was definitely the conquered one in this encounter.

He turned his face in to her neck, mouth on her skin like he'd been dying of thirst and had found the fountain of life. She moaned, the grip on his hair changing until her short nails grazed his scalp and sent sparks tumbling down his back. He kissed his way up over her jaw, finding her mouth and euphoria a moment later.

Goddamn. She tasted like ecstasy and felt like salvation.

She slid closer to him, and he caught her against his chest, wrapping his arms around her and smoldering everywhere her body came up against his. Somehow, she ended up on top of him, and next thing he knew, she had him down on the floor, straddling his hips, her hands on his chest the way he'd been wishing for when she'd given him the impersonal bucket bath.

He slid a hand to the back of her neck, deepening the kiss as she pressed down against him. *Oh yeah.* She set herself right on his hardening erection and, despite the layers of clothes between them, he pumped against her like it was a simple matter of thrusting himself to heaven. Her breath coming short between kisses, Kira rocked against him in response, the low sexy noise of approval from her only kicking his desire harder and higher.

Hell, they couldn't take this any further, not here and now

with half the *Imojenna*'s crew sleeping a few feet away, leaving every chance someone would wake up and catch them mid-orgasm. But she was unrestrained lightning ecstasy on top of him, the spark to the acetone in his veins, making him want to explode in the most violent way possible.

He grabbed her wrists and tugged her hands away from his body but then had no way to stop kissing her. Or prevent the unrelenting, maddening way she slid against him.

Pulling back from her and breaking the kiss, he gulped in a desperate breath. Except she wasn't giving him any quarter, she simply slipped down his body a little, lips, tongue and—*christ save him*—teeth grazing his skin without mercy. An inevitable chain reaction was building within him, one that would see a short, blistering end to this unexpectedly intense moment.

"*Goddamn.* We have to stop," he said.

A low seductive laugh was his only answer, and a sharp dose of incredulity rounded out the unbelievability of the moment, giving legitimacy to the parts of himself that wanted to let her take him over the edge.

He had one last rational thought that he should roll them over and climb off her, except there wasn't enough room in the narrow floor space between rows of seats where they'd ended up. Her lips found their way back to his mouth and, though he tried to fight it, like a ship already in a planet's atmosphere, he couldn't do anything but streak through the burn and hold on as she undulated against him with wicked, unapologetic intent.

"*Dammit, Kira.*" He clenched his jaw, locking both hands on her hips to keep her still. He gulped in a breath and held it, fighting to regain control of his body that wanted to go over the edge.

She moaned low in his ear, and it only sent a second, harder surge of mercury flooding his veins until he almost lost the fight against the soul-searing pleasure simmering in every cell of his body.

When the flare died down and the burn receded, he lifted her, the unsatisfied swelling below his belt almost painful. Damn this skimmer and its lack of privacy to hell. He needed somewhere to take her and finish this properly right now.

Still perched on top of him, she let out a frustrated sigh, and he cracked his eyes open to look up at her. Her cheeks were brushed with the slightest flush, and her heated gaze held a definite note of triumph.

"Underneath that starched doctor's coat, you're a total degenerate. Is this my punishment for disrespecting you?"

"If you don't know, then I'm not going to tell," she murmured, repeating his words from earlier.

*Frecking hell.* If he hadn't already been thinking the woman needed a lesson in fair play, then that sealed the deal. He slid her off him and climbed to his feet, pulling her up with him.

"What are you doing now?" She used her free hand to tug her clothes straight.

"We have unfinished business." He towed her out of the rows of seats, toward the back of the shuttle. As they passed by the bunks, he made sure to check the others were all still sleeping.

"Varean, I'm meant to be keeping watch of the helm."

He tabbed the controls to open the closet-sized privy. "You should have thought of that before you decided to try to get me off on the floor."

With both hands on her shoulders, he spun them around and walked her into the tiny room, letting the door slide shut behind them, catching her mouth in a hungry kiss.

# Chapter Thirteen

Oh god, that had been such a bad idea. Actually, it had been a very, *very* good idea, but so not the right time.

Kira let Varean hoist her up onto the edge of the sink, not pausing as he kissed her right back into a storm of heat. Not that it took much. She was aching all over with unsated lust. So maybe she hadn't argued all that hard over him bringing her in here when she technically had other duties, especially if he was planning on doing something about the unassuaged throbbing for her. Besides, they wouldn't be more than a few minutes, and the others would never know.

He tugged at the top fasteners of her shirt, releasing only half before he kissed a wet, hot path down her neck, pushing the cup of her bra out of the way to get his mouth on her nipple.

She sagged back against the mirror behind her, clenching her jaw over crying out, trying to keep quiet with the last fraying threads of her logic.

Varean had moved to work on unfastening her pants next, but instead of pulling them off, he slid his hand inside her underwear.

She blew out a ragged breath of relief and anticipation as he slid his fingers into her, nerves so oversensitized she bucked against the single, simple touch. He gave a low, graveled laugh as he set the knuckle of his thumb against her in the exact right spot, clearly enjoying the fact he'd turned the tables on her.

But she couldn't care about any of that, could barely breathe as he set to stroking her with a maddening rhythm, not fast enough, but inexorably building her up in a way she couldn't escape.

Capitulating, she gave herself over to him, sinking into the moment, relaxing in his hold, and embracing the delirious pleasure rolling through her.

He increased his tempo, maybe because he'd sensed the last shred of resistance drain right out of her.

"That's it, Kira, I want you to melt all over me." The low murmured words were like taking a shot of pure dopamine, making her blood rush and her skin tingle.

She anchored herself, one hand on his shoulder and the other gripping the edge of the basin as the immersive glow surged through her with a burst of molten heat. At the last second, he covered her mouth with his, taking the unguarded, unintentional cry that escaped on her next exhale.

He released her mouth, and she gasped in, fighting for air as the atmosphere seemed to lose all oxygen. And then she did exactly what he'd demanded and melted into the last ebbing flow of the torrent, letting it sweep her into enraptured oblivion.

As she let out a long sated breath of relief, Varean kissed her just beneath her jaw slowly, tenderly, bringing her down with gentle handling, giving the whole thing a delicious end instead of an abrupt withdrawal.

Varean was probably the last person she should have

been doing this with, but in his arms, she'd never felt a rush so deep and intense or been able to instinctively let go and lose herself so completely to pleasure.

She'd slept with a total of two men in her life. Both had been long-term partners, every intimate step considered and decided well before the act. Never before had she so rashly given in to such consuming passion. But when she'd realized Varean's intent, realized that whatever she'd started feeling for him went both ways, it was like someone else had taken over her body, making decisions and acting in ways she would have been mortified about in the past.

She wasn't embarrassed. No, far from it. There was a heady satisfaction in what they'd done, despite the fact—or maybe because of it—that they hadn't even taken things all the way.

Varean stepped back from her and leaned over to tab the shower on. Water shot down and cascaded over him, back-spray hitting her like a fine mist. He braced one hand against the wall and used the other to sluice water off his head.

After fastening her shirt, she slid down to stand on the floor, more than a little tempted to join him under the warm water.

"What are you going to do for clothes now?"

He hadn't removed his pants, which were getting soaked. They were the only thing he'd been wearing when they'd come aboard the skimmer.

Wiping a hand over his face, he shrugged. "They needed a wash almost as badly as I did. Don't know how the other three will feel about it, but I'm sure you won't mind if I have to go naked until we reach Barasa."

Reaching down, he flicked free the fasteners on his pants and then paused with the top open but not revealing anything. However, the outline of his erection was unmistakable. When she realized she was practically drooling to see him strip off the sodden garment, she snapped her gaze back to his face.

"You being naked will be a huge problem. How about I go see if I can find you something?"

"Huge is definitely a good word for it," he murmured as she turned and groped for the door control.

She threw him an unimpressed glare over her shoulder, but he just grinned in return, shoving his pants down far enough for her to get a glimpse of his lower abdomen and dark hair, but nothing else.

Forcing herself to turn away and escape—because if she watched him take off those pants there was a very good chance she'd throw what little respect and dignity she still had to the stars and join him in the shower, despite the risk of getting caught.

She couldn't begin to imagine what the others would say if they found out about what she and Varean had been up to.

Back out in the main cabin, she was relieved to find that no one seemed to have stirred from their sleep. She went to one of the lockers. Rian usually kept a stash of emergency supplies in the skimmers in case they ever had to do exactly what they'd done a day ago and abandon ship without grabbing anything. She found a pair of pants and a T-shirt, and though they were probably Rian's, looked like they'd be kind of small on Varean.

Well, if his other choices were wet pants or naked, she guessed he wouldn't complain. She didn't go inside when she returned to the privy—she totally didn't trust either of them. Instead, she opened the door far enough to lean in and set the clothes on the sink, all without looking at him. His low laugh followed her out as she firmly closed the door and went to sit in the pilot's chair.

They were still twenty hours out from Barasa, but it didn't seem like enough time. Somehow, she had to come up with a convincing argument so the others would let her take Varean to a lab.

Honestly, it was going to be a fine line, coming up with a reason that sounded logical, not emotional, especially since she was clearly so far beyond the bounds of doctor-patient relations when it came to him. If nothing else, she'd proven that to herself just now when she'd climbed on top of him and let her hormones do the flying.

And then when he'd taken her into the bathroom— A low echo of gratification rolled through her, and she couldn't regret her out-of-character recklessness. Not when the conclusion had been so very rewarding. She only felt sorry that Varean hadn't found the same fulfillment. Of course, he was now alone and very naked in the shower...

She tightened her fingers into the armrests and took a deep breath against the crazy pound of her heart. That thread of thinking was not helpful in any way whatsoever. This wasn't about the irrational and likely foolish attraction that'd sprung up between them. This was about what was best for Varean after everything he'd been through.

With a goal in mind, a purpose to focus on, she had something else to think about rather than dwelling on the fact that she'd had to leave behind everything—leave behind the only home she'd known for the past three years. Though she hadn't signed up for war when she'd joined the *Imojenna*'s crew, she'd found herself in the middle of a fierce battle, which definitely wasn't what she'd envisaged for her life. But the morbid joke was on her, because though a smart person might have walked away, she couldn't. Not even to save herself.

• • •

SKIMMER ONE, DUNHAM

Rian blinked against the shaft of sunlight shining in his face, bringing up a heavy arm to shield his eyes as he rolled away into the shadows. Both arms went with the movement, since apparently they were attached to each other, bringing back his last clear memory with the head-aching alacrity of putting down the entire bottle of Violaine and then having Callan cuff him.

With a low groan for the fact he ached everywhere, he pushed himself up, half turning to lean against the bulkhead behind him. The skimmer was empty, light shining brightly through the single viewport, rimmed in blue sky and edged on either side by slim buildings reaching upward into the ether.

Obviously they'd arrived on Dunham while he'd been out of it; he only hoped the half of his crew he had with him hadn't ventured too far from the skimmer. One, because he wanted these cuffs off *now*. And two, because Dunham was an outer-central systems planet with a large military population—they were at risk of being grabbed by any number of any IPC officers, UAFA agents, Reidar, or all of the above.

He dragged both hands over his face, the hangover from Reidar-induced blackouts far worse than anything he could inflict on himself with Violaine. Which was partly why he preferred to put himself down with the hard liquor, rather than go through this particular type of purgatory.

His wrists chafed, slippery under the cuffs, and he glanced down, unsurprised to find his hands and forearms streaked with blood where the metal had bitten into him. Closing his eyes, he blew out a hard breath and leaned his head back against the wall behind him. If Callan, Jensen, Nyah, and Ella hadn't been afraid of him before, they sure as hell would be now that they'd gotten to witness his meltdown firsthand. A few times he'd questioned the intelligence of keeping an entire crew, when the past had proven that literally no one was safe when the darkness took over, and no one could bring him out of it.

Until this little episode, he'd thought a steady regime of

Violaine, bloodshed, and keeping focused on the singular goal of bringing the Reidar down had helped him get a handle on things.

If he'd been a spiritual kind of person, he might have taken losing the *Imojenna* as a sign he needed to cut everyone loose and strike out on his own. But selfishly, he'd come to realize he couldn't take out the Reidar alone. He needed people at his back to do that. So he told himself that he was well enough contained, not as bad as he used to be.

But it had all turned into one giant cosmic joke, with him as the punch line. He'd had his wings clipped, because without the *Imojenna*, he couldn't do frecking much of anything.

A heavy-treaded fall of boot steps echoed from behind him, and he glanced over his shoulder to see Callan emerge from the single narrow ramp access to the skimmer.

"Good. You're awake. Was starting to think someone would have to go all prince charming and kiss that ugly face of yours." Callan tossed him a bottle, which he caught against his chest.

A moderately expensive brand of vodka. It wasn't Violaine, but it also wasn't watered down backworld moonshine. He twisted off the lid and raised the bottle, chugging down half a dozen long mouthfuls before coming up for air.

"Knew that would perk you right up." Callan shoved a hand in his pants pocket and produced the key to the cuffs.

Rian wiped his mouth with the back of his hand and took another quick mouthful of the vodka while Callan crouched down and unlocked the bloodstained cuffs.

"FYI, I don't think these were necessary, but you were damned insistent." After the cuffs were free, Callan sat back, taking the vodka and helping himself to a long swallow. When he handed the bottle back, there was something a little too much like concerned caring in the guy's mindful gaze. "I ended up knocking you out with my pulse pistol. If you're aching all over, that'd be why."

"Thanks." His voice came out a bit on the gravelly side, so he took another drink of vodka to wash away the tightness. It was a relief to know he hadn't tried to hurt anyone, but he hated that Callan and the others had seen him like that—nothing more than a rabid animal, a messed-up, deranged product of the frecking Reidar. At least Callan wasn't outwardly treating him any differently.

If anyone so much as even looked at him with a hint of pity, it would tip his recently patched temper right back into fraying. Yeah, what the Reidar had done to him, what he was now stuck living with, sucked ass. But he would not—nor would he ever—tolerate being pitied. If they wanted to feel sorry for someone, they could waste that sentiment on the who-knew-how-many-thousands of people the Reidar had already killed.

"How long ago did we land?" He handed the half-empty bottle off to Callan and pushed to his feet, clenching his jaw over a groan. Aching all over was a vast understatement. He felt like someone had put his insides through a meat grinder and then unceremoniously stuffed the minced leftovers back into him.

"About four hours."

He dragged himself a few steps over to the privy and slapped at the door controls.

"Where are the others?" He shuffled inside, leaving the door open as he tabbed on the faucet over the sink to splash water on his face. Goddamnit. Even his skin hurt.

"We got a layover room in the spaceport under a false identity of mine." Callan stepped up beside him, shoving a cloth under the running water to wet it down then wiping the blood off the cuffs. "They're safe for the time being. I ordered them some food and told Nyah to buy supplies online to keep them distracted."

"Good plan." He glanced down at the abrasions on his wrists, debating whether or not they were serious enough that he needed to do something about them. No doubt if Kira had been here, she would have insisted on patching him up. But the doc had taken the other skimmer with his sister, her fiancé, and Lianna. He only hoped they stayed safe on Barasa while Tannin followed up on his childhood friend and the possible Reidar connection. Of course, if Kira and the others hadn't loosed that commando, and the authorities found someone locked in the bowels of his ship, it was going to be one more reason for UAFA to hunt them all down.

He cleaned the worst of the blood off his hands and forearms, poured some vodka on the wounds with a hiss through clenched teeth at the sting, then splashed more water on his face, wetting his hair and letting rivulets drip down his neck, onto his back and chest under his shirt, before rinsing out his mouth. He needed to get his shite together, get himself cleaned up, and then contact Commander Captain Colter Routh and hope to god the Reidar hadn't already gotten to the guy.

Colt had been the leader of his original military unit, the one he'd trained with as a green recruit when he'd been just a rich kid who'd run away from home at the age of sixteen and used a fake ident to join the military. The same unit where he'd met Zander, who'd been on leave for an injury and helping Colt get the newbies into shape. Zander had been the first one to work out he wasn't as old as he'd pretended to be, but he and Colt hadn't kicked him out. The two of them had kept quiet, made sure he got his ass through basic training, and survived the first eye-opening years of war.

Being that Colt was only a commander captain, he was hoping the guy wasn't ranked high enough to have attracted the Reidar's interest. He was also hoping the guy didn't believe the BS charge of intergalactic terrorism that frecking

Baden Niels had brought against him. He was taking a huge chance even setting boots on Dunham—half the planet was basically one big military outpost. If going onto Kalaheo had been like flipping off the authorities, coming to Dunham was like stripping himself naked and running right through the middle of a Yarinian government sitting.

Still, there was very little he wouldn't do in his efforts against the Reidar. And having recently succumbed to the demons inside him, they'd be quieter for a while. So he was less likely to flip out and kill anyone with an overabundance of stupid today.

He shrugged out of his shirt, clenching his jaw at the rippling ache through his upper body. As he came out of the privy, he took another hit of vodka, then searched through the meager emergency supplies for a new one.

Once he'd drunk a few more mouthfuls, which started doing a damn good job of dulling the aches and lessening the pounding of his head, he slipped on a cleanish T-shirt and followed Callan out of the skimmer.

Mysteriously resourceful as always, Callan had fake UAFA idents for them to pass through the security checkpoints, all without needing any kind of palm scan or DNA test. On the other side of the terminal, they took an elevator up to the fourth level where the others waited in a layover room.

As he stepped in after Callan, he didn't meet anyone's eyes and refused to feel guilty or ashamed about his little meltdown. It was what it was, and if they didn't like it, they knew where the hatch was.

Callan joined the other three at the table where they were eating, while he made a beeline for the single smallish crystal display in the room, tabbing up the comm system. As he dropped into the chair, he could feel that now-familiar tingle buzzing just in the periphery of his awareness and knew that Ella was looking at him. He'd been trying not to think too closely about it, but ever since she'd healed him a few months ago, it was like she'd somehow forged a permanent link of consciousness between them.

Though they hadn't talked about it, and he sure as shite hadn't asked, he got the sense she always knew exactly what was going on with him, while he could unfailingly tell exactly where she was at any given time. The only good thing about it had been his advantage in avoiding her.

Shaking off the distraction, he accessed Dunham's public comm network and looked up Colt, gratified to discover he was currently stationed at the Succession MTB—military training base—just outside the capital city. He'd heard Colt had permanently moved into overseeing the training of new recruits, which hadn't been a surprise; the guy was a natural leader and always cared more than most people about the others in his unit at any given time.

It took him a few minutes to come up with a way to send the message for a meeting so Colt would know it was him, while ensuring any random security checks wouldn't pick up the same thing. The last thing he wanted to do was get Colt in hot water over meeting with a wanted terrorist. But that concern didn't reach far enough to make him hesitate about meeting up with his old buddy.

He was going for broke here. If he couldn't get Colt to help him, he had no frecking idea how he'd otherwise get the components.

Once he'd sent the message, he took himself over to where the others sat and helped himself to the food. The table sat only four, and though Callan had left the last seat vacant—instead balancing a plate on his hand, eating as he looked out the window across the city—Rian didn't sit, either, taking his meal to join Callan.

"I know it's kind of obvious, but the question needs to be asked," Callan said between bites of food. "What the freck are we going to do without the ship?"

"I don't plan on being without her for long. And, lucky for me, I happen to have one of the universe's most wanted marauders for a cousin. Once I've made this contact and the others have concluded things on Barasa, we'll organize to meet up with Qae and see how he feels about going on a good old-fashioned pirating raid of whatever IPC impound yard the *Imojenna* ends up in."

Callan sent him an exasperated frown across his plate. "If I'd wanted to be a pirate, I would have made my way to the Barbary Belt years ago. A man's got to have some respect. No offense to your cousin, but pirates are like the bottom-feeders of the universe."

"Why do you think Qae hates anyone calling him that?"

Callan coughed a short laugh, scraping the last of the food off his plate. "You can put a monkey in a dress and call it Sally, but it's still going to be a monkey."

"I'm going to tell Qae you said that next time I see him. The look on his face will be priceless."

Balancing his empty plate on one hand, Callan leaned over and grabbed a beer off the table. "Speaking of pirates, are you sure aligning ourselves with Rene Blackstone is such a good idea? You might be a deranged sonuvabitch on your best of days, but Blackstone is a total sociopath."

"I'm sure we don't have any other choice, unless we want to sit back and watch the Reidar make the universe their bitch." He helped himself to one of the beers as well, feeling a little more like himself now he'd had a meal and the vodka had taken the worst of the edge off his blackout hangover.

"Yeah, but on the other hand, we end up being Blackstone's bitch." Callan shook his head, returning his gaze out the window as he took a contemplative swallow of beer. "You know, some days I think we're the wrong people for the job. Saving the universe wasn't one of my life goals."

The revelation came as no surprise. Callan was a good soldier, and he didn't want to lose the guy. But Rian needed to know that the people he took into this fight had his back all the way. By the same turn, this was his personal crusade and at the last stand, he didn't expect anyone else to take the fall with him.

Callan had given him three good years. If the guy felt like it was time to move on to different hunting grounds, he wasn't going to cry into a gallon of ice cream about it.

"Can't say it was one of mine, either. My goals are more along the lines of slaughtering every last frecking alien I can get my hands on. If the universe gets saved in the process, I guess that's a bonus."

Callan sent him a grin with a definite bite of viciousness to it, as if he didn't really believe the declaration, but was up for killing a few Reidar all the same.

"Anyway, if you've got better prospects elsewhere, don't feel like you owe me anything."

"Better prospects than killing aliens?" He shook his head, draining the last of the beer. "Don't think I could come up with anything more entertaining. And if I didn't know you better, I might think you were trying to get rid of me or being some noble asshat."

"Noble?" He scoffed, setting his empty plate aside. "There're a lot of interesting words you could use to describe me, but noble sure as shite isn't one of them."

The crystal display chimed an incoming message alert. Rian went over and tapped the screen, bringing up a reply from Colt, who was ready and willing to meet. Except the location wasn't what he'd been expecting.

Colt had suggested a bar just off base, one frequented by mostly the military crowd blowing off steam, the other half of the patrons the kind of people looking to hook up with said military personnel. He'd been there a few times in the past while he'd still been IPC himself and all respectable-like. He considered that it might be some sort of trap, thought about replying with a different location.

But wherever they ended up, this wasn't his dirt, and the risk of being captured or taken out was already astronomical. So he returned a confirmation, hoping this latest risk didn't screw him like the last one had.

# Chapter Fourteen

The bar hadn't changed one bit since the last time Rian had been there—five years ago—just before he'd given up his commission and struck out on his own. During the day, a lot of military personnel came to eat or play pool, and though the interior seemed to absorb the sunlight, leaving the room dim, it was still hard not to notice the stains here and there on the floor or that the furniture had seen better days. At night, with the liquor flowing, music thumping, and lights turned down, it was exactly the kind of place a soldier wanted to be to get himself lost.

Callan had wanted to ride shotgun on this little jaunt, but he'd ordered him to stay back. If something went down, he needed to know the guy would be there to get Jensen and Nyah to safety.

As for Ella, her well-being was all on him. The rest of his crew wouldn't be a target if Ella wasn't with them—the Reidar wanted the two of them, and anyone else was collateral.

When he'd told her she was coming with him, she hadn't said a word or even looked surprised. She'd simply nodded serenely and come along like they were on a frecking Sunday picnic.

Considering that he'd been working so hard to avoid her, and she'd so recently gotten another glimpse of how thoroughly the Reidar had bent him over and ruthlessly screwed him, one-on-one time was about the last thing he wanted with her.

But the surprises just kept coming, because she didn't say a single word—no cleverly disguised platitudes, no sanctimonious advice cloaked in innocent conversation, not even a tension-breaking comment on the weather. Her distant indifference pissed him off more than if she'd tried talking to him. With little to no resistance, she'd seemingly given up on him.

She'd vowed once to help him even if he didn't want it, didn't deserve it. He'd warned her, but she hadn't listened, and he'd formed a weird kind of hate-love for the fact that she believed there was something inside him to be saved.

It was like he'd been in the dark, only to be given a single candle. And when the wick had burned out to plunge him back into the darkness, he was left wishing he'd never seen the light in the first place.

The bar was less than a quarter full as he entered with Ella and swept a gaze around the room, cataloguing every person, weapon, and their combined prospect of threat in the single glance. Colt wasn't here yet, not surprising since Ella and he had arrived fifteen minutes before the agreed time.

He picked a seat in the far left corner of the room, cutting around the outer side of the tables to make his way over. Halfway there, a soldier staring at him snagged his attention. He knew the face, but couldn't remember the man's name.

The soldier's expression hardened as he stood. "Rian Sherron."

Silence dropped over the room like plunging into a void.

Making sure Ella stayed behind him, he stopped and turned to face the man, four tables separating them. It was the first time he could ever remember another soldier addressing him without adding his former rank or without a note of awe or admiration.

He didn't answer the guy, but let his shoulders relax and stared him straight in the eye as he set his palms on the grips of his holstered guns.

"It *is* you." The man stepped out from behind his table, and tension all but rippled through the other dozen or so soldiers in the bar.

"I'm not here for trouble, just looking to meet an old friend."

The man laughed, but the sound held a note of incredulous contempt. "Well, I guess the rumors are true. You must have some serious metium-lined balls to meet an old friend in this bar, right outside an MTB, considering you're a wanted terrorist."

"Come on, Newberg." Another soldier at the bar spoke up, swiveling on his stool to face them. "You know those charges have to be a load of shite. Whatever Major Captain Sherron did, there had to be a reason. No one really believes he's a terrorist."

A few others chimed in with opinions, but Rian kept his gaze fixed on Newberg. Captain Garvin Newberg, at least he'd been a captain years ago when Rian had still been with the IPC. Judging by the stripes on his uniform, it looked like Newberg had risen to lieutenant marshal. One step up of rank in five years was pretty pathetic, but Newberg had always been more brawn than brain.

"If there's a warrant with Sherron's name on it, then it's our duty to hand him in," Newberg said over the low swell of chatter. "Whether or not he's guilty, they can sort it out when he gets to Erebus."

Rian tightened his grip on his guns, resisting the urge to simply yank one out and solve his problems the easy way by putting Newberg down.

But the soldier at the bar — couldn't have been more than a second officer — stood up, and was joined by several others. "You try to take him in, you're going to have a fight on your hands."

Newberg glanced over at the small group, expression tightening in disapproval. "You said something, officer?"

"With all due respect, *sir*." The last word sounded more like an insult than a deference to rank. "I think most of the men in here would agree that if Major Captain Sherron wants to have a drink and catch up with an old war buddy, then he's got every right. And we're all off duty, so if we happened to see him, then there's a pretty good chance that by the time we return to base, we'll have forgotten all about it."

Newberg's posture became even more rigid, obviously realizing he was outnumbered. "Well I sure as hell don't have to stay in the same building as some terrorist piece of shite."

Rian jerked out his pulse pistol as Newberg stepped away from his table.

"Sorry, Newberg, but I can't have you heading back to the MTB and telling the first person with two ears and no brain that you saw me here." He steadied his aim, thumbing the setting to stun. "So, sit the hell back down, and I'll buy you a brew. Your other option is unconscious on the floor, and we both know a pulse pistol blast can make even seasoned soldiers piss their pants at the most inconvenient times."

Newberg's taut expression had gone from pissed-off to enraged bull. But he sat without a word, and Rian flicked a hand at the bartender as he put his pulse pistol away. Stepping to the side, he ushered Ella ahead of himself to the table he'd picked out earlier.

Just as they sat down, Colt walked in, nodding a greeting

to another table of soldiers as he came over. Rian stood, accepting Colt's handshake but dodging a buddy-buddy man-hug.

"Rian, man it's good to see you." He slid into a seat, passing an entirely not-subtle, curious glance over Ella. Not surprising. Ella was damned gorgeous, and people noticed wherever the woman went.

"She's an Arynian priestess, so keep your tongue in your head or she'll melt your brain."

Instead of seeming abashed, Colt simply grinned. "The way I've heard it, she could melt my brain and I'd love every minute of it."

"You never did have a lick of sense when it came to women."

"Any man who claims sense around a beautiful woman is a pathological liar." Colt reached over and wrapped his fingers around Ella's. "Commodore Captain Colter Routh. But call me Colt. The rest of it's too much of a mouthful."

Ella sent him one of her signature still-as-frecking-frozen-water smiles. "Miriella Kinton, but everyone calls me Ella. Nice to meet you."

The bartender set a tray of drinks on the table. Beer all around, but no Violaine to be had. Nope, no illegal liquor in this goddamned upstanding corner of the universe.

"So, Colt, we couldn't maybe have had this catch-up in a more inconspicuous place?" Rian glanced over to where Newberg sat, untouched beer in front of him and baleful expression on his face.

Colt followed his line, looking over his shoulder and sending Newberg a sardonic wave. "Newberg, you're not being a douche-bucket toward the IPC's most infamous war hero, are you?"

Newberg's expression hardened. "No, sir."

"Because Sherron is an old friend of mine, and I'd be

mighty unhappy if I found out any fellow officers weren't being polite."

"I'll be sure to keep that in mind, sir." Newberg started going an interesting shade of red, and Rian wondered if it'd be worth pushing him a little farther just for entertainment's sake, but Colt had turned his attention back to him.

"It was a calculated gamble, meeting here. I haven't got much time between sessions with the recruits, and I figured you still had enough supporters in the military that you'd be safe enough showing your face."

"So glad you were willing to risk me ending up in prison on the capricious opinions of people who don't know how to do anything except follow orders."

Colt took a swig of his beer. "Hell, Rian, so inconsiderate of your old compatriots."

"You would be, too, if they wanted to see you buried," he muttered into his own bottle.

"It's not like that." Colt's expression became more serious. "There are people working to get the charges dropped. Having the IPC's most respected war hero charged with intergalactic terrorism doesn't look good for anybody, especially when the accusations are totally unfounded and coming from the private sector."

Though he'd heard a similar rumor two weeks ago, he hadn't put much stock in it, given the source had turned out to be a lying sack of Reidar shite.

In all truth, he didn't get why a bunch of people he didn't know and had never met had such a hankering to see his name cleared. So he'd turned the tide of the war and made sure the IPC had their victory, and all the boys and girls could go to bed at night knowing their every move was governed across all the known worlds. That single suicidal act he'd pulled off to the finish the war had worked as effectively as a ball and chain, keeping him tethered to the IPC military no matter how many years went by or where he went in the galaxy.

"What do you think they'd say if they knew I didn't give a shite? Maybe being a wanted criminal is working real nice for me. Maybe if people think I'm a regular asshole they'll stop lining up to see my ship dock wherever I go."

Colt shot him a grin. "Talk about ungrateful. What's wrong? The fame isn't all it's cracked up to be?"

He glared over a mouthful of beer. Colt knew full well what he really thought about his ill-gotten notoriety. "Anyway, if you're so short on time, we should get down to business."

Colt seemed even more amused, and he waved a hand magnanimously as he leaned back in his seat. "By all means, change the subject. I won't call you on it, and I'm sure Ella here won't, either."

A quick smile flashed across her face, a more genuine expression than any he'd seen on her features since they'd left the *Swift Brion*. The thought that Colt might be charming her turned the beer in his stomach to acid. He swallowed down the unpleasant and unwanted sensation in annoyance, setting his half-empty bottle on the table and sliding it away.

"I didn't risk flying into the central systems just to catch up with old friends, Colt."

"Yeah, I thought as much," he replied, picking at the edge of the ever-changing micro-crystal display label on his beer. "So what is it you need, exactly? I'd actually thought you might be looking for someone to help you get those terrorism charges cleared."

"Believe me, the charges are the least of my problems."

Colt gave a disbelieving laugh. "Intergalactic terrorism charges are the *least* of your problems? Jezus, you must be into some serious shite."

"You can't imagine the half of it," he muttered, clasping his hands on top of the table, the beads on his wrist digging into his recently stripped flesh. "So when I tell you exactly what I'm after, I need you to believe that the only ones who are going to get hurt are the ones who deserve it."

"Well now, I'm positively enthralled. Just what are we talking here?"

He pulled his commpad from his pocket and tapped the screen, bringing up the list of specs. "I need these items, in bulk."

Colt took the comm. As he read down the list, his eyebrows got higher and higher. "Freck me, Rian. I'm assuming you're full well and good on exactly what a person gets when they put all this together in a certain configuration?"

He nodded, taking a sweeping glance around the bar to make sure the lay of the land hadn't changed and that no one seemed overly interested in their conversation.

"I'm aware, but the kind of *configuration* we'll end up with won't hurt anyone."

Colt handed back the comm. "If it's harmless, then what's the point?"

He leveled a sharp eye on his buddy. "If I tell you—"

"You'd have to kill me?" Colt picked up his beer to finish off the dregs, grinning like a moron.

"Yeah, you'd probably end up dead, but not by my hand. For now, the less you know, the better."

Colt's amusement morphed into an unimpressed glare. "Don't pull that less-you-know crap with me, jerkwad. And I mean that in the most agreeable way possible. You know as well as I do how hard these items are to procure in bulk. So tell me what the hell I'm putting my career and freedom outside of Erebus on the line for."

Rian glanced at Ella, and she gestured like maybe she thought he should tell Colt the full story. But he didn't have the time or inclination to give the truth-about-the-dark-corners-of-the-universe speech here. Besides, if Colt knew, they'd more than likely have another defector on their hands.

While he'd be more than happy to have Colt join their ranks, it was becoming more and more obvious that having someone on the inside might end up coming in handy. Maybe it wasn't fair on Colt to keep him in with no frecking idea what he was inside of, but the guy could look after himself. If Colt came through on the components, he'd fill the guy in and hopefully convince him to keep his IPC position for the time being.

He pulled the razar out of his thigh holster, setting it in the middle of the table. "This is what we're making."

Colt picked the weapon up, bringing the razar to eye level to examine its lines then testing its weight. "Nice design, good balance. What does it do?"

"Technically, it doesn't do anything. It's a failed stun weapon prototype."

"Then why the hell do you want to mass produce it?"

He sent Colt the ghost of a smile—the closest he ever got to grinning.

"That's a long story for another day." He held out his hand and Colt returned the gun. "To prove my word."

He turned the barrel of the gun and pressed it into his shoulder, letting off a single round with a muffled buzz. The energy passed through him on a low vibration.

Colt regarded him with an exasperated frown, a hint of conjecture in his gaze.

"I didn't need a display of how well it *doesn't* work."

"Then you won't mind?" He pointed the razar toward the middle of Colt's chest.

Colt gave a lazy shrug. "Sure, go right ahead. I still don't get what the point of all this is."

He squeezed off a round, breath stalling in his chest for half a second as the pulse of energy hit Colt. Nothing happened

"Wow, tingly. Now will you tell me what the freck, man?"

Blowing out a low breath of relief that Colt, at least, hadn't been permanently disappeared by the aliens and replaced by a meat puppet, he shoved the gun away.

"Get me these components, and we'll have a conversation. In the meantime, watch your back. Even with all the idiots who apparently want to see me restored to hero status, there are people who want me dead. A lot of people. And they're everywhere."

"Now you sound paranoid." The gleam in Colt's gaze proved he'd take the warning seriously, though.

"I'm down half my crew, so I'm heading to Forbes to meet up with them. That's where I'll be if you can get my merchandise."

"Going all provincial? I hear its berry season out there." Colt sent him a grin that was nothing but smart-ass all the way.

Forbes was one of Dunham's six moons, all of which were dedicated to specific types of farming, with Forbes being famous for its fruit and wine. Besides the farmers who lived and worked the land, the uber-rich liked to holiday there, taking weekends for winery tours or short getaways at harvest times for the festivals.

"I'll be sure to send you a crate," he replied dryly as he stood. "Thanks for putting yourself out for me. I owe you one."

Colt pushed to his feet and held out his hand. "Tell me what the hell is going on next time we see each other, and I'll call it even. I've got to get back to the MTB anyway. Ella, nice to meet you."

Ella sent him a polite nod in return. "And you, Commander Captain."

Rian stepped away from the table, indicating Ella should go ahead of him. He shot a pointed glance at where Newberg still glared daggers at him. "You mind hanging back and making sure we don't have company on the way out?"

"Sure thing. I'll comm you in a day or two about your shopping list."

He headed across the bar, one hand on the butt of his pulse pistol until Ella and he stepped outside. Though he trusted Colt to keep a handle on things, he'd still half expected Newberg to make a move, moronic wanker that he was. No doubt the guy would tell *someone*, even if it wasn't in an official capacity.

Though it seemed the threat of being captured for the intergalactic terrorist BS wasn't as immediate as he'd thought, he still wanted to get boots off Dunham ASAP. Since Forbes was mostly working folk, farmers, and cashed-up tourists, it was about the best place within the skimmer's limited reach they could bunk down until the others finished on Barasa and Colt got back to him.

So a plan for the short-term. Those plans were the easy ones. Those plans didn't require strategy and deft maneuvering like trying to land a battle cruiser. The bigger plans, the ones that might make a difference in his carcinogenic campaign against the Reidar, they required more finesse. One of these days, he was probably going to have to stop making shite up as he went along, especially considering the growing number of people relying on him not to get them killed.

For now, he was going to go collect the measly half a crew he had with him, send a message to his sister, and hope they could all get to Forbes in one piece.

"Your friend seems commendable," Ella commented out of the blue. It was the first time she'd spoken directly to him in days.

"*Commendable*? You always come up with the most colorful language, princess."

"You should confide the truth to him sooner rather than later. He could be a worthy asset in the long run." Her serene expression didn't change in the slightest.

Until the little skirmish they'd engaged in on the *Swift Brion*, he'd thought they'd be seeing less and less of that damned priestess mask. But she'd reverted right back to the aloof, untouchable idol persona, like she'd been when she'd first come aboard. Of everything, that was what pissed him off the most—her walking around like she was so damned above everything. Like none of the muck he was mired in could possibly touch her.

"Yeah, he'll be a real good asset until I get him killed as well," he muttered, clamping his muscles against a surge of frustration.

Ella shot him an unreadable sideways glance, and he almost wanted her to argue that he wouldn't get Colt killed. But she didn't say anything, and once again he was left with the reality that she'd apparently abandoned all inclination to help him.

# Chapter Fifteen

A large warm hand on her shoulder and the murmur of her name in a low voice that sent shivers rippling through her roused Kira. She blinked to find Varean leaning over the narrow bunk she'd fallen into a few hours ago.

"We're coming up on Barasa. Lianna will be contacting the spaceport tower for landing in a few minutes."

She pushed her hair back as she sat up, reaching into her pocket for a couple of pins, and then haphazardly securing the shorter strands away from her face. "Did you get any sleep?"

He nodded as he scooted back to sit on the bunk opposite. "A few hours. But it's kind of hard to sleep, considering my life resembles a crater-pitted asteroid at the moment."

She sent him a sympathetic frown, reached to take his hand, but then thought better of it. She glanced toward the front of the ship to see if anyone had noticed, but Lianna was set at the helm, concentration on the viewport, while Tannin and Zahli seemed to be absorbed in a conversation.

She looked back at Varean to find a rueful half smile on his face. But there was a slight shadow in his gaze as he regarded her, like maybe she'd inadvertently hurt him.

"Worried about what the others would say if they knew?"

A sharp jab of guilt rammed right into the middle of her chest. "I'm sorry—"

He sat back, scrubbing a hand over his hair and avoiding her gaze. "Don't be. I understand. You might trust me, but they don't, and they care about you. If they found out, it would probably cause you nothing but trouble. Forget about it."

She hadn't meant to hurt him—not that the stubborn military-to-the-toes guy would let her see it. But she'd gotten to know him well enough that she could tell he'd taken her hesitation the wrong way. Unfortunately, they didn't have time to be hashing out such things right now.

"Anyway, try not to worry about the tests. Whatever we find, we can deal with it. Okay?"

He nodded, standing and folding the bunk into the recess on the bulkhead. She sighed, annoyed he could dismiss her so easily after what they'd shared a few short hours ago. But she could understand his position, relate to him wanting to isolate himself in the face of an unsure future.

Maybe once she had irrefutable proof Varean was a victim of the Reidar, Rian might be more willing to help him, since they'd have that tragedy in common. Perhaps if Varean wanted to return to his old post onboard the *Swift Brion*, they could get him back there after they'd solved the current issues of being split up and having no ship. Whatever happened, she had no doubt that he'd want to join the fight against the aliens, especially if it turned out they'd done something to him that he had no memory of.

Stretching her stiff muscles, she slowly pushed to her feet, missing her comfortable bed on the *Imojenna* more than ever. She helped Varean fold up the rest of the bunks and then went to the front of the ship with the others.

"Breakfast? Chocolate or caramel?" Zahli held out a packet of energy bars. Made of a protein powder composition, they were okay in a tight spot or as a snack, but didn't have much taste. Damn, she could have used a coffee and bacon right now. One positive about living on the *Imojenna*, Rian had never scrimped on the essentials like real coffee, never making them drink the cheaper repli-coffee like most shipbound people put up with.

But she was hungry enough that she took one of the bars and ripped it open. Through the viewport, the burn of Barasa's upper atmosphere streaked past the skimmer, Lianna communicating with the spaceport tower for landing.

"We heard from Rian." Zahli cut Varean a wary look as she set the bars aside.

Kira sat down adjacent to her. "He wants us to get things wrapped up on Barasa ASAP and meet him on Forbes. Seems like he might be able to get what we need."

"Well, that's a nice change, something actually working out like it's meant to." She took a bite out of the protein bar as they cleared the burn and emerged into blue skies, the skimmer settling into a smoother descent. "Have you and Tannin come up with a plan to track down Quaine Ayden?"

Zahli nodded, glancing at her fiancé. "Tannin is going to hack Barasa's cities' surveillance networks and run a facial recognition program, see if he can track Quaine's movements after he arrived onworld a few weeks ago."

"While you guys are doing that, I've got something I need to do."

Zahli raised an eyebrow. "And what might that be?"

"Rian wanted answers about Varean, and I intend to get them. An old friend of mine from med school works at one of the hospitals here. I want to see if she can get me into a lab so I can run some blood tests."

"And I suppose you need the commando to go along?" Lianna asked, a hint of skepticism in her voice as she guided the skimmer toward the landmass below. "I bet he jumped at the chance."

She tried to keep the frustration out of her expression. Varean stood nearby, arms crossed and expression shuttered, not looking like he intended on contributing to the discussion.

"He wants the answers about what's going on with him more than anyone. Rian brought up the possibility that the Reidar did something to Varean, even though he has no memory of it, and I think he's right. We just need to work out what."

"We're not doing anything until we've cleared it with Rian." Lianna shot a stubborn glance over her shoulder as Barasa's world-capital city came into view.

"No offense, but Rian isn't here." She took a breath to keep her temper, not wanting the others to work out how important this had become to her. She still didn't really understand it herself, so trying to explain it to them would be impossible. Which was why she'd hesitated in taking Varean's hand before, not because she was ashamed of him like he probably thought.

Besides, Rian wasn't a god, but all too often, people treated him like he was. Lianna, in particular, was loyal to a fault.

"He's still the captain." Lianna's voice was tight with tension. "Off the ship and split up, we're vulnerable. Following orders, even if Rian isn't here to oversee them, is the only thing that's going to keep us alive. He expects us to find Quaine Ayden, so that's what we're going to do. The last thing we need is to go looking for trouble. Well, any more trouble than we're already aiming for, considering we're tracking a guy who was probably killed by the Reidar."

Kira continued with determination, "We hardly know

anything about the Reidar. Whatever they did to Varean, it could give us information we didn't have before. If we're ever going to have even half a chance against the shape-shifters, we need to know everything we can about them."

Lianna sighed as she set the skimmer down. Once they were fully grounded, she glanced at Zahli and Tannin as she powered off the shuttle. "What do you think?"

Zahli shot a considering look at Varean, who stood tensed and detached a few steps away. "We've already divided the crew once. I don't think it's a good idea to split up again."

"This isn't a debate. I'm taking Varean to run those tests. If you don't like it, kick me off the crew."

Stunned silence met her announcement.

Holy crap, had she just said that? Yep. By the way Lianna, Tannin, and Zahli stared at her, she really had. So much for keeping under wraps how important this was to her. But while she hadn't meant to blurt out the ultimatum, she found that, upon reflection, she meant every word.

Despite the dangerous and unfortunate circumstances they'd met under, she'd never met anyone like Varean, and that was saying something, considering she was on a crew with Rian Sherron, a universal-class forger in Callan, a hacking genius in Tannin, not to mention the numerous other larger-than-life men who regularly marched on and off the *Imojenna*. But there was something about Varean none of those other guys had. Something in his loyalty, in the secrets of his past he'd held onto for half his life, in the way he'd put up with crap that might have made another person lose their head, figuratively and literally.

"Kira, I'm not worth you losing your place here."

She turned at Varean's low words to find he'd stepped closer to her. "Yes, you are."

He shook his head, jaw clenching. "They're right not to trust me, and neither should you. Maybe the best thing would be to let me walk. Tell Rian I fought my way free or you left me on the ship. Just promise you'll forget all about me as soon as I step foot off the skimmer."

She shifted closer, shortening the gap between them. "Maybe you don't think it, but you need someone on your side, Varean. If you leave, how are you going to find out the truth?"

A strange kind of desperation had settled into the pit of her stomach, like she'd swallowed meteorites. It wasn't only the ingrained need to help a patient, especially one who'd been taken advantage of or put into a terrible situation not of his own making. She couldn't watch him walk away into the unknown and possibly right into the Reidar's firing line, couldn't imagine him walking out of her life and straight to his death.

God, she was such an idiot to let him get under her skin like this. She'd come to care about him more than she should. Whatever happened, Varean would leave. Rian didn't trust him, and even if they found out he'd been subjected to god-knew-what kind of Reidar experimentation, it wasn't like the captain would get all chummy-chummy over their matching torture scars and give Varean a place on the crew.

The best Rian might be willing to do was return him to the *Swift Brion*. And even that wasn't a certainty. He pretty much never apologized to anyone for anything. It was more likely Rian would consider cutting him loose without killing him a magnanimous act.

Varean glanced past her, presumably to where the other three stared at them and then returned his gaze to her, silver-blue eyes wary with uncertain shadows.

"Fine. I'll stay, because I already gave you my word. But only if your shipmates decide they trust you to know what's right."

She crossed her arms and turned to face them, the only

friends and nearest thing she'd had to family in the last few years. She felt like an invisible wall had sprung up between them, solid and sure as ancient stone, forcing them apart.

However, Zahli, at least, looked like she might agree. "You really think the Reidar might have done something to him like they did to Rian?"

Of course, this would be a sore subject for Zahli, who worried about her older brother every day and had only the shadow of a clue what the Reidar had subjected him to or why.

"I really do. And if we can find a way to help Varean—"

"Maybe we can find a way to help Rian," Zahli finished.

"Zahli…" Tannin took her hand.

"We need to give them a chance." Zahli's tone had become resolute, matching her firm expression. "Kira is right. We probably owe Varean that after what we put him through."

Frowning slightly, Lianna didn't look so convinced. "Just because they played the we-can-help-Rian card, you're going to go along with it?"

"It's not that simple, and you know it." Zahli crossed her arms. "And I'm not going to apologize for wanting to do everything in my power to help Rian. He's my brother, and after all he's done for us, we owe him that."

"And the fact we're doing it behind Rian's back doesn't matter?"

Zahli's features only got more stubborn. "If you're so worried about what Rian will think, comm him. I'm not trying to hide anything from him. I trust Kira. If she thinks the Reidar did something to Varean, then we should let them go and run the tests."

Lianna glanced away and, though her expression remained obstinate, Kira could see that logic was winning out. "Fine. But we shouldn't split up. We stick together, first to track down Quaine Ayden, then to get the tests done."

An automatic disagreement surged forward, but Kira

swallowed it down. Yes, it would be more difficult to go unnoticed as a group of five at the hospital—if her old med school friend even agreed to help her—but getting them to make this much concession was probably as far as she could push things. While she might have told them they could kick her off the crew, the last thing she wanted was to be homeless again… Well, more homeless than she already was, considering they'd lost the ship.

"Okay, sounds like a plan." She glanced at Varean, who nodded.

Apparently satisfied, Lianna turned her attention to Tannin. "I'm assuming the skimmer's onboard computer isn't going to cut it for whatever super-hacking you've got in mind?"

Tannin gave her a sharp grin "Not even in the slightest."

"Where do you want to do this from, then?"

"We can either get a hotel room under the false idents Callan made or break into my parent's house."

Zahli shot him an incredulous look. "Why would you want to break into your parent's house?"

Tannin shrugged, the movement careless, but his expression troubled. "There are a few things of mine I wouldn't mind grabbing, assuming they didn't trash-compact everything when they disowned me."

"I'm sorry. I knew coming here wouldn't be easy, but I guess I never considered exactly what it meant for you." Zahli reached down and twined her hand with Tannin's, stepping closer to him.

"It's fine, Zahli. It's been over twelve years."

"If you're sure this is what you really want."

He sent her a tender, reassuring smile. "It is. Besides, they have heaps of priceless stuff just sitting around the house, and we need money. Stealing a few things to sell is the least I owe them for failing to act like parents."

Great. The felonies kept stacking up—they were docked

under forged ident files and hacking into government surveillance systems. Might as well add breaking and entering to the list, because at this point, it was their least serious crime.

"Before we go," Kira said, interrupting them before they could come up with more illegal activities. "I need to send a message to the doctor I know, see if she can help me get access to a lab at the hospital where she works."

Lianna waved toward the skimmer's helm. "Go ahead. The comm system is still online."

She made her way to the front of the ship and looked up Doctor Melyssa Kendrick, finding her at one of the smaller outer-suburban hospitals.

She and Mel had been pretty good friends at med school and interned together. They'd spent a lot of nights studying, made it through thirty-hour shifts together, and on more than one occasion, drank way too much at the on-campus bar.

Mel had left to take a job on her home planet of Barasa about a year before everything had gone down and Kira's life had irrevocably changed.

She was taking a long shot, requesting that Mel get her access under the name Doctor Kat Allen. Since she'd been barred from practicing medicine at any hospitals or clinics within the central systems, Callan had created an entire false medical ident for her. She'd had to use it only twice before now, both times to get supplies on planets at the very edge of the central systems, and it had held up with no problems. Hopefully the same would apply for actually going into a hospital on one of the inner central worlds.

Mel might or might not have heard what had happened to her. Either way, asking her to allow them access to the Dalton Memorial Hospital genetics lab, knowing she was using a fake ident and banned from practicing medicine in the central systems, was a huge favor from someone she hadn't seen in five years.

Message sent, she joined the others outside the skimmer. As she stepped out, Zahli held up a Reidar stunner for her, while Lianna used her commpad to close the ship.

She shook her head. "You know how I feel about guns."

Varean grabbed it, instead. "Whether or not you like guns has to come second to your safety. Besides, this one won't hurt anyone unless you happen to shoot me with it. At least if you have this and come across any Reidar, you'll be able to slow them down."

He took her hand, bringing it up to gently set the weapon in her palm.

She closed her grip around it with a small sigh and then reluctantly secured it in the back of her pants like the others had. The cold surface of the gun pressed uncomfortably into her skin, while the slight weight of it felt awkward and unnatural. Though it had been years since the incident that had ended her medical career as she'd known it, being in the central systems, heading for a hospital, brought back a lot of things. The frustration, disgust, fear, and utter devastation—she hadn't felt that particular mix of emotions for ages, making it seem like it had happened only a few months ago.

Something must have shown—her features did feel tight and drawn—because Varean stepped closer as they set off across the docking hangar.

"Is everything okay?" he murmured, presumably so the others wouldn't overhear.

"No, everything is not okay." It would have been easy to pretend otherwise. but being honest with Varean felt good, gave her a small moment of relief. He'd trusted her with the truth of his past, it seemed only natural for her to do the same.

"Does it have something to do with why you need a friend to help you get clearance at the hospital and you can't go yourself?"

She glanced up at him, expecting to find intense curiosity

or scrutiny in his regard, but instead, she saw only warm concern.

"That, and pretty much everything else in my life."

He nodded. "Do you mind— Can I ask why you're flying around the universe in an old Nirali classer under a captain who is clearly on the deranged side of psychotic, when you're obviously a highly trained doctor?"

She took in a deep breath, and it caught as she tried to exhale. Rian had never asked for the full story, she'd told him simply that she wasn't able to practice medicine in the central systems, so he'd had Callan make the fake ident for her. After she'd been on crew for two years, she'd told Zahli everything, and it was the one and only time she'd spoken of it.

She wanted to tell Varean. He would understand, wouldn't view her any differently. But just the thought of speaking the words made her stomach tighten. She would tell him, just not here and now.

"Something happened, and I was barred from practicing medicine in the central systems." Her voice came out on an uneven note, and she swallowed down the anxiety.

It had been years ago; she'd dealt with the fallout of grief and rage and then picked up the pieces as best she could to move forward. Finding a place on the *Imojenna* had been close to a miracle. If not for Rian, she wouldn't even be a doctor anymore, or she would have ended up on one of the almost-lawless outer planets where modern medical supplies were considered a luxury. So while it might not seem like it to Varean, onboard the *Imojenna* with friends she could basically call family, she was actually happy and content. If not for the threat of the Reidar, life would have been just about perfect.

Varean's hand touched hers lightly on the outer side of her thumb, before he caught her fingers and twined them with his. "Whatever happened, you don't have to tell me. I already know it wasn't your fault. I'm guessing you got screwed by the system or some individual. Either way, it doesn't change who you are where it counts."

Her heart skipped a few rushed beats. As a commando, as a guy who looked like he did—tall, broad-shouldered, rippling muscles, and intimidating when he was pissed about something—it was unexpected and surprising to find he was insightful, compassionate, and pretty much seemed to have a big squishy heart underneath his tough exterior. Which only made her burgeoning feelings toward him that much more acute. And, most inconveniently, it made her want to kiss him the second they were alone. Heck, maybe not even when they were alone. She was pretty well tempted to stop right in the middle of the spaceport walkway, throw her arms around his neck, and show him exactly how much those simple words meant.

Warmth brushed her cheeks, and she glanced away. At least she wasn't caught in the cold grip of her unchangeable past any longer. "It's more complicated than that, and I could have made different choices. But thanks for saying it all the same."

"I'm sure it was in the best interest of someone, totally disregarding your own well-being."

"There are some people who'll never see it that way, and I don't blame them."

Would he still regard her with the same warmth when he heard the entire story?

They arrived at a security checkpoint, saving her from any more conversation. Once they'd made it through the usual checks, Lianna led them outside to hire an aerosphere car, Tannin entering the address of his parent's house after they were onboard.

As the aerocar took off, rising vertically into the flow of traffic skimming above the city, Kira closed her eyes, took a few deep breaths, and put her memories back to where they usually lived—in the deep, dark corners of her mind where they couldn't affect her.

# Chapter Sixteen

Varean had to wonder about the crew of the *Imojenna*. When they'd treated him like crap and had him locked in the bottom of the ship, he hadn't cared about anyone except Kira, because she'd been the only one willing to stand up for him.

But since they'd had to abandon ship, he'd learned some mighty interesting tidbits. Added to the few snatches of things people had said in front of him since he'd been dragged half-conscious from the *Swift Brion*, he'd become more than a little intrigued with the disparate group of people Sherron had collected.

First, there was Kira. From early on, it'd been clear she was a highly skilled, well-trained doctor, so it made no sense for her to be living on the fringes of society aboard a decommissioned war supply ship for what he guessed was very little money.

There were only a handful of scenarios that would see a doctor banned from practicing medicine in the central systems, and none of them painted her in a good light. But he'd meant every word—whatever had happened, he refused to believe she'd done anything wrong. It seemed more likely someone had either blamed her for something that hadn't been her fault, or she'd done something in the best interest of her patient, which resulted in the same thing.

Then there was Rian. From what he could glean, most of the guy's problems stemmed from a bad run-in with the Reidar. Now, the captain not only had the authorities after him, but the aliens as well. Talk about living life on the edge. By all rights, it was probably amazing the guy was still breathing.

Next came Callan, because the gorilla was a universal-class forger and made sure the fugitive crew of the *Imojenna* could blatantly go wherever their wanted hearts desired without fear of being identified. He'd been surprised the security specialist—or whatever title the guy used—knew how to work anything that didn't involve ammo, a charge pack, or a blade.

Varean hadn't worked out whether Zahli or Lianna had any kind of shady pasts, but there was definitely a story behind Tannin's spot on the crew. Hacker extraordinaire who'd been disowned by one of Barasa's most prominent, wealthy families and now engaged to marry Rian's sister. The guy must have had one giant pair to even think about touching Major Captain Rian Sherron's baby sister, let alone enter into any kind of relationship with her. Varean had to hand it to the guy, he must be one steely sonuvabitch, if he was willing to take Rian as family.

Speaking of Tannin, he was the reason they were flying in an aerocar above the fanciest neighborhood he'd ever seen. No simple houses here. Not even any large family residences. Every single dwelling on this street was a mansion, the kind of palatial living reserved for less than one percent of the population.

The car lowered to the street, entering the parking lot of a public garden with a playground filled with under-school-age children and adults who were more than likely their nannies.

"My parents' house is two blocks back that way," Tannin said, gaze on the playground, expression shuttered. Had he played here himself as a child?

Varean tried to imagine what it would be like to have parents only to be disowned by them. Suppose it'd be worse than never having them in the first place. His mom had died before he was old enough to remember her. With no other family and no clue as to who his father was, he'd ended up in the foster system, his longest residence lasting two years. He had no concept of a permanent home or what it would be like to have the constant care and attention of a parent. Without knowing these things, he didn't have a reference for exactly how Tannin might be feeling, but assumed it probably sucked big time.

He could kind of understand the guy's decision to break in and help himself to a few things. Plus, if the authorities got wind of whatever hacking Tannin planned on doing, the guy's olds would have a few awkward questions to answer.

Varean had promised Kira he'd stay until she'd run her tests and found out what the freck was going on with him, even though there was a solid-metium weight in his gut telling him he didn't really want to know the answer. He didn't want to believe it, but he couldn't shake the notion that Sherron had been right, and the damn aliens had done something to him at some stage that he had no memory of.

After he got the results, he'd no doubt have some decisions to make about how to live his life going forward in the new universe he found himself in, where every single person he came across could be a shape-shifting alien in disguise. The only thing he knew for certain was that, for Kira's safety, he had to walk away from the *Imojenna* and never look back.

The aim to be gone should have filled him with a sense of relief. Instead, his brain oh-so-helpfully reminded him of the way Kira had moaned his name when he'd had his fingers inside her, taking her right over the edge he'd so desperately wanted to plunge off himself.

What did he really think could happen here? He'd never been boyfriend material and never would be. The best he'd ever done was casual hookups over a few months. He didn't do relationships or family. Growing up in the foster system, he didn't know how. And he sure as hell hadn't tried once he'd become an adult and joined the military. He'd found his sense of belonging in a unit, in formations, and regulations.

Besides, no doubt Sherron wanted him around about as much as he wanted to be around. Yeah, maybe he'd be missing out on something he could have had with Kira, something he'd never experienced before. But the reasons to leave stacked way up against the one reason to stay.

As they left the aerocar and headed out of the park, Tannin and Zahli took point, while Lianna brought up the rear in a way that told him they were used to being on guard.

Though he didn't have a weapon, he was definitely on alert as they walked along the block edged by high fences, the yards so big the houses were hardly visible from the street.

"So is there some kind of plan here?" he asked as they turned a corner. "Do any of you have B and E experience, or is this just a winging-it-as-you-go kind of thing?"

"Just because you're not chained up any longer doesn't mean I want to hear you talk," Lianna said from behind him.

"Lianna, really." Kira tossed an annoyed glare over her shoulder.

"Wow, you really don't like me, do you?" He glanced back at the nav-engineer, but she was too busy scanning the street like a pro, hands on the weapons holstered low-slung around her hips. Seemed like she had a few more skills than a regular ship navigator or engineer. Color him *not* surprised.

"I don't know you," Lianna replied in the same prickly

voice. "And considering your last place of residence was our brig, and the stunner affects you and no one else, I'm a long way off trusting or liking you, Command Donnelly."

"It's Lieutenant Captain," he muttered.

"What?" This time, Lianna actually looked at him, confusion creasing her brow.

"My rank? It's Lieutenant Captain Varean Donnelly, tier one commando, Armed Forces unit Alpha-Alpha. I'd nearly worked my way up to getting my own unit to command when you all so very politely asked me to join you for this little excursion on your superior vessel. So glad I came along."

Lianna scowled, but he caught an amused glint in Kira's gaze.

"Well then, Lieutenant Captain Donnelly, sir." Lianna gave a sarcastic salute. "You're welcome to take your commando assets and get lost whenever it suits you."

Really, Lianna's insults didn't bother him.

"Looks like I'm multitalented," he murmured to Kira.

She regarded him with a conspiratorial look. "How so?"

"I can talk and piss Lianna off at the same time."

She started to laugh, but caught it with a badly covered cough, putting her hand over her mouth.

"While I'm glad some of us are having fun," Tannin interrupted, "I'm sure you won't be insulted if I suggest you shut the hell up, since we're here."

Tannin paused just a few steps down from a large ornate security gate.

"So what's the plan?" Lianna asked, as if he hadn't just said the same thing.

Kira wrapped a hand around his elbow and shook her head, as though she thought he was going to say something. He liked way too much that she was apparently watching out for him. Instead of saying anything, he sent her a heated look, back-burning with exactly how damn good it had been when she'd taken him for a ride.

Her eyes widened, and she glanced away, a light brush of rose coloring her cheeks and leaving him more than a little gratified. Maybe he planned on disappearing sooner rather than later. But before he did, they needed to finish properly what they'd started onboard the skimmer.

"You guys just hang here for a minute," Tannin was saying to Zahli and Lianna, pulling his commpad out of his pocket. "My parents have an extensive surveillance system like all the other paranoid, uber-rich people around here. I should be able to override it if I splice my commpad into the gate control and ident screen."

Zahli murmured something he didn't quite catch, but was probably along the lines of *be careful*, then Tannin headed for the huge double gate. The fence had an old-fashioned gatehouse built into it, but he doubted anyone ever stood around in there, considering tech security was so much more reliable.

The four of them remained silent for the time it took Tannin to hack his way into the house's surveillance program. He waved them over after about ten minutes, looking more apprehensive than satisfied with his efforts at circumventing what was probably an expensive and sophisticated system.

"We're in luck. Logs show my parents have been offworld all week and won't be back for a few more days. There's a skeleton staff, but they leave at six in the evening and come back at eight in the morning. We've got the house to ourselves for the night."

"How long do you think it'll take to track Quaine?" Lianna asked.

"A few hours, if I'm lucky. Probably longer, if he was trying to keep a low profile."

Lianna glanced at her comm screen. "It's nearly four thirty. What are we going to do until the staff leave?"

Zahli glanced between him and Kira. "Should we go to the hospital and get the tests done?"

Kira's expression tensed. "I'd need to check if my friend Mel has messaged whether or not she can help me. But the tests could take a few hours as well."

Lianna tapped her commpad screen. "I've got the skimmer's system linked to me. Logs are showing no message has come in."

"It's probably a long shot, but I want to give it a bit more time to see if my friend will come through."

"Okay. We'll head back to the skimmer and wait it out."

"How about we find a bar and decompress for an hour or so?" Everyone looked at him after he'd made the suggestion as if he'd grown a second head.

"What?" he demanded after a long second of silence. "We just spent two days stuck on a skimmer the size of a tin can, and I don't know about you guys, but before that, I'd been posted on the *Swift Brion* for three straight deployments without any downtime. Last time I saw a bar, it was a crappy one on some random waystation, and I was still getting carded."

"We could probably do with some downtime," Tannin agreed at last, though he sounded hesitant.

Lianna gave him a full-on evil eye. "First we bring him along on our little mission to find Quaine, and now we're going to take him out drinking? What the freck? I mean, seriously, if Rian knew about any of this—"

"But Rian isn't here, and he's not going to find out," Zahli said in a hard voice—one that was scarily similar to her brother. "At least not until we have some answers."

Muttering a curse and looking skyward as if praying for divine guidance, Lianna obviously realized she was outnumbered. "Fine. But if he starts a bar fight, I'll shoot him myself."

She brushed by them, stalking back down the block the

way they'd come earlier.

"Jezus. I don't think I've ever seen Lianna in such a bad mood," Tannin muttered.

Zahli watched after the nav-engineer with a concerned gaze. After taking Tannin's hand, she tugged his arm to get him to go along with her. "Lianna loves the ship almost as much as Rian. Actually, there's a good chance she loves it more than Rian, no matter how much she bitches about having to fix it. And I'd guess she's also stressed about the fact we've split up. She's used to being there for him, both on the ship and as extra backup. Since he's currently on a whole other planet, I'd say she's worried about him, though she'll never admit it."

Varean slowed his steps to put some distance between him and the couple a few paces ahead.

"Are Lianna and Rian a thing?" he asked Kira in a low voice. Not that it was any of his business, but the crew of the *Imojenna* had proven to be way more interesting than they'd appeared on the surface, and he found himself wanting details.

Both her eyebrows shot up. "*Lianna and Rian?* No!"

Consternation etched her face, as if the notion had never occurred to her.

"No," she repeated, though this time she sounded more unsure. "They couldn't be. I mean, someone would have worked it out. Living on a ship the size of the *Imojenna*, it's impossible to keep anything a secret. And Rian's never shown the least interest in anyone or anything except his obsession to track down the Reidar. I guess she could have feelings for him, but they'd be deeply buried, and she's never acted on them. So, no, it's not like that, they're just friends. We're all close, in different ways."

"Wow, that was like so convincing."

She glared and then gave him a light shove in the side. "Shut up! And stop deconstructing my life as I know it, putting weird ideas in my head about Lianna and Rian."

"Hey, I'm just trying to work out what the hell I landed in the middle of." He shrugged, trying not to grin like a moron, but probably failing.

Seriously, he should not be having a good time right now. He should be trying to decide how he was going to pick up the atomized pieces of his life after Kira finished running her tests. He should be making a plan A through to frecking Z, but all he could do was enjoy the way the sun made her skin glow and how the light breeze tugged at the strands of her hair, like he was living some damned sappy love song. And the small, intimate smile she sent him in return just about made his heart flatline.

He'd been unceremoniously ripped out of his life, threatened repeatedly, and nearly killed a few times. Any sane guy would not have started falling for a woman in the middle of all that, no matter how gorgeous Kira might be. But it was like his senses had gone into hyperdrive in the last few days, his mind receiving and processing information like it was all new.

Obviously the multiple razar hits had scrambled his brain worse than he'd thought. Maybe he really, really just needed to get her naked somewhere and work this out of his system. It was more likely to be a thank-god-still-alive-suckers thing. He'd experienced it before, after nearly getting taken out on a mission a few years back, and had found a sweet little ensign comm officer who'd been more than willing to help him take the edge off. Only this time it was more acute, lighting him up and billowing through his body like steam off hot pavement.

No one said anything else as they made their way back to the aerocar and Tannin put in directions to some bar near the spaceport. It wasn't the fanciest place, but neither was it a crater dump. Most of the patrons seemed to be travelers, with a few people scattered about who were probably having early after-work drinks. They found a table without too much trouble, and Tannin went to get the first round.

Sitting at a bar, drinking with half the crew of the *Imojenna*, hadn't factored into his reality less than forty-eight hours ago. Then, he would have said he'd rather do three straight shifts of babysitting bridge officers duty in the command center of the *Swift Brion*.

But here he sat. And without Sherron or his gorilla getting in the way—plus Lianna's bad mood aside—he could almost see the appeal, understand why Kira didn't seem unhappy with her lot in life.

With his place in the commando unit and the knowledge he had his teammates at his back, he'd felt fulfilled and hadn't ever thought about needing anything more. But what Kira had with the crew of the *Imojenna*, it was totally different, more than just people working together.

They didn't protect one another because they'd been trained to do so, they did it because they cared. Sure, he had a bond with the guys in his unit, but not to the depth Kira treasured the others on the ship. She'd mentioned them being like family, and the more time he spent with them, the more he could see how true the sentiment was. And it had opened up something within him, a chasm he hadn't realized existed. It had been covered by the insubstantial assurance that he'd never had anybody and been just fine, so clearly he didn't need anyone to continue living his life.

But had he been living? Or merely existing? The question made him uncomfortable, made him get tight and prickly all over, like there were thorns beneath his skin.

Hell, that goddamn razar must have knocked more than a few frecking screws loose, because introspection was not for him. So, instead of dwelling on it, he took a long swallow of the beer Tannin brought him and washed the inconvenient thoughts away.

The hour went by surprisingly fast, while he tried not to

get absorbed in the nuances of expressions that crossed Kira's face when she spoke, or getting himself distracted and wound up over what they'd been doing in the bathroom onboard the skimmer. A few times, she'd caught him staring, but instead of being embarrassed or trying to hide the fact, he'd simply held her gaze and enjoyed the light of awareness in her gorgeous eyes.

Before he knew it, Tannin suggested they get moving. Kira shot him glances all the way to the exit as if she had something on her mind.

"Something wrong?" he asked as they picked a spot off to the side of the walkway to wait for the others.

"Actually, I was about to ask you the same thing." She leaned against an exposed-brick column that he supposed was meant to give the bar a kind of rustic or old-world feel.

"You realize asking me that is totally redundant, right?"

"How so?"

"If everything was right in the universe, I'd be onboard the *Swift Brion*. Given, I apparently would have had to make the decision on whether or not to defect with Captain Admiral Graydon. But things would still be familiar. They'd still be sane. Mostly." He dragged a hand over his face, the frustration, the wearisome uncertainty of his situation, the questions of those hallucinations, the language, the knowledge that'd started filtering into his mind, all crashing down on him like an asteroid.

"I know I've said it already a hundred times, but I'm sorry, Varean. And I promise to make it better." She took his hand, no hesitation like when she'd woken up on the skimmer and been worried her crewmates would see. It shouldn't have bothered him when she'd changed her mind about touching him then. But stupidly it had. He'd thought—or more like hoped—whatever this thing was that had developed between them would be stronger than her worry about what the others would think of her.

But logic had won out, and he'd understood her caution. Couldn't say he wouldn't have done exactly the same thing.

However, when she took his hand now—as if it were the most natural thing to do and she had every right—it soothed some of the wildness in him, the desperation to escape the mess he'd fallen into. Which was a problem, because the mess was his entire life, and there was no escaping that.

"You're going to make it better by running the tests?" He sent her a casual smile but got the feeling he missed the mark entirely. "Sorry, Kira, but whatever those tests prove, I don't think it'll make anything better."

"Whatever the results are, at least we'll have answers, and then we can make a plan."

Her expression wasn't sympathetic or falsely optimistic, it was simply realistic and practical, which was exactly what he needed. And he liked her use of *we* way too much, even though there wasn't actually any kind of *we* at all. But it was helpful to imagine for a moment that she cared deeply about him, that there was a *we,* and would be, going forward. Something indefinable he could rely on, no matter what other crazy was happening in his life.

Kira glanced around the faux-brick column, probably to see where the others were—Tannin and Zahli waiting in line to pay, Lianna nowhere to be seen.

Before he could even begin to wonder what was going on in that too-intelligent mind of hers, she grabbed the collar of his shirt and pulled him toward her, right into the kind of kiss he'd been imagining for hours.

He set a hand on the bricks by her head, bracing himself as he pressed into her from thigh to chest, the other hand on the back of her neck underneath the fall of her shoulder-length dark hair.

Despite the unfortunate public setting, Kira was no-holds-barred as she pulled him closer, her tongue sliding against his in a way that nearly made his knees buckle.

Just when the rest of his body shook the surprise and started catching up with the program, she broke the kiss, pushing him back a step and blowing out an uneven breath.

"What the hell was that?" His voice came out like cheap scotch. No doubt because the way she'd so abruptly stopped kissing him had spun his head almost as much as when she'd started.

"I couldn't stand seeing that look in your eyes anymore, the one that makes me worried you're going to run off and get yourself killed the second I'm not watching you like a hawk. That seemed like the easiest way to fix it."

"Well I guess that's one way of doing it," he muttered. He sucked in a long pull of air, willing his heart rate to settle and certain appendages to cool it, because there was clearly nothing doing in the middle of a crowded bar, with Tannin, Zahli, and Lianna in their pockets.

And with perfect timing, said pocket-people came over, ending the conversation and any imbecilic thoughts he might have about grabbing a second kiss.

Never mind going crazy over what the tests might reveal, Kira and her sweet, sexy lips were more likely to drive him right out of his head before they got anywhere near the hospital. She was a force to be reckoned with, and on every front he'd been besieged. For the first time in his life, he found himself ready and willing to lay down arms if Kira was the one taking the victory.

Whatever happened, one thing had become blatantly clear. Where his heart was concerned, he was already totally screwed.

# Chapter Seventeen

Rian sat drinking some kind of red wine straight from the bottle on a sturdy swing situated on the porch of a little out-of-the-way cabin they'd rented after arriving onworld a few hours ago.

He couldn't remember the last time he'd drunk wine, but with a decided lack of beer or goddamned Violaine in the cabin, red wine had been the only other viable choice. Seemed marginally better than drinking white wine, or god forbid, champagne.

The short half hour it had taken to fly from Dunham out to this farming moon had been uneventful, however, he could still feel the tension of the half crew he had with him creeping down the back of his neck like marching ants. So, instead of parking the skimmer at a spaceport to wait for the others to meet up with them or Colt to contact him about his shopping list, he'd splashed out some credits he couldn't afford on this cabin to give everyone some space and a break from traveling.

They'd been ship-bound for weeks, making only the shortest stops at the most backwater worlds and stations ever since the Reidar had tried to take them out on his home planet of Dalphin. His crew was good, and they'd taken it well. But there came a point where even the most well-adjusted, optimistic person was in danger of becoming a serial killer and stabbing them all in their sleep. Besides, it was pretty clear from his little meltdown earlier that he was the one who needed to get his shite together, or he'd end up adding more beads to the band he wore around his left wrist. The weight of the ones he already had felt as if they dragged him down like a black hole most days, without upping the tally.

So here he sat, on this countrified porch swing, swigging his fancified red wine, listening to the frecking birds sing, getting some damned frecking fresh air, and pretending like he could maybe take some sanity with him when he was done here.

As for the rest of his crew, they seemed to be making the most of things. Jensen and Callan were inside sleeping, while Ella and Nyah had wandered into the nearby, thinly treed woods to pick the berries Colt had told him were in season. They hadn't gone all that far, and he could still see the two of them standing in the dappled shade eating berries and chatting about god knew what.

Between keeping watch of things and emptying the bottle, his gaze kept wandering back to Ella, catching on the way she moved across the short grass, bending every now and then to drop berries in the container she'd found in the cabin. Lingering on the way she smiled so damned reservedly at whatever Nyah was chattering about. How her smooth, dark golden-toned features never once lost that serene countenance.

After a while, as he drank more wine and sank deeper into the porch swing, he gave up pretending he was paying attention to anything else and gave in to the insidious urge to lose himself in her simple, elegant beauty. So when they finally seemed to have picked themselves enough berries and made their way back toward the cabin, he felt like he'd fallen into some kind of honey-thick trance. As she and Nyah came up the four steps to the porch, he couldn't take his eyes off her, and his initial judgment of her returned. Not priestess. *Enchantress.* A siren leading him from the path of sanity to a wild, uncharted course that would be the ruin of what little he had left.

Ella handed the container of berries to Nyah. "Would you mind taking these in? I'll join you in a moment."

Nyah shot him a wary look, then made her escape. He sighed and leaned down to set the half-empty bottle of wine on the porch, scrubbing both hands through his hair.

Ella had stopped a few steps in front of him, hands clasped behind her back. He couldn't see any higher than her damned dainty feet, but didn't need to see her face to know she'd be regarding him with that detached observation, like she was cataloguing each moment of his decline into wretchedness to use if she ever returned to Aryn, as a warning to others of everything wrong with mankind.

"Something on your mind, princess?" He straightened, shoving his hair off his forehead as he lifted his head to meet her gaze.

"Not at all." She shifted to stand near the porch railing, bracing both hands on the smooth surface, staring into the surrounds and not offering anything else. No reason as to why she'd stayed out here instead of going in with Nyah or any of the usual unwanted counsel she'd given him in the past.

Like everything else she ever did, it only made the frustration within him wind tighter.

"Is this your new tactic?" He surged to his feet, stooping to pick up the bottle and setting it on the nearby table. "Just stand around silently until I spill my guts, or beg for help, or admit all my sins, or whatever it is you think I need to do?"

She hadn't shifted from her position and from where he now stood, he could see nothing but the slim line of her back and tousled fall of her dark brown hair, the mid-afternoon sun catching fiery red highlights.

"Despite what you may think, Rian, I do not spend my days trying to come up with ways to trick or lure you into meaningful discourse. My thoughts and actions are my own, with no reference to manipulation."

He gave a short, humorless laugh, his damned feet taking him a few steps closer to her. "We both know that's not true. You said yourself that you intended to help me whether I wanted you to or not."

"So I did." Her head lowered, as though she'd dropped her gaze from the horizon to her hands on the railing. "Perhaps I was mistaken in my belief that I could avail you of all that has come before, and all that is to come in the future."

And there was the sucker punch, catching him low in the guts and stealing his breath. Though he'd suspected as much, hearing her say out loud that she'd given up on him was like an arctic torrent swirling up from the depths of him and billowing outward, all sharp ice and cutting wind.

For half a second, he was actually at a loss. He had no words and no direction because astoundingly, there'd been a tiny shred of hope that if Ella thought he could be saved, then maybe everything wasn't lost.

Except the old familiar rage descended, reminding him that he'd been doing just fine before she'd come along, and just because she'd ended up on his ship it hadn't changed him or his situation. If anything, it had made things a whole frecking lot more complicated, because now the Reidar weren't after only him, they were in double the danger because the shape-shifters wanted her as well, maybe even more than the hard-on they had to see his head mounted on a wall.

Which brought him right around to the fact that he spent most of his days on his own damned ship avoiding the woman, including dodging his vow to find out what the aliens wanted with her. And after months living on his boat, he still had no accounting of what exactly she was capable of, what with all those mysterious Arynian abilities of hers.

He stepped forward, clamping a hand on either side of her on the railing, trapping her in place with her back to his chest, though they weren't quite touching. The top of her head only just reached his chin, and the now-familiar moon jasmine scent of her washed over him, except this time it was underlaid with the wild summer-sweetness of the berries she'd been eating.

"Maybe you don't want to talk, but we're long overdue for a conversation about you."

"Are we?" Her voice came out totally neutral, no hint of concern over his close proximity or his suggestion of topic. "What would you like to discuss?"

"Don't play dumb." He lowered his head until his lips were against her ear. "It doesn't suit you."

"You expressly forbid me from reading your mind, yet you expect me to know what information you desire?"

He slid his hands in closer, bringing his arms tighter on either side of her, easing the slightest bit nearer, until his chest was only just against her back. "Trying to talk me in circles isn't going to work this time. I want to know why the Reidar want you so badly."

She took in a deep breath, and he felt every atom of it as her body shifted imperceptibly against him. "I told you, I don't know."

"Yeah, you told me." He pressed closer, unable to help himself, the feel of her against him consuming every lick of sense and fragment of anger and frustration, melting into something just as hot but totally impossible to define or contain. "But see, I don't believe you."

"What would I gain in hiding anything from you?" She stiffened, not enough that anyone looking at her would have noticed, but he was aware of her on a level that defied explanation, like the closer he stood the more he could sense, until the separation of them as two distinct people became blurred. It was the same thing he'd been running from since she'd healed him, the invisible tie that meant he always knew exactly where she was on the ship. But now, he didn't want to escape it, he wanted to sink deeper, the high sharp and clear like a hit of the purest Violaine.

"Okay, I'll go along with your claim that you don't know. But you must have a theory."

She didn't answer, but not because she was trying to avoid the question. Somehow, he knew she was considering her answer.

"I'm a second generation Arynian, and that is a very rare thing," she said at last. "When two Arynians have children, it almost always results in a child with absolutely no abilities whatsoever. I am one of very few successful outcomes and was trained from a very early age. Because my powers are much more acute, they are harder to control, but also hold more potential. I can only guess one of those two reasons has something to do with it."

Nothing he hadn't heard before, except that she was born of Arynian parents. And with this newfound, other-level consciousness he had of her, he also knew she'd told him everything she could.

She truly didn't know what the Reidar wanted of her, but in her darkest moments, it scared her more than anything had in her entire life.

He shook his head, a shot of dizziness spilling through him. Where the freck had that thought come from? Ella had once gotten inside his head, read his mind, spoken telepathically to him. Could the connection go both ways?

She sucked in a sharp breath. "You shouldn't be able to read my mind. Not even other Arynians should be able to do that."

Which meant frecking what, exactly?

"What the hell is going on?" he muttered, more to himself. Because he'd ended up against her with his arms around her, hands on her hips, holding her firm against him, the curve of her back fitting against his chest. And for the first time, he wasn't consumed by the desperate need to escape her. Everywhere they touched sparks bloomed and flared into intense heat. Warm rapture built, blasting back the ice within him. Instead of flinching away, he embraced the solace, the heat, the uncomplicated simplicity of the buzz. It had been too long since he'd felt anything other than fear, loathing, rage, or pain. Maybe Ella thought him lost, maybe she didn't want to help him break out from the pits of his own personal hell, but he was exhausted from it all. He just wanted one moment to forget, to be above it, to feel the euphoric torture of something purer than he had any right to aspire to, let alone actually hold.

Ella's breathing hitched, her hands tightening where she still held the railing, yet she pressed against him, her head falling back to rest on his shoulder, exposing the slender line of her neck, down into the swells of her upper chest. And he'd never seen anything more beautiful, her eyes closed, lips parted on a ragged exhale, a light flush coloring her cheeks.

She was firm against him, everything of them connected in high-vibrating harmony while the heat within him teetered, ready to crash into unadulterated pleasure he knew would bring him to his knees. He couldn't imagine anything except falling into her and losing himself, needing her in a way that went far beyond physical longing.

But something within him fought against it; that inherent darkness the Reidar had planted deep within him pushed back, threatening to rise up and turn his reality into nightmare. And he sensed a different turmoil within Ella, a kernel of some fixed logic that held out against him in much the same way.

This couldn't ever be anything, but for a second he considered plunging into recklessness, the temptation so much more enticing than he could have possibly anticipated.

"Rian."

Callan's voice shocked his system like a bomb exploding, yanking him out of his dangerous yearning.

He released Ella and stumbled to the side, knocking against one of the porch posts. Like waking up from a deep, drugging sleep, he couldn't get his brain to function at speed. Ella lowered herself on the porch swing, looking as dazed as he felt.

"You left your comm inside. There's a message from Colter Routh on it."

Expression blank, Callan glanced at Ella and then headed back inside.

Rian dragged both hands over his face, feeling cold down to his core, like leaving a warm, toasty room and stepping into a snow flurry. And now that he was back to himself, hard logic tore through him like lightning. Whatever the freck was going on with Ella and him, touching her sent it spinning out of control. Obviously, avoiding her had been the damned smart thing to do. Until he worked out what he was going to do with her, he needed to stay away from her at all cost.

He didn't let himself glance at her as he forced his unsteady legs to cooperate and take him inside. He found his comm where he'd left it on the kitchen table, hand shaking as he reached down to grab the device. He took a second to inhale and clamp down all his muscles, forcing himself into something close to normal equilibrium.

Across the room, Callan stood barefoot next to the condiments dispenser, running a finger down the list of options on the screen.

"Repli-coffee." The look on Callan's face matched the disgust in his tone. "Guess it's better than frecking nothing."

"Pull a second cup for me." Rian tabbed up the message on the display of his commpad. Short and sweet—the commander captain had found a way to get everything in bulk quantities on a continuing basis, if he needed that option. Colt wanted Rian to organize a way to pick up the first shipment.

For a start, without the *Imojenna*, taking a shipment was going to be that much frecking harder. And second, his paranoia was kicking up big time, telling him this was too fast, too simple. He'd expected it would take Colt days, if not weeks, of wrangling and secretly pulling in favors, yet only a few hours had gone by, and already his buddy had handled it.

The way he saw it, there were two possible explanations. Either the Reidar were behind this and they'd gotten to Colt after he'd left Dunham, or they were using Colt and the guy had no idea. Or second, all that stuff Colt had said about believing Rian was innocent of the intergalactic terrorism charges had been bullshite, and this was the IPC's way of capturing his entire crew at once. Either way, this had come together like a hooker on a planet-leave soldier, quick and easy.

Callan handed him the fake coffee. "Did your IPC friend have any luck?"

"He says he can get what we need."

"But you don't believe him." Callan took a gulp from his mug, not seeming the least bit surprised. Of course, he trusted any IPC officer about as much as a rat in a cargo hold full of food stores.

"What I believe doesn't count for shite. Cold hard facts are worth their weight in Violaine." He took a mouthful of his repli-coffee, the brew bitter and scalding hot, but with the usual not-quite-coffee taste the fake stuff had.

"So what are you going to do?" Callan took another sip, then made a face and dumped the rest of his drink down the drain.

That was the million-credit question. How did he play this? Because if his old buddy were innocent and being used by the Reidar or IPC, he didn't deserve to get smashed. On the small chance it was legit, he didn't want to screw up the single thing that had gone his way in recent times.

"I think the best thing to do would be to invite Colt out here for another chat, to pick some berries, and enjoy this frecking quaint little cabin we've found ourselves."

Callan shot him a grin. "Yeah, it's all quiet and remote-like. I'm sure he'll have a great time."

Rian sent Colt a short message saying he was eager to take possession of the shipment, but wanted to organize the particulars in person. If Colt made a big deal about not being able to spare an hour to fly out to Forbes, if he insisted on arranging a time and place immediately, there was a good chance this was a trap.

Each passing day, it seemed like his list of enemies grew exponentially, with more and more people he'd known getting lost in this frecking war he didn't even want to be fighting. If Colt turned out to be one of those victims, maybe it was finally time to reconsider just what the freck he was doing and how much more this had to cost before he was done.

# Chapter Eighteen

Breaking into Tannin's childhood home didn't turn out to be as difficult or exciting as Kira had thought it would be. He'd already circumvented most of the security system on their first visit, so when they arrived back in front of the huge gates, it was just a matter of him logging in to the program and shutting down everything from silent alarms to cameras. After that, he opened the gates and they simply strolled up the long driveway and through the front door.

Tannin had set himself up at the crystal display in his father's office, while the rest of them settled in an adjoining room in front of a large viewer screen, watching different programs before Lianna flicked it over to a movie.

At first, Kira found it uncomfortable and weird to be sitting in someone else's home watching TV and snacking while Tannin hacked all kinds of government systems in the next room. She'd been sure the authorities would turn up at any minute to arrest them. Yet, as the hours crept by, well into the middle of the night, she'd slowly relaxed and started thinking about other things—mainly Varean.

He was worried about the tests—understandably so. Truthfully, it was grating her nerves as well. Not because of what they might divulge, but how Varean would take it and what he'd do after that. Commandos had no fear of death, and he'd certainly proven that.

While she'd come to terms with the fact that there was no version of a future where she would see him again once they went their separate ways, she'd realized she could deal with it as long as she knew Varean was alive somewhere in the universe. If he discovered the Reidar had done something to him and went on some sort of suicidal quest to find out when and how, or to get revenge, he'd more than likely end up dead.

And the thought of a galaxy without him left her aching and cold, like someone had rammed an icicle through her chest. Kind of like the desolate look he'd gotten in his gaze back at the bar, the one that told her he couldn't see any kind of outcome for himself besides despair and death.

He didn't owe her anything. Nevertheless, she was becoming more and more desperate to make sure that whatever happened after the test results came in, he didn't rush off and get himself killed. She just had no idea how to convince him.

The movie credits started rolling, and she blinked, stretching her arms above her head. She couldn't have said what happened in the film, she'd been too caught up in her thoughts. She glanced over to find Lianna had fallen asleep in one of the recliners, while Zahli had disappeared into the office where Tannin was working. The low murmur of their voices floated through the open doorway, though she couldn't quite make out what they were talking about.

Varean reached over and snagged the remote, switching the channel and lowering the volume. Pushing to her feet, she stretched a little more, feeling stiff all over. She crossed the hall to the bathroom and splashed water on her face. Tannin didn't seem like he'd be finishing anytime soon, so maybe she could take a cue from Lianna and get some shut-eye. The way things were going, she had no idea when they might get any more downtime.

When she stepped out of the bathroom, she found Varean leaning against the opposite wall, one boot kicked over the other with his arms crossed.

"Sorry, I wouldn't have taken so long if I'd known anyone else was there." She gestured back toward the bathroom, indicating he could go in.

"I was waiting for you." He pushed up from the wall and stepped toward her, running a hand over his already disheveled short hair, messing it up even more. "I've been thinking about things for the last few hours and I need to know, whatever the tests show, you'll let me walk when it's time to go."

She opened her mouth to reply, but he held up a hand. "I know you said if it turns out the Reidar did some kind of experiment on me, the best place to get answers is on the *Imojenna*. Aside from the fact that you left the ship somewhere in another system, I don't trust Rian or Callan, which makes it hard to live in close quarters. Plus, for all I know, Rian will still want to lock me up if he finds out I've been messed with by his mortal enemies."

She wanted to argue, but instead took a short breath. She couldn't blame him for not trusting Rian and Callan after what they'd put him through. But after Rian's experiences with the aliens, he couldn't justify locking Varean up.

She crossed her arms over her middle, a low wave of apprehension swelling in her stomach. "What will you do?"

"Honestly, I don't know. I can't go back into the IPC military knowing half of the commanding officers are probably shape-shifting aliens. I suppose I could rejoin the *Swift Brion*, but—it's probably totally stupid to say—I don't feel like that person any longer."

"It's not stupid at all." She closed the distance between them, setting her hand on his arm, apparently unable to help touching him, the instinct to comfort him driving her beyond logic.

His gaze roamed her face as though trying to work something out. "Actually, what's stupid is, despite everything, I wouldn't change a second of it because I got to meet you."

Her heart leaped like she was fifteen and it was the first time a boy had told her he liked her. She couldn't have picked a worse time to decide she was going to free-fall over someone. If she was smart, she wouldn't let things go any further, because it would make it that much harder at the inevitable end. Yet, she wanted everything of him she could get while she had the chance.

"You're going to leave. Probably tomorrow." She said the words more to keep herself in check.

He nodded, gaze becoming grim. "Yes, I am."

"I was thinking of getting some sleep. It's most likely going to be a long day."

"It's probably a good idea," he replied in a banal tone.

How had she ended up here all of a sudden, not knowing what to say to him, their conversation edging toward awkward?

"Okay, well—" She went to take a step, but Varean grabbed her upper arms and before she could work out his intention, his mouth found hers. His hands cupped her face as he plunged them into a decadent kiss without any warning.

She pressed up against him, one arm around his shoulders and the other hand finding his hair as she returned the kiss with all the desperation she'd been trying to push down in the past few hours.

But just as she was ready to lose herself in the way his mouth consumed her, he pulled back a fraction, breaking the kiss on an uneven breath.

"Kira, my life is in pieces and I don't know who I am anymore. I can't give you anything except for a good-bye tomorrow."

For all the perfectly logical reasons she'd given herself not to do this, not to let herself fall any further, now she couldn't remember a single one of them.

"I know. I can see what's coming. But I don't need anything except you right now."

"Thank god." The words were murmured against her lips as he tightened his arms around her and dragged them right back into the heady kiss.

He tugged her backward and she went with him, slamming through the nearest door into a dimmed room where he spun them and pushed her up against the wall. As his mouth left hers to kiss a frantic path down her neck, she took a second to glance up, finding they'd ended up in what looked like a library, shelves covering the walls with countless old-fashioned books and other items displayed, two lamps on a couple of low, small tables the only light.

But then Varean's hand closed over her breast, squeezing lightly, and even with all her clothes on, the sensation was enough to make her close her eyes on a shudder. His hand shifted from her breast to the edge of her shirt, slipping underneath and skimming across her overheated flesh. A second hand joined the first, and then her shirt lifted, disappearing, leaving welcome, cool air swirling over her skin.

His mouth found hers again, firm and insistent against her lips, leaving no doubt where he wanted to take things. After their little caper on the skimmer, she'd craved more, but forced the need to the back of her thoughts behind the other pressing issues they faced. However, now that she'd let her guard down, made the decision that she'd give and take everything in the short time they had, the smolder of longing roared up through her, leaving nothing but a fine, light ash in its wake.

She pushed up his T-shirt, and he oh-so-obligingly helped by taking over and yanking the garment off one-handed, tossing it aside, and then his hands were on her again. This time, he caressed his way to her upper thighs, where he gripped her and lifted her against him.

Wrapping her legs around his hips, her breath caught when he eased her onto the nearest couch. The cushions gave way as he lowered his weight on top of her, lips skimming across the top of her chest while he tugged at the clasp of her bra.

In a blur of half breaths and light, teasing strokes, the rest of their clothes disappeared and when Varean pressed naked against her, a deep shiver of anticipation rocked her all the way to her soul. He was hard, heavy, and hot all over, but she didn't feel trapped or intimidated, instead she relished the secure, delicious feel of him on top of her.

His lips and hands moving over her had slowed, become measured, almost reverential with every breath he took.

"You're so damn beautiful," he murmured against her collarbone. "I don't deserve this, not when I'm going to walk away from you."

She set her hand against his jaw, forcing him to look up at her, astonished at the weight of emotion she saw in his gaze.

"It is what it has to be, and I don't think either of us deserves that, but I don't want to think about tomorrow."

She pulled him toward her, and this time when their lips met, it wasn't with the same desperate burn of what they couldn't have. Instead, it was slow, tender, filled with the knowledge that this was right in a way nothing else in her life had been for a very long time.

Varean sighed, as if he was letting go of the last thread of conflict holding out against this. His hips pressed in closer and she welcomed him, widened her legs and sucked in a breath as his hardness came up against her core. Her fingers dug into his shoulders as he set himself at her entrance and then pushed in by slow gradual degrees until she wanted to scream with frustration.

But then he was inside her, and the sensation of him filling her was beyond description, so amazing and complicated and consuming everything that she'd felt before, replacing it with something deeper and more brilliant.

He rocked back, and she tilted her hips to meet him, altering the angle of his thrust from good to somewhere around the level of mind-blowing. She bit her lip on crying out, even as he groaned low in her ear, as though the slight shift had been just as good for him.

The next thrust came shorter and harder, and the urge to moan long and loud was almost too hard to resist. But Varean saved her, catching her mouth beneath his on the next reckless plunge, taking the cry she couldn't hold back.

She was lost, but she didn't care and let herself go, Varean her only reality. The detonation came sudden and intense even though she'd been expecting it. She couldn't breathe, but it didn't matter, as she shot into the stratosphere and burst into a shower of stars, powdering the darkness with a million pinpricks of brilliant, twinkling light.

Varean groaned her name on a shuddering breath, pinning her into the cushions with one last explosive piston of his hips, filling her with swelling, rolling waves of delirious aftershocks.

With a long, ragged exhale, he dropped against her; the weight of him relaxing into her was beyond gratifying as she, too, sank boneless and replete into the couch.

Only a few seconds had gone by before she felt him

tensing.

"No, don't move, you're not too heavy, I promise." She tightened her arms around him, not ready to give up the sated glow of the moments after.

"It's not that." He secured her more firmly to him, gently rolling them off the couch, onto the floor, so she ended up on top of him. She let her cheek rest on his chest, as he smoothed a hand over her no-doubt tangled hair.

"Then you better not be feeling guilty. I told you, I wanted this and I don't regret it. I never will."

For a moment he was silent, the steady stroke of his hand mesmerizing, lulling her toward the sleep she'd been thinking about earlier.

"I grew up in the foster system. My mom died when I was too young to remember her, and I had no other family. I never got adopted, and the longest I was ever in one place was about two years."

Her breath caught at the sudden avalanche of information, and she went totally still, desperate to hear what he'd say next, unable to imagine not having a family or home. Was that why he'd been such a successful commando, why he didn't value his life, because no one else had? Her heart ached for him, and in that moment, she wanted nothing more than to wrap her arms around him and never let go until he realized he was worth everything.

"It probably sucked compared to having a normal childhood, but I never knew any different, and once I got too old for the system and they kicked me over, I bounced to the military. It gave me a place to sleep, regular meals, and something to do with my life. In all the years I've been old enough to understand the concept of regret, I've never wished for anything to be different."

He seemed to run out of words after that, and for a long moment, silence stretched between them. But she'd never been one for tiptoeing around things.

"And now?" She tensed, worried about what his answer would be. Did he regret what they'd just done?

But his hands moved to smooth up and down her back in calming strokes, and she relaxed against him.

"I don't regret us, Kira. But for the first time, I am wishing things could be different."

He didn't elaborate further, but he didn't need to, because she was feeling the same thing.

. . .

Varean ducked his head out of the room, glancing up and down the hallway before stepping out with a light tread. Kira followed a moment later, shooting him a small, intimate smile then disappearing into the bathroom.

He took a second to tug his borrowed clothes straight— the damn things didn't fit him all that well, plus they'd dressed quickly, not wanting any of the others to realize they'd both been missing for a while now.

When he returned to the main room, he found Lianna still dozing in front of the viewer. He sat down and flipped through a few channels disinterestedly.

Maybe he should feel bad things had gone so far between them when they both knew he had to walk away in the next few hours. But she'd said she accepted their fate, the same as he had. And finding contentment in each other for that short amount of time had been something he wouldn't ever regret.

"Where's Kira?"

Varean glanced over his shoulder to find Zahli standing in the doorway of the room Tannin had been using.

"Bathroom, I think."

Gun in hand, Tannin appeared next to his fiancée a second later, checking the power chamber, his expression taut.

Battle-honed instincts flipping on like a flare, Varean put down the remote and pushed to his feet.

"What's going on?"

Tannin slipped the gun away, glancing at Zahli, who sent him a confident nod, and now that he was standing, he could see she gripped her own pulse pistol.

"We've got company. Someone sneaking around in the yard," Tannin replied.

"What's the plan?" he asked as Kira came back into the room.

Zahli stepped forward and shook Lianna's shoulder, rousing her, then turning off the nearby lamp.

"We're going to find out who it is and what they're doing." As he said the words, Tannin moved over to the window, inching the curtains aside to look out while Zahli filled Lianna in.

"Maybe we should just leave." Apprehension replaced the contented expression Kira had had when he'd been alone with her. He wanted to cross the room, wrap an arm around her, and tell her everything would be fine. Except now was definitely not the time to be distracted by her.

Tannin turned from the window, shaking his head. "We can't go yet. I still haven't found Quaine. I've got a few leads, but I need the next few hours until the house staff turn up."

Lianna nodded her chin toward the room Zahli and Tannin had emerged from. "You get back to it, then. Zahli and I will take care of the intruder."

Tannin crossed the room, pausing to kiss Zahli. "Be careful."

She murmured an agreement as he continued back toward the crystal display screen in the study.

"Kira, you and the commando stay here. I don't want to shoot either of you by mistake…" Lianna paused. "Actually, him I don't care about. But we need our doc, so keep out of trouble."

A familiar pulse of frustration flared within him, the same one he'd had countless times since encountering the aggravating crew of the *Imojenna*.

"As hilarious as I find your lack of concern, why don't you let me come? I can take this guy down before he even knows anyone is here."

Lianna bristled, her stance tightening as her hand landed pointedly on the butt of her gun.

"And you don't think a couple of *girls* can do the same thing?"

The irritation burned hotter. It was really starting to get on his nerves how she had decided to hate his guts without reason.

"No, that's not what I'm saying. This is what I'm trained to do, and if it were Rian and his gorilla standing here, I'd probably suggest the same thing."

Lianna's tenacious expression didn't alter. "Well Rian and *Callan* aren't here, and that leaves me in charge. You're not crew, and I don't know you. So do us all a favor and stay out of the way."

Zahli got between them. "And while we're standing here arguing, the intruder is doing who-knows-what. Lieutenant Captain, I appreciate you wanting to help, but you understand why it would be better to stay here. Besides, someone needs to stand guard while Tannin is working, and no offense, Kira, that's obviously not you."

Though he was well aware Zahli was pandering to his *delicate* soldier ego, offering him the runner-up-bitch award of "guarding" Tannin against the solitary intruder who would probably turn out to be some lowlife burglar taking advantage of the offline security, he backed off and sent her a nod of agreement.

That apparently settled, Zahli and Lianna hurried from

the room. He turned on his heel and headed into the office where Tannin was working.

"You got security feed of the intruder?"

Tannin didn't glance up from whatever he was doing, but pointed to one of the three screens he was working with. "Here."

Varean moved partway around the desk to get a better view, Kira coming up beside him. And while Tannin was still running some kind of program that seemed to be searching a database, his attention was mostly focused on the person jimmying a door in the kitchen.

On the inside, Zahli and Lianna were taking up covert positions. Didn't seem like much of a fair fight—the intruder wouldn't know what hit him. Lianna already had her pulse pistol out and steadied across the edge of the bench. She'd no doubt stun him unconscious as soon as the door swung shut behind him.

However, burglary couldn't have been this guy's regular gig, because it seemed to take forever before he got the lock undone. And the first thing he did when he got inside was trip over a bucket of cleaning products the staff had probably left for the morning shift, sending him stumbling into the bench and knocking off an empty vase to shatter, the noise echoing through the otherwise silent house.

On the screen, Zahli and Lianna exchanged a short glance, which he imagined was probably filled with the same exasperated puzzlement both Kira and Tannin had on their faces.

A nanosecond later, Lianna squeezed off a round, hitting the intruder dead center of his chest. He staggered a step and then fell back, half landing in the broken glass of the vase.

As his head flopped to the side, giving a clear view of his face to the security feed, Tannin suddenly shot to his feet.

"Goddamn!" Tannin bolted out of the room.

Kira followed, so Varean fell into step behind her as they hustled to the kitchen. By the time they arrived, Tannin was kneeling next to the fallen intruder, lightly slapping him on the cheek.

"Jase. *Jase.* Come on man, bring it around."

The man groaned but didn't look like he was going to wake right away. Getting knocked unconscious by a pulse pistol blast hurt like a bitch. Some people could come right out of it, especially if they'd been hit by one before. But if a person wasn't used to it, they could take up to half an hour to rouse from the stupor.

Tannin glanced at Lianna. "Help me get him up."

"Who is he?" she demanded instead. Varean skirted around Kira and went over to the fallen man's side. As he took the guy's arm, Tannin shot him a grateful look.

"His name is Jase Nevan. He's a guard from Erebus. He was the closest thing I had to a friend the entire twelve years I was there."

"He's an IPC officer?" Lianna half brought her pulse pistol up as though she was considering hitting him with a second shot, which would definitely kill the guy.

"He was last time I saw him, but he's not wearing a uniform now." Tannin huffed the words as the two of them carried Jase toward the stairs. "Let's not jump to any conclusions until I can talk to him."

They took the man back to the room they'd been occupying and laid him out on the couch.

"Is this really a good idea?" Zahli's voice held a deep note of concern as she flicked the lamps back on to brighten the room. "The IPC think you're dead. That was your ticket to staying out of Erebus. Once this guy knows you're alive—"

Tannin cupped Zahli's cheek. "He won't tell anyone. We can trust him."

"You can trust him all you want"—Lianna took up a

stance next to the couch, pulse pistol still in hand—"but I'm not taking that risk. Don't forget, we're still wanted for intergalactic terrorism."

Tannin stepped into her line of fire. "Jase isn't a typical IPC military droid. He was my friend, and he won't betray me."

As Lianna glared at Tannin, Varean tugged on Kira's arm to get her attention.

"Tannin was on Erebus. As a prisoner?"

Kira nodded, keeping an eye on the pair facing off.

"Then how is he free? No one escapes and lives to talk about it."

"It's a long story," Kira replied in a low voice. "Suffice to say, Rian decided he was useful. And so far, I've never seen Rian fail at anything. Tannin is the only person ever to escape Erebus successfully, but he couldn't have done it if Rian hadn't agreed to help. Somehow, Rian rigged the system so the authorities think Tannin died on Erebus."

Before Kira could expand or Tannin and Lianna argue further, Jase started coming around with a muttered curse, reaching down to clamp a hand on his side.

Kira quickly brushed by Zahli and knelt on the floor next to him.

"Are you injured?" She pulled a small med scanner from her pocket and held it up in front of his forehead, concentrating on the readings that flashed up on the small inset screen.

"Feels like it," Jase replied in a hoarse voice, still a little groggy. "My side."

Kira reached down and gently moved his hand, his fingers coming up covered in blood.

"He must have caught some glass from the broken vase when he fell. Tannin, would there be a med kit somewhere in this house?"

"*Tannin*?" Jace surged up, becoming lucid in a second flat.

Kira set a firm hand on his upper arm before he could get up. "I really need to check your wound."

"Zahli, you'll find a med kit in the bathroom on the ground floor," Tannin instructed, then moved around Kira to crouch in front of Jase.

What little color the man had washed out of his face, leaving him looking on the verge of passing out again.

"Holy jezus above. It really is you." Jase gripped Tannin's shoulder, as if he needed to anchor himself to the guy to make sure he was real. "They told me you were dead. I saw a body."

"Sorry, Jase. But being dead was the only way I could stay free." Tannin stretched out a hand and returned the guy's shoulder hold, then they grinned at each other and followed through with a hug.

"Seriously," Jase exclaimed as he sat back again. "I can't believe you're alive. And *free*. Mind blown."

Kira shifted to elbow Tannin out of the way. "Now that the reunion hugs are all done, you mind if I do something about your friend bleeding all over the place?"

Tannin shifted sideways and sat on the couch next to Jase as Kira lifted his shirt to examine the wound.

"Looks like there might be a shard of glass still in there," Kira mumbled, seemingly more to herself.

Zahli returned with the med kit, crossing the room and handing it to Kira.

"What are you doing here?" Tannin asked Jase as Kira rummaged through the kit and came up with a pair of tweezers.

"I came to tell your parents that you'd died and give them the few possessions you left behind. Except they full-on did not give a shite. They refused to even see me. Which kind of pissed me off." Jase winced as Kira gave no warning before going in with the tweezers and plucking the bloodied shard free. "I know you told me they disowned you, but talk about heartless. Anyway, I came earlier to see if they were back from being abroad yet and noticed the security system was down—"

"And then decided a spot of B and E was just the thing?" Lianna interjected.

Jase shoved his hand into his pocket and pulled out an envelope. "I was just going to leave this in the old man's office. It's all they kept when Tannin was indentured."

Kira swapped out the tweezers for a small multifunction remedial device with a fine laser to close the wound.

"But I left months ago. Why come now? And what about your post on Erebus?" Tannin asked, taking the envelope Jase held out and slipping it away without even looking at it.

Jase made a grunt of pain when Kira set the MRD against his skin. "Maybe I asked too many questions about your death. I mean, in all the years I'd known you, when did you ever pick a fight, let alone one bloody enough to get you killed? It wasn't the first time I'd been reprimanded for putting my nose where it didn't belong. Guess I'm not the kind of guy to take orders without thinking about the why behind them. They offered to put me on box duty, but I declined with a very polite *screw you guys* and then resigned my commission with the IPC."

"And came here with Tannin's possessions to give to his parents," Zahli finished. "That was very considerate of you."

"Despite being a prisoner, Tannin was my best friend. I knew he wasn't guilty and hadn't deserved anything that'd happened to him. I thought making that last contact with his parents was the least I could do. I couldn't believe his parents would repeatedly refuse to see me, unless there was something else going on." He glanced back at Tannin. "What are you doing here?"

"Looking for Quaine Ayden."

Both of Jase's eyebrows hiked up. "Quaine Ayden, who killed your friend and framed you for the murder?"

Tannin's expression shifted into a grim kind of rueful. "Turns out that wasn't what happened. Quaine's father was behind the murder. After I got free and started poking around into things, it flushed out Quaine, who'd had a falling out with his old man over the whole thing. He came back here looking for answers and disappeared. So we're looking to find out what happened to him."

Jase nodded, passing a glance around the room. "Looks like you made quite an interesting bunch of new friends since you left Erebus."

Tannin glanced at Zahli, a spark of amusement in his gaze. "You can't imagine the half of it."

Kira removed the MRD and took a piece of gauze to wipe away the last of the blood. "All done."

"Thanks." Jase stretched out his arm, grimacing a little as though it had pulled. "And about Quaine Ayden. I might have a clue for you."

# Chapter Nineteen

The low trill of the commpad near his face roused Rian out of the red-wine-laced doze he'd fallen into. He batted at the noise, sending his comm clunking to the floor. But it didn't stop the trilling and, with an annoyed curse, he half rolled on the couch, groping for wherever the stupid thing had landed. His hand knocked into the two bottles of wine he'd put down trying to escape the lingering prickle under his skin from the run-in with Ella, and the gnawing cold belief that however things went down with Colt, it wasn't going to end well.

He finally got fingers on the comm and grabbed it, cracking his eyes open to glare at the screen. Colt messaged that he was about to leave Dunham and would be there in half an hour.

He dragged a hand across his face, rubbing away the last dark vestiges of the usual dreams he had no matter how lightly he slept. The room was dim, the only illumination slicing in from an adjoining hallway while the low familiar drawl of Callan's voice, followed by Jensen answering, came from the kitchen.

Sitting up, he shoved his hair off his forehead, taking a moment to put the creeping darkness that always rose with the dreams back into the dungeon in the lowest pit of his consciousness.

Once he was about as stable as he ever got, he shoved to his feet and went into the brighter hall, blinking as his eyes adjusted to the light. In the kitchen, Sen and Callan were playing cards, while in another room that opened out past the bench, Nyah and Ella were watching something on the viewer. Outside, night had well and truly fallen.

"Colt will be here in half an hour," he said to no one in particular as he went to the coldstore and pulled out a bottle of water. He twisted off the lid and set to downing the icy contents in a few long swallows.

"Do we need some kind of contingency for that?" Callan asked, throwing his cards on the table, apparently losing the hand to Sen.

"I hope not." He crumpled the empty bottle and dropped it in the waste chute. But he still felt sticky, felt like his clothes were too tight, like something was trying to break free of his skin. "I'm going to hit the shower before he gets here."

He didn't wait for anyone to answer, leaving the room with an even stride, good at pretending like nothing in the hell was going on with him, when really it was all he could do not to run as far and fast as he could until he collapsed into nothingness.

Finding the bathroom, he released a long breath of pent-up tension as he stepped in and stripped his clothes like he couldn't get them off fast enough. He lurched into the shower and tabbed on the cold water to high, letting the chill hit his almost fevered skin until he had his shite more together.

Shutting the water off again, he flipped a towel around his

hips and started toward the door but paused as he reached it. A light trickle of energy passed over his skin like a shiver, and he knew without a doubt Ella was out in the hallway, coming closer and pausing outside the door, even though it hadn't been her intended destination.

He wanted her to keep walking, to continue toward the bedroom he somehow knew she'd been heading for. But then he was reaching out, twisting the handle, and pulling the door open to find her standing near the opposite wall, stance relaxed and expression serene as always. Except now, he got the feeling the seemingly unperturbed countenance of the Arynian priestess was nothing but a façade.

"When you first came onboard my ship, you were determined to help me, even though I didn't want it."

Something that could have been surprise flashed through her eyes as she nodded, but it didn't last, leaving him unable to read her, as usual.

"I thought that was why I ended up on the *Imojenna*, that it was my destiny."

He stepped out of the doorway, but kept a good few feet between them. He didn't need another demonstration of what happened when they got within touching distance.

"And now?"

She glanced away. "Now, I am reminding myself of my teachings, of what is expected of me as an Arynian."

He crossed his arms, muscles tightening on a wave of dissatisfaction. "That tells me absolutely shite-all, and you know it."

She snapped her gaze back to him, the light of something nearly fanatical kindling in her gaze. "Do you *want* help, Rian?"

The direct question cut through him like a red-hot blade, burning and slashing in equal measure, laying him open and leaving him blackened. No one had ever actually asked him if he wanted help…well, not the kind of help Ella meant.

And he didn't. What was the point when he couldn't be fixed? There was no salvation for him and the things he'd done. Only a merciful death once he'd found his bloody vengeance.

"That's what I thought." She turned away from him and walked the rest of the way down the hall, not looking back as she stepped into a bedroom and closed the door.

He hadn't realized until this second that, since Ella had come aboard, a small part of his old self had been partly revived, and maybe that was why he loathed having her around as much as she intensely fascinated him. But with the knowledge that she really had given up on him substantiated, he got the sense of that last shred falling away. The hollow numbness returned, but this time he didn't welcome it.

• • •

Rian waited down the block from the spaceport where they'd left the skimmer that morning, sipping an expensive cup of real coffee as he waited for Colt to arrive. Shortly after his weak moment with Ella, a comforting sense of the usual low-simmering rage had reignited, leaving him on familiar, manageable ground.

He'd left everyone else at the cottage to pick up Colt, since they were about as safe there as they could be anywhere that wasn't the *Imojenna*.

There weren't many people on the street; it was edging toward midnight, and while there was a trendy, late night café nearby, this clearly wasn't a restaurant or club district. Most of the shops were dark and closed, only a handful of couples and small groups of people walking the block.

When Colt turned the far corner leading from the spaceport, Rian pushed off from the sign he'd been leaning against.

Colt gave a short wave with his free arm, other hand carrying a rucksack.

"Evening," Rian greeted as they got within speaking distance. He nodded toward the bag. "Decided to stay a few days to pick some berries after all, huh?"

Colt sent him a grin, switching the bag to his opposite hand. "Decided to take a few days, yeah, but not to pick goddamn berries."

"Let's get on with business then." He led Colt to the aerocar he'd hired and set off in the general direction of the cottage. They didn't make much in the way of conversation during the trip or the walk after they left the aerocar some ways off from the cottage in case anyone was tracking it.

The silence was partly because he was never exactly chatty at the best of times, but it was also a test to see if Colt seemed nervous or on edge. People who were anxious often got more so when left to their own thoughts. But Colt was easy, as if he didn't have a care in the world. Which he probably didn't, the lucky son of a bitch.

Back at the cottage, Jensen, Ella and Nyah were nowhere to be seen, likely in bed, while Callan greeted them at the door with a hard, jaded expression and kitted up with a few more weapons than usual, probably because they weren't on the ship. Plus, Callan had trust issues the size of a flagship.

Rian did the introductions and then led Colt into the kitchen to sit at the table still littered with the containers of takeout they'd had earlier in the evening. He hadn't eaten anything himself then, more interested in downing those ineffective bottles of red wine. He picked through a few of the wrappers and boxes until he found a burger and cold fries.

"Leftovers?" He held a second, half-empty carton of fries out toward Colt, who was in the process of dropping his rucksack just inside the doorway.

His old buddy waved him off, and with a shrug, he turned

to reheat the food.

"So you said in your message you could get a regular supply of what we needed. Got to say I was a bit surprised. I thought a single shipment would be hard enough to come by and would take you days, if not weeks."

Colt pulled a chair for himself and sat down. "Maybe for most people. But you remember my brother, Arlo? These days, he's working in military munitions and supplies. You wouldn't believe the amount of perfectly good merchandise that gets junked because of all kinds of reasons like oversupply or shipping damage."

Rian studied Colt closely, but saw nothing except a genuine offer in his open expression. Jezus, had he actually stumbled onto a stroke of luck for a change instead of getting bitch-slapped by it like usual?

"And Arlo can send it to us without anyone knowing?"

Colt nodded confidently. "Once Arlo strikes supplies as unusable, he nominates a vetted company to dispose of it. That's the only thing we've got to get around. If you've got some way to get a ship or crew cleared to handle sensitive IPC materials, then you've got as much as possible of whatever you need coming your way."

Rian glanced over his shoulder where his very own universal-class forger stood behind him. "Callan?"

"Consider it done. Just point me in the direction of a ship."

"We obviously can't use the *Imojenna* or Qae's *Ebony Winter*. Besides the fact we've temporarily misplaced the *Imojenna*, either of them would be recognized in any kind of IPC depot."

"We could repurpose one of the *Swift Brion*'s shuttles," Callan suggested. "Hull works, rip out the guts, the whole pimp-out."

"Good plan. I'll comm Zander and give him the heads-up. He should be in the Barbary Belt by now."

Colt was clearly taking in the exchange with unconcealed interest. "None of that made any sense, unless we've somehow slipped into an alternate universe where you're working with one of the IPC's most wanted marauders. Not to mention Graydon taking the *Swift Brion* into the Barbary Belt? That can't have been sanctioned. Rene Blackstone will blast the flagship into space debris well before they get within spitting distance."

Callan shifted to brace both hands against the surface of the table and leaned forward slightly. "He knows too much. You want me to take him out to the woods and kill him all quiet-like? I'm sure he'll make great fertilizer for next year's berries."

Colt tensed, hand dropping below the line of the table, presumably for a weapon.

With a shrug, Rian turned and took out his reheated leftovers. "I dunno, you think he's worth the ammo? He said it himself. Who's going to believe Zander is taking the *Swift Brion* into the Barbary Belt?"

"Pretty sure the IPC brass will, once they realize Graydon took the entire crew and the flagship AWOL," Callan replied conversationally. "And Colt here could tell them all about how it was Rian Sherron's idea."

Colt shoved to his feet. "You're shamming me, right?"

Rian shoveled a handful of fries in his mouth and chewed thoughtfully.

"About which part? Callan wanting to quiet-kill you, or Zander stealing the *Swift Brion*?"

But Colt didn't seem to be fully listening, realization dawning in his expression. "I heard a report just before I left. The IPC had lost all contact with the *Swift Brion* after a scheduled stop at the Beta Seven Waystation. They were scrambling to find some trace, going on the assumption they'd been attacked or suffered some kind of catastrophic accident.

But now you're saying—"

"Nothing happened to them," Rian confirmed around a mouthful of burger. "They went off the grid on purpose."

"Zander Graydon *stole a flagship*?" Colt ran a hand back and forth over his short hair, almost looking dazed. "Holy mother of jezus, what the freck is going on around here?"

Rian yanked out the chair across from his buddy and sat down, putting aside his half-eaten food. "Look, Colt, I really need this thing with Arlo to go my way. I want to trust you and need to know that you trust me."

"That's a complicated question to ask considering I haven't seen you for over five years, you're a wanted intergalactic terrorist, and I just found out you've got something to do with Zander Graydon stealing an entire frecking IPC flagship."

Rian clasped his hands together on the tabletop, leaning forward a little. "Actually, if you put all of that aside and remember that once you were like an older brother to me, it's not complicated at all. It's simple. Do you trust me, Colter?"

For a long, weighted moment, Colt stared at him, no doubt recalling those early years when he'd been nothing but an oblivious, runaway rich kid who thought joining the IPC and going to war would solve the problems in his life, not completely destroy it.

Colt released a harsh breath and dropped back into his chair. "Okay, yeah, I trust you."

"Then before you leave here, we've got to have a conversation. But first, I want to organize that shipment."

# Chapter Twenty

Kira covertly studied the latest complication in their already convoluted situation. Jase Nevan had caramel-toned skin, dark hair and eyes, possibly a number of different heritages mixed into his family bloodline so that it was hard to pinpoint any one in particular.

After announcing he might have a clue about Quaine Ayden, Tannin had led them all into the office where he'd been working, while Lianna kept close, looking nothing short of suspicious.

"Don't you think we need to clear him before we start taking his word on anything?" Lianna swapped the pulse pistol she'd been holding for the Reidar stunner.

Tannin glanced up as he sat behind the display screens. "Sure, whatever you think."

He was already tapping away before he'd even finished saying the words, not looking the least bit concerned his old prison pal might be Reidar. Despite how many years she'd spent on the *Imojenna* and had known about the Reidar, she still couldn't get her head around suspecting every single person they came across of really being a shape-shifting alien.

Jase had stopped next to the desk, stiffening when Lianna brought the razar up and aimed it in his direction. "Wait. What—"

Lianna squeezed off a round. The energy passed through him without any discernable effects, leaving him looking more than a little confused.

Kira let out the breath tightening her chest, not even realizing she'd been holding it. In these close quarters, she hated to think what would have happened if Jase had been an alien.

"What was that?" Jase looked down at Tannin, who had his attention on the screen in front of him.

"A security measure. Don't worry, you passed. Now tell me about what you saw."

Jase eyed Lianna for a second as if he thought maybe she was going to shoot him a third time while he wasn't looking then braced one hand on the desk and the other on the back of the chair Tannin sat in.

"This rough-looking guy came here a bunch of days in a row, demanding to see your father. Apparently refusing to see people is a thing with your dad. But this guy was pretty insistent for nearly a week. I don't know whether he got his meeting, but he stopped turning up, and I haven't seen him since. I overheard one of the staff say he was a childhood friend of the chancellor's son."

While Jase was talking, Tannin had taken to the house security archive files. "How long ago was this?"

"A week ago, maybe a bit more."

"That fits in with the timing." Tannin leaned a little closer to the screen, fingers moving in a blur as he accessed the stored footage. On the screen, an image came up of a man standing outside the gates. He had a mop of shaggy hair falling around his ears, well-worn but neat clothes, and the wiry muscled build of a laborer. From the angle, it was hard to see his face, so Tannin flicked through several different views until he found a clear one.

When the shot of his face came up, Tannin blew out a hard breath and sat back. "That's him. That's Quaine."

"What do you think he wanted with your father?" Zahli asked.

"I have no idea. But maybe we can find out."

Tannin dove back into the archives using some kind of facial recognition program to zero in on Quaine's face. "According to the logs, this is the last recorded image of him."

"Of him entering?" Lianna asked. "What about inside the house or leaving?"

Tannin worked at another screen. "No, nothing, and there's a whole chunk of archives missing. Which probably means someone deleted it, but the backup files are still here."

There was no audio, but on the screen, Chancellor Everette came out into the foyer to meet Quaine, not looking all that friendly. The chancellor led Quaine through the house into the very office they were all sitting in.

"Can we get audio, hear what they're saying?" Lianna asked, shifting closer, like they all had, watching Quaine and Tannin's father arguing.

Tannin shook his head. "I probably could find it and match it with the—"

He broke off when, on the screen, Quaine advanced across the room, clearly enraged, and attacked the chancellor. But he'd barely gotten within reaching distance when his father grabbed Quaine and brutally snapped his neck like it was a twig.

Jase made a low noise of surprise, while Tannin glanced away from the screen.

"Well…" Lianna cleared her throat. "That was unexpected."

Tannin reached out and slapped off the footage, blanking all the screens, then shoving to his feet.

"My father killed Quaine. Guess at least now we know what happened to him." He paced a few steps away, clearly struggling with what he'd just witnessed.

"Did you see how fast he moved," Lianna said when no one else offered anything. "I don't think that was your father, Tannin."

Zahli stepped over to intercept Tannin's pacing. "This wasn't your fault, and you couldn't have saved him. None of us could have known—"

"That my father is Reidar?" Tannin gave a hollow laugh.

Zahli caught his hands, shifted closer, nothing but love and concern in her expression. "So maybe it wasn't really him who abandoned you all those years ago."

"And that's supposed to make me feel better?" Tannin ducked his head, but Kira caught the sheen in his eyes before he lowered them. She grabbed Varean's hand and tugged, nodding toward the door.

As they started making a hasty exit, both Lianna and Jase got a clue, following them out.

"Well that sucked," Jase announced as Lianna pulled the door shut. "But I need some blanks filled in. I thought the chancellor was Tannin's father, but now you're saying he's not? And what the hell is a Reidar?"

Lianna pulled out her comm, glancing at the screen. "Sorry, that's not a conversation I'm willing to have with you."

She held her comm up to her ear and turned away.

Jase looked to Varean and her, but before the baffled guy could even say a word, Varean held up both hands. "I'm not saying anything that'll risk me getting shot again. Technically, I'm their prisoner."

Jase's expression twisted into one of confused puzzlement, but he didn't reply as Lianna put her comm away and stepped closer.

"Rian sent a message. He's made some progress on the shopping list and wants us on Dunham's moon, Forbes, ASAP."

"What about the tests?" The words were out of Kira's mouth before she'd considered if she should bring it up at all, after this latest revelation and Rian's demand.

Lianna's expression turned tense, and for a second Kira thought she was going to renege on the deal. "How fast can you get them done?"

"With the right equipment, two hours." She clamped down on the urge to simply launch into an argument. Lianna was stubborn and one tough chick. Head-butting her in the face with a demand wouldn't get her anywhere.

"We still haven't heard from that friend of yours, the one you're relying on to get you into a lab." Her words weren't an accusation that her plan had failed, more a question about what it might mean without Mel's help.

"It would have been easier to get in with Mel organizing clearance, but Callan's forged med ident should hold up either way. I'll just have to talk my way in. It's the next best option."

At her last few words, the door opened, Zahli and Tannin emerging.

"Come on, let's get out of here," he said, his tone understandably grim, not waiting for anyone to answer as he headed for the corridor.

"What about Jase?" Lianna asked, making Tannin pause.

The ship's tech analyst glanced over his shoulder, eyes red-rimmed but no less resolute. "Bring him with us."

"Seriously?" Lianna muttered, as they left the house and stepped into a peach-colored dawn. "How many more strays are we going to take in?"

• • •

Despite the fact that she'd gotten nothing but silence in response to the message she'd sent Mel, the first thing Kira did when she got to the hospital was look up her old friend's private consulting rooms. Mel had ended up specializing in neonatal pediatrics and, as well as treating patients on the wards, also saw patients in her clinic.

It was still early as she led the others up three floors, the consulting rooms devoid of patients but lights on with doctors and nurses getting ready for the day's sessions.

When they reached Mel's rooms, she paused, surveying the group behind her, which now included Tannin's ex-IPC friend from Erebus, Jase, who was obviously curious about what he'd inadvertently landed in the middle of, but to his credit hadn't asked a single question since they'd left the house.

"You all mind waiting out here for a minute?"

Everyone agreed, taking seats along the corridor walls.

Tightening her grip on the container with Varean's blood, Kira continued into the office, half hoping that Mel wouldn't be in yet. She didn't want to get her old med school friend involved in this mess… But there was more to her reluctance than that.

Part of her was deeply worried she was about to find out Mel was no longer her friend, that the things she'd escaped when she'd joined the *Imojenna*'s crew had completely destroyed everything she'd left behind. Not that she ever planned on going back, but it left a gaping hole in her chest to think that everyone she'd ever known now hated and believed the worst of her.

There was no receptionist at the desk, so she went through the second waiting room and knocked firmly on the door.

An old familiar voice bade her to enter and, with a ripple

of apprehension, she stepped through.

Mel sat behind a neat desk, features freezing with surprise. She stood slowly when Kira stopped on the opposite side of the desk.

Mel hurried around the desk and pulled her into a tight hug. Kira returned the embrace fiercely, not realizing how much she'd missed her until that moment.

"I can't believe you're really here." Mel pulled back, but held on to her shoulders. "After you left Jacolby and no one knew what had happened to you, I didn't think I'd ever see you again."

"You probably wouldn't have, if I'd never had good reason to step foot on Barasa." Despite the hug and Mel's apparent happiness at seeing her, she still felt on edge. Mel hadn't answered her message, and every minute she spent in this hospital with the advanced security system came with the risk of her or the others being recognized.

"I never believed it, you know." Mel leaned closer, as if they were at risk of being overheard here, even though they were alone. "Everyone heard the whispers about Doctor Eon. I knew whatever happened, you weren't the one at fault."

Ice rippled beneath her skin at Mel's mention of Doctor Eon, and she crossed her arms, holding the case to her chest to clamp down a shiver. "I didn't come to talk about that."

Mel shifted away from her and sat in one of the two patient's chairs in front of the desk. "You need help. I read your message last night. I'm sorry I didn't reply right away. I was going to. Believe me, I didn't think about anything else all night. I just didn't know what to say."

She dropped into the other seat, sitting stiffly on the edge. "Because you didn't want to help me?"

Really, she couldn't have expected Mel to put her job and career on the line for a doctor who was both banned from practicing in the central systems and wanted for intergalactic terrorism.

Mel placed a warm hand over her own cold fingers.

"No, that wasn't it at all. I felt guilty I hadn't tried to find you or help you after what happened. I didn't know how I could ever apologize or make up for that. I was going to answer you today—it just took me a while to work up the courage."

Kira blew out a breath of relief, sagging into the chair. Hell, she'd been half convinced they'd have to make a quick getaway from the hospital without Varean's tests when Mel reported her to the authorities.

"You don't know how much it means to me that you didn't believe the news reports."

Mel made an indignant face. "Of course I didn't."

"So you'll help me?"

"What do you need?"

Kira straightened, running a hand over the smooth top of the case. "These blood samples I have, I need to run DNA and genetic sequencing on them."

"You want me to push them through the lab under my own name?" Mel started reaching for her commpad, but paused when she shook her head.

"The results might be…sensitive." Maybe that wasn't exactly the right word, but it was the best she could do right now. "I need to run the tests myself."

Mel sent her a half smile. "You took an interest in genetics since you left Jacolby? I seem to remember that sort of thing used to put you to sleep. You were more interested in the high-risk, innovative surgeries."

The smile she sent Mel in return was underlaid with the shared memories of her friend helping her get through the subjects and classes she found snooze-worthy, when all she wanted was to get into a hospital, get her hands dirty, and start saving lives.

"Not in the least. But this is important. *Really* important, so I can't leave it for anyone else to do."

Mel pushed to her feet and rounded her desk to face the inset display screen in the surface. "Let's find you a lab then."

Pulling the case closer to herself, and all but white-knuckling the handle, she shifted to the edge of the seat, while Mel worked in silence.

She was so close to being able to get the answers for Varean. The closer they became, the more he trusted her, the weightier her responsibility to help him find the truth. She'd been his one constant since they'd taken him off the *Swift Brion*—she couldn't fail him now. And considering the depths of her emotions for him, she'd no doubt feel the results almost as acutely as he would.

Whatever the tests revealed, it would change everything for Varean. It was almost like she held his future in her hands, and it was nothing but doom and disenchantment. Somehow, she had to make sure that wasn't his fate.

"Okay, I got you a free lab on the fifth floor. It's an entire pathology and screening unit that was closed down several months ago due to lack of funding. That entire half of the floor has been decommissioned, pending a review next year. You won't be disturbed."

Kira pushed to her feet as Mel took a blank ident card out of her desk and flipped it over to write on it. "Use these codes once you get on the elevator, and you won't trip any alarms."

"Thank you." The words didn't seem like enough as she took the card.

"It's the least I could do. Come and see me before you leave? I'll be here until at least eight tonight. Maybe we can get dinner."

She tucked the card into her pocket. "I can't stay that late, but I'll definitely come back and say good-bye before I leave."

Mel nodded, seeming a little disappointed. "Well, good

luck with those tests. Comm my office if you need anything."

Mel sent her a wave as Kira stepped out the door and quietly pulled it shut.

One more obstacle down.

# Chapter Twenty-One

Varean pushed to his feet as Kira emerged from the offices she'd disappeared into a few minutes ago, her expression far less tense than it had been since they'd come here.

"There's a vacant lab on the fifth floor we'll be able to use."

Her words sent an unexpected jolt of apprehension through him, the sensation unfamiliar and unwelcome. It had been a damned long time since he'd felt anxious about anything. Commandos were taught to fear nothing, and with nothing to lose in life, he'd been better at that aspect of training than others.

But getting that much closer to the truth stirred a kind of fear he'd never experienced, never considered could affect him—fear of himself.

If he were a different kind of person, he might have been running as far and fast from this as he possibly could. Found a dark corner of the universe to lose himself in and never face the light of reality again.

But the swell of trepidation instead made him want to

fight, probably a response conditioned into him by his military training. And that was fine; the instinct had kept him alive all his years in the IPC. Except he was fighting only himself.

Whatever the results revealed, they wouldn't change who he was, who he'd been, and what he'd done until now. Except the banality of those assurances sounded hollow.

They stepped out on the fifth floor, which was completely deserted and dimmed. Tannin accessed and looped the security feed in the lab so it would look like the room was empty if anyone happened to check. The ex-Erebus inmate had some serious tech skills, certainly coming in handy for these types of jaunts. He could see why Rian had deemed him useful enough to risk breaking him out of the infamous prison world.

Once they entered the lab, Kira visibly relaxed, clearly feeling at home surrounded by the medical equipment. She did a lap of the room, turning on lights, machines, and display screens, bringing the lab to animation in an almost indiscernible buzz of mechanical life.

A door opened into what turned out to be a staff room—a table with six chairs, a single small couch, and an empty fridge. Luckily the condiments dispenser was still connected to the hospital's main supply, and the others didn't waste any time helping themselves to the repli-coffee, tea, and juice.

Though he hadn't eaten much in the last twelve hours— only a few snacks at Tannin's parents' house—Varean didn't bother making himself anything. He did grab a juice for Kira, figuring her brain needed a sugar hit to work on whatever it was she planned on doing with his blood samples. He took the drink back into the lab as the others switched the viewer on and looked to be settling in for the next two hours.

Kira was already accessing some kind of program on one of the crystal screens, and while the case with his blood stood open, she hadn't done anything with the samples yet.

"Thanks," she said without looking as he set the juice on the desk next to her.

"So?" He shifted to the adjacent empty desk and hopped up to sit on it.

"So you might as well go hang out with the others. It's going to be at least two hours, if not longer." She still didn't look at him as she took one of the blood samples out and shifted to a nearby machine.

"What if I'd rather hang out here with you? The company might be better."

"The company will be busy. And if you distract me, this will take even longer." She turned from the machine to scrutinize him. "I know you're probably nervous about the results—"

"Nervous isn't quite the right word."

"Sorry. I'm sure the big tough AF commando never gets nervous about anything."

He caught a hand on her hip.

"I never said that." Tugging her closer, he lowered his head. "Truthfully, I'm petrified of what you're going to find out about me."

She cupped his face with both hands, expression taking on a tender edge. "Whatever the results are, we'll deal with it."

Her utter confidence that these tests weren't going to be that big a deal clashed into the knowledge that as soon as he had the truth he was walking away.

Closing the short distance, he caught her mouth beneath his, tasting the reprieve against the sins of his possibly Reidar-corrupted body only she could deliver. The kiss had a definite edge of somberness to it, as if maybe she knew as clearly as he did there was likely no help for him, no matter what she said.

He pulled back, taking in a choppy breath. "I appreciate you trying to soften it for me. But when this is done, I'm going to leave, and you're going to forget about me. You're smart enough to realize there's no other option."

There was a stubborn gleam in her gaze, but she nodded, not offering a single argument. Leaning up, she pressed a kiss onto his cheek and then returned to her work.

Despite the few short steps separating them, it felt like he'd already said good-bye.

• • •

Two hours later, Kira roused Varean from where he'd slipped into a very light combat nap on a nearby stool.

"Is it done?" He rolled his shoulders, feeling stiff from dozing upright.

"I've done my part, yeah. Now we have to wait for the computers to finish analyzing and compile the report. Hopefully it'll be ready in another fifteen or twenty minutes."

He crossed his arms, his brain clearing the remaining tendrils of sleep on a small spike of adrenaline. They were literally on countdown to getting the truth.

Kira sat on the stool next to him, pinning her hair back from her face where it had fallen loose while she'd been working. When she was done, she placed her hand on his knee.

"I don't want to scare you, but I want you to be prepared. From a few anomalies I've found, I'm already certain the results are going to confirm that at some point, you were altered on a genetic level." She had her doctor mask on as she said the words, the one she'd probably perfected while she'd worked out of a prestigious central systems hospital. However, he needed her to be more than just his doctor.

"I'm ready for it, Kira. But do me a favor, let's talk about something else until the results are in."

She nodded, a gleam of detached understanding in her gaze. "Okay, sure, what would you like to talk about?"

"I want you to tell me what happened to you, why you

got banned from practicing medicine in the central systems."

Surprise shoved the detached professionalism right off her gorgeous features. She audibly swallowed.

Glancing away from him, this time her distance was completely different.

"That's not something…" She took a deep breath and closed her eyes. "I've only ever told one person since it happened. Not even Rian knows the truth."

"I'm not trying to upset you, and I'm not asking because I think it's some trivial thing. Whatever it was, I can't believe you did anything wrong. I just want to know who I have to track down and kill for ruining your life after I leave here today."

She snapped her eyes open and stared at him with so much disbelief, it almost made him laugh. "You're kidding, right?"

He allowed himself a grin. "Mostly. Unless there really is someone you want me to take out. I would do it if you asked."

"No! Please. There's been enough death."

He traced a finger along her jaw. "You're a better person than I've ever been. I can't believe that, with everything you know, everything you've seen, you still have such a pure light of optimism in you."

"I'm stuck in the dark like everyone else."

He shook his head. "No, you're one of the ones who keeps the light burning for the rest of us poor damned souls."

She leaned in to his touch for a brief moment, then straightened, visibly preparing herself.

"We had a patient come in from a sister hospital that specialized in rehab and psychiatrics. While she was physically capable, able to understand and follow direction, years of drug use had made her paranoid, prone to periods of delusion, and at times she talked nonsensically of things that had never happened. She had fallen in the shower and broken her collarbone. We did a very minor surgery to repair the break and admitted her as a day patient to give her a few hours while her body adjusted to the rapid heal and regeneration."

Kira shifted on the stool, hands gripping the edge of the seat near her upper thighs, posture rigid and expression distant. Instinctively, he wanted to reach out and comfort her, but he instead crossed his arms and kept his hands to himself.

"That day wasn't anything out of the ordinary. We were slammed in the ER, and I missed lunch. Later in the afternoon, between patients, I managed to take five minutes to get some fresh air and eat a protein bar. On the way back, I decided to check on the female patient. When I walked into the room I caught Doctor Eon—" She clenched her jaw, taking a quick breath. "He had given her a sedative and was performing some kind of unsanctioned internal examination of her uterus and vagina. Not only that, he was clearly enjoying it the way a doctor shouldn't be enjoying that kind of thing."

"Jezus," he muttered, though he doubted Kira heard him. Of all the things he'd imagined her telling him, this hadn't factored.

"I demanded to know what he was doing, but he said it was a top secret program funded by the government, that the hospital board was aware of it and kept his work quiet for reasons of intergalactic security. I was shocked, so I left. But when I thought about it later I got angry, and I didn't believe what he'd told me. He'd clearly been getting off on whatever he'd been doing to that poor woman."

"Did you report it?"

She shook her head, her gaze becoming haunted. "This is when I made the wrong choice. When it was time for the woman to be discharged, I went back to see her, to find the nursing staff struggling to keep her from getting hysterical. You see, the sedative Dr. Eon had administered only made her unable to move, while still being fully aware of what was happening to her without her consent. Of course, the other attending doctor and nurses didn't believe what she was saying about Dr. Eon, they just thought she'd been having delusions, since there was no record of him entering her room that day."

"So what did you do?"

"I confronted him. I demanded to see some evidence of his supposed top secret program. He handed me a sedative to give her and said once she wasn't causing a ruckus anymore, he'd tell me everything. I didn't second-guess him, didn't even think…" She pushed back a few strands of hair with an unsteady hand, and this time he couldn't help but catch her fingers, squeezing them gently.

"It wasn't a sedative. It was five times the amount of the painkiller I'd been giving her while the fracture finished healing after the surgery. She died, and when I went looking for Dr. Eon, a couple of CP officers found me instead. They escorted me from the hospital grounds, and I was questioned by IPC planetary law enforcement. A week later, when I faced the hospital board for a hearing, they had files of evidence that I'd mismanaged over a dozen patients in less than a year, resulting in death, never mind that none of them had actually been my patients. They'd been in the care of Dr. Eon, but my name ended up on the files. My name on the orders of drugs, the administration of medications that had killed them. The board wanted to send me to Erebus for being some kind of sociopathic serial killer, but since they couldn't prove intent, I was instead banned from practicing medicine in the central systems."

Varean clenched his jaw, fighting down an intense wave of anger—he could have quite happily gotten up, headed for Jacolby, found Dr. Eon, and separated a few important appendages from his body.

"I'm sorry, Kira."

She shook her head, as though physically removing

herself from the memories, and looked up at him. "It was years ago, and I've come to terms with what happened. Most days I think I'm far happier on the *Imojenna* than I would have been if I'd spent my life in that hospital, never leaving the central systems."

"Still, to have your life torn apart like that—"

She shrugged. "I guess it makes me uniquely qualified to understand exactly what you're going through."

"I'm one lucky bastard then." He smoothed a hand up her arm to her shoulder, leaning closer. "Did you ever consider, in the years since, that Dr. Eon might not have been human—"

"That he was Reidar?" She shifted forward to meet him halfway, wrapping her arms around him and setting her chin on his shoulder. "It had crossed my mind, yes. But there was nothing I could do about it, and dwelling wouldn't help anything. I always figured if Rian ever got anywhere with his plans against the Reidar, I might find some sort of revenge. Of course, there's always the possibility Eon was your garden-variety sicko. Reidar aside, there are still a few of those lurking in the universe."

"Unfortunately, yes." He tightened his hold, enjoying the simplicity of having her against him, nothing between them, and nothing owed.

She turned her head slightly and then the warmth of her lips was against his neck, sending a shiver rippling through him.

"What are you going to do when you leave here?" Her words were a low vibration against his neck.

"I don't know. I was thinking about rejoining the *Swift Brion*, but if the Reidar did something to me, I'm going to need to find out how and when, and why I don't remember. Unless you want me to go find Dr. Eon and kick his ass into the next galaxy for you first."

He felt her smile before her mouth trailed lightly upward.

"Satisfying as that sounds, I wouldn't want you to risk getting caught and ending up on Erebus. I've been there, and it's not a place you want to spend an hour, let alone the rest of your life."

He urged her head higher so he could look into her eyes. "Worrying about where I end up is useless."

Her expression was grim as she stared back at him. "It's too late for that. No matter what happens after today, I don't know how to stop worrying or stop caring about you."

"I'm damaged goods. Growing up in the foster system made sure of that, and if the Reidar did something to me, it only sealed the deal." The words were resigned but not miserable. Simply a fact of life.

"You're trying to convince me that I'm better off without you, but you're better off without me. There's a good possibility you'd be killed sooner rather than later if you stayed with our crew, given Rian's ambition. Sure, we're on different paths, but that's not going to change how I feel about you."

She closed the distance between them and, without resistance, he embraced the hard and fast burst of desire and emotion as their mouths fused.

He tugged her forward, and she slipped off her stool to stand between his thighs, pressing her chest against his, her hands in his short hair. For a wild moment, he was desperate for more of her, wanted to stay for a few more days; if only he could lock them both in a room somewhere and simply enjoy everything of her—wit, fortitude, and every gorgeous inch of her body.

A low chime sounded, and it took a few long seconds to register the sound and pull himself back from where sensation was the only reality.

Kira broke the kiss before he did, turning to look over her shoulder.

"The computer has finished compiling the report."

His hands contracted where he held her hips, squeezing tighter for a second as though afraid he was about to lose her for good. Which was the undeniable truth. That inoffensive, low-volume alarm had signaled the end of whatever this had been between them for the past few days. He would leave, and she'd have to go forward with whatever her life would be now that they'd lost the *Imojenna*.

She looked back at him. "Do you need another minute?"

Locking himself down before any futile emotion or apprehension could swell up, he forced himself to let go of her. He was an AF commando, for jezus sake. He'd faced far worse things in this universe than a damned test result.

"No. Let's see what all the fuss is about."

She walked over to one of the screens. He took a second to drag a hand over his face, tug his clothes straight when he stood, and put up a final wall of military-grade fortitude to deflect whatever was about to come his way.

He stepped next to Kira, who had downloaded the files onto her commpad and was reading the screen intently. Nothing on there looked like actual language to him; it was all just scientific terms, numbers, and symbols.

She stiffened, the utter shock on her face highlighted by the blue-white glare from the screen. No matter how much he'd retreated behind his training, her expression sent his blood running cold. Christ, what had she seen?

"What is it?" He clamped a hand on her shoulder and spun her to face him.

"The results…they're nothing like I guessed." She studied him as if really seeing him for the first time…or maybe seeing him as something else entirely. The chill in his blood turned to a full arctic blast, freezing his heart mid-pound.

"What does it say?"

She took a half breath and retreated a step from him. "You're not human."

# Chapter Twenty-Two

Kira locked her knees, not letting herself move another inch. She was being ridiculous. This was *Varean*. She knew him more intimately than she'd come to know anyone in a long time. But this was bad. If Rian found out Varean was half Reidar, he'd probably kill him without a second thought. God, she had to help him get somewhere safe. Except, where the hell could that be, when Rian seemingly had an endless reach through his various contacts throughout the universe?

"What do you mean I'm *not human*?"

A belated tremor of shock rolled through her. "Your DNA— I thought I was going to find genetic mutations. But that's not what your bloodwork shows. I mean, you are human, but not fully."

He closed the space between them and gripped her upper arms. "I've told you a thousand times I'm not one of those aliens. I have no idea—"

"I believe you." She covered one of his hands with hers. "The truth is, you're half Reidar, half Mar'keish. You said you didn't know who your father was and that your mother died—"

"And now you're telling me one parent was from an isolated race of mystics who died out decades ago and the other was a frecking *shape-shifting alien*?" He released her and paced several steps away, shoving a hand through his hair, his movements jerky.

The Mar'keish had been a race of people rumored to have even more powerful abilities than the Arynians. After humans settled the planet of Mar'kei, something about the environment produced generations of people with abilities like mind control, telekinesis, and various other abilities. The old legends went that some Mar'keish could kill a person with a single thought. And since people feared what they didn't understand, the Mar'keish were persecuted and hunted. They'd eventually closed any interplanetary trading and kept to themselves. Which had seemingly worked out, until they'd been one of a handful of planets wiped out by a super virus, leading the IPC to enforce the zone of cold-space where no person was allowed, to keep the deadly disease from spreading. The Mar'keish were thought to have died out. So it was harder to decide which half of Varean's DNA was more shocking.

"Could your mother have known? How did she die?"

He dragged both hands over his face. "Jezus, I don't know. I don't remember. Whenever I asked, they always told me it was an accident, but no one ever explained what that meant. By the time I was seven, I stopped asking."

Chest tight and aching, she went over and intercepted him before he could stalk back across the lab. "This doesn't change anything. It doesn't change who you are. We knew the results were probably going to be ugly. I don't care if you're half mystic, half Reidar."

"He's half *what*?" Lianna's voice cut loud enough through the lab to probably be heard in half the hospital.

Kira glanced over her shoulder to find the nav-engineer had come in while she'd been distracted by Varean's turmoil. And her exclamation had gained the attention of the others. They poured out of the staff room to stand behind Lianna.

"Are the results in?" Zahli asked, expression creased with consternation, probably picking up on the tension that had spiked in the room like a stun grenade exploding.

"Apparently they are, and Kira was just about to explain," Lianna said in a steel-capped voice.

Varean stepped forward, brushing by her shoulder and putting himself in the middle of the lab. "You were right about me. I'm an alien. Not only that, but I'm apparently half Mar'keish. Have we reached the super-fun part of this adventure where you want to kill me?"

Lianna had a hand on the razar and leveled at Varean.

"No!" Kira rushed forward and put herself in the firing line. "He's not Reidar. But he's not human either. And he had no idea until now. This doesn't change—"

"Like hell it doesn't." Lianna grabbed her arm and jerked her aside none too gently, leaving a dull pain radiating down her arm. "Mar'keish or Reidar, he'll never be one of us, and we can't trust him."

Varean's expression hardened, and he took a menacing step forward, halting only when Lianna thumbed the power tab on the razar to fully charge it for a shot.

"Hurt her again and that buzz-gun isn't going to stop me."

Surprise flitted over Lianna's face, and she passed a slow look between the two of them, no doubt putting a few things together and coming up with an answer they'd all be aghast about. Especially now in light of Varean's true origins. But Kira didn't care what they thought, she cared only that Varean got to walk out of here in one piece.

"Everyone just calm down." Zahli held up both hands, playing peacemaker like she often did on the ship. "Yes, it's shocking, but we can take a minute to consider what this really means."

"It means he should have walked when he had the chance," Lianna muttered.

"You have every right not to trust him, considering all the old rumors about the Mar'keish and knowing what we do about the Reidar," Kira said, making sure her voice was extra calm and soothing, the one she'd used to pacify agitated patients. "So how about we just walk out of here and leave Varean to go his own way?"

Before Lianna could answer, the door to the lab cracked open. Varean shuffled her behind him, while Lianna, Tannin, and Zahli had their guns out and pointed in a second flat.

A figure slipped in, followed by another, both holding their hands out as they let the door click shut again. They weren't wearing lab coats or IDs and didn't act like hospital employees. In fact, they didn't seem at all surprised to find them in what should have been a disused lab and were both focused on Varean, despite the multiple guns pointed at them. They looked like regular, unremarkable people apart from their eyes—they were silver mercury, like Varean's had been that moment she'd felt him use his abilities. And it hit her then, why that fact had been familiar—it'd been an old rumor about the Mar'keish, that they were easily identifiable by their unique, silver-mercury eyes. If she wasn't mistaken, Varean's long-lost relatives had somehow found him.

"We don't want any trouble. My name is Ko'en. This is La'thar."

Both unusual names had slight inflections of accent.

"If you don't want trouble, you stepped into the wrong lab," Lianna replied.

Ko'en lowered his hands slowly. "We're not in the wrong lab. We're here for Va'ran."

It took Kira a second, but without the inflection separating the two hard sounds of his name… "You mean Varean?"

Ko'en nodded. "We've been tracking him since we became aware of his existence around a week ago."

And how exactly had that happened?

"Who are you?" Zahli asked.

But Lianna, apparently, was over the whole polite-conversation-with-weird-strangers thing and shot both men with her razar. Except nothing happened. They simply stared back with unruffled expressions.

"Who are you?" Lianna all but spat the words.

Ko'en held up his hands again. "We're Mar'keish. We don't want to hurt you. Our intentions are not to cause conflict." Ko'en eased back a step, obviously trying to appear as unintimidating as possible.

"You know about Varean? What he is?" Kira asked, not caring about anything other than they'd said they were here for him.

La'thar was the one who nodded. "We have been looking for one such as Va'ran for a long time. We heard they existed, but thought the Reidar had managed to wipe them all out. When we discovered Va'ran's unique energy, we began following your ship to observe him. But, as he has just discovered the truth of himself, we felt it was time to intervene."

"You mean there are more like me, half Reidar, half Mar'keish?" Varean's question sounded a little dazed.

"The Reidar have been experimenting with human-Reidar breeding for decades, and they were particularly interested in the Mar'keish because of our abilities," La'thar replied. "But something about the half-breeds scared them, and they shut down all the programs, destroyed most of the research…and the results."

"And you turn up now, just in time for us to find out what he really is?" Lianna demanded. "That's a little convenient, don't you think?"

"Though Va'ran does not realize it yet, all Mar'keish share a connection, which is how we knew what was happening here." Ko'en inclined his head. "I understand your cynicism, given the reputation of our race. It's why the few of us who remain stay in hiding. But we know about the Reidar and their plans, and we also know humans don't stand a chance against them."

"Thanks for the vote of confidence, but we're doing just fine," Lianna snapped.

"Are you, though?" La'thar asked. "Our intelligence gathering indicates the Reidar have already infiltrated all the most important government and military assets. A final invasion may be imminent."

Kira glanced at Lianna, Zahli, Tannin, and Jase who all had varying expressions of alarm and desolation. It was what they'd feared as more information about the Reidar had come to light. Rian had been right—they were beyond screwed.

"We won't go down without a fight." Lianna's voice held not a single note of doubt.

"The Reidar will make sure there is no fight. Your defeat will be swift and brutal," La'thar said, as though the entire thing were nothing but a formality.

"And we're just supposed to take a Mar'keish's word for it. You know people used to call you mind-wraiths for a reason." Lianna swapped her razar for a pulse pistol.

Neither man seemed particularly worried.

"Believe what you will." Ko'en shrugged as if he couldn't care less. Which he probably didn't. "We didn't come here to aid you. We came for Va'ran."

"It's *Varean*." He crossed his arms, pushing his shoulders back like he was daring them to take him. "What exactly do you want with me?"

"We would like you to come with us to a secure location.

We can teach you about your abilities, how to access and use the shared consciousness of our people. We hope to find out exactly what it is about the mix of Mar'keish and Reidar DNA the aliens wanted to hide. We also believe you may be able to access the shared Reidar consciousness, something we've been aware of for a long time, but unable to exploit."

"Wait. What do you mean *shared consciousness*?" Kira asked, mind skipping and landing on the recollection of Varean's dreams he insisted seemed real, of people he didn't know and places he'd never been, of hearing and speaking a language he said he didn't understand.

"All Reidar share one pool of memory, intent, and will. An advanced hive mind. Humans are far less evolved, unable to successfully access theirs, yet it does exist. It is where both Mar'keish—and to an extent, Arynians, though they don't comprehend it—draw their abilities. Humans have referred to this energy in the past as God, or a number of Gods. Some of your most famous personages in history were adept at manipulating a small portion of it to influence people and manifest their desires, though they were unaware and didn't understand what they were doing. It is an energy that runs through us all, through every speck of matter in all galaxies. It is what keeps the multiverse together. A person who can access and wield this energy can manifest anything they desire. So, it can easily be misused."

Wow… Just wow. She had no other words as her brain tried to make sense of a truth she felt in her soul was right.

"That's totally nuts," Zahli uttered, sounding about as bewildered as she felt, as they no doubt all felt, at their entire theological and spiritual beliefs being blown into the stratosphere.

"Nonetheless, it is the truth. Va'ran— Sorry, *Varean*. We became aware of you through this shared consciousness because you opened yourself up to your abilities. But it may not be long before the Reidar become cognizant of you in the same way. And I am not exaggerating when I tell you that they'll stop at nothing to track you down and kill you. If you want to survive, we may be your only option."

Kira glanced up at Varean, waiting for the inevitable *screw you* with some fancy expletives thrown in for good measure. Why were they here now? Why hadn't they found Varean as a child, leaving him all alone in the foster system? But the harsh rejections weren't forthcoming. In fact, Varean actually looked like he was considering their offer.

A hot burn of denial lit in her chest, but her mind was already telling her this was exactly the answer they needed to save him. She'd been worried that Rian would kill him when the truth came out, and there definitely wasn't anyone in the universe Rian Sherron was afraid of, but maybe the prospect of taking on the mind-wraiths might at least make him hesitate. Besides, everyone thought the Mar'keish were long dead and gone, but they'd been successfully hiding for decades. If Varean needed to disappear, this was the way to do it.

"You should go with them." The words were out of her mouth before she'd let herself think any more about it.

Varean speared her with a disbelieving look. "Just like that? No question of whether they're who they claim or if I should trust them?"

"I think you already know the answer, Varean. And whether or not you can trust them has to come second to what's best for you, especially in light of—" She swallowed, words deciding to abandon her.

"The fact that I'm half alien and a damn lot of people will probably want to kill me for it?" He finished for her. He glanced over at the waiting pair, then closed his eyes on a curse. When he focused on her again, maybe she was imagining it, but his eyes seemed more silver than blue. "You're right, like always. My gut feeling is this is legit and probably my best chance at getting any answers. But is this it? Am I really supposed to just walk away?"

"We both knew this was coming today, one way or another." She crossed her arms, pressing her wrists into her abdomen, wishing she could push back the ache rising up within her just as easily.

"Yeah, but not like this." He shifted closer to her, leaving barely any space between them, though he didn't touch her. "Not with you still in danger. I need to see you somewhere safe."

God, why did he have to be so damned noble and wonderful? It only made things that much harder. Couldn't he see that she wasn't the one they needed to worry about?

"I am safe. I've got Lianna, Zahli, and Tannin." She took a breath, calming her emotions. She had to make him go, because he'd never be safe anywhere else, and she wouldn't be able to live with it if something happened to him because he was trying to protect her. So she pulled on the only armor she had. "I've done all I can for you. They'll know more about your Mar'keish genetic makeup than I ever will. As your doctor, it's my recommendation that you go with them."

Utter bewilderment crossed Varean's face. "As my *doctor*? After everything, that's what you're reducing this to?"

Her stomach churned, but she stiffened her posture and called on every shred of professionalism she had. Maybe he was going to hate her for this, but at least he'd be safe.

"Yes, that's what we were. I was your doctor; you were my patient. I crossed a line, took advantage of you. That was wrong of me when you were in a vulnerable position."

"*Vulnerable*?" The disbelief in his voice almost made her wince, but she was determined not to react. "I might have been a lot of things, but I sure as hell wasn't vulnerable."

"Weren't you?" She tipped her chin up slightly. "You said

it yourself, you didn't know how much longer you would be able to control the rage inside you, that you might be capable of hurting people. You were worried about hurting me."

His lips pressed together, and she could tell the way his features hardened that—whether intended or not—she'd burned him, bringing up in front of the others the things he'd confided to her.

"Yeah, well clearly neither of us will need to worry about that any longer, will we?" He turned away from her, making her chest ache. "I thought you trusted me, even when I didn't trust myself. Looks like my DNA wasn't the only hard truth revealed with those tests."

The hit landed a little too well, sending her resolve crumbling. She hadn't meant to use his fears against him, it'd just been the first stupid thing that'd blurted out of her. Damn her impetuous need to always retreat behind her doctor's mantle. She should have just told him straight out why he should go with them, why it was important to her.

But if he knew she cared so deeply, maybe he wouldn't have been walking away from her so easily now. Too easily. Yes, she'd been trying to push him away, but an idiotic small part of her had wanted him to fight for them, not give up at the slightest resistance.

He had to go; it was the only way he would be safe, but after everything they'd been through, she couldn't let him leave thinking that his heritage was the reason she'd pushed him to this.

"Varean, wait, I didn't mean—" She started forward, but Lianna caught her arm and held her back.

"Good-bye, Kira." Varean went to join Ko'en and La'thar where they stood by the lab doors, speaking in low tones with them.

"Let him go." Zahli's voice was soft, but held a note of sympathy. "It's best for everyone."

Varean glanced at her one last time, his expression blank and devoid of emotion, just like when she'd first seen him in the brig onboard the *Imojenna*. Without a word or even a wave, he turned away, following the two Mar'keish out of the lab and disappearing forever, leaving her with nothing but the hollow comfort that she'd done the right thing in pushing him away. Maybe he was hurting—maybe they were both hurting—but at least he'd be alive somewhere. She could live with that…or at least find some way to be okay with it one day.

"I'm sorry. I didn't realize how close the two of you had become," Zahli murmured, no judgment in her tone, only empathy. She supposed Zahli knew a thing or two about falling for someone forbidden, since Rian had done everything in his power to keep her and Tannin apart when the ex-Erebus inmate and tech analyst had first come aboard.

"You're better off without him," Lianna put in, little compassion in her voice, as though getting over him should happen in exactly five seconds and there would be no need to cry into a pint of ice cream or steal a bottle of Rian's Violaine to drown her sorrows in the most toxic way possible.

"Thanks," she muttered. Lianna's lack of empathy had worked in distracting her, after all.

Lianna sheathed her weapon and glanced around the lab, as though checking they weren't about to leave anything behind. "Come on. Let's get to Forbes. We've got four days on that skimmer to meet up with Rian and the rest of the crew."

# Chapter Twenty-Three

FORBES

It had taken several days of going back and forth with the *Swift Brion*, but the shipment was organized, Zander overseeing the fit out of a larger shuttle to take the shipment.

Callan had spent hours forging the paperwork. However, uploading them into the IPC systems had proven complicated, so they'd commed Tannin, who talked them through it from the other skimmer. The rest of the crew had been traveling for a few days and hoping to join them by dawn. Which, by Rian's estimation, was now less than an hour away.

Colt had flaked out on the couch in the front room a while ago, and though he'd been obviously curious and impatient to know what was really going on, the guy hadn't demanded answers, contacting his brother without question when they'd needed him to.

He would have to tell Colt the full story before they parted ways, let the guy decide what he wanted to do with that bitch of a reality check, but for now he didn't have the energy to give someone the monsters-in-the-dark-corners speech.

With the bedrooms taken up by Ella, Nyah, and Jensen, Callan had said he'd take the floor once he was finished double-checking his forged files, and while Rian wasn't exactly in the mood for sleepy-time himself, he went to the front room where Colt was snoring and dropped himself in an armchair.

But he'd barely gotten his ass on the cushions when the stairs creaked softly, and a glance revealed Ella and Nyah coming down. The pair of them tended to be early-to-bed, early-to-rise like some kind of old-fashioned Puritans. So he wasn't surprised that with dawn about to come, they were up for the day.

As the two of them went into the kitchen, Callan came out yawning, flopping into the armchair opposite him, and pressing the tab to recline.

"There's something wrong with those two." Callan yanked a frilly cushion out from beneath himself and tossed it, before settling back. "Don't they know five a.m. is still the middle of the night?"

The scent of a generic black tea wafted from the kitchen, Ella and Nyah murmuring in quiet tones.

"They'd probably tell you it's the best time to be doing all sorts of goody do-gooding things like baking and saving the damned."

Callan gave a short laugh, kicking his boots up on the footrest. "If they're planning on putting all those berries to use to make some muffins for breakfast, I'm not saying a word."

Soft, hurried footfalls brought his attention back as the two women returned to the sitting room, tension in their postures, Nyah looking downright scared.

"There are two figures moving out in the yard just beyond

the tree line in back." Though Ella's words were clipped, they had only the slightest hint of urgency. And if he hadn't gotten to know her so well, he might have missed the shadow of worry behind her otherwise calm expression.

Rian leaned over and shook Colt awake. "We've got uninvited guests."

Callan slid off the recliner, right hand gripping a still-sheathed gun. "I'll head upstairs and get Jensen."

He nodded. Callan staying stooped and moving off before he'd even finished agreeing.

Motioning Ella and Nyah over, he ordered them to get down behind the couch. While Colt strapped on the single gun and knife he had with him, Rian went low, scrunching his way over to the window and slitting the curtain slightly to look out into the gray pre-morning light. It took his eyes a second to adjust, but he counted four moving in the trees. Four more, or four altogether? There was no way to tell.

As he let the curtain slip back into place, he sensed Ella shifting up beside him.

"Rian, we need to get out of this house right now."

Her expression was cast in shadows, but her eyes caught the faint light coming from the kitchen, and there was a definite gleam of alarm in her gaze. In fact, he could all but feel it rolling over his skin.

"There are at least four men out there. When Callan and Jensen get down here—"

"No." She clamped a hand on his forearm, and a cutting sense of foreboding almost flayed his composure. Something was about to happen. "We need to leave. *Now*."

He jerked a nod and caught Colt's attention. His buddy gently took Nyah's arm and brought her over.

"We're going to make a break for it," he said as they huddled in a group.

"Why? We've got a defensible position here, and once

Callan and your mechanic get their asses down here—"

"There's no time." He glanced up the stairs, willing the other two to appear. What in the hell was taking them so long? "Trust me. We're better off out there than we are in here."

He unholstered one of his pulse pistols and handed it to Colt, then palmed his other two guns. "We're going to face heavy fire, so be ready to shoot, and aim straight."

Colt nodded grimly, tugging out his other gun. The two of them ushered the girls to the front door.

"On my count," he said in a low voice that barely carried. "One… Two… Three."

He yanked open the door and went out low, darting over to the verandah post and waiting a split second for the others to join him. They'd barely made it to his position before he was up again and leaping down the stairs, opening fire on the shadowy figures as a shout went up.

Hell, there were definitely more than four of the bastards, and whoever they were—he was betting Reidar, being the obvious answer—they didn't hesitate in returning fire.

Nucleon blasts lit up the lavender-gray shrouded yard, spitting up dirt as they peppered too close to his feet. There was a squat stone wall another fifty yards to the right, and he cut at an angle to head for it, glancing over his shoulder to make sure the others followed.

A few short steps to go, and Colt cried out. As he paused, shoving Ella past him and propelling her toward the wall, a blast grazed his thigh just above his knee, sending him stumbling. But he didn't stop running, instead reversing direction back to where Colt had gone down. He didn't bother to check if his buddy was conscious or even alive, simply hauled him up over his shoulder like a sack of bricks and sprinted for where Ella and Nyah crouched behind the stone wall.

As he arrived and dropped Colt to the ground, a high whistle skimmed above them. His body reacted on instinct, the sound straight out of the wartime scars he never fully remembered, and he half ducked over Colt, pulling Ella against him before his mind even registered the sound of the low-intensity, compressed-ion antimatter missile. Once used as a kind of nuclear propulsion system, it hadn't taken some genius long to retro-fit the tech into contained bombs with a small but effective blast radius for precision damage.

They were only a hundred yards or so away from the house and on the exposed side of the stone wall, and when the missile went up, a reverberating boom rumbled through the atmosphere.

There was no outward blast radius, only the residual heat as what remained of the structure exploded in flames.

He raised his head, but only far enough to check on Colt. The guy had a chest wound the size of his fist, scorched around the margins and pumping blood out in rivers. If his buddy's heart hadn't already stopped beating from losing too much blood, it soon would.

"Ella." He leaned over to where the priestess had shifted to comfort a sobbing Nyah.

She turned to him with a resolute nod, apparently not even needing him to tell her to heal Colt.

Rian got out of her way, quickly assessing his weapon situation. While he still had both of his guns, the power packs were down by about a third. Colt had lost the two he was carrying. Without Callan and his usual one-man-army arsenal—

He glanced back toward the blazing remains of the house. In the middle of the yard, there was a crumpled, smoking, blackened body. From the slighter build, it had to be Jensen, likely thrown clear when the blast had detonated, but most certainly dead. While there wasn't a second body on the lawn, he had no doubt Callan had shared the same fate. When the fire burned itself out, they'd find the remains of the ship's security specialist in the ruins.

Clenching his fists around the grip of both guns, he took a moment to let the anger burn harder and hotter than the flames dashing over the black skeleton of the building. Callan and Jensen had been integral to the crew—Sen because there wasn't anything he couldn't fix, and he kept the *Imojenna*'s engines running in peak condition with only the bare minimum in new parts and tools. As for Callan, he'd never met a tougher son of a bitch who hid his smarts so deep it had been kind of scary to think what he could be capable of when he set his mind to it.

When he got his ship back, it wouldn't be the same stepping onto her decks without those two behind him.

The hot rage extinguished into ice-cold intent, and he shifted to the end of the wall, glancing out to assess the enemies' positions. They were moving in, at least eight. With Jensen and Callan gone and Colt down, he wouldn't be able to hold this ground for long.

"Ella, can you heal Colt, or is he already dead?" he asked without taking his eyes off the group swiftly closing in.

"He's on the brink, but I should be able to save him."

The small bluish light in his peripheral vision told him she'd already started. "How long is that going to take?"

"Ten minutes, at least, maybe longer." Her voice wavered, as though it was hard for her to talk and heal at the same time.

"We don't have that long, princess, so you're going to have to speed it up a little."

If she replied, the words were lost under the whine of weapon fire as he opened up on the approaching Reidar. Before he'd even gotten three shots off, sparks exploded on the stone around him from return ammo.

Nyah squealed, and Ella murmured a calming order, but all of that was inconsequential background noise as he concentrated on picking off as many of the bastards as he could before his power packs were drained.

By the time his guns started clicking empty, he'd put down four and a half Reidar—one of the bastards had dragged himself back up after being down for a few seconds.

He tossed his guns and palmed his knife, waiting as the Reidar realized he had no ammo left and rushed their position. He came up at the last second, catching one in the gut with his knife and shoving it back again, then turning on the other three.

He fought his way to the already-injured guy, stabbing him in the neck and putting him down for good this time. The other two came at him from opposite sides, and while he deflected the one on the left who tried to punch his lights out, the one on the right caught Rian's forearm in a bone-crushing grip and left him open to a fist rammed into his solar plexus. The impact hammered the breath out of his chest, leaving his lungs stalled. He wheezed and hunched forward to protect himself from a second blow but jerked his elbow up and out, catching the son of a bitch in the nose.

The injured guy fell back, leaving him free to spin an attack on the other one. Except at some point that Reidar had pulled his own knife, and while Rian saw it and shifted his weight to avoid getting stabbed, the guy compensated with lightning-fast reflexes that definitely weren't human. The knife slammed into a rib and deflected off to jab deeper into his chest. The pain ripped through him like getting struck by lightning, except he'd been conditioned not to react to any kind of hurt and shoved the attacker back.

But while he'd been distracted by the whole getting-stabbed thing, the one he'd elbowed in the nose, plus two other less seriously wounded, had dragged themselves over, leaving him with four opponents again. Frecking resilient parasites.

Blood was running down his side, soaking his shirt, and

a cold sweat rippled over his skin in waves, blooming like clouds of noxious gas.

The four slowly shifted into formation, surrounding him on all sides.

"Ella?" He risked a glance over his shoulder, but from here, the wall blocked her, Colt, and Nyah from sight.

"I still need another few minutes."

"And what happens if you don't get a few minutes?" The men started circling, and he resisted the urge to clamp a hand over his wound, since he'd need both fists free for when they decided to attack.

"He could still die."

He clenched his jaw, glaring at the Reidar as they edged closer. He'd already lost Jensen and Callan. He wasn't about to lose Colt as well.

One of the bastards sent him a cutting grin and backed off a step, veering toward the wall. Black fury descended, and he lost all higher reasoning. Felt nothing. Existed as nothing but raw violence. He lunged forward, rounding the wall in pursuit, but just before he got within reaching distance of the bastard, the other three fell on him, dragging him back and down.

Ella glanced up at the Reidar now standing above her. As the alien reached for her, she pressed her hands down on Colt's chest and a single, nearly blinding pulse of light passed through him, making his whole body jerk like he'd been shocked. He gasped in a cutting, panicked breath, eyes snapping open. But he wasn't fully healed, not the way Ella was capable of doing if she'd had the time. The ragged wound still marred the middle of his chest, though it was at least closed over. Yet, after seeming as though he'd woken up for a moment, Colt collapsed back into unconsciousness.

The Reidar grabbed Ella by the back of her neck and yanked her away from Colt, sending her sprawling.

A new surge of dark rage boiled up within him, and he

jerked forward, but the three Reidar held him down, and the blood he'd been losing was slowing his body's systems.

Ella didn't resist, but when the Reidar produced a pair of blue-tinged thick bracelets—no doubt a special blend of metium, sapphire, and micro-crystal components that would dampen her abilities—energy sparked off her skin, lighting up her eyes with beautifully awesome animosity.

However, when the Reidar bent down, she didn't blast the sonuvabitch like he'd hoped. In fact, she didn't move, letting him snap the bands around her wrists and extinguishing the light of her powers.

That damned Arynian conditioning and its stupid rule about not retaliating unless her life was directly and undoubtedly threatened. She'd alluded to the fact that she'd been all but brainwashed into not using her powers in reprisal. *Jezus*. Even in a situation like this, with two of his crew were already dead, she still couldn't bring herself to help either of them.

The Reidar who'd cuffed her stepped back with a satisfied smirk, then pulled out his nucleon gun. His heart flatlined.

"No—!" He wrenched forward, managing to pull free from two of the aliens holding him.

But the Reidar with the gun half turned and shot Nyah, who'd been whimpering, scrunched up against the wall on the other side of Colt.

Ella cried out as Nyah listed sideways and crumpled forward, while the Reidar calmly put his gun away again.

The Reidar holding him managed to cuff his wrists, double securing them with a short length of metium-reinforced chain. They hauled him up and unceremoniously dumped him next to Ella.

"The two of you are long overdue for a meeting with Baden Niels."

Rian clenched his fists, making the chain and cuffs bite in

harder. Frecking Baden Niels, one of the head douche-Reidar who'd tried to have Ella kidnapped all those months ago.

"Good. Let's get to that meeting. It'll make it easier for me to kill him."

The Reidar hooked a boot into him, almost dead-on where he'd been stabbed. He coughed, struggling to breathe through the pain while stars dotted his vision with blackness.

"You're going to kill. But not any Reidar. Once Niels has gotten what he needs from you, it'll be time to hit the reset button on your inner assassin."

Ice clamped on every vital organ, nearly sending him into a panic for the first time in over five years. *No.* He wouldn't let himself be reset as a Reidar assassin again. He would die before they did that; he didn't care who he had to take with him to make it happen.

A light, gentle hand touched the side of his neck. "Rian, don't sink back into the darkness. That's what they want."

He closed his eyes for a long second, letting Ella's words wash through him. But without her abilities working, there was no comforting warmth flowing through him like her touch usually brought. And words alone were not enough. The darkness was already winning.

The Reidar snapped an order in its language, and the others pulled Ella and him up, marching them off through the trees.

He glanced back at what was left of the house, now a smoldering orange glow through the thin forest. He hoped Colt lived, hoped he told Zahli and the others not to come for them, because they would only meet the same fate as Jensen and Callan.

But it was a hollow wish. He'd known for some time he'd get his crew killed but thought they'd at least achieve something first. In this, they were all nothing more than fodder for the invisible war.

Maybe getting killed trying to free Ella and him was their best option. Because if the Reidar succeeded in turning him back into a soulless tool without his own will or conscience, his crew—what was left of them anyway—would be the first ones the Reidar sent him out to destroy.

# Chapter Twenty-Four

Varean had thought training to be a commando had been hard—as psychologically demanding as it had been physically. Learning about his Mar'keish side was proving to be infuriatingly harder in that he pretty much sucked at it.

The past few days since he'd left Barasa with La'thar and Ko'en had dragged, especially since his patience seemed to have abandoned him and his frustrations kept getting the better of him.

The two Mar'keish had brought him to what was apparently one of many bases and safe houses they had across the galaxy. The Mar'keish might have been in hiding, but they certainly didn't seem to be lacking funds. The penthouse suite they'd brought him to in one of the fanciest buildings he'd ever seen on the central systems planet, Kestrel, lacked for no luxury or amenity. It even had a lab-slash-medical room, which he'd spent more time in than he would have liked.

La'thar had explained that Varean's Mar'keish abilities were inherent and instinctive—his body should know how to use them the same way he knew how to breathe. And while he'd been accessing the basics like healing himself since he was a teenager, the majority of whatever the mysterious Mar'keish abilities were remained locked away within him somewhere.

Ko'en had reasoned that maybe his Reidar side was somehow blocking it, and it seemed the two were more interested in seeing him harness his Reidar abilities anyway. For the past day or so, they'd focused on the alien consciousness that had been creeping deeper and deeper into his psyche since the first time he'd been hit with the Reidar stunner. La'thar and Ko'en theorized that somehow his Reidar DNA had come out of dormancy—probably as some kind of self-preservation. He speculated it had something to do with that damned razar, closely followed by the multiple times he'd nearly died.

But his Reidar DNA came with its own downside. He was half human, with human limitations, and the testing had taken a physical toll on his body, leaving him with pounding headaches, to name just one of the fun side effects. His Mar'keish ability to heal had definitely come in handy. Plus, thankfully, they'd also helped in teaching him how to keep a rein on his ingrained aggression.

He finally felt like he wasn't about to snap at the smallest provocation.

Though he'd finished up the latest session a while ago, Varean hadn't left the lab and joined the two men for dinner.

He hated this time of day. At least when La'thar and Ko'en were melting his brain with their tests and experiments, he had something to focus on. And at night, when he was sleeping—peacefully, since the Mar'keish had shown him how to put a barrier up in his mind to keep the brimming Reidar consciousness out—it saved him from having to think about things.

But during the in-between times, short as they were, his

mind tortured him by swinging from moods of righteous indignation at the things Kira had said before they'd parted ways, to regret that he'd walked out on her and left things so broken when he'd vowed to see her safe. For the first time since becoming a commando, he'd let his emotions get in the way of logic and had failed to see out the duty he'd sworn to.

He'd replayed that conversation over in his head a million times, because her words hadn't matched with what he'd come to know of Kira in the time they'd spent together. She wasn't petty or mean, she wasn't shallow or fickle, though he'd taken her short argument that way.

In fact, he now had a sneaking suspicion that if he'd bothered thinking about it, he would have realized that underneath her hurtful revelation of his deep-seated aggression in front of the others, she'd actually been doing a pretty typical Kira-like thing—pushing him away because she believed he was better off with the Mar'keish.

She hadn't said it straight out but, reading between the lines, it'd become pretty damn clear she'd been trying to protect him, force him to walk away with the only ammo she could think of, because they'd both known he would put himself at risk to make sure she was safe before he looked to his own welfare.

Well, her plan had worked perfectly, because here he was, cushy in some high-end penthouse while she—

Hell, he had no idea where she'd gone or what she was doing, and it was starting to drive him full-on mental. He didn't know how much more he'd be able to take before he completely caved and went looking for her, just to make sure she was okay.

Sitting there obsessing and going hungry obviously wasn't going to help anyone so, with a long sigh, he left the lab-slash-medical room and headed down the short hallway that opened into the main sitting rooms.

La'thar and Ko'en weren't serving up dinner like he'd expected, but having a low, intent conversation that ceased the second he walked into the room.

"Don't mind me, continue with whatever you were arguing about." He walked over to the screen built into the kitchen wall, checking the day's menu. The building had its own food service like a hotel, and it was just a matter of tapping a few buttons to have a five-star meal sent up. Apparently the other two men had been too distracted to see to it yet.

"We weren't exactly arguing," Ko'en replied, shooting a quelling look at La'thar. "Just having a polite difference of opinion."

"Well that's a civil way to put things. You want fish or chicken tonight?"

"Varean, there's something you need to know." La'thar came up on his side, distracting him from the food choices. "Ko'en was just worried about what you'll do when you find out."

"Find out what?" He passed a look between the pair, but couldn't get a read off their expressions.

"We got some intel from a source of ours watching one of the Reidar in the top echelon of their power structure. His name is Baden Niels. He's been after an Arynian priestess named Mirellan Kinton for a long time."

"Ella?" The same priestess Sherron had on his crew?

"Niels just launched an attack on the crew of the *Imojenna* to take both her and Rian Sherron," La'thar answered, reluctance clear in his voice.

*Kira.*

Fear, the likes of which he'd never felt in his entire life, zapped through to every nerve ending in his body. Why the hell had he let his damned pride and insecurities get in the way of protecting her? Kira had needed him, needed someone to be there for her, and he'd selfishly walked away.

"What kind of attack?"

"We're not sure exactly." This time Ko'en answered, and he seemed more resigned, probably already guessing Varean's intent. "Only that it happened on one of Dunham's moons, Forbes, and they were successful. Niels has both the priestess and Sherron in custody, which is not good news for the universe."

Instead of asking what Ko'en meant by that, he sprinted to the hall cupboard and yanked out a jacket from the stack of new clothes he'd bought the day before.

"I need to go, right now."

"Of course you do," Ko'en muttered, trailing La'thar over and also grabbing their jackets.

He paused as he hit the door release. "What are you doing?"

"Coming with you," La'thar answered.

Perhaps he should have asked why or questioned their sudden buddy-buddy act, but he couldn't think of anything beyond getting to Forbes ASAP and making sure nothing had happened to Kira.

God help him if it had, he would never be able to live with himself.

# Chapter Twenty-Five

The sun had just topped the horizon, golden yellow streaks of light stretching out through the thinly wooded landscape, as the aerocar set down exactly where Rian had instructed them earlier. They'd be walking the remaining distance to the cabin, none of them in the mood to defy his usual, precise security measures to make sure they hadn't been followed.

As Kira stepped out of the aerocar, the acrid scent of smoke hit the back of her throat instead of the fresh dew-laden country air she'd expected. The others glanced warily at each other as they joined her, but no one said a word as they set off through the trees toward Rian's secluded hideout.

But really, what was there to say? Especially as her thoughts were all about Varean. Maybe she should have feared a man who was half Mar'keish, half Reidar, because she couldn't imagine what that made him capable of. But it hadn't changed how she felt about him. Though she'd convinced him in the cruelest way possible that he'd be better off with the Mar'keish, part of her wished things could be different, that there'd been a way for him to stay.

She'd probably never see him again, never know what happened to him. The notion made her chest ache in a way she had no right to feel, since she barely knew the man.

"Someone's burning the home fires a little too enthusiastically this morning." Jase Nevan gave a cough after the comment, the only one of them who hadn't been in a dour, silent mood since leaving Barasa.

He was right—the smoke was getting thicker the farther into the woods they went. And it wasn't just the scent of a typical wood fire, it was laced with the noxious undertones of burning plastic and other materials that stripped the back of her throat as she inhaled.

"You don't think—" Zahli broke into a run.

"Wait!" Tannin launched after her without hesitation, leaving the rest to get their tired legs with the program and chase after them.

Zahli and Tannin arrived in the clearing a few seconds before Kira did, skidding to a sudden stop. Beyond them, there was nothing but blackened, charred, smoking ruins where the cabin had presumably stood. Disconnecting from the jarring sight, Kira scanned the ruins, then shifted her attention to the neatly cut grass, her mind picking through the debris, looking for—

"Oh god." She shoved past Jase, who'd stopped next to her, and darted into the yard, dodging broken and burned pieces of the house that weren't recognizable.

Even as she made it to the prone figure, she knew there was no hope. There was nothing left but bloodied and charred skin, no way to survive such extensive and horrific injuries. Hand shaking, she gently pressed her fingers into a wrist, but found nothing.

As she swallowed against the tightening, rising churn in the back of her throat, she reached over and turned his head toward the morning rays of golden sun warming her back.

*Jensen.*

She had to close her eyes, had to let him go and press her hands into the damp, cool grass beneath her.

"Oh no." Zahli's voice struck the same chord of disbelief that was echoing through her body. "No, no, no. *Jensen*—"

Forcing her eyes open, she reached over and caught Zahli's hand before she could touch him. "He's gone."

Zahli gulped in a ragged breath as Tannin pulled her up, easing her a few steps back from the horror of Jensen's fate and wrapping his arms around her.

"What about the others?" Lianna asked from behind, voice uneven.

She pushed to her feet, turning to find the nav-engineer, along with Jase, standing a few steps away.

"I don't know. If they were inside—" At her words, the rest of the crew looked over to the remains of the house, but she couldn't bring herself to even glance in that direction. If everyone else had been inside, then whatever remained of them would be in worse condition than Jensen. As the ship's doctor, it would be her responsibility to deal with that. But they wouldn't be the faceless victims of an accident; they were her family.

All of the turmoil and shock of the last few days—Varean leaving, weary from days of traveling and arriving to find tragedy instead of asylum—slammed into her like heavy grav. She stumbled a few steps away, making it to a low stone wall. She braced a hand against the rough edge as she leaned over, gulping air and ordering the contents of her stomach to stay exactly where it was.

"Are you okay up there?" The unsteady voice coming from beyond the fence yanked her out of the tailspin as effectively as taking a hit of sedative. She looked down to see a man propped up against the wall. His shirt was torn, bloody, and gaping open in the middle, though whatever wound he'd sustained had somehow healed to an angry red scab.

A woman lay across his lap, and he had his hands pressed against her bloody shoulder. It took a second for her mind to kick the shock and recognize Nyah.

"Guys, over here!" She rounded the wall and went down on her knees, pulling Nyah out of the stranger's grasp and laying her flat so she could do a proper examination.

The girl was unconscious, but breathing steadily, her color good. The shoulder wound looked nasty, no doubt requiring surgery to stop the bleeding and repair the damage. But she was stable for the moment and not in any immediate danger.

"Who are you?" Lianna demanded, her gun out and pointed at the man as the others surrounded them.

"Commander Captain Colter Routh."

"You're Colt?" Zahli knelt down next to him.

He shot her a wan smile. "You must be Zahli. Heard so much about you from Rian, I feel like we should have met long before this. And under better circumstances."

"What happened?" Again, Lianna with the demands. It seemed to be her default setting when things got messy—she turned into a demanding hard-ass entirely worthy of being Rian's backup.

"I have no idea. I was asleep on a couch in the front room. Rian woke me up, said we had company. Before I knew it, that priestess says we've got to leave the house, and Rian just goes along, no questions asked, even though we were outnumbered and had no cover out here. We made a run on this wall. The last thing I remember is taking a nucleon blast to the chest." He motioned to the starburst-patterned wound between his pecs. "Pretty sure this should have killed me."

Reaching forward, she pushed his shirt out of the way, studying the margins of the injury and its placement. "You're right. It should have killed you. Ella must have healed it."

He nodded, though his expression had a dazed, confused edge to it, like he had the facts, but couldn't quite assimilate the truth of the answer. "Yeah, I guess she did."

"So where are they now?" Lianna swapped her gun for a razar.

"Whoever attacked us, they took both of them, Rian and the priestess. I heard them mention someone…Niels."

Tannin cursed under his breath, while Zahli shot a worried look at Lianna.

"You know who that is?" Colt pushed straighter, grimacing at the movement.

"Yeah, we know who that is," Lianna answered. "What about Callan?"

Colt's attention shifted past them to the smoldering ruins. "He was still in the house with Jensen when they shot a compressed-ion missile into it."

The words washed over her, but it was like her body had gone numb, not able to take another blow. Lianna's expression tightened, but she didn't say a word, simply brought the razar up and aimed it at Colt.

"Hey! Just wait a—" The pulse hit him, passing through his body with no apparent effects.

Colt blew out a ragged breath, dropping his chin to his chest for a long second. "Jezus, what is it with you people and those guns?"

"Rian didn't tell you?" Zahli asked.

"I'm sure it was on his to-do list, but some guys with a hard-on to blow shite up got to us first."

"And now is not the time to be having that conversation. We have to move." Lianna shoved her razar away, scanning the clearing.

"Where are we going?" Zahli asked as she pushed to her feet.

"I don't know. But we can't stay here."

"Nyah needs medical treatment," Kira added. The bleeding had definitely slowed, but the wound still needed attention.

"You'll have to make do with whatever's on the skimmer. I don't think we should risk going to a hospital," Lianna answered.

It wasn't ideal, but she was right. Going to a hospital presented too many risks, and besides, she didn't trust anyone else to treat Nyah.

"Here, I'll take her." Tannin carefully lifted Nyah into his arms.

Zahli helped Colt up, and Jase came over to sling an arm over his shoulder, taking a majority of the commander captain's weight as they headed away from the house. With two injured, and all of them no doubt processing the shock of losing both Jensen and Callan, they wouldn't have put up much of a fight if the Reidar found them.

Lianna kept up a fast pace at the front as they navigated the woods back to where they'd left the hired aerocar. But just before they broke through the tree line to the road, Lianna stopped and held up a hand to silently halt their procession. She yanked out her razar, half turning to aim to the left of their group.

"I know you're there. You might as well come out."

A figure emerged from the thicket, hands out and steps slow. The face was familiar—achingly so—but with all the shock of the last few minutes clogging her brain, she couldn't process the how or why.

"I thought we left you on Barasa." Lianna leveled off her weapon, shifting to take up a more protective position as the two Mar'keish they'd met appeared as well.

Varean nodded, slowly lowering his hands. "You did. But when Ko'en and La'thar got intel about Niels launching this attack, I convinced them to hop a shuttle, and we took a transit gate to get here. I had to make sure—"

His gaze focused on Kira, and despite the numbness and

exhaustion and sheer emotional fatigue, her stupid, *stupid* heart leaped against the inside of her chest.

"You had to make sure we were all dead?" Lianna shot back. "Sorry to disappoint."

A flare of frustration tightened Varean's features. "I had to make sure you were okay."

"Sure, by creeping around the woods all stalker-like. How did you find us?"

"*I* didn't." He gestured to the two Mar'keish behind him. "They did. I needed to know Kira was safe."

Lianna frowned. "This has become a real thing for you, hasn't it?"

"There's nothing you can do here, Varean. In fact, you're probably the one who isn't safe. You should go, before the Reidar find you." Without waiting for him or anyone else to say anything, Kira brushed past Lianna and headed for the aerocar. The others came after her…but so did Varean.

"Kira, wait."

At the aerocar, she had to stop because Tannin had the keys to unlock the vehicle. *Damn it.*

"Just go away, Varean." She closed her eyes, wishing she were anywhere else in the galaxy, that anything else was happening right now except this—two of their crew members dead, Rian and Ella in the hands of the enemy. Why did he have to come back? She'd already watched him walk away once; she didn't know if she had the strength to do it again, not when everything was falling down around her.

"I can help you." He'd stopped by her side, voice low, not quite imploring, but begging her to understand nonetheless. "I know you didn't mean what you said, about the doctor-patient thing. Like always, you were trying to do the right thing, sending me off with the Mar'keish. I know you, Kira. Know that you care about what happens to me as much as I care about you."

The others were loading Nyah and Colt into the aerocar, shooting wary glances at the two of them.

"But it doesn't change anything, does it? None of it matters, because after this, you're going to leave again. You were right, I'm a coward, because I don't want to face that. I just want you to go."

The door in front of her opened, and she stepped forward, but Varean grabbed her arm.

"I know this sucks, and it hurts, but you're not the only one who feels that way. You might not want to admit it, but you need me right now. You helped me, now stop being so damned stubborn and let me help you."

"Don't you get it? You can't help us. You're half Mar'keish, half Reidar, how can you possibly do anything except make it more complicated and put us in more danger?" If the Reidar got him because he had some noble idea about saving her, she'd never be able to live with it. She pulled out of his hold. "I don't have time for this. The Reidar have Rian and Ella."

She had to suck in a breath, some of the gruesome details from the alien lab reports she'd read bursting into her mind in a flood of grisly narrative.

Everything around her shifted, leaving her swaying, until a firm arm caught her weight.

"Kira, are you okay?" Varean's gaze traveled over her face, nothing but concern in his silver-blue eyes.

She pushed his hands away. "I'll be fine once you leave."

His expression shut down, like hyperdrive engines going cold. "Fine, maybe you want me gone. But I can help you find them. I can figure out where Rian is."

That got Zahli's attention at least. "How?"

"By accessing that shared Reidar consciousness Ko'en and La'thar mentioned." His tone was unapologetic, as if daring anyone to call him on the irony of him wanting to use his apparent newfound Reidar abilities and the inherent

Mar'keish powers he'd ignored all his life to help them rescue Rian and Ella. "I can do it, with their guidance."

"So, what? A few days with them and you've fully embraced your Mar'keish dark side, know all of their mind tricks? And let's not forget the part where you're half Reidar." Lianna scoffed from where she stood on the opposite side of the car. "You know we'll never, *ever* trust you, right?"

Varean clenched his fists, shooting a brief, icy look at Lianna then returning his attention to Kira. "I don't need you to trust me. I just need you to believe me."

"Why the hell would you want to help Rian, of all people?" Lianna marched around the aerocar, gun out again. "You missing all that fun time you spent locked up in the brig and getting shot at?"

But Varean wasn't looking at the nav-engineer, didn't seemed the least bit fazed by her weapon. His attention was fixed on Kira, stirring emotion deep within her that she wanted to keep locked away if she was going to get through the day. "I'm not doing this for Rian. I'm doing it for Kira. She's lost enough—you all have. So if I can make that even a little better by helping you get Sherron back, then it's a lot less than I probably owe her for everything she did for me."

"We should let him help us," Zahli put in. "I don't care why he's doing it, as long as he does."

Lianna shot Zahli an incredulous look. "We'll find some other way."

"How?" Zahli stalked forward, using one hand to push the razar down. "You tell me. How are we going to find them when we've got absolutely no clue where the Reidar might have taken them and an entire galaxy to search?"

Lianna swept an apprehensive look over Varean. "You know what he is: half Mar'keish, half Reidar. Either of those things by themselves is bad enough. But put them together? How the hell are we supposed to trust him?"

She was torn, herself, because as much as she wanted Varean to leave and get somewhere safe, far away from the Reidar, she would have made a bargain with Baden Niels himself if it meant getting Rian and Ella back in one piece. They'd already lost so much. Without Rian, there wouldn't be a crew left whenever they got the *Imojenna* back.

"This is my brother we're talking about," Zahli continued. "I'm making the call. They come with us. We use him to find Rian and Ella."

"Zahli—" Tannin set a hand on her shoulder, but she cast him a desperate glare.

"I don't care. It's a risk I'm willing to gamble on. I'll do whatever it takes for Rian."

Lianna muttered a curse, holstering her gun. "Fine. But if he screws us over, I get to kill him."

"Great incentive," Varean muttered darkly, shoving his hands in his pockets.

Lianna pointed a finger at him. "You don't talk unless someone asks you a direct question. And even then, keep the commentary to yourself. Got it?"

"Ma'am, yes, ma'am." He added a sarcastic salute after his words, which only made Lianna frown at him.

"Let's go before I decide to gag and cuff you."

"We have our own transport parked nearby. We'll follow you." Varean cut Kira a brief, unreadable look as he passed then headed back over to where La'thar and Ko'en waited. Everyone else piled into their aerocar a moment later, leaving her to climb in last.

As the door closed and Lianna used manual drive to get them off the ground, she kept her gaze trained out the window as a second aerocar lifted a little way off and swung around to follow them. She wanted to wish that she'd never let herself fall for Varean in the first place, but even with her fractured emotions, she couldn't deny what they'd had together had been remarkable.

She'd connected with him in a way she'd never done with another person before. How the hell was she supposed to give that up? But the question was useless. It was because she cared so much that she needed to know he was safe from the Reidar and those throughout the galaxy who'd fear him if they knew he was Mar'keish.

One thing was painfully clear—he'd never be safe with her, and it wasn't like she could stage-exit on her life and go live with him wherever the Mar'keish now resided. They could heal themselves—what use would they have for a doctor? And if she wasn't a doctor, if she didn't live to her calling, then what kind of existence would she ever have?

"Can we get a secure channel from here, or will I have to wait until we get back to the skimmer?" Zahli asked Lianna, pulling her out of the spiraling thoughts.

"Your personal comm should still be connected to the skimmer's systems; we're not that far out from it. So, yeah, you can access a secure channel. Why?"

Zahli leaned sideways and pulled her commpad from her pocket. "I'm going to put a call through to Qae. The *Ebony Winter* will be faster and safer than traveling in the skimmer. And whatever goes down, we're going to need the backup."

"Good idea," Lianna murmured.

Yeah, calling up Zahli's infamous cousin, Captain Qaelan Forster—who was technically a pirate but hated being called one—was probably their best option. She only hoped, for all their sakes, that Varean could come through on his promise and use his abilities to find Rian.

But whatever plan he had in mind, she just wanted to be left out of it and get this over quickly so they could go their separate paths again. The only way to heal the wound in her heart was to move on, and she couldn't do that until he was gone and firmly in her past.

# Chapter Twenty-Six

Light fingers tugged at the blindfold across his face, pulling the material up and away. Ella motioned for him to stay quiet, the manacle on her wrist catching the light from the bulkhead above them.

Rian snatched a quick glance around, finding their surrounds reinforced and obviously kitted out for this exact type of jaunt—kidnapping and slave trading.

As soon as they'd reached the small Ambit class ship the Reidar were using as their transport, the bastards had blindfolded him then dumped Ella and him in the hold. It seemed they hadn't bothered blindfolding or even restraining the priestess. Obviously they didn't view her as much of a threat.

On one hand, he wanted to say that was ill-advised of them, because in her time on the *Imojenna* Ella had proven to have a pure metium-forged will. But with her powers outed, the frecking aliens were probably right on the money about her being more useless than a pulse pistol mounted on a battle cruiser.

"Are you all right?" He finished his inspection of the hold—barred and locked down with no obvious means of escape—and turned his attention to the priestess.

"I'm not the one who got stabbed and shot." Her voice came out even, tone mostly calm. So what? Even after getting nabbed and knowing they were facing a probable hell of god-knew what kind of torture, she could keep up that still-as-frecking-water thing?

"I've had worse." One good thing he could say about what the Reidar had done to him all those years ago, he'd been left with the weird ability to dull down physical pain. If he didn't think about it, it didn't really hurt, was more like a niggling strain in the background.

"I would heal you if it wasn't for these." She touched her fingers to the cuff on her left wrist.

"Let's talk about those, shall we, since we've got nothing better to do and all." He pushed himself straighter, shifting his leg with the nucleon blast wound. At least that injury had mostly stopped bleeding. His side, however, was still dripping.

Ella didn't answer, simply cast him a wary look, as though she could guess what was coming even without her mind-reading abilities.

"I mean, what the freck, princess? We both know you could have blasted those Reidar into next month. Yet instead, you thought it'd be a good idea to sit back and let them snatch us."

"I couldn't—"

"I don't want to hear another word about your frecking training." He leaned closer, the anger and frustration at being the last place he'd vowed to ever find himself—in the custody of the Reidar—tipping toward her. "No one is making these choices for you. If you wanted to enjoy the Reidar's special spa treatments so much, you should have said so when I met you on Arleta. I would have happily left you if I'd known you were eventually going to land me here."

She clasped her hands in her lap. "That's not true, Rian, and we both know it."

"Isn't it?" He shot back, voice going up a few notches.

One of the Reidar sitting in the cockpit banged hard on the mesh cagelike door. "Keep it down back there or I'm coming in."

"Be my guest," he yelled back. "Come down here and knock me out for all I care. It's got to be better than sitting here talking with this Arynian prig."

Ella's lips pressed together, the only outward sign that she hadn't been impressed by his snark. But then the cage door was opening, one of the Reidar he'd gotten down and dirty with earlier limping in, palming a pulse pistol. Under the harsh light of the bulkhead, the guy's mug was all kinds of messed up. Cheered him right up like a bride getting a face full of confetti.

He pushed to his feet unsteadily, his bound hands making things a little awkward. But when he got upright, he sent the Reidar a cutting grin.

"Hey there, big fella. What's a guy got to do to get in-flight entertainment around here? Maybe a few chicks, bottle or two of Violaine. You feel me, right?"

The Reidar stopped a few steps away and raised the pulse pistol, aiming it at his chest. "Neils wants you alive, but he didn't say anything about being in good working order. So keep your mouth shut, or I'll break your jaw and shut it for you."

"You Reidar aren't so much into the people skills, are you?"

He shuffled half a step forward, bringing himself almost within reaching distance. If he could distract this moron, get his hands on a pulse pistol, make a rush on the bridge—he'd still be left with three or four aliens to overpower if he wanted to take this vessel. But he had to try. He couldn't just sit back and enjoy the trip to another Reidar lab or base wherever they planned to brainwash him right back into a jacked-up, cracked-out droid with no other purpose but to kill.

"Rian, please sit down."

Ella's entreating words almost distracted him, but he kept his gaze locked on the Reidar and that gun.

"You should listen to what the bitch said and sit down."

Despite the fact that he'd readily insulted her himself just a minute ago, the Reidar's words revved the anger already humming loudly through his veins.

This time he took a full step closer, ending with the muzzle of the pulse pistol pressed to the middle of his chest.

"Call her a bitch again. See how that ends for you."

The Reidar laughed, jamming the gun harder against his sternum. "She's nothing but an uptight Arynian scrog, and when we hand you over to Niels I'm going to enjoy watching every second he plays with the bitch."

The anger coalesced into a single white-hot burst, and he clamped his cuffed hands over the pistol, forcing it downward as he head-butted the bastard, breaking his nose with a satisfying crack.

A pulse pistol blast flashed through him, but not from the gun he and the now-bleeding Reidar were both still holding. His knees gave out, and he tried to resist collapsing, but the heavy bastard he'd head-butted had also taken the pulse blast and dragged him down when he collapsed. The two of them fell in a heap, and Rian rolled away to avoid getting flattened by the bigger man. He clenched every muscle in his body against the razor-sharp twitching of his muscles as the pulse subsided.

A second Reidar marched in, muttering under his breath. He grabbed his fallen partner by the collar and dragged him out of the cage. As soon as he stepped foot on the other side of the door, he dropped his burden and slammed the hold closed again.

Rian blew out a pained breath, lying on his back and shoving the new assault to his central nervous system down.

"Was there a point to that?"

He lolled his head to the side, where Ella had shifted closer, sitting cross-legged next to him.

"I thought if I could get his pulse pistol and make it out of the hold, I might have a chance of taking the ship." He dragged both hands over his face, fatigue ramming him like an asteroid. His muscles were weakening, aching, that pulse blast stealing the last of his energy. His chest felt too tight, making it hard to breathe, and in the back of his mind, he knew he'd probably lost more blood than he could afford to part with.

"Thank you for trying."

He opened his eyes and forced himself to sit up, despite the way everything tilted and spun around him. "I didn't do it for you. No offense, princess, but right now, the only person I'm interested in saving is myself."

"And you think I'll believe it a sin that your priority is to save yourself?"

Damn it to hell, his brain was not up to the task of sorting out the meaning in her Arynian speak.

"Honestly, I don't care what you think. I only care about escaping these bastards before we arrive wherever they're headed."

"Why?" She studied him as though she could still see into his very depths, despite the band on her wrists keeping her abilities at bay.

"Besides the obvious torture?" What exactly was she looking for him to admit? And why did he even let himself get drawn into these convoluted conversations? He should have been conserving what energy he had and formulating a plan.

"Besides the obvious," she repeated with a nod.

He didn't need to answer, didn't owe her any explanation. Yet the words were there, despite his aversion to any touchy-feely-sharing-time stuff.

"Reidar assassins are highly trained, highly skilled, single-minded in their focus." He dropped his gaze to the metal grate floor beneath him, clamping a hand over the stab wound in his side that was aching with more insistency. "There's a lot I don't remember from that time, but I know I wasn't just a single Reidar assassin. I was the perfect assassin. The one they'd honed to precision with their brainwashing and reprogramming and god-knows whatever else they did to me."

"Rian—" She reached for him, but he shifted away from her touch. He didn't deserve even the most basic human decency. Not after everything he'd done, everything he was capable of. In the intervening years, onboard the *Imojenna*, he'd actually managed to somewhat remove himself from the reality of the monster he was, separating it to a different entity that existed deep inside him. But there was no division, no two separate halves. It was only him.

"If the Reidar succeed in turning me back into what I once was, no one in this universe will be safe. Not my sister or what's left of my crew. And especially not you."

He cut off the last weak parts of himself that shied away from the truth. Because there was only one path he could take. He had to escape. Or die trying.

# Chapter Twenty-Seven

Kira wrapped her fingers around the handle of her med case, finally feeling anchored in a whirling storm that only kept getting darker and more chaotic.

Tannin had laid Nyah down on one of the bunks in the back of the skimmer, and she was finally showing signs of coming around. Not that it would do her much good. She was about to knock the poor girl out again so she could use an MRD to repair the nasty wound.

The skimmer's control panel chimed with an incoming message, and Lianna pulled her comm out as Zahli crouched down near Nyah's shoulder, reassuring her with quiet words.

"Message from Qae. They took the *Ebony Winter* through a transit gate, so they're in-system. Should be here in about half an hour," Lianna reported.

As Kira set her medical kit on the bunk opposite Nyah and started pulling out various items she'd need, arranging them in order, she couldn't decide if she'd be relieved or sad about leaving the skimmer. The craft was way too small and not made for the kind of travel they'd likely have to do when they went after Rian and Ella, especially now that they'd added Jase and Colt to their traveling band. But it was also the last link to the *Imojenna*, and she was missing her home more with every hour that passed.

Putting the dismal wish out of her mind, she shifted over and knelt next to Zahli.

"How are you doing, Nyah?"

"It hurts." Her words were strained, running together, as she shifted restlessly on the cot.

"I know. I'm going to do something about that right now, okay?"

Nyah gave a jerking nod, and Kira leaned over, shooting the dose of sedative and painkiller into her neck. Almost immediately, she relaxed, body going limp until she fell still and her eyes slid closed on a long exhale.

"How long will she be out?" Zahli climbed to her feet, moving to stand with Tannin, where the others were all watching from the last row of seats in the front half of the skimmer.

"Probably about two hours, but it won't take me that long to repair the wound. I've got to do a scan, but I'm pretty sure the injury is mostly superficial."

"Will you be done by the time Qae arrives? I want to go as soon as the *Ebony Winter* lands."

She nodded absently as she used the handheld scanner to confirm what she'd suspected about the shallow injury. "It'll be close, but yes, I'll be finishing up around then."

"Good," Zahli replied, resolution in her voice. "Now, tell us how and where to find Rian."

Zahli turned toward Varean—where he stood slightly apart with La'thar and Ko'en—a formidable glare aimed in his direction. Kira needed to concentrate on healing Nyah, as she swapped the scanner for the MRD and picked the apparatus to connect for healing a wound of this type. But she was too damn interested in exactly how Varean and the two Mar'keish were going to help them.

"It'll take some time for me to find the information."

"Of course it will." Lianna cocked a hip, hand pointedly resting on a razar. "Maybe you just need some extra motivation."

"You want to find Rian, shooting me with that damned stun gun is the last thing you should be doing. Accessing the Reidar's shared consciousness isn't exactly easy. I'll need my strength, not be half dazed from my brain getting scrambled."

"And how do you expect us to trust anything you say?" Lianna shot back. "Forget the half Reidar thing for a minute, and we're still left with a mind-wraith. And everyone knows the old stories about them."

Varean's stance was tense with frustration, but his expression remained patient. "If that were the case, I could have already used those abilities to get anything I wanted. Instead, I'm standing here with an offer of help."

"How is accessing the Reidar's consciousness going to help us find Rian?" Zahli asked.

"It'll take some searching, and it's going to expose my existence to the rest of the Reidar, but all knowledge of the Reidar is pooled there. As long as at least one Reidar knows Rian's whereabouts, I should be able to find that information."

"How?" Zahli pressed, voicing the same thought she'd had at Varean's explanation, even though Kira was pretending to ignore the conversation as she worked on Nyah. "If all Reidar knowledge is in one giant bubble—"

"Like I said, it's hard to explain. There are actually no real words for it. The whole thing is so alien. But to simplify, it's kind of like a search engine on the net. Type in Rian's name then search the hits that come up until I find what I'm looking for."

"Psychic Reidar internet?" Lianna muttered from the

front of the skimmer. "That doesn't sound stupid at all."

Zahli shot Lianna a brief, annoyed look. "How long will it take you?"

"I have no idea." Varean dragged a hand over his hair.

Her heart squeezed. She had to clamp down on the urge to tell him not to do this, to say she agreed with Lianna, that they'd find Rian some other way. What would it mean for him once the Reidar at large knew of his existence?

The two Mar'keish had said those who'd been responsible for creating Varean had otherwise destroyed all the others like him, along with the evidence that the hybrids had ever existed. Why?

The scientist in her desperately wanted to know the answer. What if there was a chance that whatever the Reidar had been trying to hide about hybrids was the key to their undoing?

What if Varean was the single element they needed to bring down the Reidar?

But she was biased when it came to Varean and this situation. What if she was just looking for reasons for him to stay? She couldn't let herself go there. Varean was safer with the Mar'keish. If she started thinking there was a chance of him not needing to disappear from her life, it was only going to hurt that much more when he inevitably walked away.

· · ·

Varean had never been one to regret his decisions, and he certainly wasn't going to start now. But Kira's cold shoulder act was definitely making him wonder if coming back had been the best idea. Maybe he could have found some way to help them without actually being here.

His Mar'keish abilities continued to elude him, but apparently, for better or worse, he was completely open to his alien self. In this instance, though, it was probably exactly what he needed.

La'thar and Ko'en had instructed him how to skim the edges of the Reidar consciousness and keep his existence hidden. They'd warned him not to dive into the seemingly infinite depths of knowledge and spend only short amounts of time connected or risk the Reidar becoming aware of his presence.

Unfortunately, in order to find Rian like he'd promised, he was going to have to risk everything the pair had cautioned him not to do.

But it wasn't as simple as it sounded, his human side continuing to limit his effectiveness. And the one thing he hadn't mentioned to Kira, the one bitch of a drawback, was that his brain wasn't designed to withstand accessing that level of consciousness or process that much complex information. The result was an increasing ache in his head that eventually turned into a migraine.

La'thar and Ko'en had only started to do a full medical work-up, beginning with basic tests, before they'd discovered intel about the attack.

La'thar had warned him not to push himself, because the results could end up being bad. As in, his brain melting out his ears bad. He didn't want to think the worst of the Mar'keish, but he got the feeling their offer to "help" was more about not letting him out of their sight.

So yeah, this all might end messy and painful for him, but he didn't for a second consider not going through with it. He owed Kira for every moment she'd stood up for him. For helping him discover the truth of his origins, even if it wasn't exactly the stuff of fairy tales. Yet it went deeper than simply owing her, to a place no other person had ever touched—a depth in his soul where she'd compromised him, and he'd enjoyed every second of it.

Zahli had left the other two Mar'keish and him alone a while ago, and the others were obviously wary of the pair. While their race had supposedly died out decades ago, the shocking stories had lived on. Rumors abounded that the Mar'keish could make a person do almost anything with mind control or cause a person to stroke or have an aneurism to kill them without a trace. La'thar and Ko'en hadn't said anything about those kinds of abilities. Of course, they hadn't really said much of anything, initially focusing more on his Reidar side.

They'd taken seats in the last row of the skimmer, but he was aware of the attention and scrutiny. The *Imojenna*'s crew was waiting for him to come up with the answer to Rian's whereabouts. And he had no doubt that if he failed, Lianna would happily follow through on her promise to kill him.

He forced himself to breathe evenly, putting aside the knowledge that Kira was just a few feet behind him and, more than anything, he wanted to make things right with her. But if this worked and he didn't happen to turn his brain to mush, he'd have to go on the run and never look back. The Reidar would never stop coming for him. Anyone close to him would be in danger.

"You remember how to turn your mind inward?" La'thar asked, keeping his voice low.

He nodded, trying to get a handle on his racing thoughts. "It's not so easy here, with all the distraction."

"The Mar'keish side of you is all about intuition," Ko'en said. "You've felt your abilities within you all your life, became good at hiding and ignoring them. When you find that spark, that path inside you, everything will open up, and you will know our ways without having to practice or be taught."

He clenched his fists on the armrests of the chair, the frustration making what he had to do that much harder. They'd said it a dozen times already, made it sound so easy, like he could look into his mind, flip on a switch, and suddenly be able to do all kinds of tricks.

"Though easier to access now, your Reidar side will be more difficult to master," Ko'en continued. "There is a component of utter darkness in the Reidar soul. If you take too much of that into yourself, you will become the darkness, become like them."

Okay, that was new information. And now he had confirmation that was what he'd felt deep within himself on the *Imojenna*. The uncharacteristic aggression, the urge to lash out of control, the desire to use violence instead of calm logic…it was his Reidar side.

"You know of what we speak," La'thar concluded.

He would have been surprised, but he'd worked out in the first two minutes in their company that they could straight-out read his mind.

"Yeah, I've felt that. How do you know all this stuff?"

Ko'en and La'thar shared a look, expressions shifting as though they were having a conversation, which they probably were.

Finally La'thar looked back at him. "You are not the first of your kind we managed to track down. There was one other, a woman. But she became lost to the darkness."

Right. That made him feel so much better. "So you're telling me that by accessing the Reidar consciousness, I could become like them? A sociopath who likes to invade other galaxies?"

"It is a risk, yes. But if you are so set on finding Rian Sherron, this is the only option. No one else can access the Reidar consciousness and discover his whereabouts like you can."

Something about the way La'thar had said *Rian Sherron* made him think the Mar'keish knew a little something about the infamous ex–war hero.

"Why did you come with me? And why are you willing for me to take this risk?"

"It's a long story but comes back to the Mar'keish who were able to flee our homeworld before the IPC created the no-fly zone of cold-space. Those who went to ground and let the universe believe the Mar'keish were no more. Even back then, they knew about the Reidar—the first of the aliens who came to this galaxy. We have been fighting them in secret ever since."

"And what has that got to do with any of this?" He glanced toward the back of the skimmer, where the remaining members of the *Imojenna*'s crew were sitting or standing around Nyah while Kira worked to repair her shoulder.

"Rian Sherron is unique. He was able to break free of the Reidar's mind hold where no others had been able to. We are beginning to realize that if we want to win the war and rid the galaxy of the parasites, Rian Sherron may be one part of the key. But if the Reidar succeed in turning him back to darkness, all hope may be lost."

He scoffed. "So the fate of the universe rests in the hands of one man, and that man is Rian Sherron? How comforting."

La'thar gave a quick smile. "It is not so simple as that, but we believe Rian has his role to play."

"Have you found anything yet?" Zahli had come over, impatience in every line of her body.

"Not yet." Not that he'd been getting anywhere.

"It's been twenty-five minutes. We're getting ready to move Nyah over to the *Ebony Winter* while Lianna docks both the *Imojenna*'s skimmers in a long-term berth."

"I'll be able to do it once we're onboard the *Ebony Winter*." There was too much going on here, too many distractions, all of them starting and ending with Kira.

When they got onboard the larger ship, he could find a quiet room by himself and have more luck. That was after he punched Qaelan Forster in the face.

Repeatedly.

"We won't be coming with you," Ko'en said as Zahli

returned to Nyah's side.

He passed a look between the two men, surprised they were leaving.

"We're needed elsewhere. But when you have found Rian Sherron, contact us. We can continue helping you on your path to fulfilling your potential."

"And to make sure I don't go dark-side like your last hybrid?"

La'thar's smile widened to a grin. "Something like that."

The two men bid him good-bye, extending their courtesy to the rest of the crew before departing.

Varean pushed to his feet as everyone else grabbed the few possessions they'd brought onboard when they'd fled the *Imojenna*. Kira was overseeing Tannin, who carefully picked up Nyah.

"Can I help with anything?" Damn it, he didn't want to sound like a pathetic, overeager puppy looking for approval or attention, but he was pretty sure that's how he came across. Kira shot him a brief glance — at least she actually looked at him, which he was going to count as an improvement — before handing over several medical bags.

"No problem. Happy to carry the luggage," he muttered as she followed after Tannin down the narrow ramp.

Outside, the *Ebony Winter* perched two docks over. Though less than half the size of the *Imojenna*, the Sylph class ship had a definite elegance to it, unlike the Nirali class that had been built to run supplies and withstand war.

The ghostly image of a woman wearing white was painted on the side of the infamous marauders' ship, no doubt adding to whatever reputation Qaelan Forster liked to uphold. Didn't exactly make the ship ideal for stealth. So just how in the heck had Forster managed to land here without bringing every IPC officer and UAFA agent on Forbes running to apprehend him?

As their little group approached the ship the ramp lowered, the noise of the engines still winding down. Forster stood just inside the atmospheric doors, arms crossed and feet braced wide. The undeniable urge to shoot the bastard swelled in a flooding tide, but he didn't have a weapon, and shooting the man they'd called for help wouldn't win him any favors with the crew.

Forster wasn't besieged with the same qualms, since he yanked out a razar and a pulse pistol as soon as their gazes clashed.

"Hold it right there. What the mother of all that is frecked, people? No one mentioned that shag we trussed up on the *Swift Brion* was still around."

Zahli sent him an annoyed look as she continued up the ramp. "He's helping us find Rian. So if you shoot him, Qae, I'll have to shoot you."

"What do you mean he's *helping* us find Rian? What the hell happened since we split up?"

She stepped in front of Forster and pushed his guns down. "We'll explain everything on the way. Can we just stow it for now and get off this damn moon?"

"I'm not letting him on my ship unless he's cuffed—"

"Not this again." Kira expelled a sharp breath. "He's not the enemy and definitely didn't deserve the way you treated him. No one is cuffing him or tying him up or restraining him. He came to us with the offer to help find Rian, and we are *not* repaying that by treating him worse than an animal. Again."

Kira standing up for him made him get a moronic case of the warm and fuzzies. If nothing else, he could still count on her, even if she was eager to push him away.

Scowling at him, Forster holstered his gun. They glared each other down as he walked past, before he went deeper into the cargo bay following Kira, where she was leading Tannin to find Nyah a bed. Lucky he had his hands full of the medical kits or he definitely wouldn't have made it onto this ship without a few fists being exchanged.

Kira and Tannin walked into the tiny medbay with a single bed. Tannin set Nyah down gently and then left the room.

While Kira ran her scanner over Nyah, he inspected a couple of lockers and found somewhere to put the kits. That done, he shoved his hands in his pockets as he turned to focus on Kira. He watched, keeping silent as she fussed over Nyah, finding her a blanket and then strapping her down to the gurney. That done, she went to where he'd stashed her bags, sorting through them, pulling out a few bits and pieces, and leaving them on another shelf for easy access.

Finally, she turned to him, frustration tightening her features. "Is there something you need?"

"To talk."

The look she shot him said he was all kinds of crazy to expect any kind of conversation.

"Can we just not? It'll be easier when you leave again if we don't complicate things in the meantime. In fact, how about we just avoid seeing each other altogether." She hurried out of the room before he could so much as take in a breath to answer.

"Kira, wait." He followed her out and caught her arm.

She tugged out of his hold and crossed her arms, avoiding his gaze. But she did stop, and it was probably the best opening he would get.

"I shouldn't have been so quick to leave you on Barasa the way I did, not when I knew you weren't safe. If you'd arrived at that cabin half an hour earlier, it could have been you in the house when—"

"This is pointless, Varean." She shifted away from him, closing herself up. "I've told you before, I was doing fine before you came along, and I'll be able to look after myself when you've gone again. I'm not your responsibility; it's not up to you to keep me safe. I wish you hadn't come back, and that makes me selfish, because I know you're our only hope of finding Rian and Ella."

The totally logical and true statement hit him like a blow to the gut. Damn it, she wasn't his responsibility, but christ, did he want her to be. Considering who and what he was, he couldn't give her anything except danger and death, couldn't expect her to live a life on the run. And though he'd known all those things on some level, now it really sunk in, like claws digging into his chest, sliding deeper and deeper until he couldn't deny the reality of it.

"You're right. This was pointless. Avoiding each other is probably the smartest idea."

Before she could reply, he walked away, following the drift of voices as he headed up into the ship. He emerged in a small kind of common room and galley, to find Lianna, Zahli, Tannin, and Jase chatting with people he assumed were Forster's crew, plus the marauder captain himself. Silence dropped like a stone when they saw him, the tension in the room spreading like a frost.

"Are we about ready to launch?" The familiar voice shocked his system, almost sending him to automatic attention from years of military training.

Captain Admiral Zander Graydon entered through the opposite, wider passageway, which presumably led to the bridge. However, the captain admiral wasn't wearing an IPC uniform. The matching black shirt and pants did appear to be some kind of uniform, with a red six-pointed star insignia the only decoration, but it wasn't any military outfit he recognized.

The captain admiral paused when he saw him. "Donnelly. Can't say I expected to see you here."

"Because you thought I was dead, or that I abandoned my post on the *Swift Brion*?" The words came out before he'd really thought about them. Once he would never have dared to talk trash to the captain admiral. But by all accounts the man had gone AWOL, and, after everything Varean had been through recently, he was left feeling like he didn't owe anyone a single damned thing. Especially since Graydon hadn't tried to intervene when Sherron decided to take him.

Graydon clasped his hands behind his back, raising a single eyebrow. "To be honest, I hadn't given it much thought. Your name came up as unaccounted for, but between getting stabbed and stealing a flagship, I hadn't found the time to follow it up."

Some of his indignation drained away. "You mean you didn't know Sherron and Forster forcibly removed me from the *Swift Brion* and locked me in the brig of the *Imojenna*?"

Graydon shot an incredulous look at the marauder. "They did *what*?"

"I reacted to the alien stunner. Sherron wanted to know why." He couldn't exactly have stayed pissed off at the man if he hadn't known anything about it.

"For the record, I think numbnuts is an alien," Forster put in, his glare all kinds of suspicious.

For the first time, he took a tiny flare of enjoyment out of his hybrid DNA as he sent Forster a cutting grin. "Actually, dick-face, you're only half right."

Forster scowled. "What's that supposed to mean?"

"Kira ran some blood tests on him," Lianna interjected. "Turns out he's the result of some kind of Reidar freak show breeding experiments, and he's half alien. Not only that, but he's also half Mar'keish."

"You brought a mind-wraith onto my ship? A frecking *half alien* mind-wraith?"

It might have been frosty before, but at Forster's exclamation, the temperature in the room dropped about a thousand degrees.

He held up his hands, gesturing his surrender. "Don't get

your guns out on my account. I'm not working for the Reidar. Finding out I shared some DNA with them was news to me."

Forster took an aggressive step forward, palms on his weapons. "Well, isn't that frecking convenient—"

"How about I show you just how convenient I find this whole thing?" He matched Forster's step forward, nearly putting the bastard within punching range, until Graydon got between them.

"Stand down!" Graydon used his captain admiral voice, effectively grabbing everyone's attention. "Donnelly, I understand better than anyone about getting the urge to take a swing or two at Forster. But since we're currently standing on his ship, it's probably not going to leave the moron in a helpful mood."

"Jezus, Graydon, you make it sound like I'd let my ego get in the way of saving my cousin."

Forster and Rian were *cousins*? Well, that explained a few things.

The look Graydon shot the captain in return asked *wouldn't you?* loud and clear.

Forster's glare deepened. "I'll do anything to get Rian back from those crazy-pants aliens, apparently even let some Mar'keish-Reidar-hybrid freak on my ship. But if he leads us into a trap, I'm going to put a round of ammo into his face."

"Already called dibs," Lianna put in conversationally, as if they were talking about the last slice of cake instead of killing him.

Forster's attention sharpened on Lianna, a hint of intrigue in his expression. "Well freck me Friday, woman. What's a man gotta do to kill people on his own ship? Everyone's got a price—name yours."

"You couldn't afford it, believe me." Lianna gave him a patronizing pat on the shoulder as she passed.

"We'll see about that," he muttered as she disappeared.

A second later, he clapped his hands, rubbing his palms together. "So, someone have a destination in mind for this circus of death?"

"That's why I'm here." He crossed his arms, not really wanting to explain the whole Reidar-consciousness thing again. "I just need a little time to work out where Rian is."

Just as he guessed, Forster went right back to looking unimpressed. "And how are you going to do that?"

"You don't want to know," Zahli said from where she was sitting with Tannin and the rest of Forster's small crew.

"What kind of risk are we talking here? It's not going to clue the aliens into our whereabouts or the fact we're coming for Rian?"

And this is where things got even more complicated. "I can't make any assurances. But if you want Sherron back, this is probably the only option."

"Lucky for you, terrible plans are my forte." The captain swept a glance around the small room. "Let's at least get off this planet before the authorities work out we're not really a machinery hauler and our registration papers are forged."

Forster sent a nod to Graydon, and the two of them headed up to the bridge while everyone else settled in for launch. Instead of joining them, Varean went back out into the passageway. On a lower level, he found two cabins with multiple uncomfortable-looking fold-down racks—not much better than many troop transports he'd been on during his years with the IPC.

He took himself into the second cabin and plonked his ass down on the nearest cot. Really, he could have used a combat nap, but everyone was waiting for him to provide the information he'd promised, and he doubted they'd be impressed if someone came looking and found him sleeping. So instead, he got himself into a comfortable upright position and then closed his eyes, following the instructions La'thar and Ko'en had given him to delve deeper into his own mind, access parts of his brain humans never used.

Without Kira's distracting presence or the watchful stares of the others, he was able to sink into the stream of higher awareness more easily. La'thar and Ko'en had helped him create a kind of barrier to keep himself from slipping into the Reidar consciousness accidentally, as he apparently had while he'd been sleeping. That was what the hallucinations had been—memories and information literally leaking into his mind. The language he'd heard was Reidar, and now his mind had processed enough that he was able to fully understand it.

Accessing the Reidar consciousness was almost like having an out-of-body experience. Like his mind had gone to a completely different plane of existence and left his physical form behind, though he was still aware of his body anchoring him to reality.

Once he brought the barrier down, he could feel the complex pool of energy and knowledge, as though it was brimming at his feet, just waiting for him to dive in. He reached out and touched it, connected, felt himself altering in a way he didn't understand or have words for, as though he'd become one with something far greater than himself. He could receive small amounts of information by keeping himself separate, but to find what he needed specifically might take too long.

He hesitated, remembering La'thar and Ko'en's warning not to fully access the consciousness because the Reidar would become aware of his presence. Not to mention the added bonus of the risk he took in getting lost to the darkness.

But something good had to come out of this mess, and if that single good was helping Kira put what she considered her family back together, it was the price he'd pay.

Bracing himself—because he had no idea what this was going to do to him—he fully opened his mind, immersing his entire being into the ethereal energy.

# Chapter Twenty-Eight

Rian had examined every damned square inch of the hold and found it to be brilliantly seamless. On the bright side, he could now make some improvements to the *Imojenna*'s brig to make it inescapable. On the downside, Ella and he were totally screwed and not getting out until the frecking Reidar let them out. Which was probably why the bastards hadn't said a word about him prowling the cage, because without a laser torch or ion blaster, he wasn't going anywhere.

From what he could overhear on the bridge, the aliens were getting ready to land on a station, though he didn't think this was their final destination. They were either swapping transports—which would give him an opportunity to escape—or getting supplies, which made escape a little less likely. Either way, he was calling the break in the trip a win. The only downside to his not-quite-a-plan? His frecking ribs were burning like a white star, his ability to numb the pain not working so well anymore, which told him the wound was worse than he'd thought. Plus, slowly but surely, his lungs strained more and more, as if with each breath, they held a little less oxygen.

Ella had stayed sitting in the middle of the hold, silently watching him as time marched by and he'd failed to find a way out. Now, as the ship shuddered into its station docking berth, she got up and came over to him.

"Don't you think you've wasted enough energy trying to find a way out of here?"

He scoffed, but the sound turned into a cough. And coughing sent one mother of an agonizing spasm ripping through his middle. He doubled over, the pain made worse by the vise squeezing his lungs, leaving him unable to breathe properly.

Ella caught his arm with surprising strength, keeping him from collapsing face first. But she wasn't strong enough to keep him from going down altogether, and the two of them ended up sitting on the floor, her arms around him, propping him against her. Usually he would have been scrambling to escape anyone touching him, especially her, but he couldn't find the stamina to care.

"Rian, you should have conserved your energy." She splayed one hand against the middle of his chest, as if checking his heartbeat.

"What for? All the fun torture and brainwashing? No thanks. I'd prefer to check out before that." The back of his throat dry, his words came out rough.

She shifted them slightly, settling herself back against the bulkhead and taking his weight more easily against her smaller frame. He should get up; he was probably too heavy for her, and he still had to find a way out of this. But it was as if his arms and legs had disconnected from his brain and left him with an "out of order" sign.

"The others will come for us—"

"Yeah, they probably will, the idiots. And they'll get themselves killed."

"You don't know that." Her voice was quieter, simmering with determination.

"Don't I?" He let his eyes slip closed. Just for a second. Just to get some energy back. "Anyway, I thought you didn't care. I thought you'd come to realize I'm a lost cause."

"I never said I didn't care or that I'd given up on you."

Though the bands were keeping her abilities dampened, he could have sworn her touch was taking away some of the pain. Or maybe he was just that far gone. Maybe he'd get his wish and die before the Reidar could turn him loose on the galaxy again.

"You might not have said the words, but your actions told me loud and clear. Despite the fact that it's impossible to avoid people onboard the *Imojenna*, where we all live in one another's pockets, you did a pretty impressive job of keeping out of my way after we took the *Swift Brion*. Because of what I did to you."

He thought she might have shaken her head; he felt it in the subtle movement of her against him and where her long hair brushed over his upper arm.

"It wasn't because of what you did, Rian. It was because of what *I* did."

Well, nothing much surprised him these days, but that sure as shite did. He cracked his eyes open and shifted to look up at her. "What do you mean?"

If he hadn't already been having trouble breathing, seeing her up close, her gorgeous mossy-hazel eyes fixed so intently on him, it definitely would have stolen the air right out of his chest.

"The way I retaliated when you had me trapped. I got angry and I used my abilities against you, to bring you down. It went against all of my training, showed me that I was capable of things I'd never considered before, that I was weak and prone to emotion as my teachers always accused."

He reached up and caught her hand where she still had it pressed against the middle of his chest. "That's what you think happened?"

She gave a single resolute nod. "I discarded my training and acted on impulse. All those months onboard the *Imojenna*, the farther I got away from Aryn and my life there, I started forgetting who I was and what my purpose is. I became weaker, began letting my emotions come before logic—"

"No." He squeezed her hand, and she returned the gesture, hanging onto him tightly, like he was her only lifeline. "You're not weak. Using your abilities against me, that was the right thing to do. That is your strength. You stand up for yourself and never let anyone hurt you or put you down. Especially me. That's what I've been trying to tell you this whole time. Whatever those frecking idiots on Aryn told you, they were wrong. The universe is a harsh, dark place, and the only way to survive it is to use whatever tools you have at your disposal."

Her gaze searched his, as though looking for redemption, looking for a truth she needed, to justify the person she kept hidden behind her priestess mask.

"But what if I hurt someone? What if I do something atrocious to those undeserving?"

"You'll never hurt anyone, princess. Not anyone who doesn't merit it, anyway. Like I said, this universe is a dark place. But you are the light, and nothing will ever change that."

She exhaled, as though his words had released something within her.

"Is that why you didn't use your abilities to stop the Reidar from taking us?" he asked, struggling to keep his eyes open, the lids feeling weighted, dragging downward.

Her gaze cut away from him. "No. I became emotional when the Reidar hurt you. Emotion means loss of control and my abilities fail me. I'm sorry I couldn't save us."

"It doesn't matter now." He gave in and let his eyes shut him into the black again. "This probably isn't going to end in fairy tales and rainbows for me. The best I can do is make sure I don't take anyone else with me. But promise me, if you get those cuffs off, you'll try to stay calm, use your abilities, and do whatever it takes to get yourself free."

Ella tightened her arms around him, letting go of his hand to cup his cheek. "I'll promise to do better next time, if you promise to stay awake. The others will come for us, Rian."

"That's what I'm afraid of," he murmured, before sinking deeper into nothingness.

# Chapter Twenty-Nine

Kira ventured up into the ship, her stomach rumbling at the scent wafting down the passageway. They'd left Forbes about two hours ago and since then, Nyah had woken up, clearly not any worse for wear from her injury. She'd given her a light painkiller, though since the MRD had done most of the work in knitting tissue and flesh back together, she shouldn't have been in as much pain.

Now she was on the hunt for some food for both Nyah and her, while her patient rested in the medbay. Plus, it was probably about time she stopped hiding out.

After Varean had walked away from her in the passageway, she'd returned to the medbay and given in to the tears she'd been holding back for what seemed like forever. She'd cried for Callan and Jensen, for Rian and Ella, and the fact that she hurt so much over Varean, over something she'd always known couldn't be, but had fallen into anyway.

She wasn't sure what he'd wanted to achieve from talking to her—he knew just as well as she did there was nothing to be said or done to change their situation. Dwelling on it would only make things messier, and with everything else going on, she couldn't handle that.

She came into a small common area, about a quarter of the size of the one on the *Imojenna*. The room was packed full of both the *Ebony Winter*'s crew, plus what was left of their own crew, Commander Colter Routh and Tannin's friend Jase. The mood was nothing short of dour, only a few quiet words exchanged as the food was served.

"Where are we headed?" she asked Zahli as she stopped next to her friend and accepted the plate Tannin handed her.

"We still don't know." Zahli's expression was drawn, as though she fully expected to find Rian dead and was already grieving.

"But I thought Varean—"

"That's just it. He went down into one of the lower cabins and when he didn't come back, Lianna and I went to check on him. We found him in some sort of trance or coma, and we can't bring him out of it."

She set down the plate carelessly, almost dropping it and making it clatter against the bench, her heart going in the same direction. "Why didn't you come and get me?"

"You were looking after Nyah." Zahli shrugged, clearly unsure of what decision she should have made, which was totally out of character. Usually Zahli was the first one to make a choice and stick with it. "I was going to give it another half an hour, and then get you if he still hadn't come around. I just thought after everything, you wouldn't want to deal with him."

"Whether or not I want to deal with him comes second to finding Rian." She pushed off from the bench and hurried out of the room, Zahli on her heels.

Down on the lower level of the ship, she found Varean in the second of two cabins. He was sitting propped up against the bulkhead on one of the cots, eyes closed, yet body tense.

A trickle of blood tracked out of his nose.

"Was he like that before?" She got onto the cot, kneeling and checking his eyes. His pupils were totally blown. "Damn it."

"He looked fine before." Zahli stood at the edge of the bed. "What's wrong with him?"

"Mydriasis."

"Which means what to those of us without a medical degree?"

"It can be an indicator of intracranial pressure or impending brain herniation, among other things. It's bad. Help me lay him down."

Between the two of them, they managed to shift Varean around and lay him flat on the cot. "Zahli, run to the medbay and get my med kit."

She pressed her fingers into Varean's neck to measure his pulse then leaned down and listened to his chest. His heart rate was up and his breathing shallow. His body wasn't going to be able to take much more before his systems started to fail.

"Varean, if you can hear me, you need to stop. You need to come out of this or it's going to kill you."

His muscles twitched, though she couldn't have said whether it was a response to her demand or simply his body beginning to hit critical mass.

Zahli returned with the med kit, slightly out of breath.

Kira grabbed a scanner and switched it on, monitoring first his head and then moving down his body. Just as she'd expected, his brain was swelling, restricting his oxygen and blood flow.

Her first instinct was to give him something to bring down his heart rate and possibly reduce the pressure on his skull, but his hypersensitivity to medication might only make things worse.

Her chest got tight, like her ribs were clamping down on her lungs. Varean couldn't die. They needed him.

After everything, she refused to let it all end like this.

"What are you going to do?" Zahli asked, expression edging toward desperation. Not because she cared about Varean, of course, but because he was her best chance of finding Rian.

"I don't know." Not the words people wanted to hear a doctor say. But the unknown variable of Varean's Mar'keish and Reidar DNA made doing anything a risk. Without medication, the only option was to drill a hole in his head to release some of the pressure. But that came with its own risks. Doing nothing wasn't an option.

"Okay, Varean. I hope whatever you found out was worth it, because this isn't going to be pleasant." She pulled out the MRD and searched through the case of fittings until she found the one she needed to perform this little surgery.

She sifted her fingers through his hair, mentally mapping the skull and brain, recalling her training to locate the exact spot.

Varean groaned, shifting beneath her touch and making her pause.

"Here, Zahli, hold this for a second." She handed the MRD off to her friend and lifted Varean's eyelids again. His pupils were normal and reactive now, irises completely mercury silver. When she checked the second eye, he swatted her away.

"My head is killing me, and that's not helping." His voice was rough and gravelly, but steady. He blinked open his eyes and then pressed the heel of his palm into his forehead. "Christ, it feels like someone used my skull for batting practice while I was out of it."

"Did it work? Did you find out where Rian and Ella are?" Zahli knelt down next to the bed, gaze searching Varean's pale face.

"I know where they're headed, but they haven't arrived yet. They're in transit." With a harsh exhale, he pushed himself upright but then swayed, almost pitching right off the edge of the rack.

"You should stay horizontal for a while." Kira set a hand on his shoulder, urging him to lie back down. "Your brain was under a tremendous amount of pressure. I thought it was going to kill you. And lucky you came out of it when you did. I was about to drill holes into your skull."

He cut her a sharp look, laced with disbelief. "As fun as that sounds, next time, just give it a minute."

"A minute?" Zahli's voice went up several octaves, making Varean wince. "You've been out for over two hours."

"Damn it, sorry. Time passes differently over there."

"And we still don't know exactly where Rian is. But you said you know where they're going? Maybe we can beat them there, set an ambush—"

Varean shook his head. "No, we can't. They're headed for cold-space."

*Cold-space?* The bottom dropped out of her stomach.

Back when she'd still been in med school, they studied a module on the super virus that had ripped through four planets decades ago and left less than 5 percent of the population alive. The IPC hadn't wanted to risk the virus getting out into the rest of the galaxy and defended the system with deadly force with no warning. A ship tried to cross the lines, it got blasted. Which begged the question of how the Reidar planned on getting into cold-space and why.

"Why the hell would the Reidar take them into cold-space? And it seems like more than a small coincidence that the Mar'keish have resurfaced after decades, and now the Reidar are heading to what used to be their homeworld," Zahli stated, voicing Kira's own thoughts aloud. "If Rian and

Ella end up in cold-space, they'll never be able to leave, and that's if they don't die."

"The Mar'keish aren't working with the Reidar, if that's what you're thinking. That's about the only thing I know for certain," Varean shot back, his tone defensive. "If we're going to get them back, we have to do it before they cross into the no-fly zone."

Zahli pushed to her feet, posture taut. "But you said you don't know where they are, only that they're in transit. How the hell does that narrow it down?"

Kira set a hand on Zahli's shoulder. "We know they left Forbes, and we know where they're heading. Lianna can plot a probable course to narrow it down."

"And what good will that do when we don't even know what kind of ship they're on?"

Varean released a short breath that sounded part pain, part resignation. "Just give me a little while to recharge, then I'll try again. I'll find something more specific."

Zahli stared at him then gave a tight nod and left the room. Once she was gone, he threw an arm over his face, shielding his eyes. A swell of worry crested within Kira, despite wanting to stay detached and view him as nothing more than a means to an end.

"Is it really a good idea to do that again? It seems to have taken a lot out of you." She couldn't help the words escaping.

"The headache is just part of the fun. It happened when La'thar and Ko'en showed me how to do it, too."

Why did she get the feeling he was leaving out something?

"And the brain swelling? Your head nearly exploding, was that part of the fun as well?" She crossed her arms, wishing she could see his eyes, wishing there were some way to make him tell her the full story. But he didn't owe her anything, and if he didn't want to tell her, that was his prerogative.

"I spent only a few days with the Mar'keish. We didn't

exactly get to work through everything. Still pretty much don't understand anything about me and what I can do."

"So is there a chance this could kill you? Because it certainly looked like things were heading that way." And why did that have to make her chest hurt like taking a blow to the sternum? If only she could sever her feelings for him, like performing surgery. Neat, painless, over and done with in a short span of time.

Varean dropped his arm and focused on her with bleary eyes. "Since we've got no other way to find Rian, and we're on the clock and running out of time, I don't see any other option."

She sat on the edge of the cot. "But when you're doing this, aren't you aware of the strain it's putting on your body?"

"At first, yes. But this time I went deeper, so I was more disconnected from myself, if that makes sense."

"Not really."

He let out a low sigh and closed his eyes again.

"I'll let you rest. But when you're ready to try again, let me know so I can monitor your vitals this time."

"Sure, Doc," he murmured, sounding half asleep.

She left the room, ducking in to check on Nyah and coaxing her up to the galley, since she'd failed to bring any food down for her like she'd intended.

As she headed up-ship, she tried not to think about what Varean was doing for them, the risk he was taking, and why he was apparently willing to sacrifice himself. But no matter how she tried to push them down and away, the nagging questions hooked themselves into her mind like burrs and refused to dislodge.

Like the commando she'd first met, Varean seemed all set on throwing himself headlong into death, probably thinking it was a misguided way of saving her by saving Rian. Or maybe he thought it was the only way for him, being that he was a hybrid and possibly the only one in the entire universe. Or maybe he was reverting to his training and willing to face death as long as he saw the mission through. Whatever the case, she didn't intend to sit by and let him die for this cause, no matter how important Rian and Ella were to the crew of the *Imojenna*.

. . .

Varean didn't need a watch to tell him that he'd slept for exactly forty-five minutes. He'd trained his body to combat nap for no longer than half a sleep cycle. Surprisingly, he wasn't feeling too bad. His head didn't ache any longer, and he felt more rejuvenated than he'd expected, considering how he'd been after coming out of the last bout of the mind-benders.

Swinging his legs off the cot, he pushed to his feet and stretched. Kira had said she wanted to monitor him the next time he went under, and the way things had gone down, it was probably a good idea.

He'd been deep in the network of ebbing and flowing energy and knowledge, not realizing he'd almost disconnected from the anchor of his body. He'd waded through a lot of information, including snatches of the hybrid breeding experiments, the Reidar's plan for the galaxy and human race, plus bits and pieces about Sherron's time in Reidar custody. And while he'd found confirmation of where Baden Niels planned on taking the abducted pair, he'd still been searching for an answer to why and where they were, exactly, when he'd heard Kira's voice.

At first, it'd been like a distant echo, but it had tethered him as surely as a safety line on a spacewalk, drawing him in and bringing him back to solid ground, just like it had in those hazy days after he'd first been hit with the stunner. If not for her, he might not have come out of it before his body hit critical mass or before he became lost to the darkness.

When he stepped into the common room, he found only Kira and Nyah, the others nowhere to be seen, though a drift of voices came from the bridge.

"You're looking much better," Kira said as he went to the coldstore and got a bottle of electrolyte water.

"That's not going to last long. If you're ready, I'd like to go back under again."

Her expression tightened, but she nodded and stood.

He headed out of the common room, but as he turned toward the cabin with the racks, Kira stopped him with a hand on his arm.

"We're better off doing this in the medbay." Without waiting for him to agree, she disappeared down the passage.

He opened his water and took a long swallow as he followed her, thirsty but not hungry, even though he couldn't remember when he'd last eaten a decent meal.

In the medbay, Kira remained silent as she set things up, so he put his half-empty water aside and got onto the slim gurney, unhelpfully remembering everything that had gone down last time he'd been in a medbay on the *Imojenna*—getting tied up, the fight with Callan, and almost getting killed more times than he cared to think about.

Putting aside the recollections, he breathed out and forced himself to relax. Kira finished her preparations and looked down at him, doctor mask firmly in place like when he'd first met her.

"Okay. I've got two different scanners ready to monitor your vitals. So how is this going to work?"

"It'll be just like last time, except if I've been out for too long, or you think things are getting critical, I need you to bring me right out of it."

"And how am I supposed to bring you out of it? I can't

give you any medications. Last time, I was about ready to drill holes in your head."

He clenched his fists, fighting the urge to reach out and take her hand. But he had no way of resisting the smile tugging at his mouth. "Yeah, that would have been one hell of a surprise to wake up to."

"You're lucky you did wake up." She clamped her lips together, as though she wanted to say more.

"Don't worry, Kira. This is going to work. I've got a better idea of what I'm doing this time. If you need to bring me out, just call my name. I can hear you, loud and clear. That's how I came around before. Your voice is like a light leading me back."

She took in a quick breath, her gaze cutting away from him. Okay, so he was obviously making her uncomfortable, which didn't really run with the whole plan of avoiding each other. But he couldn't let their personal complications get in the way of what he needed to do.

"I'm ready when you are." He closed his eyes, preparing to sink into his mind.

"What if it doesn't work?" Her words were quiet, but they jolted his body like she'd shouted them. Her fingers wrapped tightly together with his. "What if simply talking you out doesn't work? What do I do?"

He couldn't open his eyes and look at her, because if he did, all the things he wanted to say to her would come spilling out. And they'd already established that was pointless.

"If it doesn't work, you let me go. There's nothing else you can do."

Her hand slipped from his, leaving him feeling alone in the dark. But since it was self-inflicted, he wasn't going to waste time lying there feeling sorry for himself. Instead, he found the thread he needed in his mind and followed it.

When he reached the threshold, he was shocked to find

the barrier La'thar and Ko'en had instructed him to keep up was entirely missing. Because of the way he'd come out of it last time, chasing Kira's voice after being so disconnected? He put the worry aside, but made a mental note that when he came out this time, he had to make sure the mental barricade was in place.

Without hesitation, he immersed in the stream of consciousness, taking himself right to where he'd left off— pursuing a line on Sherron. There was so much to wade through because of the years the guy had spent in Reidar custody. But slowly, he was able to recognize old information, which had a different quality to it compared to new information.

Finally, he came across something he could use. Sherron and the priestess were being transported on a tiny Ambit class ship called the *Marsala*. Now all he needed was an exact location, and they'd be set to snatch the pair back.

A prickle of awareness bristled across him, making him pause. And then— It was almost something he couldn't explain, but like another reached out and touched him with icy fingers, leaving chills racing through him. In a split second, he felt the entity go from curious to hostile.

*Oh crap.* The Reidar—at least one, anyway—had become aware of his presence. Like a tornado touching down, a swirl of antagonistic energy surrounded him, restricting him from accessing any more information. Or finding his way out. He could feel multiple consciousnesses prodding him, poking him like sharp little jabs from a razor, trying to get into his mind, trying to steal images and memories. They were trying to work out where and how to find him.

Time to get the hell out. Except the churning vortex of energy left him disoriented, completely disconnected from any tether or direction. It was getting harder to keep the jagged assault of power from completely overwhelming him.

And then he felt it—a tiny glimmer of light. It was Kira

calling him, but he was so far gone, he couldn't hear her, could only feel the echo, almost too far away for him to reach.

With effort, he blocked out everything and focused on that miniscule flicker and then hurled himself toward it. His body jolted, pain exploding through every cell of his being as he slammed back to himself. Kira was shouting his name, tone just shy of outright panic, her fingers digging tightly into his shoulders.

He couldn't find his voice, couldn't breathe, couldn't open his eyes, the agonizing burn in his brain radiating through the rest of his body. Gradually, with each sluggish thump of his heart, the pain receded, and he was able to suck in a long breath ending on a cough, because his lungs had been deprived of oxygen too long.

"Damn it, Varean." Kira sounded really pissed, practically slapping an oxygen mask on his face.

He slitted his eyes open, expecting the light to stab through his retina like a white-hot flare knife, but not prepared for the exact torture.

"Do you want to risk some pain meds? I could give a very small dose, see how it affects your systems."

He shook his head, grimacing at the extra hurt that inflicted. "It'll pass in a second."

She huffed out a long sigh, and he made his bleary eyes focus on her as she dropped onto the stool next to the gurney.

"How long this time?" he asked, swallowing against the dryness in the back of his throat.

"An hour and a half. But something different happened. One second you seemed to be fine, then you started seizing."

"They found me," he murmured, more to himself. And damn it to hell, but again, he'd come out too fast and hadn't made sure the barrier was in place. Even now, he could feel the consciousness in the bottom of his mind rising up like lava in a volcano, the sinister drive to know where and how to find him so they could see him destroyed. He had to shut them down, re-erect his barricade—if it wasn't too late.

"What do you mean they found you?"

"La'thar and Ko'en warned me if I did this, I risked exposing myself to the Reidar."

"And now they know where you are?" She paced a few steps away, anger in her tight movements. "How could you risk that?"

He pushed upright on the gurney, ignoring the aching slosh of his head. "What else was I going to do?"

She spun back to face him, incensed. "How about not putting yourself right in front of danger, like staring down a battle cruiser, for once?"

"Except then I wouldn't have been able to help you. I wouldn't have been able to find Sherron."

She sucked in a sharp breath, hope leaping into her gaze like a kindling flame.

"You found Rian?"

"Not his exact location. But he and the priestess are on an Ambit class ship called the *Marsala*."

"And what about you?"

"I'll disappear with the Mar'keish. Hopefully they'll help me stay one step ahead of the bastards."

She closed her eyes. "This wasn't worth your life."

"Wasn't it?" His life had been over the second he'd been shot with the razar back on the *Swift Brion*. He had nothing and no one to hold on to. Whatever the Reidar did to him seemed like little more than a formality.

Besides, if he wanted half a chance of going on the run—whatever kind of existence that would provide—he needed to go back in and slam up that barrier as hard and solid as he could. Even now, he could feel tiny worming threads of other entities searching the outer edges of his mind. Only a matter of time before they found a clue that would tell them where to find him. And considering all Kira had put on the line for him, he didn't plan on getting her killed.

"Comm up to the bridge and give them the information. Every minute counts if you want to get Sherron back before he and the priestess reach cold-space."

In a matter of moments, she'd informed Forster, the captain ending the call with an order for Kira to go up to the bridge. There certainly hadn't been any short supply of suspicion in the guy's voice. No doubt they were going to discuss what to do with him now.

Kira didn't look at him as she shoved her comm away, but paused at the medbay doorway. "You're going to rest, right?"

He contemplated telling her a small, easy lie. That, of course, he was going to rest. But she deserved the truth.

"I have to go back in."

"*What*?" She stepped toward him, fists clenched and green eyes flashing. "You think you came close to dying before? This time you were circling the drain. You stopped breathing and your heart rate dropped to nothing but a few beats a minute. And that was before you started seizing. You can't do it again."

"If they find me while I'm on this ship, that puts you and everyone else in danger. They won't hesitate to blow the *Ebony Winter* to pieces just to kill me. La'thar and Ko'en instructed me to keep a kind of mind barrier in place, and when I came out, I don't know if the barrier stayed up. I'm not going to go deep like I did the last two times, just enough to make sure I can keep them at bay until I get somewhere far away from you."

She pointed a finger at him. "Don't do anything until I come back."

He shook his head. "I don't have time to wait. I've done my part, so your obligation to deal with me is over. Head up to the bridge, and don't worry about me."

She muttered a string of curses that sounded more like something Callan would have said, then left the medbay at a run.

Still swimming in pain and exhaustion, Varean blew out a hard breath and collapsed on the gurney.

There was no choice, however, no second-guessing. He'd vowed to keep Kira safe and that included from himself. He'd go back, no matter the cost, and make sure the Reidar didn't find him.

Focusing on that single determination made it easy to ignore the aches and fatigue to put himself down again. Streams of consciousness brimmed out from beyond where he'd erected the barricade before. They were in the outer reaches of his mind already, and it wouldn't take long before they found what they needed and everything was lost.

He'd have to partly immerse himself to put the barrier back up. He didn't know what that would mean for him, but he didn't hesitate and rammed against the surging tide of energy.

At first, he met resistance. But as he struggled to bring up the mental blockade, the drag switched directions, hooking into him and trying to tow him deeper. Was this what the Mar'keish had warned him about, the risk of getting lost in the darkness?

What if the Reidar took over his mind, and he woke up only to hurt Kira and everyone else onboard this ship? The thought made ice crystalize within him, all the way to his soul.

Like a swimmer trying to stay above choppy storm water, he fought to keep himself from getting sucked under, even as he desperately used every mental faculty left to get the barrier up. But he was steadily losing. Inch by inch, falling deeper. And this time there would be no escape.

He surged up and outward in one last desperate attempt, but he couldn't get free.

Something caught his attention.

The blue star. Except now it was more like a nebula swirling with untamed vitality, bright and seductive. And there was someone there. The shadow of a figure that didn't belong.

His instincts told him to reach out, that it was as trapped as he. Switching tactics, he pitched toward the figure and as soon as they connected, he realized who it was, though the answer made no damn sense.

But now wasn't the time to play a round of what-the-hell.

He felt like he was being torn in two as the Reidar consciousness refused to let the shadow and him go, but he joined his last ounce of energy with the other presence, forcing them both into the blue star.

The familiarity of it struck a chord deep within him, just like La'thar and Ko'en had said it would when he at last found the path to access his Mar'keish abilities. That's what the blue star had been all along, his own inherent potential, hovering just out of reach. With nothing but sheer determination, he forged ahead deeper into the mercury light, dragging the other presence with him.

And then every atom in his body exploded.

# Chapter Thirty

Rian came around coughing, lungs aching and side burning like someone had injected lava into his chest. He'd been dreaming of gray-and-yellow tinted shadows, of the Reidar dragging him back into the deepest hells of his own mind.

"Breathe, Rian. Take a second and then breathe." Ella's words anchored him, and he did what she said, willing his body to stop the instinctual panic of not having enough oxygen and sucking in what air he could. But it wasn't enough. Like they'd been stuffed with cotton, his lungs wouldn't fully expand.

He wasn't a doctor, but he'd punctured a lung before. And while that had been worse and taken him down faster, it seemed this stab wound had created a slow leak, gradually but surely filling his chest cavity. He probably didn't have long before he suffocated in his own body, which he found laughably ironic… Or, at least he would if he could get enough air to laugh.

After everything, after all of his bloody plans for revenge and intentions to go out as messy and destructive as possible, he was going to lie in the hold of some random ship and quite simply stop breathing.

"You're okay." Ella tightened her arms around him where he was still propped up against her. "You're okay. We'll be fine. The others will be here soon."

She still thought that? Well, he wasn't going to burst her bubble, not until he kicked it, anyway.

"How long was I out?" He rasped the words, despite how they made the whole breathing thing harder still, and his throat ache like he had a flu.

"Around two hours, I think. We haven't moved, though. The ship is still docked."

"Wonder what they're waiting for."

Because if they waited much longer, he was going to be too dead for whatever plans Baden Niels had in mind. He got a flare of dark satisfaction, imagining the look on Niels's face when he found out Rian had thwarted him by dying. Except that was quickly followed by the notion Ella would be left to face the psychotic bastard by herself. A surge of determined protectiveness fed him a swell of energy, and he forced his eyes open.

The view stole what little air he'd managed to save. Ella stared down at him, watching him breathe, no doubt knowing he had too few breaths left.

"I'm sorry I couldn't save you," she whispered, her voice catching.

"You tried, even though I didn't want it."

"Didn't you?" She brushed his hair back from his forehead.

He swallowed, the truth of hope he'd kept buried in his soul rushing up. "I did. Somewhere deep... Even though I couldn't face it...there was a small shred of hope you could save me. But I always knew I was doomed."

He focused on her face, for once letting everything go. Nothing else existed. No monster lurking inside him that he feared would consume everything and everyone he cared about. No revenge, no vendetta, no war, and no impossible quest he was desperate to see through.

No rage, no desolation, and no pain.

*No pain.*

Everything was rushing away from him, leaving nothing but a vast darkness. When he went under this time, he wouldn't be coming back. The inevitability of that knowledge gouged his soul.

"Tell me again," he gasped out, the words running into one another. "Tell me that if you get the chance…if you get those bands off…you'll use your abilities to escape …"

She nodded, the movement causing her brimming eyes to overflow. "I promise, I won't fail again. I'll do whatever it takes."

He brought a heavy hand up to brush the tears from her cheeks. "Don't cry for me, Ella, I was lost a long time ago."

She leaned in to his touch, closing her eyes on a hiccupping breath. "You were never lost, Rian, just on a dark path."

Her ability to see the best in him, to believe he was capable of good, after everything he'd done, was a gift he didn't deserve. And now he was repaying her by dying, leaving her alone in the captivity of the Reidar.

He trailed his hand from her cheek to the back of her neck. She opened her eyes, drenched gaze making his heart skip a beat.

"I never asked for compassion," he murmured, fatigue dragging at him, the lack of oxygen making everything swim.

"But you *did* deserve it. I shouldn't have withdrawn from you the way I did. It was selfish. I would give anything—" She gulped a breath, desperation in her gaze for the first time since he'd known her. "Please don't die, Rian."

In that second, he would have done anything to promise her that he'd stay alive, promise he wouldn't leave her, get up and fight any Reidar who came near her. But all he could do was struggle against the consuming darkness for another few moments.

"You're strong, Ella. Remember that, and you'll survive this."

"No—" She shook her head, pain suffusing the shadows in her eyes.

He pulled her down, tilting his head to catch her lips, in his last breath taking the salvation from her that he didn't deserve. Heat and light rippled through his body like nothing he'd ever experienced, a kind of pure euphoria he'd never aspired to touch.

She cupped his jaw, deepening the kiss, until he could taste her sadness and desperation. And though he wanted his last moment of lucidity to be nothing but rapture, the old fury at the Reidar—for the fact they were stealing yet another facet of his life, for knowing Ella would be at their mercy— flashed through him in a final burst of futile vehemence.

The next breath he tried to take didn't come, and he lost his grip, hand dropping away from Ella as he went limp in her hold. She sobbed his name, and it was the last sound he heard.

# Chapter Thirty-One

It'd been twenty minutes since Kira had rushed up-ship at the summons of Captain Forster. Even as Lianna had started searching for the vessel holding Rian and Ella, the others had been arguing about whether they could trust the intel and the chances of it being a Reidar trap, given that Varean was half Reidar. Qae had wanted to lock Varean up again and told her to stay clear of him.

Lianna discovered the ship docked at Itzac station in the Nabyl system, close to cold-space, and Zahli had shut down the argument, telling her cousin she was going with Varean's lead whether the rest followed or not. After that, they'd set the *Ebony Winter* on a course to the nearest transit gate, Callan's forged documentation helping them get through the tight security measures and putting their arrival into the Nabyl system expensively, but instantly.

With everything under control and nothing else for her to do while the others formulated a strategy to storm the *Marsala* to take Rian and Ella back, Kira had snuck out and returned to the medbay, finding Varean had put himself back into the coma or trance, or whatever it was when he accessed the Reidar consciousness. She might be on Qaelan Forster's ship, but she'd tell him the same thing she'd told Rian—Varean was in need of medical care and there was pretty much nothing the captain could do to stop her from providing it, apart from chaining her up as well.

But now, as she paced the short length of the medbay and prayed he woke up, she second-guessed every choice she'd made since Varean had returned and offered to help them. She'd pushed him away, trying to keep him at arm's length because she'd known on some level that if she didn't, all those feelings she'd been fighting would take over and she'd end up begging him not to leave again.

But they'd ended up here, and this was so, *so* much worse. If he died—

If he died, she'd go through the rest of her life with his death as a dark shroud on her heart and soul.

The temptation to call him out of his trance—as he'd told her she should be able to do—was getting harder and harder to ignore. But if she brought him around and he hadn't done whatever it was he thought he needed to do, there was every chance he'd simply put himself back under again.

An alarm sounded from the inset screen above the bed, cutting off her agonizing. She rushed over, studying the readouts. His heart rate was dangerously high, almost four hundred beats per minute. Enough to make him arrest or stroke out at any second. His brain waves were also going haywire, the readings like nothing she'd ever seen before.

"Varean!" She clamped her hands on his shoulders. "Varean, wake up!"

Last time, he'd somewhat calmed at her voice, but now it didn't seem to be working. "Varean, wherever you are, you need to come out of it."

The tone of the alarm cut out and then chimed a different

sound. She knew what it meant without even looking at the screen, and it made her stomach drop and slam into the floor.

He was flatlining.

Though panic surged through her body in an acidic flood, she kept her movements calm and efficient as she set the gurney for resus—securing the low sides and stepping clear. She accessed the inset screen and tabbed in the command. The system whirred and then delivered a low pulse of energy through his body. This was followed by a series of clicking as the system reset and rescanned to check for vital signs.

"Come on, Varean," she muttered, her insides churning as the system delivered a second pulse, gently jolting his body.

Again, no results were displayed, as the system reset for a final time. If this didn't work, the protocol was to call time of death. If a resus and regen unit couldn't bring a person back after three attempts, no modern medical technology could save them.

She held her breath as the system delivered the final pulse. Sound zoned out, replaced by a rushing in her ears as she stared at the screen, waiting, praying for the tiniest beat.

But the line of his heartbeat remained steady and straight, while the words "no signal recorded" flashed at the bottom of the screen.

As she blew out a hard breath, rigidity left her body, and she dropped heavily on the stool. The doctor side of her had calmly catalogued that she couldn't have done anything else and had expected this might be the result of him going under again.

But a deeper part of her was screaming in disbelief and pain. For all the death and tragedy she'd endured in the past days, it was like her body just didn't have the energy to expend on the grief.

"Kira, we've docked, and we're heading onstation." Zahli came into the medbay, concentration on the weapon belt she was strapping around her hips. "Colt said Rian might be injured, so we need you to come with us."

Zahli paused, her gaze shifting over to the gurney. "Oh my stars. Is he—"

"He didn't make it." Her voice came out monotone.

"I'm sorry, Kira." Zahli stepped closer and took her hand. "I know you cared about him, despite what he was."

From anyone else, the words might have been empty platitudes, but she could see from the shadows in her friend's gaze that she really meant it. She might not have understood what had developed between them, but it was clear she didn't wish this pain on anyone.

"He knew the risk and took it anyway." She didn't know what the point of saying that was; it was just the first thing that came into her mind.

"Regardless of everything Rian did to him, he still helped us find him. Varean was a good man, Kira. I can understand why you loved him."

The *L* word stabbed right into the middle of her chest, releasing the emotions that had been trapped behind the numb disbelief. And it hurt. God, it hurt more than she'd expected it to. Had she loved him? She didn't know, and now she'd never get the chance to work it out.

Zahli continued, "This is probably the last thing you want to be doing right now, but we have to get Rian and Ella."

Having a task helped stabilize her emotions, gave her a reason to shove them down and something to focus on. "No, we need to go. That is exactly what I need to be doing right now. It's what Varean gave his life for, so we could save Rian and Ella. If we don't see this through, what he did will be for nothing."

She wiped both hands over her face, even though her eyes remained achingly dry, then took a breath to clear her mind and went over to grab a med kit. But then she paused, unable to leave Varean just lying there. She pulled a light blue sheet out from one of the recesses and handed her med kit off to Zahli while she flicked the material over his body.

Something about the action was so final, making a hard lump swell in her throat and tears well at last. But she swallowed down the emotion and took the med kit from Zahli, putting everything out of her mind as she left the medbay, just like she would have when she'd been working the ED on Jacolby.

Occasionally she lost a patient, but that didn't mean everything stopped. Varean was gone, she couldn't do any more for him, but Rian might be injured, might need her help when they found him. That was what she focused on as she joined the others waiting to disembark.

Zander and Qae were there, plus Lianna, Tannin, Jase, and Colt. When Zahli and she approached the group, she ran a gaze over the commander captain.

"Your wound might be mostly healed, but I don't recommend coming along, Commander. You should be resting."

Colt sent her an indulgent, amused smile. "Noted, Doctor. But we need every able-bodied man on deck to take on these aliens, so there's no way in hell I'm sitting this one out. Plus, one of those bastards put a hole in my chest, and I'd like to return the favor."

"Speaking of bastards," Qae interjected. "Where's that hybrid freak? He gives us a lead and then hides out on my ship while we put our asses on the line? That's not suspicious at all."

Zahli had been making very unsubtle gestures at Qaelan to shut him up, but the marauder didn't take the hint.

"What?" Qae scowled at Zahli, who glared right back at him. "Am I not allowed to call him a hybrid freak? Isn't it PC enough? What about half-breed mongrel?"

"Varean is dead." Kira's words had all the effect of a bomb, leaving everyone stunned.

"Well shite, why didn't you say so?" Qae muttered to no one in particular as he released the atmospheric doors.

Everyone stared at her, like they expected a different response, but no one said a word. Their awkward attention—clearly not knowing what to do with this news—sparked her temper. So it was probably lucky they didn't try something stupid like offering their condolences, otherwise she would not have held herself accountable for whatever screaming or violence followed.

She headed over to where Qae stood in front of the atmospheric doors as they slid open with a hiss of equalizing pressure.

"Sorry for being a dick," Qae murmured, loud enough for only her to hear.

"You mean just now, or always?"

Qae winced. "Ouch. Nice jab."

The doors finished opening, and she didn't bother replying or waiting for anyone else as she stepped into the tubeway that temporarily connected the *Ebony Winter* to the space station.

Everyone else emerged, and Lianna gestured deeper into the docking arm, instead of toward the station security gateway.

"The *Marsala* is about a dozen berths out. I got us as close to her as I could."

"You mean *we*, of course," Qae shot back with a suave grin. "After all, it was my smooth talking to station control that got us a slip on this level."

"Can we just get on with this before I have to punch you in your smarmy face on principle alone?" Lianna shoulder-checked the marauder as she strode by, leaving Qae rubbing his upper arm.

There were only a handful of people on the gangway—
which had been set out in a kind of zigzag pattern to
accommodate more ships—as they made their way along.
Itzac wasn't exactly a bustling central system station; most
of the other crews they passed looked like they were rough-
living and hard-working. Luckily, they weren't the only crew
moving about as a group, so they didn't attract much attention.

They'd gone past about eight docking hatchways when
Lianna slowed to a stop. "The *Marsala* is just around the
corner. Tannin, you're on recon."

The tech analyst hastened down the remaining gangway
and disappeared around the corner. Everyone was silent for
the minute or two it took him to come back.

"Hatchway is closed and locked up," Tannin said as
he stepped back into the group. "One armed guard sitting
outside. Doesn't seem to be anyone else nearby."

"Only one guard?" Zander muttered. "That seem a bit
easy to you?"

"You still think it's a trap?" Lianna asked, not seeming
too worried about the prospect.

"Of course it's a trap," Qae replied, his tone indicating it
should have been obvious to anyone with half a brain. "You
really think your dead hybrid intel is solid?"

Zahli elbowed him, ending his words with an *oomph*.

Maybe Qae's snipe should have made Kira angry, should
have upset or incensed her, but she'd left her emotions back
on the ship and was focused on nothing but helping Rian.
Whatever anyone else believed of Varean, she didn't care.
He'd vowed back on the *Imojenna* that he'd protect her with
his life. She didn't believe for a second the information he'd
given them would lead into a trap.

"It doesn't matter." Lianna took out her razar and nucleon
gun. "If there's even a chance Rian is on the ship, we're not
walking away until we know for sure."

The nav-engineer stalked to the corner of the gangway and leaned around it with her razar. She let off a single shot, then tossed a hard glance over her shoulder. "Reidar."

Before anyone could reply, she stepped out, this time leading with her nucleon gun. The others had their guns out but pointed down as they followed her.

Since she was unarmed, Kira waited a beat before falling in behind the group. The last thing they needed was for the only person with medical training to take any stray ammo. But it seemed there wasn't much of a threat after all. Lianna had made sure the Reidar who'd been guarding the hatchway was messy-dead, and no others appeared to back him up.

Tannin was already accessing the screen to open the hatch to the tubeway, muttering something about it being partly Reidar coding. Most of the others took defensive positions in case some kind of reinforcements turned up.

Time dragged by, but finally Tannin got the hatchway open, revealing the empty tube leading to the atmospheric doors of the *Marsala*.

Lianna and Zander went in first, followed by Zahli and Tannin. She stayed securely in the middle of the group, while Colt, Jase, and Qae formed a defensive line behind her.

Tannin took to the control panel of the *Marsala*'s atmospheric doors, seeming to have a better idea of what he was doing. It took half the time to get the ship's hatchway open.

When the hatch slid back, a few short feet in was another door, this one appearing to be metium-reinforced mesh, kind of like would be fitted in a prison transport. Off to the left, near the far bulkhead, Ella sat, Rian sprawled across her lap and very definitely not moving.

"Oh god." Zahli rushed up to the door. "Ella, is he okay?"

The priestess wiped tears off her face with an unsteady hand. "I can't heal him, these cuffs—"

"We're going to get you both out of there. Just hang on for a second." Zahli turned to Tannin, who was already working on the electronic lock. "Hurry."

His shoulders were tense, his expression grim as he hacked the controls, breaking through the coded ciphers.

Finally, the door clicked and swung free. Zahli dashed through first, but Kira was right on her heels as they ran over to where Ella gently laid Rian on the floor. Her heart hiccupped in her chest as she took in his gray complexion and blue lips.

"How long has he been like this?" she shot at Ella, yanking the med scanner out of her kit.

"Just a minute or so." Ella's usually calm voice was ragged, thick with emotion. "But he was having trouble breathing for a long time before that. He was stabbed."

She didn't need the med scanner to tell her he'd probably suffered from a collapsed lung. But she waited the second or so it took for the information to scroll across the screen before she dove back into her med kit, snatching out the things she'd need to put in a chest tube.

"Someone get his shirt off." As she got the MRD ready to make an incision, Zahli and Ella ripped and tugged the cloth out of the way, revealing the stab wound and several ugly bruises covering his abdomen.

"He did *not* go quietly," Zander muttered from where he stood a few steps away, gun in hand, his attention clearly not focused on keeping watch.

Kira lifted Rian's heavy arm away from his chest and then ran her fingers over his ribs, counting the spaces between bones until she found the right one.

"Wait." Ella grabbed her wrist before she could make the first cut. "What are you doing?"

"His chest cavity is filled with air. That's why he can't breathe. I need to release the pressure."

"But I can heal him." Ella glanced up at the others standing around. "If someone can get these bands off, I can heal him."

"I can try." Tannin came over and knelt down next to the priestess.

"We don't have time to wait."

She tugged out of Ella's hold and opened a small hole in Rian's side so she could insert the tube. In a hospital, this sort of thing would have been done from a distance, using robotics that left no room for error. But with only the most basic medical tech, she'd have to trust her judgment and skills and hope it was enough to save him.

As soon as the tube was in, the air released with a hiss. She secured the line and checked his vitals. He hadn't started breathing on his own, and the med scanner informed her that the last activity from his heart had been ninety-three seconds ago.

"I am not losing anyone else today," she muttered, tugging her med kit closer. "We need to get him back to the *Ebony Winter*. Someone find me a hover stretcher."

While Lianna hurried to comply, Kira grabbed the small automatic resus unit out of her med bag. One part went over his mouth and nose to breathe for him, the other onto the middle of his chest to stimulate his heart.

Tannin cursed under his breath where he was still trying to free the bands from Ella's wrists. When the priestess had first come aboard the *Imojenna* all those months ago, she'd been wearing something similar.

"Damn it, Ella. It looks like these things are coded to Reidar DNA. We'll have to cut them off like we did last time."

"But Rian—" She glanced down at him, shadows of desperation in her gaze.

"He's stable for the moment." Kira clasped Ella on the forearm in reassurance. The small automatic resus unit was a temporary measure at best and not designed to be used for more than a few minutes on a patient with wounds this extensive. They were probably lucky it worked at all.

Lianna returned with a hover stretcher. While she monitored his vitals, Tannin and Zander got Rian strapped on quickly. They formed a protective group around her as she guided the stretcher out of the ship.

This time, they did get curious stares from the few people they passed as they dashed along the gangway toward the *Ebony Winter*.

Halfway there, the resus unit gave a small warning beep, indicating things were getting critical, and it wouldn't be able to sustain Rian for much longer. His injury was bad, but she'd seen him recover from something like this before—Ella had brought him back from a wound just as nasty, if not worse, shortly after she'd joined them on the *Imojenna*.

She'd just have to keep Rian's heart beating and oxygen circulating until someone could get those damned bands off the priestess's wrists.

The stretcher jolted to a stop. Zander had stepped in front of it, facing outward, his stance protective as the others closed into a tighter group.

Up ahead, at the hatchway of the *Ebony Winter*, a group of at least twenty station security guards and UAFA agents blocked their way. A single man in a slick business suit stood just in front of them.

She'd seen the guy only once before, and that had been on a viewer screen, but she'd never forgotten Baden Niels's face, since the man who was the CEO of a multiversal corporation, Dieter Industries—who also happened to be a Reidar—had sent a team of aliens in to try to take the *Imojenna* by force.

"I knew this was a trap," Qae muttered as Niels stepped forward.

Whether or not they'd walked into a trap was incidental

now.

Rian needed immediate medical attention if he was going to survive. With all those guards and UAFA agents—who were more than likely Reidar as well—standing between them and the R and R unit onboard the *Ebony Winter*, Rian's chances of survival were getting slimmer by the second.

# Chapter Thirty-Two

Everything was so shimmery bright, blue tinted, and pleasant, it made Rian's body ache. Or maybe that was the stab wound. Either way, a second ago he'd been in that hold with Ella and now he was—

Actually, he didn't know where the freck he was. It wasn't a ship. It wasn't a planet. It wasn't anywhere. It was like existing without being.

"Sherron?"

He turned around, but hadn't heard the voice as if through his ears. It was just kind of there, like receiving audio directly into his brain.

The commando he'd locked in the brig of the *Imojenna* stared at him with more than a little confusion on his face. Or, kind of not. The guy was there, but not fully formed or maybe not solid.

"What the freck is this, and why are you here?" His own voice didn't come out as though he'd spoken it, more like an echoing thought.

"Hard to explain. And I was going to ask if you knew how

you got here."

A few things clicked together in his mind, including the last second he'd been staring up at Ella then hadn't been able to breathe any longer.

"Hang on a damned second. Am I dead? Is this some kind of afterlife?" Wouldn't that just beat all, if he'd kicked it and now got to spend eternity with a guy he'd locked up and let Callan almost kill repeatedly. Was this some kind of weird punishment because the commando was the last person he'd wronged in life?

"This isn't the afterlife. At least, I don't think it is." The guy grinned, as if he found all this amusing. "I found you in the Reidar consciousness, or a shadow of you, anyway. We got out, but you disappeared on me for a while. Now I'm pretty sure we're in the shared human consciousness that the Mar'keish can access."

Okay, that was…something. How the freck was he meant to make sense of anything the guy had just said? "I'm still not getting how this is any different from the infinite hereafter."

"Technically, you shouldn't be here. I must have given you access when I pulled you out from the Reidar hive mind. Anyway, what makes you think you're dead?"

He touched his side where the stab wound should have been.

"I got knifed. Think my lung collapsed. I couldn't breathe, and I blacked out."

"Listen, Sherron. You're not dead yet, but it sounds like that's an imminent possibility." The commando came closer to him. "I've learned a hell of a lot in the last few days—about you, the Reidar, and myself. You can't die. There are too many important reasons why you need to continue this fight. And if you want to win, you're going to need me."

He scoffed. "*I* need *you*? And how exactly did you come to that adorable little conclusion?"

"Because of this." The commando clamped a hand on his shoulder.

In a wave of energy, an overload of information flooded his mind—things about the commando and the reason the aliens wanted to exterminate Varean Donnelly at all costs. Snippets of intel about the Reidar's plans and the things they'd done to Rian all those years ago, some of which made sense and some of which were out of context and meant nothing.

The commando released him, leaving his mind spinning. The one thing he knew for certain—they needed him if they wanted to win. And despite Donnelly being half Reidar, he could trust the commando. The guy had access to the combined abilities of both Reidar and Mar'keish. Talk about super-soldier. As long as he kept it under control and didn't go all dark-side on them, he'd be one hell of a weapon.

"Jezus, that's one way to get your point across." Rian shifted out of reaching range in case the commando decided he needed to impart any other information. Words would be more than adequate next time.

"Things are going to change now, Sherron. The Reidar know about me, but they also know I found out what they were trying to hide, why they destroyed all the other human-Reidar hybrids, particularly those who were Mar'keish."

Rian sifted through the info the guy had just shot into his mind. The Mar'keish could have defeated the Reidar, which is why the damned aliens had engineered the virus to wipe them all out decades ago.

"This goes back so much further than I ever thought," he muttered. "At least we know what that freak-show breeding program was all about."

"They thought if they could isolate the gene that allows Mar'keish—and to some extent the Arynians—to access the human consciousness, they could add it to Reidar DNA and would have access to the same mind-control abilities the Mar'keish have," Donnelly replied. "But they found something far more powerful and far more dangerous instead. They discovered the hybrids had the potential to become unstoppable."

Did that answer the question as to why the Reidar were so desperate to get their hands on Ella? As a rare second-generation Arynian, she was probably the next best thing to the Mar'keish. Shite, he needed to get some answers about that girl, because there was no way in hell he was going to ever let the Reidar do to her what they'd done to him—brainwash her, control her, get access to the untapped human consciousness. And for that he needed weapons...weapons like Donnelly.

"So we might have one advantage over the bastards. But I still don't get how you found me in the Reidar-whatever. I don't remember being there."

Donnelly shrugged. "My guess is they did something to you all those years ago to make it possible. It was probably how they controlled you."

"Well that's a frecking comforting thought. I'm on some Reidar wavelength and don't even know it?"

"Now you see where I'm coming from?" Donnelly sent him a genuine smile, one edged in the new hope that they could be allies instead of the enemies he'd made them into.

"Yeah, I get it. Just one problem, how the hell do we get out of this consciousness thing?"

The commando didn't look the least bit worried about that not-so-small obstacle.

"Leave that to me." A shimmer of blue-silver power seemed to ripple around the guy. "I'm going to put those new abilities to good use."

Before he could reply, Donnelly straight-up disappeared.

"Donnelly?" He glanced around, but not only could he not see the guy anymore, it was like he couldn't feel him, either. In the same way he could sometimes sense Ella. It was a similar thread of awareness, just slightly different. Whatever the hell that all meant.

So was leaving him here alone part of the commando's plan, or had he just been shafted by the guy?

The only thing he hated more than being backed into a corner was being powerless to act. But in that second, all he could do was swear loudly and inventively into the twinkling blue-lighted nothingness.

# Chapter Thirty-Three

Keeping hold of the hover stretcher, Kira shuffled back when Niels took a few steps forward, as though the guns Qae, Zander, Lianna, Zahli, Colt, Jase, and Tannin had pointed at him weren't a threat. Of course, since the Reidar were far more resilient, and quicker to heal than humans, he probably didn't consider them to be.

"If you would all be so kind as to relinquish your weapons to these officers?" Niels spread out his hands, indicating the guards and agents standing behind him. "This doesn't need to be unpleasant."

"Like hell it doesn't." Lianna started to bring up her razar, but Zander stayed her hand.

"You shoot him with this, we've given away our secret weapon," Zander muttered, casting an implacable captain-admiral glance around their small group, causing everyone else to put away their stunners.

"Not if he's too dead to tell anyone," Lianna snapped back, apparently not ready to stand down.

"We're outgunned, two to one. This isn't the place to take

a stand."

Lianna took her gaze off Niels long enough to shoot Zander a glare. "So what, we're just supposed to surrender?"

"You got a better idea that doesn't see us all dead on this gangway?"

The resus unit on Rian's chest began chiming insistently, and Kira looked down at the screen, where the readings showed the device wasn't sustaining his heart any longer.

"Rian needs the resus and regen system on the *Ebony Winter. Now.*" She maneuvered the stretcher, intending to push it past Zander and right through the middle of those Reidar. There was no way she was going to stand here and do nothing while Rian died.

But Zander clamped a hand on the rail, stopping her from going anywhere.

"Rian was stabbed. He needs medical attention or he's going to die." Zander directed the statement at Niels.

But the alien only shrugged. "Unfortunate. I had some interesting plans for the former assassin. But dead seems like a fairly good consolation prize. Hand over the priestess, and I'll let you organize the funeral."

White-hot anger, the likes of which she'd never experienced before, stormed through her, leaving her flash-heated like she'd stepped into a furnace.

"I am not letting Rian die here. You won't let us on the *Ebony Winter*? Fine, I'll find some other ship with a medbay."

She yanked the hover stretcher back, and Zander let it go, closing ranks with the others, obviously prepared to stop anyone from following her.

Unfortunately, she'd managed only to turn around and take three steps when she pulled to a stop again. Another ten UAFA agents had come up behind them and formed a line to block the gangway.

"No one is going anywhere until I get the priestess." This

time when Niels spoke, all feigned affability was gone from his voice.

"I will go with you." Ella stepped forward, her voice sounding stronger, more assured than when they'd found her in the *Marsala*. "If you promise not to kill anyone once I'm in your custody."

Niels sent her an oily smile. "So charming that you think you've got any leverage to bargain. Take the priestess, kill the rest."

He stepped behind the line of agents and guards as they raised their guns.

Kira clamped her fists tighter around the handle of the stretcher, her flight response kicking in. She sucked in a breath, air catching in her lungs as a weird kind of numb disconnection suffused her body, like her mind understood too well she was about to meet her demise and wanted to shield her from the worst of it.

Beyond the line of agents and guards, the hatchway to the *Ebony Winter* slid open. Some of Qae's crew had stayed on the ship, but even with their added numbers, they were still outnumbered, which would only lead to more people dying today.

Yet only a single figure emerged from the shadowed passage, and Kira swore she was hallucinating.

Varean strode out, determination and anger brimming in the set of his shoulders, his eyes pure mercury and swirling with power.

"Get down!" he yelled as he brought up his hands.

She didn't hesitate. She dropped, pulling the stretcher down with her to protect Rian, everyone else in their little group hitting the deck as well.

The UAFA agents and security guards were thrown into momentary confusion—some still with their guns aimed, while others turned to Varean.

Streaks of yellow and blue light rippled over Varean's body, coalescing toward his hands and then blasting outward. The energy wave went above her head and took out every single guard and agent standing, sending them sprawling across the gangway.

In the aftermath, there was utter silence and no one moved a muscle, the guards and agents all either unconscious or dead. She knew what she'd just seen, but her brain couldn't assimilate it. Varean was *alive*. Not only alive, but he'd harnessed some kind of energy and taken out the threat in a single, effective blast.

A chiming near her left ear registered, kicking her brain back into gear, shedding the last of the numbing shock.

She looked down at Rian, the readouts on the small screen of the resus unit dire. He was out of time, the R and R onboard the *Ebony Winter* too many steps away, even if she ran as fast as she could.

"I've got this, Kira." Varean crouched on the other side of the stretcher, sparing her only a quick glance before pulling the resus unit off Rian.

"Stop! That's the only thing keeping him alive." She went to grab his wrist, but instead Varean bundled the device into her hands.

"It's okay, he's going to be fine." He set one hand on the middle of Rian's chest and the other over the stab wound. Just like when Ella had healed him all those months ago on the *Imojenna*. Except, what had taken her a number of long minutes and concentration took Varean a single, intense pulse of blue and yellow energy. It suffused Rian's body, making his skin glow as though his very cells had turned to pure light.

When it faded away, he sat back, and Rian drew in a long breath, looking perfectly healthy, as though he'd been asleep, not mortally injured.

The captain blinked his eyes open and sat up, looking at

Varean.

*Oh no.* This was not going to end well—

"I can explain—" The words exploded out in a rush, but Rian was already reaching, hand extended to—

Take Varean's offered arm, as the two of them got to their feet.

*What the hell?*

"For a minute there, Donnelly, I thought you'd shammed me." Rian clapped him on the shoulder, expression as close to happy as their captain ever got.

"I had to wake up and work out what was going on first." Varean grinned, apparently in as good a mood as Rian.

"If you really want in on this, you've got it. You're welcome to join the crew, once we get the *Imojenna* back."

Varean's grin widened. "Thanks. Though I'm requesting better quarters than my last rack onboard your ship. It was kind of uncomfortable."

"Sure, smart-ass, I'll get you a better bunk."

Everyone standing around in a loose circle looked nothing short of shell-shocked.

"Okay, did I get put into stasis and lose a few years?" Qae asked, breaking the silence. "Since when are you two not on shooting-each-other terms anymore? What's with the buddy-buddy act? And also, newsflash, hybrid freaky-pants. You were dead."

"Not quite, apparently." At last, Varean glanced over at Kira, and it was like getting hit by an electric current, his gaze leaving tingles chasing beneath her skin. "It comes with a really complicated explanation I don't have time to give you right now. Niels is planning on blowing this space station to hell and beyond. We've got less than two minutes to get the *Ebony Winter* free of her moorings and clear."

"How do you know—" Even as Qae started asking the question, Rian and Varean were already moving, heading for the *Ebony Winter*'s hatchway.

"Let's just add that to the list of things we need to sort out later," Rian tossed over his shoulder, stooping to help himself to a few guns as he stepped over the prone figures of the UAFA agents and security guards.

"How the hell did Niels even escape? He was right here a second ago." Zander followed Rian's example, grabbing guns and spare ammo clips.

Before she reached the hatchway, Kira bent down to check one of the sprawled figures. They were more than likely Reidar, so she shouldn't care. But part of her needed to know whether Varean had just killed thirty armed and hostile men with nothing more than a flick of his hands. The UAFA agent she checked wasn't dead, just deeply unconscious, it seemed. If what Varean had said was true, however, they'd die when Baden Niels blew up this station. And so would they if they didn't disembark quickly enough.

She ran with the others down the short tubeway and through the *Ebony Winter*'s atmospheric doors. Qae was barking instructions through his comm to the crew he'd left onboard, ordering them to do an emergency breakaway. It would probably damage some of the *Ebony Winter*'s docking clamps, but that was better than getting caught in the explosion.

She followed the others up-ship, everyone cramming into the bridge as the *Ebony Winter* whined and gave a sharp jerk, the screech of shearing metal echoing through the hull.

Qae muttered a few curses but didn't say anything else as the engines flared to maximum capacity, no doubt burning the tubeway and part of the docking arm they'd been attached to.

On the control console screen, an alarm of incoming weapon fire clanged, and through the viewport, several other ships that had been docked at the station made similar hard and fast launches, leaving trails of debris from broken moorings.

As the *Ebony Winter* blasted into open space, an IPC flagship hovered in the distance, thin flares of light trailing the missiles streaking toward the station.

"Give it more," Qae ordered.

"We could burn out sub-light engines," the crew member at the helm replied in a strained voice.

"They can be fixed later. If we survive. Punch it up."

The *Ebony Winter*'s engines roared, and they shot up at three times the speed, putting them out past the flagship in a matter of seconds.

"It's the *Marshal Beacon*," Zander muttered.

"We had a run-in with them when we lost the *Imojenna*," Rian replied, tone grim.

"Guess it's a safe bet Captain Admiral Barias isn't human any longer. She was a damned good soldier." Zander shook his head, looking hard-hit by this news.

The viewport flickered and switched over to show the vision from behind the ship as they zoomed farther away. Half a dozen missiles peppered the station, breaking it apart with several large explosions, setting off a chain of smaller detonations as the structure fractured and fell away into pieces.

"How many innocents do you think they killed this time?" Zander muttered, turning away from the screen.

"I don't understand how they can get away with blowing up an entire space station," Zahli put in from where she stood next to Tannin.

"They'll come up with some airtight cover story for the newsreels so people won't even think twice," Rian replied. He glanced over at his cousin. "Set a course for the Barbary Belt and put us in void-space before they start firing on the escaping ships."

Even as Rian said the words, new flashes of weapon fire

emanated from the huge flagship, this time aimed at the few other ships like theirs that had managed to disembark before the station was decimated.

Qae swore, leaning over the command console and assisting his crew to get the ship to hyper-launch.

After ripping away from the station moorings and all the destruction from the missiles, the slip into void-space and out of danger was jarringly peaceful.

Silence stretched on the bridge, everyone no doubt coming to grips with what had just happened, how close they'd come to getting killed yet again.

"Well, shite. I need a stiff drink," Qae announced, breaking the tense, quiet atmosphere. "Been saving a bottle of Violaine for a rainy day, and I'm pretty sure it's pissing down right now."

"Jezus, yes." Rian's words puffed out on an exhale. "Hit me up, cuz."

"Hang on just a minute." Kira stepped into Rian's path when he tried to follow Qae to the galley. "You were almost dead."

She glanced past Rian to Varean. "And you *were* dead. So neither of you are doing anything until I've given you a full checkup."

Rian deftly sidestepped her. "Check Donnelly all you want. I'll need at least half a bottle of that Violaine before you come anywhere near me with your medical instruments."

As Rian left for the galley, she focused a determined look on Varean.

"I'm fine," he said holding up both hands.

"Humor me." She went over and grabbed his arm, tugging him into a walk before he could think about escaping. Maybe he was fine, but she needed to see for herself. And the only words she was going to believe on the matter right now were the ones she read on the screen of the med scanner.

# Chapter Thirty-Four

Varean let Kira tow him along, back down to the *Ebony Winter*'s small medbay, where he'd woken up with that damn sheet on his face, telling him that Kira had very definitely thought he was dead. And since she was a highly trained surgeon, it probably meant that, for a little while at least, he had most certainly checked out in the final sense of the words.

So yeah, if she wanted to scan him or whatever else to assure herself he was fine, he'd humor her. But he had no doubt he was fine. Better than fine, actually. Like, operating on a higher plane of existence with abilities he'd never dreamed possible fine.

The Mar'keish had been right. Access to his inherent abilities had been there all along, in the guise of the blue star out of his reach during his earlier hallucinations. But when he'd been dragged into the dark pits of the Reidar consciousness, the fear of anything happening to Kira had unleashed the parts of himself he hadn't been able to accept before. Knowledge had flooded his mind, and he'd known what to do. All up, it was a pretty damned heady feeling.

Kira steered him to the gurney in the middle of the room, the sheet still sprawled across the end, spilling onto the ground in a light blue cascade where he'd tossed it earlier.

He obediently sat on the edge and then lay back when she gestured for him to do so, all without saying a thing. But apparently he didn't need to. As Kira fired up the diagnostic system from the screen inset above the head of the gurney, she shot him a chiding look.

"Why do I get the feeling you're totally pandering to me?"

"I have no idea what you're talking about." He almost managed to get the words out with no grin, but failed at the last second. Her scowl deepened, but he simply crossed his ankles and folded his hands on his stomach. Might as well be comfortable while she ran her tests.

Kira muttered something unintelligible, for the moment concentrating on her scanners and the readings. He didn't want to say that pretty much dying had given him a new lease on life, and everything looked all shiny and new, but he was definitely in a glass-half-full mood. So he was more than happy to lay there in the simplicity of the moment, watching her. No one was immediately trying to kill them, and for the first time in his life, he knew exactly who he was, everything he was capable of, and recognized his place in the universe.

"I don't understand." Kira stepped back after a long while, expression creased with confusion, looking at him like a puzzle she couldn't solve. "It must have something to do with your Reidar DNA. Some of these readings are impossible, others don't even make sense; they're nothing like the scans I took earlier. And you know what else doesn't make sense? How you're even lying there looking at me. You were dead. You stopped breathing, your heart stopped, there was no brain function. The R and R unit couldn't revive you. You were completely, clinically dead."

He sat up, swinging his legs off the edge of the gurney so he could face her. Reaching out, he grabbed her hands, not second-guessing the impulse.

"I can't tell you what happened from a medical point of view, but I can tell you that I was never really gone."

"But what you did when you came out of the hatchway and blasted all those officers and agents. Is that one of the things you learned after you left us on Barasa?"

"Yes and no. It's hard to explain, but I'll clarify later, once we go back up-ship, because I'm sure the others are waiting for an accounting, too."

When she began to pull back, he tightened his grip on her hands, drawing her nearer instead.

"Kira, I know we were both hurting, that we thought this couldn't be, and I honestly didn't try to fight for you the way I should have. I thought you'd be safer if I wasn't around—"

This time when she tugged against his hold, he had to let her go.

"Don't apologize for that, please." She turned away from him, and the action was like taking a knife to the chest. He'd hoped after everything, the two of them could resolve their differences. He didn't expect her to jump all in with him, but they at least needed to clear the air. If they couldn't, seeing each other every day, living on the same ship—it was going to be awkward and difficult as hell.

"I just wanted to make things okay between us."

Her shoulders tightened, and he cursed under his breath. Despite his newfound abilities, it seemed his aptitudes still didn't extend to interpersonal relations.

"I'm the one who should be apologizing." Her voice was so low he almost didn't catch the words.

He pushed up from the gurney, stepping closer to her. "I don't understand."

She sniffed then turned to him, her sage eyes filled with

remorse. "I'm such a terrible person. Back on Barasa, I tried to make you think there was nothing between us, that you were my patient and nothing more. I shouldn't have tried to hurt you like that, but I thought you needed to go with the Mar'keish to be safe, and I didn't know how else to get you to leave. I was terrified Rian would kill you, not to mention the Reidar and anyone else with a long enough memory to be afraid of the Mar'keish."

She blew out a ragged breath, dropping her gaze, as though she was too ashamed to look at him. "And when you came back to help us, I couldn't think of anything beyond my own feelings, didn't want to deal with you because I knew it would make things that much harder when you left again. I failed you as a doctor, because I should have been able to put that aside and treat you the way I would anyone else."

Stunned, he stared down at the top of her bent head, lights above them shining on her dark hair. *That's* what she thought had happened? He had never, for even one second, believed any of that about her. The notion hadn't even crossed his mind.

"Kira, you're being too hard on yourself. You're definitely not a terrible person. In fact, you're the least terrible person I know."

"But the way I treated you—"

"I realized, a day or two after I left, what you were doing. I know you didn't mean what you said on Barasa. And I understand not wanting to get close to me again when I came back, because I did plan on leaving, and you needed to protect yourself. You need to forgive yourself, because I'm certainly not holding anything against you."

Surprise crossed her features. "You're not upset with me?"

"Not for even a second."

She made a relieved noise that landed somewhere

between a laugh and a sob, and fell against his chest. He wrapped his arms around her, the acute relief at feeling her body against his again pure euphoria.

"Oh god, I thought you'd died." Her arms were tight around him, voice muffled with her face pressed into his chest.

He cupped the back of her head, cradling her against him. "I know, I'm sorry you had to go through that."

"And it wasn't until after, when I thought you were gone, that I realized how selfish I was being. I thought it was too late to ever tell you I was sorry. Then I didn't have time to process everything before Zahli came in and told me we were going to get Rian."

"I wish I could have protected you from all that." He tilted her head up so he could see her face. "While we're both onboard the *Imojenna*, following Rian around the galaxy, I can't promise that something like that won't happen again. But next time, I'll be there with you."

"Wait. What do you mean *both* on the *Imojenna*? Aren't you going back to the Mar'keish?"

"Well, if it's okay with you, Doc, I'm going to accept the spot on the crew Sherron offered me, whenever he gets the ship back."

"But I thought—"

"That Sherron and I hated each other? For now, let's just say we came to an understanding."

"So you're *staying*?" Her expression had become dazed.

"Geez, don't look so excited."

"But now that the Reidar know about you and everything you've learned, won't they be coming after you?" Kira asked, a deep note of concern in her tone.

"Not right away. They know exactly what I'm capable of, so they're not going to come charging. My guess is they'll take their time, come up with a strategy, then launch some kind of sneak attack when I least expect it."

Kira frowned at him. "And that's supposed to make me feel better?"

"Don't worry, Kira, we'll handle it. All of us, together."

She shook her head, as if to clear it. "Rian is really going to let you stay? And you're not going to try to kill each other?"

"Not even a little."

Her brow creased. "I'm missing so much here—"

"And I'll tell you all about it, but first…" He leaned down, catching her mouth beneath his, the kiss so complete and good, it speared from his lips right into the depths of his soul.

She sighed against his mouth, the sound partly of relief, partly of contentment. And he completely understood the sentiment. Kissing her now, with all that had passed between them, and the future spanning in front of them, was a coming home in a way he'd never experienced before.

There'd always been a hole in his heart, a gap in his psyche from growing up alone, having no place of his own, and no one who loved him. He'd thought since it was all he'd known, he could simply join the military, find a place to belong, and continue on in life well enough. And while he'd found that, he still hadn't felt complete. In fact, he hadn't realized how incomplete he'd really been until he'd met Kira, discovered the truth of his heritage, and awoken to his full potential.

At a knocking, Varean broke the kiss, looking over his shoulder to find Zahli standing in the medbay hatchway, clearly trying not to grin at Kira but failing miserably. She might as well have given her friend a thumbs-up and rah-rah dance.

"Sorry, but Rian and Qae have called everyone down to the cargo hold."

Kira stepped out of his arms, smoothing down her shoulder-length hair, though it wasn't any more mussed than usual.

"I suppose I should be glad Rian left us alone for this

long." She glanced up at him, setting her shoulders as if preparing for a fight. "Are you ready to face them all?"

He smiled, wrapping an arm around her upper back. "Stand down. The fight is over for today."

She blew out a breath, some of the tension leaving her frame. "Sorry, it's just after everything, I find it hard to believe they're suddenly on friendly terms with you."

"Like I said, Rian and I reached an understanding."

"Whatever that means," she muttered. "All right, let's go then."

Kira practically marched over to Zahli, shooting her friend an unreadable look, but something seemed to pass between the two women. As he stepped through the hatchway, Zahli moved in beside him.

"Varean, I'm really sorry for my part in everything you went through."

So that was Kira's play? Silently glare everyone into apologizing to him? He appreciated her attempt to make things up to him, even though he didn't need or expect it. That was firmly in the past, even though it had been only days ago. Besides, it was kind of like those incidences had happened to a completely different person.

"Thanks, Zahli, but there's nothing to forgive. I can't say I wouldn't have done the same thing if our positions had been reversed."

She nodded, stepping ahead of him to catch up with Kira as they made their way to the *Ebony Winter*'s cargo hold, where Forster's crew, the remaining members of Rian's crew, plus a couple of hangers-on were all gathered, either sitting on or leaning against the few crates clamped down to the metal grate floor.

"Donnelly." Rian greeted him with a nod. "Kira give you the all clear?"

"His Mar'keish-Reidar DNA meant half my equipment

gave readings I had no idea what to do with," Kira complained, taking a seat on a crate next to Zahli. He joined them, leaning against the side. Just yesterday, he would have been on edge, defensive about her mentioning his Reidar side aloud in front of anyone, especially the people who'd nabbed him in the first place. But now he knew it wasn't a curse, it was a blessing. One that made him a unique being.

"Speaking of Reidar DNA," Rian replied. "Think you might be able to help us with something?"

The priestess stepped forward, holding out her arms where a pair of gray-blue bands encircled her wrists.

"I tried to get them off," Tannin said from where he stood next to Jase. "But they're encoded with Reidar DNA."

Varean straightened as he gave the thick manacles a once-over and then pressed his thumb into an indent on each. The bands sprang open and clunked to the floor.

"My deepest gratitude." Ella inclined her head to him as she moved back, rubbing her wrists. But then she paused, scrutinizing him.

"You're—" Her features creased in confusion, and he felt a subtle wave of energy wash over him. "You have the aura of an Arynian. Yet it is so much more than that."

"It's Mar'keish, actually. Add it to the things I'm about to explain."

She nodded, glancing around as if only just remembering they had an audience, and then she shifted back to sit with Nyah.

"So, mongrel man, we're all here so you can tell us a story," Forster put in, a hint of cynicism in his voice. Of course, it was possible the marauder always spoke with that note of derision. "You and Rian took some Reidar pharmaceuticals and went on the magical mystery tour?"

"You are *such* an ass," Lianna muttered, but instead of seeming insulted, Forster sent her a wink.

"Settle down, children," Rian ordered. "This is going to take some explaining. I was there, and even I don't really understand it."

Varean crossed his arms, first launching into the story from where the *Imojenna*'s crew had split up, so Rian had all the details, bringing them to where he'd been approached by the two Mar'keish on Barasa and then on to how he could access the different consciousnesses of both human and Reidar, ending with finding Rian in the Reidar hive mind and bringing them both back by accessing his Mar'keish abilities.

"It's a lot to take in," Varean finished. Really, he didn't expect them to all just believe him and go along with it. This went way beyond the realms of outlandish into downright preposterous.

"If I hadn't seen that energy blast out of your hands myself, I'd be calling bullshite on everything right about now," Forster put in. "We were already like a flying bull's-eye to the Reidar. If we add some kind of super-freak to our lot, then it's going to make us that much more of a target."

"Honestly, Qae, you might be right," Rian replied. "But they won't succeed. Because Varean won't be alone. Believe me, we're better off with the doc's new boyfriend in our pocket."

A slight flush of color stained Kira's cheeks, but he tightened his hold on her, drawing her closer. Damn, he wasn't a fourteen year old, but he liked the idea of being Kira's boyfriend way more than a grown-ass man should.

"Right." Forster clapped his hands together, pushing to his feet. "We're five days out from the Barbary Belt, unless we want to pay another gazillion credits to go through a transit gate again. Much as I love you, cuz, you need to get your own damn ship back, 'cause I ain't gonna be no one's chauffeur."

"Don't worry, Qae," Rian muttered darkly. "Getting the *Imojenna* back is right up there on my list of priorities."

"I don't know about anyone else, but I could use a good meal and a decent few hours' sleep," Forster tossed over his shoulder as he headed out of the cargo hold.

The combined crews all broke into smaller groups, some following Forster and some heading elsewhere in the ship.

Varean turned to look down at Kira where she still sat on the crate.

She stared up at him, a hint of wariness in her gaze that hadn't been there before. "So you're like some kind of superman now?"

His lips lifted in a half grin. "Not even close. I'm not invincible, I can still bleed, and I can still be killed. And there is a downside to using the Reidar consciousness. Too much, and I risk getting lost to the darkness. I could end up just as evil and psychotic as the aliens. La'thar and Ko'en warned me, and I felt it firsthand before I found my Mar'keish abilities. I'm still the same man. Just consider that I have a few upgrades."

She pushed to her feet, bringing herself up against him as she wound her arms around his shoulders, her gaze becoming warm, loving, and trusting.

"Interesting. And are any of these upgrades going to be beneficial to me? For purely scientific reasons, I mean." Her irreverent grin told him the exact opposite to any of this being *scientific*.

He leaned in closer, relishing the comfort and security of having her against him. "I don't know. How about we go find out?"

# Epilogue

The infamous Tripoli bazaar bustled with late evening crowds, people coming out in the pleasant temperate night air after the smothering humidity of the day. Women in exotic and expensive clothing shopped, people from all walks of life drank and gambled in booths and through the walkways. Scents of every type of food and cuisine throughout the galaxy blended to create a riot for the senses.

Even though the *Ebony Winter* had landed less than an hour ago, after five days with too many people on his cousin's small Sylph class ship, Rian hadn't returned to the berth on the *Swift Brion* that Zander had offered him or to the mansion-like guesthouse Corsair Rene Blackstone had set aside for their use when they were in the Barbary Belt. As the sun set into an orange-pink ball behind the thick green of the jungle mountains outside the city, he left everyone wearily disembarking and going their separate ways to get himself lost in the winding streets and alleys of the bazaar instead.

He'd purchase a bottle of Violaine from the first trader he'd found, since the rest of his supply was stowed on the

*Imojenna*, wherever she was out in the universe right now.

The thought of his missing ship uncharacteristically made his insides squeeze, setting off a burn through his limbs he hadn't felt in longer than he could remember. But that was only marginally better than the acid-like smolder in his guts whenever he thought of Callan and Sen.

*Damn it.* He took a swig of the Violaine, bottle emptying too fast, considering he didn't have a second.

The crew had organized a memorial or some frecking thing for the following day. He'd join them, but he hated all that standing around and talking about people in ways that didn't really reflect the life they'd actually lived.

Take Callan. He'd been a son of a bitch on his best of days, regularly flipped off the whole chain of command, and didn't have a sensitive bone in his body, especially when it came to women. But he'd been *their* son of a bitch. And without his universal-class forgery skills, they'd have ended up on Erebus a long time ago.

So, no, he didn't really prescribe to the whole celebration-of-a-dead-man's-life thing, but he'd go because Zahli expected him to, and because it was important to the rest of his crew.

He dropped down on a vacant seat roughly carved out of a local white wood, situated under a couple of tall swaying trees, the fronds flicking back and forth in the slight breeze. This time, his swig from the bottle was more contemplative. There was something almost hypnotic, something calming, in the busy, raucous crowds. For a moment he was just a guy on a seat drinking his Violaine without a need to be anywhere else.

"Clearly I'm spending too much time around you."

Rian glanced up to see Qae standing a few steps away, holding his own bottle of Violaine. His cousin closed the distance and sat beside him.

"You know, I never thought I liked this stuff." Qae held up the bottle, still well over three-quarters full, unlike his own that was already half empty. "But I'm beginning to see the appeal. Plus, apparently pirates love this kind of poison, so as long as we're in the Barbary Belt, I've got to make like a native."

"Yeah? Well that also includes being able to walk straight once you've downed that bottle."

Qae shot him an indignant glare. "Are you saying I can't hold my drinks?"

"Drinks? Yes. Violaine… I guess we'll find out shortly."

"That we will." Qae leaned over to clink their bottles together. "Here's to those dick-faced shite-gibbons, the Reidar. May you all burn in hell."

Tipping back his head, his cousin took a long swallow of the Violaine, then wiped his mouth on his sleeve.

"So, how's your revenge plotting coming along?" Qae set his bottle on the seat next to him then clasped his hands together.

"What makes you think I'm plotting?" Not anywhere near ready to relinquish his own hard comfort, he took another drink to avoid looking at his cousin.

"Because that's what you do. People get killed, and you go off on these crazy vendettas of blood and slaughter."

He cut an annoyed, sideways glare at Qae. "Then I'm sure you'll be pleased to hear the only plotting I'm doing right now is how to get my frecking ship back. Though no doubt there'll be some level of bloodshed involved."

"Of course. I'd be worried if there wasn't." The usual cynical gleam left Qae's eyes. "What are you going to do?"

"Since I'm not the marauder in the family, I'm not actually sure." He shifted, slinging an arm across the back of the seat to look directly at his cousin. "I'm going to need you on this, Qae."

"You got it. Whatever you need."

Though he'd already assumed he could rely on Qae to help him get the *Imojenna* back, hearing him say the words quelled some of the smoldering in his guts.

"First, we need to find her." Around them, a few fat stray drops of rain splattered the ground.

"I've got people I can reach out to." Qae gripped his shoulder. "Don't worry, Rian, we'll get your ship back."

"I know we will." He didn't doubt for a second that they'd recover the *Imojenna*. The problem was, how much more would it cost him by the time he did?

Qae grabbed his bottle and stood. "There's a bar down the way me and the crew like to frequent. You coming?"

"Maybe in a few."

Qae nodded and headed off, weaving through the crowd that was starting to shift more quickly now that rain was periodically sprinkling from the sky.

After getting slowly to his feet, Rian set off in the opposite direction, checking the various displays and stands as he went. At last, he came across the kind of stall he'd been searching for—one selling wind chimes, colorful hanging decorations, woven blankets, and jewelry. But not the glitzy gold and diamond type. The earthy type made from natural products like wood, crystal, and stone. He stopped in front of the trays displaying loose beads, glancing over the options. A few moments of poking around and he found what he needed. A platinum bead, chunky, dully polished, looking like it could withstand nuclear fallout, for Callan, and a smaller, unusual bead made from rusted metium and alloy, similar to a ship's hull, for Sen.

Lastly, he grabbed a generic white crystal bead to add to the other dozen or more similar white crystal beads already on his wristband. For every time he'd been directly or indirectly responsible for the Reidar killing innocent people on a mass scale.

He set his half-finished bottle of Violaine on the table while he pulled out a few credits to pay for the beads. He glanced down at the band, hating the thing as much as he needed it.

A tingle of energy trickled down his spine, and without looking up he knew Ella was near. Unable to help himself, he glanced across the bazaar, where she appeared out of the crowd and floated toward him, no doubt totally aware of his exact location.

They hadn't spoken since the cargo hold of the *Marsala*, before he'd nearly died. Again. But not because either of them were avoiding each other or everything that had passed between them. More because nothing needed to be said.

Yeah, he'd kissed her, and it had been a kind of revelation, but compared to almost dying and everything he'd found out from the commando, one short kiss didn't need to be scrutinized and analyzed down to the nth degree.

She stepped under the awning of the trader's tent, movements graceful and efficient as always. He didn't bother greeting her. Those kinds of awkward pleasantries had become pointless. There was no denying they had a connection that transcended whatever feelings he may or may not have. He still might not understand what that connection was, what it meant, or where it would lead them. But Donnelly's blast of imparting knowledge while they'd been in the collective human consciousness had undeniably changed something within him.

Whether it was for better or worse, he couldn't say yet. It certainly hadn't taken away his bitter rage, the pain, the hatred, or his demon-self lurking in shadows at the back of his mind, bloodthirsty and yearning for death, waiting to take him over when he was at his weakest. That part he now knew was the Reidar's hold on him he couldn't shake.

Ella stopped at his side and gently took hold of the band around his wrist.

"What are you doing?" he asked, not in an accusatory

way, more with plain curiosity. He'd never let anyone witness the not-quite ritual of adding notches to his penance, but he didn't feel like Ella was butting in on his personal custom, because she understood in a way no one else did.

Without a word, she unfastened the clasp. She took the new beads from him and wove them into the band with steady, nimble fingers, taking half the time it probably would have taken him. In a matter of moments, she had the band refastened around his wrist, fingers lightly brushing his skin with a teasing hint of warmth.

Above them, on the stretched fabric of the tent, the chatter of quick splats got faster—the balmy tropical shower opening into a downpour. Ella let go of the band at his wrist and looked up at him, the lamps the trader had strung up to illuminate her wares against the night shadows casting a deeper golden glow across Ella's flawless skin, catching a deeper green in her mossy eyes.

"Why did you come here?" he murmured, stepping closer to her, leaving only a breath between.

"This time, the beads are my weight to bear, as well."

He shook his head. "You weren't responsible for Jensen and Callan. Your warning saved the rest of us."

"But as you have so readily pointed out, I could have done more. I could have acted first. I could have remembered my training, had discipline over my emotions, and not lost control when it really mattered. Next time I won't fail."

There was a boldness, a stubborn strength in her eyes that hadn't been there before.

She shifted away, holding his gaze in a way that made his heart bump against the inside of his chest. He still hated that she'd seen his worst secrets, the darkest places in his soul, the monster he lived with and barely controlled. Yet her knowledge chipped away at the wall between him and everyone else that he'd always considered to be impenetrable.

It was a long way from coming down, but the damn thing wasn't impervious, those small dents a tiny light in a vast darkness.

Ella took another step back, and he abandoned his bottle of Violaine to pursue her. Another step took her out into the warm, pounding rain, but he didn't hesitate, going after her, barely noticing the wetness soaking through his clothes.

He reached out for her, and his fingers brushed her jawline. A smile tilted her lips upward, and she shook her head. Before he could decipher exactly what that meant, she spun, slipping through the rushing crowd of people trying to get out of the rain and disappearing from sight.

Rian let his arm drop back to his side, water rushing over him, washing off the past five days of being cramped in a ship with too many other people. Cleaning off the near death, the fighting, the running and hiding they'd been doing for months on end before that.

He'd lost his ship. He still had no plan on how to stop the Reidar or get his revenge. He still didn't see any other end for himself except total bloody destruction. And he was still a broken shell of himself, bringing danger and death to everyone who followed him.

But life was fluid. He'd thought himself stuck, trapped by the past, by what the Reidar had done to him, by the things he'd done himself.

Those things still existed inside him. But he could see now that they weren't holding him down, they were pushing him forward, that the answer didn't lay in trying to escape or outrun his past. The answer came in embracing it. In understanding and using what he'd been given to control his future.

Yes, the Reidar had remade him into a weapon in that godforsaken lab.

And the only thing more deadly than a weapon used against others was a weapon turned on its creator.

# Author's Note

"Well, is Rian next?" I hear many of you asking. Just how much longer can I possibly drag out this story before the crew finally get their shite together?

Sorry, but that's going to have to remain one of life's mysteries for the time being.

I can tell you with all certainty that the hero in the 4th book, *Entropy*, will be Rian's not-a-space-pirate cousin, Qaelan. Ah, I see that perked you right up. Yeah, Qae is something else, all right. Along with Qae, Rian will have his usual page-time, but I don't imagine getting the *Imojenna* back will be all that easy or come without some cost. But that's a story for another day.

# Acknowledgments

Though my wonderful editor, Robin Haseltine, assured me otherwise, I felt like *Diffraction* was one of those books that fought hard before we were able to break it in and turn it into the story that's now on these pages. I have to say, I was very glad to see these edits behind me!

So as always and forever, thank you, Robin. You already know how awesome I think you are, and that these books would not be the same without your particular eye when it comes to my stories.

Secondly, and no less importantly, I have to say a huge thank you and shout out to my agent, Nicole Resciniti. I have come so far this year alone, learned so much, been wowed by your energy and absolute belief in me and my books. You were the missing element in my little team, and it might be a cliché to say, but under your care and guidance, I feel like the stars are the limit. I'm looking forward to reaching those heights with you, because I'm sure it's going to be one hell of a ride!

Next, I need Liz Pelletier, Tera Cuskaden, and the rest

of the team at Entangled, who have been involved in the *Atrophy* series and securing the future of my books, to know how grateful and thankful I am for your continued support and the amazing faith you've put in the continuation of this series. A few years ago, I could have only imagined such opportunities, and now through you, I am seeing my dreams come true.

And lastly, like always, thank you to my family. Without your love, without the chaos, the laughter, the mess, the general craziness of day to day life, all of this would be pointless.

# About the Author

Jess has been making up stories ever since she can remember. Though her messy handwriting made it hard for anyone else to read them, she wasn't deterred, and now she gets to make up stories for a living. She loves loud music and a good book on a rainy day and probably spends too much time watching too many TV shows. Jess lives in regional Victoria, Australia, with her very supportive husband, three daughters, two hyperactive border collie dogs, and a cat who thinks he's one of the kids.

*Discover more Entangled Select Otherworld titles...*

## FROM THE ASHES
### a *Fires of Redemption* novel by Xen Sanders

The villain known as Spark has masterminded countless crimes to build his father's inhuman empire. Yet to professor Sean Archer, this fearsome creature is only Tobias Rutherford—antisocial graduate researcher and a fascinating puzzle Sean is determined to solve. But one kiss leads to an entanglement that challenges everything Tobias knows about himself, aberrants, and his own capacity to love. When his father orders him to assassinate a senator, one misstep unravels a knot of political intrigue that places the fate of humans and aberrants alike in Tobias's hands. As danger mounts, will Tobias succumb to his dark nature and sacrifice Sean—or will he defy his father and rise from the ashes to become a hero in a world of villains?

## DRAKON'S PROMISE
### a *Blood of the Drakon* novel by N.J. Walters

Darius Varkas is a drakon. He's neither human nor dragon. He's both. He and his brothers are also the targets of an ancient order who want to capture all drakons for their blood, which can prolong a human's life. When Sarah Anderson finds a rare book belonging to the Knights of the Dragon, she's quickly thrust into a dangerous world of secrets and shifters. And when the Knights realize Sarah has a secret of her own, she becomes just as much a target as Darius. Her scary dragon shifter just might be her best chance at survival.

## Flying Through Fire
### a *Dark Desires* novel by Nina Croft

Thorne's willpower has been honed over ten thousand years. He might want Candy, but the last thing he needs is an infatuation with a young, impetuous werewolf. Candy makes him lose control, and that could have disastrous consequences. As the threat escalates and they become separated by time and space, Candy must find a way back to him, because while Thorne alone has the power to defeat the dragons, only together can they finally bring peace to the universe.

## Out of This World
### a novel by Patricia Eimer

Engaged to a murderous, intergalactic warlord, Capridocian Princess Corripraxis is running for her life and crash lands on Earth. If she can just get some help—in the form of the very attractive Earth male who just pulled up in a tow truck—she can hunker down in the Roswell Martian colony until she figures out her next move. Ex-Marine Mattias Cadiz needs to get on living a nice—quiet—life. But he pulls up to the scene of an accident, where a sexy woman asks for a lift. No way he can refuse such a gorgeous, violet-eyed beauty, even if she seems a tad confused.

CPSIA information can be obtained
at www.ICGtesting.com
Printed in the USA
LVHW03s1444100618
580220LV00001B/9/P